BRYCE MAIN spei  :fore
writing fiction full-ti   ·ime
novel. He is married   rth-
west of England.

Follow Bryce on Twitter @brycemain99

BRYCE MAIN
A TIME FOR DYING

Northodox Press Ltd
Maiden Greve, Malton,
North Yorkshire, YO17 7BE

This edition 2024

1
First published in Great Britain by
Northodox Press Ltd 2024

ISBN: 9781915179319

This book is set in Caslon Pro Std

For Denise, my wife and first reader,
who helped me bring *A Time for Dying* alive…

Dying is easy. It's living that's hard. Living with all the pain and disappointment. Living with all the love and hate.

Living with all the life that might have been and death that shouldn't have happened.

Sometimes the difference between the two is something as simple as a boy with a thought.

A thought given enough time to brew and fester. And then an action drenched in blood…

Prologue

Time is a patient killer.

Sometimes, all it takes to put the thought of bloody murder into somebody's head is a few hundred years wait and a visit to a historic building, located on the north bank of the Thames.

Then all you need are sharp knives, a strong desire to end lives, and the ability to leave no trace behind.

But before all that, you needed a King.

Preferably one who's thirty-four years old. Over six foot tall. And sitting on the throne of England a year shy of the Great Plague of London.

It was Friday August 1, 1664 and the weather in London fell somewhere in between warm and muggy, damp and dreary.

Charlie Stuart, or to give him his proper title, King Charles II of England, Scotland, and Ireland, had recently taken delivery of a new set of Royal Regalia. The old set had, over time, been lost, used as collateral, pawned, and generally buggered about with, before the most important man in the realm took his seat on the most important chair in the land.

Even at the time, the new regalia set him back a whopping £13,000. Around £1m in modern currency. Separate from the banqueting plate, golden altar, and baptismal font, which he had to fork out a further £18,000.

Charles was well pleased with all his new gear. But he was no mug. So, he stashed all his pretty valuables where nobody else could get within touching distance. The most fortified place in the land. The Tower of London.

And there they stayed. For 330 years, waiting for the right opportunity to present itself; waiting for the right mind to pick up the thread of an idea and run with it.

On 24th March 1994, the Royal Regalia, fondly and officially known by all as The Crown Jewels, was moved into the newly created Jewel House on the ground floor of the Tower.

It had six-inch-thick, two-tonne-heavy, blast-proof doors. Strong enough, experts said, to survive a nuclear clobbering. The national treasures it held were lit by state-of-the-art fibre optics and rested on the finest French velvet.

Around 20,000 people a day viewed the collection of more than one hundred priceless objects and 23,578 diamonds, rubies, emeralds, and sapphires.

But on 1st August 1995, one object more than all the others, caught the eye, and the imagination, of a small ten-year old boy, looking at it through its protective glass display cabinet.

He was there with his parents and twin brother, as a treat for their 10th birthday. He was older than his brother by two minutes. One hundred and twenty seconds. Give or take.

He had been counting in his head for as long as he could remember. Today, his head carried all the numbers he'd been counting since the four of them walked through the large, heavy entrance doors. Every breath. Every step. Every person. Every object. They were all there. Numbers were everywhere. Numbers were his passion. Numbers made sense of everything. Especially one kind of number.

Prime.

And as he looked at the golden Sovereign's Orb, he firmly believed that he'd never seen anything so beautiful in all his short life. But that beauty awoke in him other feelings. Strange, terrifying feelings. The kind of feelings that made his body buzz as if electricity was coursing through it.

He didn't just see a cross sitting on top of a ball. He didn't just see priceless jewels and a hollow golden sphere. In his warped imagination, he saw blood and death. He saw lifeless bodies, and he felt a magnificent exhilaration.

When he left The Tower that morning, he was a very different kind of animal from the boy who had entered.

Fast forward twenty-two years.

Chapter One

Everyone has a time for dying.

Some folk have a say in the matter. They can choose their time right down to the split second. Messy or not. Others don't stand a chance. The Reaper just comes out of the shadows, kicks in the front door, and doesn't even bother to ring the bell.

Joseph Miller knew a thing or two about death.

He'd seen it up close and personal enough times to recognise the look, the smell and the sound of it.

He'd been a soldier, and knew the injuries to the human body that war caused. Especially the kind caused by hand-to-hand fighting performed by desperate men who just wanted to live through the day. And the next day. And the next. Until it was time to go home.

He knew that the knife handle sticking out of his chest was in just the right place, at just the right angle, to inflict the kind of damage that there was no coming back from.

The double-edged blade had broken the surface of his skin, just left of the sternum, cut cleanly through muscle, slid neatly between the 3rd and 4th ribs near his left nipple, through the pericardium, to rupture the organ that lay between his lungs.

His heart.

Then it was ripped powerfully sideways and slightly up to inflict a catastrophic wound. Scraping the ribs in the process.

He knew all this in the space of a few seconds.

It wasn't true that your whole life flashed in front of you just before you died.

Joseph only had time for a couple of panic-filled thoughts. A look of surprise. A feeling of sorrow. And a moment of regret.

Then the knife was roughly pulled out, tearing more flesh. His chest cavity filled with blood, which spurted out to splash on his shirt front and the upper legs of his trousers.

His blood pressured crashed and he lost consciousness.

Lungs ceased to function.

Heart stopped beating.

Shortly after, his brain stopped sending signals out to the rest of his body.

And the light went out in his eyes.

Then, right on cue, he evacuated the contents of his bowels and bladder.

By the time the withdrawn knife was plunged into his brain through the top of his head, he was way past caring.

The time was 10pm on Tuesday, 1st August 2017.

In Stockport, Cheshire.

Joseph was found in his terraced home in Stockport, Cheshire, by two police officers acting in response to a 999 call, made from Joseph's house.

The killer spoke fifty-six words, ended the call, and left.

For all the trace he left behind, he might never have been there in the first place.

It took the two first responding policemen just over eight minutes to get to the address. Then another thirty seconds to realise that the door was slightly open, the curtains drawn, and the hallway light off.

They both gloved-up and switched on their Maglite torches. The senior officer gently elbowed open the front door and stepped over the threshold. The junior followed behind.

'Try not to touch a bloody thing, lad,' the senior said.

Entering the house they made their way to the living room, where Joseph was sitting, slumped to his left, on a three-seater sofa. Next to a coffee table. Facing a television that was switched off. As off as Joseph's brain. The only thing in the house that was on was a dull lamp on the coffee table.

While the junior officer hurried outside to puke on the path, the senior, with a stronger constitution, switched on the overhead light, looked closer at the knife handle, hilt, and blade wedged deep in the top of Joseph's skull.

He also noticed that in Joseph's left hand was a black leather-bound copy of the King James Bible. It was splashed with blood.

'Jesus fucking Christ,' he cursed before getting on the radio.

Looking around the room, the bloody mess and carnage centred around Joseph, the sofa, and the carpet at his feet. Everything else looked tidy. Untouched. It was as if whoever had ended the old man's life had done so quickly and with savage efficiency.

He called his colleague back and they both searched the house.

The senior officer knew SOCO would be on their way and all necessary photographs would be taken, evidence would be removed, investigated, catalogued, preserved, and stored.

He knew that a D.I. whose name he barely remembered would be there shortly. He knew that a coroner would also be there shortly and Joseph would be taken away to a place he'd never been before. To be examined by people he'd never met in his life. Then put in the ground within a month.

He knew all that.

And he also knew that, although the phoned tip-off was made by someone who didn't leave his name, the police knew his nickname.

That was the good news.

Joseph was seventy-three, a whisker over five-feet ten, and the sixth victim of the serial killer the newspapers named *The Holy Ghost*.

That was the bad news. The very bad news was that the police were no closer to catching him than when he killed his first victim.

That one happened at 10pm on Wednesday, 1st August 2012, in Halifax, West Yorkshire.

Since then, apart from a shit load of activity on August 1 each following year, the case had stayed as dead and unmoving as Joseph Miller.

Unlike Joseph, it wouldn't stay that way for long. It was about to receive a hefty kick up the arse.

Chapter Two

Things happened the way they normally happened in his house, in this room, most mornings.

A raucous bluesy Jeff Beck guitar riff shattered the silence and broke the spell. Then a hand attached to a hairy left arm snaked out from under the bed covers and stabbed the alarm into snooze cruise mode.

Ten minutes later, right on cue, the alarm went off again.

A man groaned in pain and resignation and slapped the snooze off.

'Bollocks!' a low voice coughed and cursed.

Another day started. Piss. Shit. Shave. Teeth. Shower. Moisturise. Then dress. Painkillers. Black roast coffee. Check emails on phone. Shove laptop in bag. Jacket on. Grab keys. Lock door. Start car. No radio. Not yet.

He drove to work with brain on autopilot. Ready, set, go. Only today was different. Today was cheese. Yesterday was chalk. Today was the morning after what, for others, came after a very busy night.

Only he didn't know that.

Today was going to be his first day on the task force that nobody in their right mind wanted to be on. The poison chalice.

Only he didn't know that yet, either.

One thing he knew for sure was that the painkillers he took with his coffee weren't working. The gang of bastard thugs was

9

still kicking the hell out of the inside of his skull. And every single damned one of them was wearing steel toe capped Docs.

Another thing he knew was that, as he climbed the stairs, he was about thirty seconds away from the stash of para-bloody-cetamol waiting in the top right-hand drawer of his desk.

The desk was in an open plan room on the second floor of a drab, utilitarian building in Stockport Town Centre. Right next to a taller building named after triple Wimbledon Tennis Champion Fred Perry.

This morning there was an extra buzz about the place. The kind of buzz that only happened when death came to town and life had no option but to chase after it, and hope it caught up.

There were grim, serious looks on the faces of people whose job it was to keep the peace and dispose of those who meant to disturb it.

There were no smiles. No good-natured banter.

That suited him perfectly.

Detective Inspector Tom McHale wasn't known for his cheery disposition. Especially not first thing in the morning after one of his migraines. They came fast, left slow, and took no prisoners. Even if he hadn't had one for a week, or a month, they still sat in the background, jeered, and threw rocks at him. Just to remind him they were still there. Most of them missed, but every now and then one of them hit the mark. And it had "we'll rip your fucking head off" written all over it. And it felt like bastard thugs wearing Docs.

Until the painkillers kicked in.

McHale was an easy twenty yards from his top right-hand desk drawer when someone tapped his left shoulder lightly.

A voice said, 'Boss wants to see you.'

The voice belonged to a young Detective Constable called Macbeth. McHale liked him – as much as he could be accused of liking anyone. McHale wasn't known for his cheery disposition.

If he could be described in one word, even by those who

thought they knew him well, the word would be "detached". If he could be described in two words, they would be "fucking detached". It was a persona he liked to cultivate. It didn't do to let folk get too close. Shit happened when you let folk in.

He ignored the urge to stop, turn and speak to the young DC. Instead, he kept walking.

'In a minute,' he said, over his shoulder.

'Better make it a skinny one.'

'Coffee?'

'On your desk.'

Macbeth knew the "bastard thugs" routine and he was the nearest thing to a friendly barista-buddy that McHale had.

Four 500ml tabs and two swigs of something warm and roughly resembling coffee later, McHale was ready for whatever the hell it was that Detective Chief Inspector Robert Campbell wanted to speak to him about.

Twenty feet to the corridor. Second on the right. Two knocks on the closed door. Don't wait for an answer. Walk right in and take it like a man.

Campbell wasn't alone.

A large man was sitting in one of the two chairs in front of Campbell's desk. He turned around, looked at McHale for a heartbeat, then stood up.

McHale was six two. Large man was about two inches taller and another couple wider. He was wearing a grey tweed two-piece suit over a crisp white shirt and a maroon tie. The Rock of Gibraltar looked less solid.

His mouth was smiling but his eyes were nowhere near a smile.

'Cyril, I'd like you to meet DI Tom McHale,' said Campbell.

Detective Chief Superintendent Cyril Drummond was the first to hold out his hand. He was also the first to speak.

'Aah... the man who cracked the Kirkbride double,' he said. 'Nice to finally meet someone who thinks differently.'

McHale took his hand and pumped it twice.

'We got lucky. He got stupid,' said McHale,

'Nobody that clever suddenly gets stupid.'

'We had help.'

They were referring to a double murder in Altrincham in 2010. Very tragic. Very messy. Old couple in their 70s. John and Annie Kirkbride. He was stabbed twenty-seven times and almost decapitated. She was stabbed eighteen times including once in each eye. She hadn't been raped. There was no semen in or on either of them. No witnesses. None of the neighbours heard anything.

Blood everywhere.

They were last seen alive at around 7.30 the evening they were killed.

The Kirkbride's weren't discovered until two days later when a district nurse visiting them couldn't get in and raised the alarm.

Their murderer was a fifty-six-year-old Catholic priest, Father David Black. When he was caught in 2011, he was diagnosed with Dissociative Identity Disorder. He had two distinct and separate personalities. One of these, the dominant personality, was the priest. He was of exemplary character. Caring, well-spoken, funny, and intelligent. The kind of priest loved by all his parishioners.

The other was Arthur, the subordinate personality. Arthur was twenty-five years old and was a cold-blooded killer. He had an IQ of 136. Einstein's IQ, by comparison, was around 160.

The priest didn't know about Arthur. Arthur, however, knew about the priest.

McHale was the one who put two and two (and two) together and got some sort of justice for an old couple who invited a monster into their home.

People started looking at him differently after that.

'Everybody gets stupid eventually,' he said.

Drummond nodded once. 'Let's hope so.'

Campbell indicated the spare chair and everyone sat down.

He picked up a pair of gold-framed specs from his desk, put them on, looked at a thick manila file on the desk in front of him and opened it. The file contained half a mountain of paperwork and five 8'x10' colour photographs. He picked up the top photo and handed it to McHale.

It showed a man sitting at a kitchen table. The table was one of those with painted cream legs and a naked pine top. The chair was pine. On the table top was an open newspaper and, to the right of it, a mug of tea or coffee sitting on a coaster.

Near the coaster was an ashtray and beside that was a golden pack of Benson & Hedges cigarettes and what looked like a pewter Zippo lighter. Behind the ashtray was a portable chess set. Open.

The man was slumped to his left, shirt front bloody, as were his trouser leg tops. There was a pool of blood at his feet. He was obviously dead. There was something stuck in the top of his head. It looked like the handle of a dagger.

There was no window in the shot. No clock on the wall. So, no way of knowing what time of day or night it was taken. That was left for the label on the back of the photo.

McHale didn't say anything. He flipped the photo over and saw a label with six entries.

Victim number - *1*
Victim name - *James Halliwell*
Date of Birth - *1.8.1981*
Age - *thirty-one*
Time of Death -*Approx.10.00pm, Wednesday, 1st August, 2012*
Reference and location
THG0012012/HALIFAX/WESTYORKSHIRE

Under the label was a scrawled signature and initials: *C.D.*
McHale presumed C.D. stood for Cyril Drummond. He studied the photo for a few seconds, then placed it carefully

on Campbell's desk. Label side down. Guy with a knife in his head side up.

Drummond then took the other four photos from the file and placed them alongside the first one. Every one showed a different murder.

Three men. Two women.

All photographed sitting down.

Each a different interior shot.

Each posed in the same way.

Each killed in the same way.

He flipped over the photographs and looked at each label in turn. There wasn't much to read.

The labels were brief and impersonal. McHale suspected each death was anything but.

Victim number 2 was Mary-Anne Nutall. DOB: 23.1.1958. Aged 59. Time of death: approx. 10pm, Thursday, 1st August, 2013. Reference: THG0022012/FORMBY/LIVERPOOL.

She was in her living room. On a sofa.

Victim number 3 was Deepankar Ghatak. DOB: 7.4.1950. Aged 67. Time of death: approx. 10pm, Friday, 1st August 2014. Reference: THG0032012/CAMDEN/ LONDON.

He was in his living room. On an armchair.

Victim number 4 was Calvin Miles. DOB: 24.8.1969. Aged 47. Time of death: approx. 10pm, Saturday, 1st August, 2015. Reference: THG0042015/MILNGAVIE/GLASGOW.

He was in his kitchen. On a wooden chair.

Victim number 5 was Barbara Lennox. DOB: 4.1.1976. Aged 41. Time of death: approx. 10pm, Saturday, 1st August, 2016. Reference: THG0052015/WHITSTABLE/KENT.

She was in a downstairs study. On an office chair.

Same signature and initials under all the labels.

One body a year, found on the same day each year, for the past six years.

McHale looked at them slowly and took a deep breath in.

Let it out slowly.

Looked at the other two men. Drummond last.

'The Holy Ghost,' he said, slowly. As if savouring each word.

Drummond nodded. 'You know the case?'

'We haven't been formally introduced.'

'Well... he's back.'

'You sure?'

'It's him alright. Yesterday was 1st August. He was bang on time.'

'Where?'

'Here.'

'Stockport?'

'On your bloody doorstep.'

McHale blinked twice in rapid succession, which was as close to excitement as he normally liked to show.

Drummond leaned down to his case, brought up a flash drive, and handed it to Campbell, who plugged it into a MacBook on his desk.

'All the details of all the murders are on there, along with all photographic records, sketches, the works. We're still processing the latest one. But every molecule on each poor bugger whether it belongs to them or not, is in there somewhere. Doctor Locard's rotting corpse would approve,' said Drummond.

McHale, like every good detective, knew about Doctor Edmond Locard, "the French Sherlock Holmes", and his principles of exchange. The idea that anyone who enters a crime scene takes something of the scene away and leaves something of themselves behind had always fascinated him. He'd wanted a translated copy of all seven volumes of Edmond Locard's *Treaty of Criminalistics* for years.

Campbell danced his fingers across the track pad and then swung the screen around to face McHale and Drummond.

'Gentlemen, meet victim number six. Joseph Miller,' he said. 'Found here in Stockport, last night at about 10pm. The photographer's no David bloody Bailey, but you'll get the idea.'

The screen showed a still shot of Joseph Miller's corpse. Slumped on his last resting place. His sofa. Facing the TV.

Same pose as James Halliwell.

Same pose as all the others.

Same injuries.

Blood spilled out of his chest.

Knife sticking out of his head.

McHale blinked twice in rapid succession again. He could feel his juices starting to flow.

'You're 100% sure it's the Ghost?'

Drummond looked at him and frowned. 'Aged 73. Born May 16, 1944. Died 1st August, 2017'.

McHale leaned forward and scanned the photos lined up on the desk. This time his eyes spent more time on the knife hilt sticking out of Miller's head. Then he quickly flicked through the other photos. 'The knives?'

'They're very special,' said Drummond. 'We've been keeping that bit quiet.'

McHale's fingers, which had been softly drumming on his knees, slammed on the brakes. He looked at Campbell.

'Why am I here?'

Campbell looked at Drummond, then at him. 'Because DCS Drummond here thinks you just might be the one to catch the bastard.'

Drummond turned around in his seat to face him. 'We're putting a team together.'

'Another conventional taskforce? It won't work,' said McHale, shaking his head slowly. 'We've all got bloody university degrees at being conventional. We're very good at doing things by the book. We're shit at doing things differently.'

He looked at Campbell. Campbell didn't look back.

'Did you catch the priest by being a conventional copper?' asked Drummond quietly. 'No. You operate sideways. You think different.'

McHale shrugged. 'Like I said, we got lucky.'

'Know what Thomas Jefferson said about luck?'

McHale sighed.

Campbell frowned.

Drummond smiled and looked at Campbell. 'He said, "I'm a great believer in luck. I find that the harder I work, the luckier I get"'.

'It probably wasn't Jefferson and the quote's wrong,' said McHale.

Drummond looked at McHale, raised an eyebrow, and raised his voice. 'Who the hell cares? I like the damned thought. DCI Campbell here tells me you're the hardest working DI he's ever come across. And the most unconventional. He didn't tell me you could also be a real fucking pain in the arse.'

'It's our little secret,' said McHale. The bastard thugs were yelling insults now. They'd run out of rocks for the time being. He shrugged. 'At the moment the pain in the arse has relocated to somewhere at the back of the head. But I think I've got it cornered.'

'Our golden boy has headaches for breakfast,' said Campbell.

Drummond's brows looked confused. Then he twigged and softened.

'Painkillers?' said Drummond.

'Been there. Done that.'

'How many?'

'Not enough.'

Drummond grunted and stuck a meaty hand into a jacket pocket. It came back out holding a pack of migraine tablets.

'Here. Take two of these,' he said, handing the pack to McHale. 'I've been there and done that, too.'

The two men nodded ever so slightly at each other.

'So, feel like getting lucky again?'

Two blinks.

One answer.

No hesitation.

'Tell me more about this team of yours.'

'Take those tablets first, or anything I say will just go in one ear and out the other.'

'Gents, I think maybe coffee is called for,' said Campbell. He reached for the desk phone and pressed a key. After two rings a female voice answered. Campbell went right to it. 'Alice, would you bring me in a nice strong pot of my Java and three cups, please.'

He put the receiver down and turned to McHale. 'Whatever headache you've got is going to be a piece of piss compared to the one you're about to sign up for,' he said.

Hardly a minute after Campbell put the receiver down there was a knock on the door. 'Come in Alice,' he said loudly.

The door opened and a middle-aged woman entered pushing a trolley. On the trolley was a tray, and on the tray was a coffee pot, three cups, three saucers, and a plate full of assorted biscuits.

Campbell answered the surprised look on Drummond's face with a smile. 'Alice here is our resident psychic,' he said. 'She has a supernatural ability to tell when I need my caffeine fix. So, she always gets it ready a few minutes before she thinks I'm going to put the call in.'

Alice put the tray down on Campbell's desk, smiled at everyone, and left without saying a word.

Campbell winked at her as she left. She winked back.

Campbell played mum and a couple of minutes later McHale had the fast-acting migraine tablets well and truly washed down his gullet and starting to take effect.

Drummond began to speak.

'Before we go any further, I need to know if you're interested in joining the team, or this conversation ends here.'

'Interested doesn't even come close,' said McHale.

'Good man. Right. I'm not going to start with the murders. I think the best place to start is with the knives.'

McHale felt himself begin to relax. Bastard thugs were whispering in a corner and threatening to behave themselves.

Chapter Three

Drummond reached down to a briefcase sitting by his right foot. He brought it up, sat it on his lap and opened it.

He brought out something wrapped in a dark, thick cloth. Unwrapped the cloth. Inside was a hard-plastic, see-through, Sharps evidence tube, complete with a chain of evidence sticker on the outer surface sealing the tube.

Inside the tube was a knife.

He reached back into his case, brought out a pair of forensic gloves and struggled to put them on his oversized hands. Then broke the seal on the sticker, opened the tube, and gently removed the knife.

Drummond put it on the desk on top of the photos. It landed with a thud.

McHale did the double blink thing.

The knife looked similar to the ones in the other photos.

Drummond let it sit there, silently, for a few seconds before he spoke again.

'This, gentlemen,' he said, 'is the star of the show. Well... one of them. It's called a...'

'Fairbairn-Sykes,' interrupted McHale softly. Without asking permission, he reached for the weapon. 'Thought I recognised it.'

He picked it up. Felt the weight. Tested the balance.

It was hand forged. Hand ground. Hand crafted. Blade well-polished and razor sharp. S-shaped cross-guard of nickel-plated steel.

Bowling pin handle. Lathe-turned from brass. Nickel plated and slid over the tang. Held together by a nickel-plated top nut.

McHale held it like it was worth its weight in gold. Which, to a collector, it probably was.

'Well colour me impressed,' said Drummond. 'You know your knives.'

'My grandfather had one of the later models. This, if I'm not mistaken, is a P1.'

'Correct. And it's not a copy, either. That one's the real deal. And so are the other five.'

'Six original 1st Patterns?'

'Six so far. This is from James Halliwell. Victim number one. But it's more than a 1st Pattern. It's a numbered 1st Pattern. Which means it's like having six Holy Grails. Look at the flat section under the cross-guard.'

McHale inspected the guard closely. It had the Wilkinson Sword legend etched on it. And underneath the legend was a number.

Number 1.

'Are they all numbered?' he said softly.

'Every-one.'

'Okay, this is where I butt in and say: First, what the hell is a Fairbairn-Sykes? And second, what is a 1st Pattern?'

McHale put the knife back on the desk and patted it softly twice.

The bastard thugs were conspicuous by their absence.

'I need to tell you a story,' said Drummond. 'It starts in China before the Second World War kicked off.'

McHale reached for his Java and took a fair-sized gulp, let it slide down his throat and settled the cup back on the saucer. He settled his arse back on the chair.

Drummond reached down to his case and brought out two black and white photographs, placing them on the desk.

One was a head and shoulders shot of an unremarkable looking man. Spectacles. Clean-shaven. Three-piece suit. White shirt. Patterned tie. Looking for all the world like a bank manager.

The other was a head and shoulders shot of a hard-faced man in uniform. British Army. Spectacles. Clean-shaven. Looking for all the world like someone who had seen more than his fair share of action.

'Gentlemen,' he said, 'meet William Ewart Fairbairn and Eric Anthony Sykes. Fairbairn's the one in uniform.

'Together, these two men were probably indirectly responsible for taking – and saving – more lives in close combat fighting, before, during, and after World War II than Her Majesty's Government will ever admit to.'

Campbell looked at the men on the screen for a second or two, then reached forward and lifted a chocolate biscuit from the plate on his desk, biting it in half.

McHale leaned forwards in his chair and picked up the photos again. He turned them over. Looking at the labels, He burned the details into his brain as quickly as possible. Each life reduced to a few words and numbers on the back of an 8' x 10' black and white photo.

He returned them to the desk. Each one face up. A reminder to anyone who saw them that, for all the good there was in the world, sometimes the bad made the biggest impression.

Drummond shifted in his seat. Brushed a speck of invisible lint off his right trouser leg thigh.

Outside, it was beginning to rain hard. The cold Wednesday morning drops were battering against the office's two windows. Each window looked like a sad eye peering out on the rest of the world.

'You won't find much about them in history books' he said. 'In fact, that photo of Sykes is probably the only one in existence. But in their day, they were the best close combat instructors alive. And in 1940 the pair of them got together and designed the finest damned fighting knife you ever saw. Then they had Wilkinson Sword make it.

'Back then if you asked any British Commando or US Army

Ranger what knife they'd rather have in their hands in a sticky situation, ninety-nine out of a hundred of them would have said a Fairbairn-Sykes.'

'And the hundredth?' said Campbell.

'Wouldn't say much of anything, anymore.'

'How many did they make?' said McHale.

'The first batch was produced in 1941. Those first fifty had a 17cm blade, an S-shaped cross-guard, and a flat area at the top of the blade before the hilt. After that they started churning them out, with slight modifications as time went on.

'But before that, Wilkinson made a prototype set. All numbered 1-7. Only for show. They were never used in action. After the war an official request was made for their return. The intention was to melt six of the seven down and keep the remaining one for the official records.'

McHale butted in. 'So… what you're saying is that we've got the first six and number seven still unaccounted for?

'Out there somewhere?

'Waiting to be used?'

Drummond frowned and shifted uneasily in his chair.

'That could be a problem,' said McHale. 'But it's not a problem that's going to rise up and bite us on the arse for another year, if he keeps to his schedule. So… that's how long we've got to catch the bastard.

'One knife. One victim.'

'Not necessarily,' said Drummond.

'Come again?'

'Tell him, Cyril,' said Campbell, looking at the big copper.

McHale's inner voice jumped from DEFCON five to three. 'Okay Kemosabe. I might be friggin' wrong, but I think something soft and smelly is about to hit the fan. Big time.'

'Tell me what?'

Cyril sighed heavily and looked at McHale. 'Do you know about the phone calls?'

Now it was McHale's turn to sigh. He could hear the sound of the bastard thugs tapping their Docs. 'Go on.'

'Something else we've been keeping under our hats. He calls us after each kill from the home phone of each victim. He does it so we can trace the call. But he keeps all the calls short. So, by the time we get there he's long gone. He also does it so he can say hello and leave us a message. He knows the calls are recorded.'

'That's very considerate of him.'

'Oh, he's a real saint.'

'So, what does he say?'

Drummond turned to Campbell. 'Line them up, Bob.'

DCI Campbell fiddled with the track-pad on his MacBook Pro, turning the screen around to face McHale.

He pressed a key.

Each call was preceded by a female, announcing the name of the victim.

The female was an employee of the Metropolitan Police working out of New Scotland Yard. After she finished speaking, there was a short pause, before the caller spoke.

The voice was the same in each call. Male. Not young. Not old. English. No discernible accent initially. Delivery not rushed. Not excited. Strong. Good diction. Almost as if the words were a pleasure to say.

In the first recorded call, he spoke only forty-five words. They were these.

'Hello guys. I'm calling to arrange for the disposal of a piece of meat. The meat's name was James Halliwell. You won't find me here when you arrive. But I've left a nice gift for you. I hope you like it. This is number one.'

There was a pause of a few seconds. Then the second call kicked in.

He spoke fifty-six words. They were these.

'Hello again guys. I'm calling to arrange for the disposal of another piece of meat. The meat's name was Mary-Anne Nuttall. You won't find me here when you arrive. But I've left another nice gift for you. I see the papers have given me a name. The Holy Ghost. I like that. This is number two.'

There was a pause of a few seconds. Then the third call kicked in. He spoke fifty-seven words. They were these.

'Hello again guys. This is The Holy Ghost. I'm calling to arrange for the disposal of another piece of meat. The meat's name was Deepankar Ghatak. I hope I said that right. You won't find me here when you arrive. But I've left a nice gift for you to add to the others. This is number three.'

There was a pause of a few seconds. Then the fourth call kicked in. He spoke sixty-one words. They were these.

'Hello again guys. This is The Holy Ghost. Long-time no-speak. I'm calling to arrange for the disposal of another piece of meat. The meat's name was Calvin Miles. It wasn't in very good condition. You won't find me here when you arrive. But I've left a nice gift for you to add to the others. This is number four.'

There was a pause of a few seconds. Then the fifth call kicked in. He spoke fifty-nine words. They were these.

'Hello again guys. This is The Holy Ghost. Have you missed me? I'm calling to arrange for the disposal of another piece of meat. The meat's name was Barbara Lennox. It was a whore. You won't find me here when you arrive. But I've left a nice gift for you to add to the others. This is number five.'

There was a pause of a few seconds. Then the sixth and latest call kicked in. He spoke fifty-six words. They were these.

'Hello again guys. This is The Holy Ghost. I'm calling to arrange for the disposal of another piece of meat. The meat's name was Joseph Miller. It prayed before it died. You won't find me here when you arrive. But I've left a nice gift for you to add to the others. This is number six.'

Drummond nodded to Campbell, who pressed a key and the recordings stopped.

McHale let out a long slow breath. 'Fuck,' he said, softly.

Bastard thugs were rubbing their hands in anticipation.

'We thought he was finished. But he wasn't. There was something different about last night's message,' said Drummond.

'It had a bit of an addendum tacked onto it. Long story short, he said that the next little chapter in his extended bloody shenanigans would happen not a year from now, but a month from now.'

He nodded to Campbell again, who obliged with the key pressing.

There was a pause of about five seconds, before the Ghost spoke another thirty-four words. They were these.

'I was going to wait another year before leaving you another piece of meat to dispose of. I remembered Bobby and September 1. Tick tock, guys. Tick tock. Look out for number seven.'

Campbell pressed a key and the recording ended.

McHale double blinked. 'Seriously?'

Drummond's facial expression went from being very serious to being extremely serious. 'This isn't my funny face,' he said.

There was an elephant in the room. It stayed there, looking at the three of them, for about ten seconds, before McHale acknowledged it.

'Something's wrong.'

'You think?' There was a hint of sarcasm in Drummond's voice.

McHale's mind was working overtime. 'Six murders on the same day each year for six years... then one a month from now? Why? What's changed? What's gone wrong? And why is he spilling the beans now instead of on the day like he normally does? And what the hell is Bobby and September 1 all about?'

'That's for him to know and you to get your arse into gear to figure out.' Campbell was drumming the fingers of both hands lightly on the top of his desk.

He stopped and looked at Drummond for a couple of heartbeats. Then nodded slightly. Big decisions are sometimes made with the smallest of gestures.

He turned to McHale. 'I'll shift your caseload over to Laurel and Hardy,' he said. 'Clear your desk and hand over everything to them after we finish here. Ask them to come in when you go out.'

McHale grunted. Laurel and Hardy were the pet names of Detective Sergeant Angela Connolly (short and wiry), and Detective Sergeant Stephen Wallace (tall and overweight). They were no Batman and Robin, but they were a solid crime-fighting duo.

Drummond reached into his right jacket pocket, pulled out a second USB stick, and handed it to McHale. 'That's a copy of the other one,' he said, nodding at the stick in Campbell's laptop. 'It's as near as dammit the whole bloody bible on him. It's all we have. All that's missing is nearly everything we need to catch the bastard.'

Campbell pressed a button on his phone. He didn't wait for an answer. He didn't wait for anything. He just said, 'Travel plans, Alice,' and cut the connection.

'You keep saying "him",' said McHale.

'Eh?'

'Laurel out there,' he said, nodding to the squad room, 'can bench press 200lbs without breaking a sweat. She's five-foot-five and looks a bit on the skinny side, but she's as fit as a butcher's bloody dog. You already decided it's a 'him'?'

Drummond frowned and shrugged. 'For fuck's sake… it sounds like a 'him' don't you think? Bit of a deep voice for a 'her'. Anyway, what I think isn't important. That's why you're here. But point taken,' he said.

'Just because the voice on the tape is male, doesn't mean the killer is. For the moment let's say I'm leaving my options open.'

There was a soft knock on the door and Alice came in holding a buff coloured A5 envelope. She smiled at McHale and handed it to him. Then she left without saying a word.

He recognised the scent she left behind. It threatened to scratch a small itch in the back of his memory. The moment passed faster than a sparrow's fart.

He opened the envelope and pulled out the contents.

One open-ended return train ticket from Stockport to Euston and documents for an extended stay in what he hoped would be a decent hotel somewhere near the city centre.

'There's a meeting room booked at the Yard's new home for 9am Monday,' said Drummond. 'It's yours for as long as you want it. So, it might be a good idea if you can get your arse down there ASAP.'

McHale did the double blink. Inner voice piped up. 'Okay. He definitely said who 'you' want. We heard it clear as daylight. Your team. Your game. Your rules. Light the damned blue touch paper and don't fuck this up.'

Drummond continued. 'Ultimately, they'll all be your choice… except one. The bad news is she's on board whether you want her there or not. But the good news is you'll love her. Oh… and she's a Cherokee. You're fine with Cherokees, right?'

'Last time I looked.'

Drummond reached into his inside left jacket pocket and pulled out a folded sheet of paper. Handed it to McHale, who opened it and saw three names. One below the other. Typed in black ink.

'And these are?'

'Think of them as a starting point. A few suggestions. Choose any of them or disregard them all. But have a serious look. They're on the stick.'

'And what about the Yank?'

Drummond reached down, brought up his case, opened it and brought out a manila file. Handed the file to McHale. 'Meet the first member of your team. Supervisory Special Agent Grace Lightfoot. She's part of the FBI's Behavioural Science Unit at Quantico, Virginia. She's a Native American Indian. She's forty-two and hunts serial killers for a living. If it sounds like a cliché, tough. Suck the damned thing up. You two should get on like a house on fire.'

'Does she have superpowers, too?'

'Not that I know of.'

'Is this political bullshit?'

'Don't be a smart arse.'

'When did you put her on the list?'

'I didn't. She put herself on it a year ago after Barbara Lennox became victim number 5. Called me up in the middle of the damned night. Burned my ear for an hour. Then her boss called up my boss. That lady is seriously enthusiastic. She's been following the trail of bodies left by The Holy Ghost since 2012. I got another phone call two hours ago. She's flying into Heathrow tomorrow. Staying at the American Ambassador's residence in Regent's Park. It's a nice little place. Not exactly your average B&B.'

'I thought those buggers at the BAU only butted in if they were invited. A bit like vampires.'

'You watch too much TV... just don't make any passes at her.'

'What the hell is that supposed to mean?'

'You'll know,' said Drummond, mysteriously.

McHale could hear the sound of bastard thugs approaching in the distance, somewhere above his left eye. He tried to ignore the noise. Inner voice offered a helpful suggestion; 'Note to self. Stock up on painkillers, Kemosabe.'

Drummond stood up and stuck out his right hand. McHale followed suit, grabbed the proffered mitt and pumped it a couple of times.

'I'll give you a proper briefing when you get down south,' said the older copper. 'Meanwhile, you've got a team to put together and the sooner the better. See you Monday morning.'

McHale threw a small nod in the direction of Campbell, who caught it deftly and threw it back. Then he left the room, saw Laurel and Hardy and pointed them in the direction of Campbell.

Next stop. Desk drawer. Check the blister packs. Distance, about 20 feet. Next stop. Quick pee and a slow breather. Distance one flight down. Through two doors. Back up the stairs.

Next stop. Coffee point. Lubricate throat with something hot and black.

Look around.

See Laurel and Hardy talking to Campbell.

Breathe.

The pair left Campbell and made a beeline for McHale, stopping three feet away. They were smiling.

Laurel's smile was cold and predatory. 'Bastard,' she said. Then she mouthed 'thank you'.

'Lucky fucking bastard,' said Hardy.

Two hours later McHale's desk was clear and all cases shifted over into the loving hands of a duo who, since they walked in that morning, had good reason to feel they'd been overlooked and shafted with something large and hard.

But one of the cases was the rape and violent assault of a 14-year-old girl by person or persons unknown two weeks previously. It wasn't common knowledge, but Laurel was a survivor of childhood abuse.

It was McHale knowledge, though. 'Payback's a bitch in plain clothes with a score to settle,' said inner voice.

Laurel and Hardy left with a box full of files and went on their own monster hunt.

McHale's brain went off the main road and down a darker side street.

He took the sheet of paper Drummond had given him. Opening it, he put it flat on a desktop he hadn't seen in months, maybe longer.

He took off his jacket and hung it over the back of his chair. Then parked his arse. Took a long slug of warm coffee. A deep breath. And went fishing.

'And so it begins…' said inner voice.

The three names on the sheet, from top to bottom, were:

1. *Father Steven Rice. Jesuit priest.*
2. *Detective Inspector Siobhan Kelly, National Crime Agency.*
3. *Sonny Jello. Weapons expert. Bloody good saxophonist.*

He knew the first one. Heard about the other two. Kelly for her left leg. Not the other injuries. Jello for his sax. Not the weapons.

He reached for his phone, lifted the receiver, and punched in three numbers. Alice answered after the second ring. 'I was expecting your call, Mister McHale,' she said. He liked it that she called him Mister and not DI. It was somehow both formal and informal at the same time.

'Alice, I need your help,' he said.

'I was briefed before your meeting. I have a copy of DCS Drummond's names. Would you like to speak to them personally first, or do you just want me to go ahead and arrange travel and accommodation for them on the presumption they'll accept the invitation?'

'Both. I don't think any of them would pass up an opportunity like this. But let me break the good news first.'

He could hear her nod.

Alice Kennedy. Personal Assistant to DCI Robert Campbell. Fifty-something. Unmarried in the conventional sense. But happily-so in the only sense that mattered. Keeper of the keys of all things known and unknown, for the boss she'd served and protected for the past twenty or so years.

Alice Kennedy. Intelligent. Warm. Caring. Taker of no shit. Friend to McHale.

'Let's start at the top. I'd like you to track down the Jesuit priest Father Stephen Rice. Last time I spoke to him was about six months ago. He was in Rome. I need a phone number.

'Then, I need an open-ended train ticket and accommodation arranged for DC Toby Macbeth. Same train. Same day. Same hotel. And please let the gaffer know I want the lad on my team.'

He paused. Waiting for his mouth to catch up with his brain.

'That it?' said Alice.

'No. I might have one or two others for you to track down. I'll let you know over the next twenty-four hours.'

She lingered a breath.

'Okay... what?'

'Do you have a gofer in mind?'

McHale smiled. 'You're already taken,' he said.

'I might be able to help with that. Leave it with me.'

Right.

Phone down. Eyes up. Raised voice. 'Toby?'

Ten seconds later a steaming hot black coffee appeared as if by magic on the desktop. Right hand side. Easy reach.

A voice appeared ahead of the slight but wiry frame of DC Toby Macbeth. In looks he reminded McHale of the Norwegian footballer Ole Gunnar Solskjaer who used to play for Manchester United. The one they called The Baby-faced Assassin.

Macbeth was thirty-four and as clever as the brainy one on a pub quiz team.

Soft Scottish accent. Light brown hair. Pale complexion. Single minded. Couldn't grow a beard if his life depended on it.

A whisker over five-foot-nine and about twelve stone soaking wet.

He had an almost spooky ability to know just what McHale wanted, just when he wanted it. And he wasn't a prick, which itself earned him a shitload of brownie points.

He was a Macbeth, but two 'Macs' on the team would be one too many. So as long as he was with McHale, he would be known as Toby.

'I hear you're going hunting,' he said.

'News travels fast.'

'Any particular prey in mind?'

'Pull up a chair.'

Inner voice offered a bit of advice. 'Make him an offer he can't refuse.'

'Remember the movie, The Godfather?' said McHale.

Chapter Four

Wednesday, 2nd August, 2:30pm

By mid-afternoon, the day after the sixth murder, Alice had tracked down the Jesuit, sorted out the paperwork for Toby, and put the feelers out for a suitable gofer.

She was a very fast operator.

The feelers came back with one name.

Daisy Nash.

A shade over twenty-nine. A smidge under five-foot-eight. Unattached. Very protective. Hard as nails. A little black book full of contacts. A one-woman support system, complete with Alice's seal of approval. She lived just south of Macclesfield. She was coming in at 9.30 the next morning.

At just after three that afternoon, McHale rang Father Stephen Rice. The Jesuit who had been instrumental in helping to catch Father David Black.

The priest who wanted no credit for his involvement in the hunt or the capture. The one who faded quietly into the background when the smoke cleared and the coughing stopped.

McHale counted the rings as he did with every call he made. On the eleventh ring the phone was answered. A small calm voice. One word. No information. Just as he remembered it.

'Yes?'

'Hello, Father, it's Detective Inspector Tom McHale. We worked together in 2011.'

Silence.

More silence.

'Hello, Tom. Yes, I remember. Not the sort of thing you forget easy. Hang on a sec…'

McHale heard shouting on the other end of the line. Rice was swearing. He couldn't hear a second voice. After one minute and forty-six seconds, he came back on the line.

'Sorry about that. I have a washing machine that's too clever for its own good. It thinks it knows everything but the damned thing has shit for brains. We are not on friendly terms at the moment.'

McHale smiled at the memory of having long conversations with the priest who cursed like an Irish navvy.

Inner voice came to the rescue. 'Put your damned empathy head on.'

'I have a toaster that's a bit bad tempered at times,' said McHale.

He thought he heard a sound between a laugh and a grunt.

Small voice. 'Hmm… well, you're not calling for a nice friendly catch-up, are you? You have another killer then,' he said. Not a question. A statement. A fact. One that was devoid of all enthusiasm.

'Yes.'

'How bad is this one?'

'Ever heard of The Holy Ghost?'

'That's a stupid thing to say to a priest.'

'This one has nothing to do with the Trinity, Father. Although probably everything to do with the sign of the cross.'

Silence.

More silence.

A soft 'Bollocks.'

McHale could imagine the Jesuit's bright blue eyes closing slowly as they did whenever something threatened to upset his equilibrium. It was almost as if he was on a tightrope. Holding onto the long pole. Increasing his rotational inertia. Maintaining his balance. Keeping himself from falling into whatever madness lay below.

He imagined Rice's face as he breathed deeply, keeping his eyes closed for at least a dozen heartbeats, then slowly opening them again. Just like the first time he saw the carnage of the Kirkbride couple. Once Black had finished with them.

'How much do you know about him?' he said.

'It's never what you know that's interesting. It's always what you don't know yet.'

'Well, at this point we don't know shit.'

Silence.

More silence.

'Interesting. When was the latest one? And what's the count? Officially.'

'Last night. And six so far. We're no nearer catching him, or her, now than we were in 2012. I need your help again, if you're up for it.'

Silence.

More silence.

'You're putting together another team?'

'Different kind of team. I remember something you said to me before we caught Black. You said…'

'Stop thinking like coppers. Start thinking like killers.'

'Or Priests.' McHale took a deep breath and let it out slowly. 'We've been thinking like coppers on this one since 2012 and it's got us nowhere. Time to change.'

Silence.

'I wasn't exactly flavour of the month with some of the old guard in The Vatican after our last little get together.'

'We caught a double murderer.'

'And I also betrayed the sanctity of the confessional to help do it.'

'Some things don't deserve the sanctity of the little curtained box.'

'Tell that to the Guardians of the Galaxy back at global HQ.'

'Did you get benched?'

'Do you remember who Saint Ignatius Loyola was?'

'I miss your habit of answering a question with a question.'

'One of the things he said was 'Teach us to give and not count the cost'.'

Silence.

'Words to live by,' said McHale.

'So, I gave up Black. Or rather I gave up what he told me in his confession. And I didn't count the cost.'

'And you got a pat on the back for being a good Jesuit?'

'No. I got threatened with Canon Law number 983.1. The sacramental seal is inviolable. I'm not allowed to betray what's said to me in confession. For any reason. Whether by word or in any other way. Ever. No exceptions. Under pain of excommunication. Or words to that effect.'

'So, what happened?'

'I lied.'

'You WHAT?'

'I told them I didn't spill the confessional beans on Black. Black said I made it all up and he couldn't understand why. But he forgave me anyway and thought I needed psychiatric help. Well, the priest did. Black's alter personality, Arthur, was a very clever bastard. But it was his word against mine. Black had no idea that Arthur even existed. The Vatican had no proof to the contrary. They had their suspicions, but without my own confession, they had bugger all. Canon Law, they said, wasn't broken. So, they decided to believe the guy who didn't get off on stabbing people to death and trying to cut heads off. They gave me a damned good talking to then cut me loose.

'They gave Black a permanent residency in Broadmoor with no possibility of parole. Not in this lifetime, anyway. I went to see him once, you know. In the beginning. I thought he was possibly one of the nicest men I've ever known. I never got to meet Arthur. I'd like to keep it that way.'

'I think you've got friends in high places,' said McHale.

'Just because the Pope is a Jesuit too, you think that gave me some sort of free pass?'

'I think the Soldiers of Christ stick together.'

Silence.

Then the sound of a breath being slowly released. The sound of air molecules being rearranged. The sound of a decision being arrived at.

Big sigh. Small voice.

'Oh bugger it. Okay. Where and when?'

McHale smiled as quietly as he could.

Some people know the answers before they've even heard the questions.

'You know, you can actually hear a smile,' said the Jesuit. 'If you listen hard enough you can hear the lips stretch, the cheek muscles lift, and the breathing change. They have studies that prove it.'

'I read a study once that scientifically proved the existence of Alex Ferguson's squeaky bum.'

He almost heard the smile bouncing back over the phone line. Those who said that Jesuits didn't have a sense of humour didn't know Jesuits at all.

'The New Scotland Yard building. Victoria Embankment. London. Next Monday around 9am. Check in at reception. I'll get travel and accommodation documents delivered to you by hand this week. Where the hell are you?'

'Oxford. And it's not Hell. It's a tiny patch of Heaven. Apart from the damned washing machine. See you there and then. Best wishes to your toaster.'

The line went dead.

Four down (including the man of God who speaks to household appliances, the Yank and Toby). Everyone else to go.

Alice was still hunting.

'Take a break, dammit. Grab a coffee and look for the missing one,' said inner voice

One refill. Twenty feet across the room. Stand at the window and look at the rain. Concentrate.

McHale had that feeling Charlie used to get when his epilepsy started thirty-two years ago. Before it stopped ten years ago. Forever.

Before the accident.

The feeling he had before the anti-seizure tablets set him free. Free from the damaged tongue. The lost hours. The falling down and shaking in the middle of the street and relying on the kindness of strangers to look after you until you came around. Before they got the medication right.

The feeling that something important was always just out of sight. Just out of reach. Through the mist. Through the darkness.

Charlie McHale.

Older by five years. Taller by two inches.

Charlie McHale.

The proud possessor of not only epilepsy, but also a brain cancer that was too deep to go in and look at, and too advanced to cut out. Six weeks from start to finish. From healthy on the outside to all fucked up on the inside.

Only he fooled them all. Because after that, he got the Beamer. Then he had the crash. And the pine box. And the flaming send-off. They burned him up as per his last wish.

It was still raining outside and the sky was the colour of cigarette ash when McHale turned away from the window. Still looking for the missing one.

For as long as he'd been a copper, he'd had a missing one. It was there in every case he'd ever worked on. Every major life decision he'd ever had. And it was always one of two things.

Either somebody or something that formed the last piece of the jigsaw. The last thing that needed to fall into place before the picture was complete.

It was always sitting in the background. Just of reach. Just out of sight. Parked in the fog. Just like Charlie's feelings.

Sometimes the fog cleared and sometimes it didn't.

If it didn't, you just added the latest missing one to all the other ones you had. You just left it sitting festering in a dark corner somewhere between your ears. That was the rule.

And if it did clear, the missing one wasn't way off in the distance. It was up close and personal. Right in front of your face. Looking into your eyes. Daring you to look away. Just like it did back in 2011.

Bastard thugs were whispering. They knew when to keep their voices down and when to yell their heads off.

Chapter Five

Alice stuck a yellow square post-it-note onto the wood of his desktop. The note appeared as if by magic. Hand unseen. Feet unheard. All that remained of the delivery was the faint hint of something feminine in the air.

The post-it had a name, a number and a message on it. Written in elegant handwriting. The name was Detective Inspector Siobhan Kelly. The number was for a mobile telephone. The message was 9 words long. The words were: 'So far Sonny Jello a no-show. Still hunting.'

Inner voice prepped him. 'Don't mention West Hampstead and the Brasher twins. And be bloody nice.'

He picked up the handset and dialled. It was answered after one ring. A woman's voice said, 'Hello?'

'DI Kelly?'

Pause.

'Yes?'

'My name's Tom McHale. I'm a DI working out of Stockport. I was given your name by DCS Cyril Drummond.'

'Yes, I know Cyril and the answer is no.'

The line went dead.

McHale looked at the handset as if by examining it he would gauge the expression on Kelly's face.

'Well, you bollocked that one right up,' said inner voice. 'Time to switch to Plan B.'

He dialled the number again.

This time it rung out. No answerphone.

He dialled again.

One ring. One pissed off voice. 'Perhaps I didn't make myself clear,' said Kelly.

'The Holy Ghost,' said McHale. And waited… and waited…

Eventually there was a soft 'Fuck' on the line.

It was the kind of 'Fuck' that was probably whispered by United States Marshall and Texas Ranger John Barclay Armstrong on 24th August 1877, when he came across John Wesley Hardin, the most dangerous gunman in the Wild West, on a train.

It was the kind of 'Fuck' that was a mixture of instant excitement and powerful vengeance.

A fight ensued.

Armstrong won… Hardin didn't. His .44 Colt cap-and-ball pistol got caught up in his suspenders. He was knocked out cold. The long arm of the law had a mean right hook attached to the end of it.

Fast-forward 137 years.

At 11.00am on Monday, 17th November 2014, Detective Inspector Siobhan Kelly and a team of six armed police officers, five men and one woman, were outside a large detached Victorian house in West Hampstead London.

They were members of the newly formed £450m National Crime Agency (dubbed Britain's FBI). A 5,000-strong elite force with sweeping powers to hunt down cyber criminals, drug barons, paedophile gangs, and people-traffickers.

And Kelly was their blue-eyed girl. Smart. Tough. Thirty-five. Fanatically fit with an intuition that bordered on the spooky.

They were looking for a fifty-seven-year-old convicted paedophile named Gregory Stubbs. Stubbs liked little girls. He had five-year-old twins Ellie and Samantha Brasher with him in the house. He had kidnapped them a week earlier from their home in Battersea.

The team, acting on what they believed were reliable

intelligence reports that Stubbs was inside the house with the girls, decided to mount a hostage rescue operation.

But Kelly had an itch in the back of her brain. The kind of itch that brought with it a cold, sick feeling that she couldn't nail down but couldn't dismiss either.

They had tried negotiating with Stubbs. He told them to go to Hell. He added that he would kill the girls if the police tried to enter the house.

He had never killed before.

The windows were blacked out. So, the police used advanced wall-penetrating radar technology, which told them that three individuals were inside. Size indeterminate.

Downstairs room next to the kitchen. The armed police didn't wait to be invited in. They had a court order. They had a profile. What they didn't have was the knowledge that Stubbs was suicidal.

Nowhere in his profile did it say that suicide had ever been attempted or even thought about.

Nowhere in his profile did it say that he had learned how to make bombs from visiting a variety of websites.

Nowhere in his profile did it say that he was capable of rigging a house to explode and then releasing a dead-man switch that he held in his hand at the same time that the police were gaining entry.

The moment the rescue team breached front and back doors, firearms at the ready, Kelly's itch got scratched. She was about to shout out but the machine was in motion and nothing could stop it.

Stubbs released the dead-man's switch and a series of explosions reduced the house to rubble and all life in it to the kind of human tissue that was collected in buckets, not body bags.

The tissue included Stubbs, the two 5-year-old twin girls, and three of the rescue team.

Kelly spent nearly three months in hospital and came back to ride a desk after a year. Along with a permanent limp. A permanent cane. And a permanent nightmare that time did nothing to dilute.

No amount of closure on God's green earth does that.

Payback might make it a bit more bearable, though.

Payback on someone else, for something else down the line. Not the piece of shit whose capture and punishment for this slice of horror would be forever denied the British legal system in general, and her in particular.

DC Siobhan Kelly couldn't attend the double funeral of both girls. But she did arrange for a colleague to attend in her place.

As per her instructions, and the family's consent, he dropped a white envelope, which was soon covered by handfuls of earth, into each grave on top of each small coffin.

Inside each envelope was a single sheet of paper. And on the paper were three typed sentences. Thirty-four words in total.

'Someone will pay for your death. They might be guilty of another death, but yours will be added to the bill. And I will collect. That's a promise. I'm sorry. Detective Inspector Siobhan Kelly.'

On 2nd August 2017, she was given the chance to settle the bill.

'You said you were based in Stockport?' said Kelly.

'Everybody's based somewhere,' said McHale. 'You?'

'Somewhere.'

McHale smiled inside.

'I'll be there in the morning,' said Kelly.

'No need. I'll get travel and accommodation documents hand delivered to you this week. Plus, a USB stick. Study what's on it. I need you in London next Monday. New Scotland Yard. Around 9am would be good. Sign in at reception when you get there. What's your address?'

'Alice has it.'

McHale was about to say goodbye when the line went dead.

Inner voice said, 'I like her. All business. No bullshit. Five down. If we get to seven I wanna be Yul Brynner.'

He picked up the phone, dialled Alice. One ring. 'Not yet,' she said.

'Not yet what?'

'You were going to ask me if I've managed to get in touch with Sonny Jello.'

'Did I ever tell you about my old Gypsy granny?'

'The one who could read the tea leaves?'

'No, that was my aunty Ethel. Granny Mavis was the one who did the palms in the kitchen by the back door. They sometimes lined up outside. She didn't charge a penny, so they brought food instead. She never went hungry.'

'In that case, no.'

'You remind me of her.'

'As well as being a very good detective, Thomas McHale, you might just be full of shit.'

'Distinct possibility.'

He could hear her smile.

An hour later Sonny Jello was still a no-show. So, he grabbed his jacket, threw the USB drive with all the Ghost details on it to Toby, and told him to expand his already expanded brain.

Then he headed home to a microwaved chicken pasta meal, a very large Southern Comfort (or two), a game of Internet Chess, and a little background tenor sax, courtesy of Dexter Gordon.

First track up: I Guess I'll Hang My Tears Out To Dry.

First move up, King's pawn opening.

First sip of SoCo.

Dexter slowed his pulse. The Ghost invaded his thoughts.

He hitched himself up to four small, hollow needles attached to four lengths of tubing, a large syringe, and a wind-up pump.

Then four small vials worth of pure plasma invaded his system. Below the skin of his abdomen. Above the muscle.

Subcutaneous Immunoglobulin. SCIG for short.

Every Sunday evening: 90ml.

Every Wednesday evening: 80ml.

Three hours of slow infusion two nights a week.

And all because four years ago he contracted the bastard

of all autoimmune conditions called Chronic Inflammatory Demyelinating Polyneuropathy. CIDP for short.

No cure. Yet. Just containment. Just slam the brakes on before it gets a good hold. Just tell the numbness and the tingly shocks go to hell. Just a real pain in the arse, but it didn't stop him from doing his job. Didn't stop him from driving his old beamer. Didn't stop him from occasionally riding shotgun while somebody else sat in the driver's seat.

Anyway, it was what it was. Nothing to do about it except get on with life, count the bodies, and piss on all the evil bastards from a great height.

Three hours later he unhitched the needles, cleaned up the mess, and put the whole damned medical circus on the back burner for another four days.

Last thing before hitting the sack, he checked the mantra on his fridge door. Same way he checked it every night.

It said: 'Sometimes you're the windshield. Sometimes you're the bug.'

Same thing it said every night.

Before he drifted off on his double pillows around midnight, inner voice said goodnight in its usual fashion. 'Okay Kemosabe. Put your damned sleep mask on and say Goodnight Vienna. Ready… steady… go. And… one-hundred leaping sheep… ninety-nine leaping sheep… ninety-eight leaping sheep…'

He got all the way to forty-nine before the night shift clocked on.

Chapter Six

As McHale drifted off to sleep, a British Airways 747 was leaving US airspace, skirting the Labrador Sea, and heading across the North Atlantic Ocean to the United Kingdom.

Sitting next to a window on the upper deck, eyes closed, fully relaxed, was a forty-two-year-old Native American Indian female.

Her ancestry said she was mixed-race Cherokee. Her passport said her name was Grace Lightfoot. Her FBI badge said she was a Supervisory Special Agent. She was fitter than most females her age, even most twenty years younger

Some may have regarded her as beautiful, though it wasn't a term she would ever have used for herself.

She had been asleep for just over an hour. But the sleep was the kind that could leave her wide awake at a moment's notice.

It was also the kind that brought with it vivid dreams.

The one she was having took her back to a time when she was young and inexperienced.

She was hunting with her great grandfather. She was ten and he was eighty-one. He smelled like old tobacco. It wasn't the hunting of grown warriors; it was the hunting of a teacher and a pupil.

And they were tracking a wild turkey.

They were hoping for a fat one.

So far, they had tracked down some elusive wild mushrooms. The mushrooms were easy to catch. They didn't move very fast.

During the hunt, he told her of Guwisguwi, who became principal Chief of the Cherokee Nation the year they found gold in Hall County, Georgia.

In the Cherokee tongue his name meant 'Mysterious Little White Bird.'

In the English tongue, his name was plain old John Ross.

'The date of his death is the same as the date of your birth,' he said. 'August 1. This is an important day for you. Remember it.'

Two dreams are never the same, Lightfoot thought, as she slept in her seat, high in the sky above the sea below. The old man had never told her this before.

The smell of old tobacco grew stronger, which was strange because the old man never smoked.

'John Ross was a leader during The Trail of Tears, when more than 4,000 Cherokee men, women, and children died,' he said. 'They had black slaves who died too.'

Lightfoot was listening intently to the old man's voice, when she heard a sound in the bush.

She stopped walking, reached up, and put her right hand gently on the old man's left arm. He pretended to be surprised at the gesture.

They stopped and listened, but didn't hear the sound again.

So, they carried on walking.

'On the Trail of Tears there was some singing to keep hearts happy. One of the songs they sang was the hymn 'Amazing Grace'. This is why, when you were born, your father, John Lightfoot, gave you the name Grace. This is an important name.'

The old man had never told her this before in their turkey hunt dream.

'Your parents had people in Scotland. John Ross had people in Scotland. You're both connected to each other. Never forget this.'

There was a light touch on Lightfoot's left shoulder.

So light that the skin under her thin cotton shirt almost didn't feel it.

But she immediately opened her eyes. A British Airways stewardess was standing over her in the aisle of the 747. 'Thirty minutes to landing,' she whispered. Smiling.

A pre-arranged heads-up.

Lightfoot nodded and shifted in her seat.

The echo of the dream drifted away into the darkness outside the window.

Chapter Seven

Twenty-five minutes before Grace Lightfoot's plane was due to touch down at Heathrow from Washington, McHale's iPhone alarm went off and a loud bluesy guitar riff shattered the silence and broke the spell.

He stabbed the snooze cruise, groaned in resignation, and opened his eyes. Turned onto his back. And said hello to the start of another day.

Only today his head was a million miles away from where it was yesterday. Today he was in charge of The Holy Ghost team. Today he was the Big Kahuna. Well, possibly medium-sized.

He did all the brush, rinse, shave, shower, dress, breakfast stuff he usually did. In the order he usually did them. Then he headed back into a place where, for a while at least, everyone looked at him through different sets of eyes.

Inner voice threw out a morning motivational message. 'Screw your damned head on straight and don't be a dickhead. Go get 'em!'

Right. Shoulders back. Balls adjusted. Walk through the door. 9am on the dot.

Coffee supplied by Toby, as usual. Only served up hotter. And accompanied by two 500ml Paracetamols. And one Danish pastry.

Kahunas of any shape and size are afforded certain perks denied to lesser mortals.

'You have a visitor,' said the young detective.

'She's not a visitor. She's our new firefighter. Maybe.'

Jacket over back of chair. Tabs and a gulp of coffee. Look at the Danish. Think better of it. Ignore the thought and take a large bite.

Walk about twenty feet to the far wall. Chew fast. Swallow slow. Around the corner. First door on the right. Walk in and smile.

Daisy Nash was sitting at one side of the meeting table in front of a mug of coffee. There was another coffee opposite her where McHale was about to sit. It was black.

She stood up and walked to him; hand outstretched, smile full on, head tilted upwards. 'I took the liberty,' she said, nodding towards the mugs.

She was all business. No nerves. White blouse under dark blue trouser suit. Sensible shoes. Medium brown hair, short and neat. Minimal makeup. Green, steady eyes. Pretty face. Petite figure. Bendy on the outside. Hard as nails on the inside.

'Some liberties are necessary first thing in the morning,' said McHale. He shook the proffered palm and both sat down.

'What did Alice tell you?'

'Not a lot. She thinks you're looking for an Alice clone.'

McHale smiled.

'I'll settle for a Daisy original,' he said. 'If you're good enough for Alice to recommend, then you're good enough for me.'

'That will be good enough for me.'

'She says you're one of the best firefighters she knows. I need somebody who knows how to keep their mouth shut and their mind open. Somebody with a brain like a filing cabinet, a mind like a steel trap, and balls like Red Adair.'

Laughter.

Genuine. Not fake. At ease. Confident.

He was impressed.

She took a small sip of coffee. 'Alice wanted to wait until we met before bringing me up to speed. I know you're going hunting, and I know you'll be hunting The Holy Ghost. But that's about it. No point telling me any more if you don't need me on the team. But if you do want me, then I'll work my arse off to help you catch this bastard. Just one thing.'

'What?'

'I answer to you. Nobody else. Loyalty is a big thing with me. And if anyone else wants me to answer to them, then they can politely sod off. Sir.'

McHale picked up the mug in front of him. Tested its warmth with a sip, followed by a large gulp. He could feel the heat slip down his throat.

Inner voice offered an opinion. 'I think this one's a keeper, Kemosabe. But she needs to can the suit.'

'Can the suit. Keep the attitude,' said McHale, smiling.

Daisy smiled and nodded. 'Understood, sir. When do I start?'

'Ten minutes ago. I'll ask Alice to sort out your paperwork, travel and accommodation documents, and she'll find you a desk plus all the equipment you need. Good to have you on board. I'll catch up with you later. Meanwhile, you'll find Alice two doors down on the right.'

McHale stood up and leaned across the table, shaking Daisy's hand again.

He felt the tingle of a team coming together.

There was a soft knock on the door and Alice walked in.

'Green light, Alice,' said McHale. 'Let's get the show on the road.'

Alice merely nodded. But he could see the smile in her eyes as he left the room.

One firefighter sorted out.

For the rest of the morning, McHale ploughed through the information on the stick supplied by Drummond. Toby was doing the same with a copy he'd made of the one McHale threw at him the night before. He was also supplying McHale with gallons of caffeine at regular intervals.

Daisy was given a desk ten feet away from his. She spent the morning settling in.

Around 2pm, she slipped a post-it-note on McHale's desk.

He didn't see or hear her do it. Mad ninja skills. Just like Alice.

On it was a number for Sonny Jello. He put in a call and got a personalised voicemail. An old, lived-in voice with a thin Manchester accent said, 'This is Sonny. You know the drill. Name and number. I'll call you when I get back from New York.'

Then there was a beep.

McHale left his name, rank and mobile number.

He also left a sentence twenty-one words long. The words were, 'Give me a call. I'd like you to help me catch a serial killer. And no, I'm not taking the piss.'

He ended the call. No way on God's earth was he saying goodbye to a bloody machine.

Daisy seamlessly took over coffee duties from Toby. Around four-ish she stopped by McHale's desk.

'What's your Paracetamol supply like?'

McHale grunted. 'Field medic, too, eh?' He opened his top right-hand drawer.

One fat box. Two skinny blister packs. Twenty tabs.

'Seriously depleted,' he said.

'Leave it to me,' she said.

Fast reverse to earlier that morning.

A few hundred miles down south, an almost fully laden British Airways 747 touched down at Heathrow. It had taken off from Washington Dulles International Airport seven hours twenty-eight minutes earlier.

It landed three minutes behind schedule.

It was 6.55am, Thursday, 3rd August. Greenwich Mean Time.

Amongst the first 297 passengers to alight was SSA Grace Lightfoot.

Her hair was tied back in a pony tail and she was wearing a dark cool-weather jacket over a cotton shirt, well-worn blue jeans, and a pair of soft leather shoes.

Her calm, almost disinterested demeanour belied the fact that inside she was hyper-vigilant. She always had been. Almost since the day she was born, on 1st August 1975.

She was unhitched. Unarmed. And unsmiling.

She was a people watcher. So instead of travelling the twenty miles from Heathrow to Regent's Park in the back of a cab, she decided to ride the tube for an hour and a half and watch the early morning world as it sat, stood, and hurried around her.

She stopped watching at Piccadilly and travelled a short hop the rest of the way to her destination in silence by black cab.

Winfield House, a neo-Georgian mansion set in twelve acres of Regent's Park, had been the official residence of the United States Ambassador to the Court of St. James since 1955.

The park was a natural green oasis in the middle of a concrete desert.

Amongst Winfield's previous owners was world-famous heiress Barbara Hutton who, a few years after marrying movie star Cary Grant in 1942, sold it to the US Government for the token price of one American dollar.

The US Government had since renovated, upgraded, and impressively redecorated it. And with unrivalled security specifications, Winfield House was an easy place to come to, and a hard place to leave.

Grace had friends in high places.

One of them in particular had heard stories about her grandfather, who spoke often about the Navajo Wind Talkers of World War II.

He was a storyteller, like his father before him.

So, she settled in, chewed the fat a bit, went for a walk in the rain in the Park, and waited.

At 3.25 that afternoon she got a call from McHale.

'I hope you like being wet and cold,' he said.

'McHale?'

Strong, warm voice.

'So they tell me.'

'And are they right?'

'Most of the time.'

Twenty words in and already he liked her.

'Sorry I couldn't be there in person to welcome you. I'm about two-hundred miles North of you at the moment.'

'My next-door neighbour is twice that. In my country you're in the next room.'

'What can I say? We're a small, friendly island floating in a crowded corner of a big pond.'

Silence.

'Your first time in the UK?'

'Fifth, but one of them doesn't count.'

'I had a welcome gift delivered to Winfield House for you. Have a good look at it over the next couple of days.'

Inner voice butted in; 'You forgot to say welcome to the UK, you dickhead.'

'When do we meet?'

'The team's getting together Monday at New Scotland Yard. You been there?'

'I'll find it.'

'If it helps, I'll be in London Saturday.'

'Can't hurt,' she said.

'I'll be in touch. What food do you like?'

'The dead kind.'

'Welcome to the UK, Supervisory Special Agent Grace Lightfoot.'

'Happy to be here, Detective Inspector Tom McHale.'

He had the feeling that happiness was an infrequent visitor to her tone of voice.

He cut the line, looked around, and saw Daisy, staring at a laptop screen. Almost as if she could feel his eyes on him, she looked up. A question in her eyes.

'Find me a number for DCS Cyril Drummond, soon as you can. Alice will have it. Add it to your list of contacts. Mobile and landline. Then get him on the phone.'

One nod. Two minutes. Six rings. One name.

'Drummond…'

Not a question. A fact.

'Tom McHale, sir.'

'Cracked it yet?'

'Just taking a hammer to it as we speak.'

He heard Drummond smile.

'I need one of the knives.'

'Not my first rodeo, Tom. The one I showed you yesterday never left your building. Your gaffer put it in a locked drawer in his desk for safekeeping overnight. Take bloody good care of it, please. See you Monday, if not before.'

Call ended.

McHale needed to pee.

On the way back he knocked on Campbell's office door. Silence. More silence. A finger tapped him on the left shoulder.

He turned around and saw Alice, smiling. 'He's not there. But he asked me to give you this when you finished your calls.'

She was holding a beige A3 jiffy bag.

She handed it to him. 'That thing's heavy,' she said.

McHale carefully tore open the bag's signed chain-of-custody label, and pulled out the Fairbairn-Sykes knife. Still safe inside its protective case. Still wrapped in its dark, heavy cloth.

But not for much longer. Chain of Evidence had now passed to him. So, he slipped on a pair of latex gloves and removed the blade.

It was a bit heavier than a billiard ball.

Not just a lump of finely crafted old metal. More like a very dangerous weapon about to be examined by a copper with an above average IQ and a healthy respect for sharp, pointed objects.

Inner voice said; 'Go stand by the window. Take the damned thing in your hand and see if it talks to you. Go on… do it…'

McHale smiled at Alice. Great minds think alike.

He left her standing outside Campbell's door and walked back into the open-plan office and over to the nearest window that didn't have a desk or a filing cabinet in front of it.

It was just the right height. About four feet, floor to sill. Easy to get up close to.

He held the container in his left hand. The knife in his right. Felt the weight. Tested the balance. Tried to imagine another hand gripping it where his hand was now. Looked out of the window onto a cold, dry day. Closed his eyes and let his mind drift like the clouds above.

So… which hand used it to kill James Halliwell? Right or left?

McHale put the jiffy bag and cloth on a nearby desk. Transferred the knife to his left hand. Squeezed his fingers around the grip. Then did the same with his right.

Which one felt more comfortable?

He was right hand and right eye dominant. Was the killer?

Did holding the Fairbairn-Sykes feel like he was holding onto something separate? Or did it feel more natural? More connected. More like an extension of his arm. More like it belonged. More like it was at home.

He took a deep breath. Let it out slow.

Somebody in a lab coat somewhere had pulled this knife from the skull of James Halliwell. Victim number one. Six years ago.

Did they clean it of every piece of flesh, blood, and brain matter? Did they remove every atom transferred onto it from the victim's body? Or from the killer's naked hands? Did he sweat? Were there skin cells hidden in any of the nooks and crannies?

Was there even a hint of residue left over? Something that could come into contact with McHale's hands? Something that once belonged to someone else?

Or was there no direct contact at all?

McHale spoke silently to the killer.

'Did you wear gloves? Tightly fitting ones that hugged your hands like a second skin? Or medical ones that left no prints but almost let you feel every touch? Every sensation?

'Where did you get the knife? How did you choose it? This very special knife. From a very special set. Not made for cutting. Not made for maiming. Made for efficient killing, in a war that ended over half a century ago.

'This knife that was out of work. Redundant. Useless. Forgotten. A knife that had lost its purpose. Lost its way. Until you decided to bring it out of the dark back into the light. Until you decided to put it back to work.

'Doing what it did best.

'What did you feel as you slid this knife in between the ribs of the man whose life you took? What did you feel as you pulled it out and set his blood free into the world? And what did you feel as you plunged it through hair, skin, skull, and deep into his brain?

'The man you killed didn't feel anything of that final act. By then he was dead. So, it wasn't done for him. Which means either it was done for you, or for those who would see what you did.

'Did you feel proud of your achievement? Did it feel like a job well done? Did it excite you?

'And what the hell was Bobby and September 1 about? Tell me that.'

A light double tap on McHale's left shoulder slammed the brakes on his thinking.

'Your hand's bleeding,' said Toby.

McHale hadn't felt the blade slice neatly into his right forefinger as he was passing the knife from hand to hand. The thought that it might be razor sharp hadn't even occurred to him.

'Shit. This damned thing takes victims even when it isn't in the hands of a killer,' he said, sucking the blood that was threatening to drip off his finger and onto the floor.

Inner voice had no sympathy. 'Bollocks. I've seen worse paper cuts. Be a man, shithead. You're not exactly the walking bloody wounded.'

'I would offer to make you another coffee, but I think I've

been usurped,' said Toby. He was holding a white mug with 'No Talk Before Caffeine' in large black type on the side. 'I'll see if I can get transferred to biscuit duty. Meanwhile, I think you should get plastered.'

He walked away and spoke to Daisy.

McHale frowned and examined the cut. The bleeding seemed to be slowing down. He tried to regain his interrupted train of thought. But that train had moved out of the station and was on its way to God knows where.

Toby approached with a fabric plaster. 'There, there' he said in his best motherly tone. 'We don't have any lollipops for brave boys. But you still have half of that Danish on your desk from this morning. That will have to do.'

He was a good choice, thought McHale.

Plaster affixed, he carefully popped the knife back into its jiffy bag, took it over to his desk, and put it in his top left-hand drawer. There was a fresh coffee waiting patiently.

The half Danish was looking at him. He could almost hear it begging to be eaten. A Danish, even a half-eaten one, had only one purpose in its short but high-calorie life.

He duly obliged.

His time standing by the window handling the knife had shaken something loose between his ears.

It was the kind of something that had previously been attached to lots of other somethings. Now it was attached to absolutely nothing. It was blissfully unattached, single, fancy free and interesting. Now it was a question. Now it was something to chew on.

Why the first day of August every year? What the hell was that all about? Anniversaries come in all shapes and sizes. What was so special about this one?

Birthday? Death-day? Wake up on the wrong side of the damned bed day? Who the hell knew?

He remembered a case from years ago about a Glasgow man who killed three members of his own family on 17th March because he was convinced that the world was going to end at 6pm that evening. He didn't want them to suffer. So, he shot each one in the head at 4am that morning.

One of the arresting cops asked him why he didn't shoot himself as well, if he was sure the world was going to end. He said that just in case the world decided it didn't want to end, there was a Rangers versus Celtic football match that evening on the TV and he didn't want to miss it.

Every year after that on March 17 he got ready for the end of the world from his shared cell in Barlinnie Prison. North East of Glasgow.

The first year of his lifetime sentence they put him in with a biker who strangled his girlfriend for damaging his precious Harley with a tire iron.

They became very friendly.

On 17th March the following year he stabbed the biker to death with a sharpened toothbrush. He was wrong about the end of the World again.

They gave him a cell all of his own after that.

So far, he'd guessed wrong about Armageddon nine times.

Sometimes logic and rational thinking are just all kinds of fucked up. Sometimes one plus one equals whatever the hell it wants to equal. Just because it can.

Dates are important to people for all kinds of crazy reasons, McHale thought.

Inner voice agreed wholeheartedly with an almost imperceptible nod of the inner head.

McHale spoke silently to the killer again.

'So... what happened on 1st August 2012? What shoved you over the edge on that day above all the other 364? What got up your ass and motivated you to think about joining the Monster Club?'

The silence inside his head was deafening.

The bastard thugs were otherwise occupied.

But those two words 'Monster Club' hung around like a bad echo.

McHale was all questions. The Ghost was no answers. This conversation was a one-way street.

He just needed a word from the darkness. Anything. A grunt would do. Something to let him know that a dialogue was taking place.

One that wasn't the inner voice. One that was a voice from somewhere else.

You could play Solitaire with a pack of cards. That was easy. That was a piece of piss. But to play Solitaire Chess. That was a whole new level of different.

One board. Two sets of wooden men. Thirty-two in total. One set white, the other set black.

Arrange them in their ranks. Ready for battle.

White moves first. King's pawn opening. Two squares forward. Classic. Ancient. Aggressive. Immediately staking claim to the centre of the board.

Freeing up the queen and the king's bishop.

Now...

Switch the white brain off. Swivel the board around. Switch the black brain on.

Move and repeat. Move and repeat. Move and repeat.

White asks the questions. Black fires back the answers.

Or maybe it's the other way around.

And so it goes. Back and forth. Offence and defence. Capture and advantage. Traps and twists. Loss and victory.

Dead men make no moves.

But nothing was coming back from the darkness. At least nothing he could see. Nothing he could hear. The Ghost wasn't talking.

Voice from behind. 'I never like to interrupt a man who looks like he's deep in conversation with himself,' said Daisy.

McHale looked up and frowned. 'Nobody's talking yet,' he said.

He saw the half-quizzical half-amused look in her eyes. Then the penny dropped.

'Aah… it's your process,' she said. 'Fair enough. I just wanted to tell you that I'll get the travel and accommodation details off to the other team members by courier first thing in the morning. When are we going down?'

'We'll take train down on Saturday morning. But I want to take a look at the latest crime scene tomorrow. Ask Alice about getting a pool car out. I take it you can drive?' Her scoff was all the answer he needed.

He handed her his copy of the Ghost USB. 'Make a copy of this for yourself, if you get the chance tonight, and have a quick look at it. Bring yourself up to speed.'

'Right Guv,' she said.

Now that was something new. Guv. Right off the bat. Not even Toby called him that. But he saw the young detective looking at her when she said it. And he saw him thinking. Until now, most folk here called him Mac.

Inner voice piped up, 'Keep your hair on, slick. Just because she called you Guv doesn't mean diddly bloody squat. The girl's just showing you a bit of respect. A bit of Aretha, see? Now… back to those calls.'

The phone on his desk jumped into life.

It was Alice. Sometimes she was damned spooky.

'Do you have your iPod with you today, Mister McHale?'

Alice knew every little detail about the coppers under her care. Even when to call them by their Christian name, as a mark of affection. And when to keep it official.

That's what made her so indispensable.

'Don't leave home without it.'

'Give it to Daisy. She can make a copy of all the Ghost's calls and pop them on it. Might come in handy.'

McHale smiled.

Alice the mind-reader. Alice the eye in the sky. Alice the

queen of the mother hens.

'Good call,' he said.

'Goodbye,' she said.

His right hand reached down to his right jacket pocket. Slipped inside. Felt the comforting shape of his silver iPod Classic. Wrapped in the loving embrace of a set of Sennheiser Momentum in-ear headphones. Black and chrome and, for McHale's money, the dog's bollocks.

Daisy appeared by his side.

He pulled the iPod out of his pocket and handed it to her. The buds dangled like a pair of pooch's shrunken gonads from the white cord.

'Let me guess. Eclectic taste in music?'

'Eclectic taste in everything, probably.'

She tested the weight of the iPod. As if by doing so she could tell the number of tunes it held. 'Give me half an hour.'

He nodded.

It was just before 4.10pm.

She was almost as good as her word. At 4.45pm she returned with the iPod and a smile. The office was too distracting, so he put it in his pocket and waited to listen until he reached the relative quiet of his small-but-perfectly-formed semi in Wilmslow. On the other side of the semi's walls lived an elderly couple who appreciated the safety and security they could enjoy by spending their days and nights next door to the law.

The irony was that these days even the law wasn't immune to being unlawfully touched by the long arm of the criminal fraternity.

Sometimes, late at night, even as they sat up in bed reading, the couple could hear his forays into the emotional tenor sax world of Dexter Gordon recorded in the 60s and 70s.

Dexter was six feet five inches of pure jazz inventiveness on good days and a heroin addict with diabetes, cancer of the throat and cirrhosis of the liver on bad ones.

His body gave up on 25th April 1990, in Philadelphia. Aged

sixty-seven.

He didn't do things by halves.

Neither did McHale, whose adventures into Dexter could be heard through the adjoining wall. But it was a small price to pay for the comfort his proximity brought to his immediate neighbours. And besides, they didn't mind his taste in music one little bit.

The old couple had no mortgage, no children, and no near relatives that either of them gave a damn about. He was seventy-nine and she was seventy-eight. He had a pacemaker and she was a homemaker. He was John and she was Eloise.

Of all the people in the world who would feel a measure of comfort having McHale living next door to them, these two were probably at the head of the queue.

They were second cousins and they had lived together most of their lives. But as partners, they had only loved each other passionately for a mere fifty years.

Their love might have been against the laws of some religions, some countries, and some elements of nature. But their secret was safe with McHale. John had thought it a giant risk telling him at Christmas eleven years ago. But Eloise had no doubt they had done the right thing.

She was the one who let the cat out of the bag. And she was the one who hugged him tearfully, when he said, 'I don't give a tinker's curse how you're related. Love is love. And if more folk felt as you two do for each other, for as long as you have, then the world would be a damned better place. My lips are zipped and welded shut. Now, who's for another Southern Comfort?'

That had been a good Christmas.

When McHale reached home at just after 9pm that night, the lights were on downstairs next door. But he knew they were just for show. Wednesday night was poker night for the old couple. They had a standing game the first Wednesday of every month at the home of a local restaurant owner by the name of

Louis Campanelli.

He looked like an old boxer. He had a pug nose, a cauliflower left ear, and he was as bent as a nine-pound note. He owned an Italian restaurant near the centre of Wilmslow called Da Vinci's.

It had posters of Leonardo's art on the walls, and a Michelin star chef in the kitchen. And it had food to die for on every plate that came out of it.

Eloise was a damned fine poker player. John was a damned fine chess player. Whatever he lost, she won back. They normally ended up even on the night. Life wasn't half bad, considering.

He nodded at the next-door semi. As if to tell it he was home and it could relax.

He went indoors, switched on the hall light and closed the door behind him. Picked up the single letter on the mat. Something from a company he didn't recognise offering a product he didn't want costing money he didn't have. Took a deep breath.

He went into the kitchen and threw the letter in the paper and cardboard rubbish bin. He was a fair-weather recycler; he did what he could for the good of the planet when he got around to it. Which wasn't all the time. Sometimes it wasn't any of the time. But the thought was there. That counted for something.

He made a quick microwave telly dinner, decided that it didn't have enough chicken in it to warrant the description 'Chicken Pasta' but ate it anyway. And washed it down with a glass of something white from the remaining half of a bottle in the fridge door shelf. It wasn't quite vinegary enough to pour down the sink.

Beggars can't be choosers.

Then he grabbed the iPod from his jacket, decamped to the sofa. Sat back. Switched it on. Scrolled to the downloaded calls from the Ghost and pressed go. Taking a deep breath, he closed his eyes and gave his ears a crack at the voice.

On Wednesday 30th June 1937, the 999-emergency service was set up with the help of the GPO (pre-BT). It was the first emergency services number in the world.

The moment anyone gets through, they're asked which service they require: ambulance, fire, police, or coastguard. If you're calling from a mobile, the operator can detect your approximate location. If you're calling from a landline, they have a database of addresses linked to phone numbers.

Sometimes callers aren't even asked where they're calling from. Some forces use a data exchange system called EISEC (Enhanced Information Service for Emergency Calls). Then callers are put through to the service they want automatically.

Then a call handler takes over, gets information from the caller, and decides whether the call is important enough to warrant immediate action or not.

Everything happens very quickly.

Police forces in the UK and almost everywhere else take emergency calls very seriously. Especially where death is concerned. Reporting a murder or an attempted murder is as serious as a bullet in the brain. Occasionally the reason for the call is precisely because a small, fast-moving projectile has arrived at its intended destination.

In the first week after the UK service went live in 1937, over 1,000 calls to the service were made. By 2017, the service received around thirty million calls a year.

Between the years of 1st August 2012 and 1st August 2017, six of those calls made were of particular interest to McHale.

They were the ones he was listening to as he sat on the sofa. The ones he'd listened to earlier that day. Each call was preceded by a female, announcing the name of the victim. The female was an employee of the Metropolitan Police working out of New Scotland Yard. After she finished speaking, there was a short pause, before the caller spoke.

The voice was the same in each call. Male. Not young. Not old. English. No discernible accent initially. Delivery not rushed. Not excited. Strong. Good diction. Almost as if the words were a pleasure to say.

There was a minute or so of static before the recording ended.

Inner voice broke the silence. 'Jeez Louise... he's a cheerful son of a bitch, eh? I bet he had a smile on his face when he called them in. This one's a nasty one, Mac.'

McHale gently pulled the buds out of his ears, laid the iPad on the cushion to his right and stood up.

First, pee. Second, coffee. Third, who the hell did that voice remind him of?

'Wouldn't it be cool if you could just look in the mirror, stick your tongue out, and check the tip of it to see if there was a name there?'

Right. One pee and shake later, he diverted to the kitchen and prepared a small cup of caffeine heaven. White cup. Dark brown liquid. No sugar.

Last Christmas he treated himself to a coffee machine to die for. It wasn't one of those cheap rubbish supermarket ones. This was a sleek, black, SMEG 1950's retro espresso coffee maker. It made fuck off espressos with an extra shot that put your eyeballs on red alert.

He took it back to the sofa along with a twin-stick Kit Kat and let the Ghost's voice bounce its way around the inside of his skull. Just to see if it could shake loose any memories.

Who the hell did that voice remind him of? Dammit...

'Don't look at me, Kemosabe,' said inner voice. 'I'm only the piano player. Just give me a fast-acting hit of that dark roast Italian bean juice pronto.'

McHale duly obliged.

Then he snapped the Kit Kat in half, chomped on a chocolate finger, sat back, hooked up the iPod, and played the six calls again. The first time was for listening. The second time was for hearing.

Before the third time came around, he decided to hit the sack.

Chapter Eight

Right on cue McHale cancelled the snooze cruise 10 minutes later. Then this part of the world woke up to another day.

In twenty-four hours, give or take, McHale, Toby, and Daisy would travel by Virgin Pendolino from Stockport to London Euston to kick-start the Ghost investigation with serious vigour.

Not long after that he would get his first look, up close and personal, at Grace Lightfoot.

Today he would use a pool car to visit the scene of the last murder at 16 Sullivan Street, Stockport. Daisy would drive.

They arrived at 10.35am. The murder house was a neat 3-bedroom semi with a paved driveway, a small grass area to the front, and a kitchen extension to the rear. It was bland, almost invisible, and in all ways unremarkable.

Except for the two police vehicles parked out the front.

And the crime scene tape across the road either side of the premises.

And the tented area still set up and obscuring the front door.

And the activity of various SOCO and forensics personnel in and out of the property.

And the police officer on duty by the tape signing in and out all visitors to the scene.

The officer knew McHale, nodded grimly, and produced a clipboard for all three to sign, time, and date. They'd do the same when they left.

At the entrance to the house, the three were required to don protective garments and footwear.

Cross-contamination on a murder site was a cardinal sin. It carried with it the very real threat of removal not only from the site but also from the investigation.

Inner voice grumbled. 'Sod it. I thought they'd be done and dusted by now.'

'Take a good look, you two,' said McHale. 'Drink it all up. This is the last chance we'll get to kick the tyres before this lot gets wrapped up and sent to the labs.'

Toby said, 'So we can go walkabout?'

'Eyes open, nostrils closed. Get your phones out and take photographs of everything everywhere.'

'Right Guv,' said Daisy.

She made the kind of face that left nothing to the imagination when it came to foul-smelling bodily fluids.

But she didn't back down and she didn't surrender.

Good girl, thought McHale.

He went through to the living room. At the door he nodded to a young SOCO who passed him on the way out carrying a see-through plastic sealed and initialled evidence bag. It contained a folded newspaper which been on the floor by the victim's right foot.

The paper was splattered with blood.

The body, and attached knife, had been removed from the premises. All that was left were the red stains on the carpet. And the sofa. And a few cast-off drops on the coffee table.

McHale took in the carnage like he was dispassionately arranging a series of photographs. Every one slightly different from all the others. Every detail imprinted on his mind. Record now, recall later.

After half an hour, he'd had enough.

'Come on you two. We're only in the way here.'

They drove back to HQ and the other two downloaded and

arranged the crime scene shots, while McHale opened the file on the Yank.

There wasn't much to see, but what there was made good reading.

He'd never met a Native American Indian before. He'd met a few cowboys. But the only horsepower they had sat under the bonnets of battered white vans.

When he was in his twenties, he'd been given a book called Bury My Heart at Wounded Knee: An Indian History of The American West. It was written by someone called Dee Brown. It made him feel ashamed, but the book was a favourite.

A black coffee appeared on his desktop. No words, no footsteps, no sugar; just a welcome aroma of caffeine and the promise of a warm hello.

There was a photo sitting on top of the folder contents. It was a head and shoulders shot of a woman. The caption underneath said: FBI Supervisory Special Agent Grace Lightfoot.

She had black hair, dark eyes and an earnest, unsmiling face – a little on the wide side – with high cheekbones, an aquiline nose, and thin lips.

The photo showed her wearing a dark jacket over a white shirt. Very neat. Very proud. Very business-like. Very federal.

And very native American.

McHale thought she was a singular beauty.

He turned to the bio.

Long story short. Her father was a member of the Cherokee Nation, a decorated war veteran and an Officer of the Law. Her Mother was a petite, dark-haired doctor of Scottish descent.

Grace was their only child.

Her calm, almost disinterested demeanour belied the fact that inside she was switched on. She always had been. She had a Bachelor's Degree in Criminal Psychology from Pennsylvania State University. She was smart as a whip.

She joined the US Department of Homeland at thirty-two and joined their elite Shadow Wolves unit at thirty-four. Operating along the Arizona-Mexico border, they were the Department's only Native American tracking unit.

Some said they were the best trackers of humans in the world.

She had no problem with stopping the drugs and human trafficking. She had every problem with stopping the desperate families trying to make a better life for themselves and their children.

After Homeland, at thirty-seven, she moved to Quantico, to teach bright, young, FBI agents how to hunt those who deserved to be hunted down. She was seconded to the National Centre for the Analysis of Violent Crime (NCAV). In particular, the Behavioural Analysis Unit (BAU). She specialised in the study, hunting down, capture, and permanent incarceration of serial killers. Both on and off US soil.

She was a predator with a badge and, for the past few years, serial killers had been her prey.

One in particular had intrigued her. But only from a distance. Now, over 3,600 miles from her classroom, and thanks to an open-ended sabbatical, she was getting the chance to look at him close up. Hopefully do more.

She had no problem using the term 'him', given that, on the vast continent where she was born, around eighty per cent of serial killers were men. Which still left a very lethal twenty per cent who weren't.

So, although she had an open mind, she had always regarded this particular one as male, just by playing the odds.

She didn't know who he was. But she knew what he was. He was The Holy Ghost.

But one thing in amongst all those facts and all that opinion stuck out like a lighthouse beacon on a foggy night.

Her birthday: 1st August.

The same day as all the murders. Six years, one after the other.

He felt his pulse take a leap forward.

McHale didn't believe in coincidence. But he did believe in fate.

He believed in things that happened because somewhere, out in the weird damned universe, something ticked a box or somebody nodded a head, and made them happen.

He believed in solid policework and grit and determination and never bloody giving up. But he also believed in intuition and perception and the tingles in his fingertips that were nothing to do with his CIDP and everything to do with somebody trying to tell him something.

And he had a sneaky feeling that Grace Lightfoot believed in it too.

Inner voice whispered in his ear. 'Don't fuck about, Kemosabe. Get the dame a birthday gift. Something classy.'

A double tap disturbed his shoulder at 2.10pm.

Toby's soft, breathy, vaguely conspiratorial voice disturbed the air next to his left ear.

'Wanna look at our holiday snaps?'

'That's the best offer I've had all day.'

'Walk this way, Guv.'

McHale smiled. The moniker was catching on, he thought. They decamped ten or so from Daisy's desk, pulled up a couple of chairs and began trawling the photos taken earlier that day at the Sullivan Street crime scene.

Apart from the human detritus left by The Ghost, nothing immediately stood out. Nothing immediately looked odd.

Nothing in the first trawl through any of the 237 shots of the house interior and exterior raised any flags. Red or otherwise.

Everything fitted in. Everything had its own story to tell. One that was part of the history of the house. There were no alien objects. No interlopers. No surprises.

He looked at Daisy.

'Train time tomorrow?'

'Depart Stockport 10.04am. Arrive Euston 12.02pm. Faster than proverbial shit off a shovel, Guv,' she said.

'Tickets and accommodation?'

'You've already got yours.' She picked up two buff envelopes from her desk. Brandished them. 'One for Toby, one for me. We're booked in at the Wellesley. Four-star hotel. Nice and clean, lots of facilities. Short stroll from the Yard. They're picking up the tab.'

'So… when shall we three meet again?'

'Ooooh… appropriate Macbeth quote. Very clever,' said Toby.

'Meet here at 8.30am? Or on the platform at 9.30am?' said Daisy, downloading all the new photos from her phone and Toby's onto her laptop.

'Starbucks. Platform 2, 9am on the dot,' he said. 'Pack your wheelie cases. Dress casual. Bring your toothbrush. Download everything we need onto your laptops before you go home. We're taking them with us.'

Daisy nodded. 'Right. Coffee?'

'Bloody gagging.'

Five minutes later Daisy was back with three black coffees. Two sugared. All cool enough to gulp.

'I think we should celebrate the beginning of an adventure with a McVitie's milk chocolate biscuit each,' said Toby. He produced a half-finished pack from his desk drawer and teased three out.

Some biscuits are meant to be slowly nibbled and savoured. Others are meant to be simply demolished in one mouthful. Like a chocolate assault on the senses.

'Live dangerously, eh… that's what I say,' said the young detective.

Toby's celebratory treat was of the demolition variety. But it was over too quick.

All that was left was a vague afterthought of deliciousness on the taste buds and a regret for not making the biscuit last just a little longer.

McHale noticed that Daisy was looking at him.

It was the kind of look that didn't slam on the breaks when it got to him. The kind of look that just kept on going in and out the other side. Like a fast-moving, high-calibre through-and-through.

'There was something odd about that house today,' she said.

'You mean apart from the murder and the blood, the guts and the brains, the piss, the shit and the smell?' said Toby. 'That wasn't odd enough for you?'

No reply.

Daisy was too busy inside her head, looking for something that didn't fit in amongst all the things that did.

DCI Campbell kyboshed the thought by putting in an appearance.

'You lot off in the morning?'

'Yeah,' said McHale. 'The place just won't be the same without us.'

That brought a grunt. 'Don't bloody come back until you bury the bastard.'

'Toby here is taking his folding spade.'

Campbell held out a business card and McHale took it.

A mobile number. In black. On thick white stock. Very classy.

No name.

No need.

'Twenty-four seven,' said Campbell.

'Understood.'

With that, the DCI nodded to all three and headed for his office.

Nothing more to do now. Time to let the dogs loose.

McHale's phone pinged.

He picked it up from the desk and noticed a newly arrived text message. It was from Alice. It was eight words short. The words were:

'Safe journey. Catch the son of a bitch.'

He sent six words back. They were:

'Hope for peace. Prepare for war.'

There was an extra name that he wanted her to check out.

But he couldn't remember who it was. It was simmering on the back burner in his pot of things to remember. Below the brown gravy, chopped carrots, shallots, and baby potatoes. No doubt it would show itself soon enough.

That night, as well as everything else he packed into his wheelie case, he put in his medication box. It didn't take up much space. Just enough to treat a condition for which there was no known cure.

Just enough for a week's supply. Sunday and Wednesday. Any time he wanted away from prying eyes. Precious cargo.

Eight 20ml vials of pure unadulterated human plasma.

One vial of 10ml.

Assorted needles, tubing, and tape.

All safe and snug in a tough, crushproof container.

After that, assorted casual clothes. A second pair of black jeans. Three black shirts. Various underwear. Shaving kit and smellies.

One box of a hundred Paracetamol.

Ten blister strips of ten 500mg tabs should do it.

One laptop. Very small on the outside. Very large on the inside.

One Grace folder. And one Fairbairn-Sykes combat knife.

Original. Estimated age, about seventy-seven years.

When that was done there was a late microwave supper to come to terms with. Washed down with a large coffee followed by a single Southern Comfort.

It slid down too easily. He made it a double.

After that, he let his mind chill with a move or two in his latest game of online chess. The game was new. Battle hadn't commenced in earnest.

The opponent was an old guy from Wales. At least the impression he got was that he was old. And a guy. The truth was that nobody knew. Online chess was an anonymous club. You knew as much, or as little, about the person you played as they let you know. McHale was okay with that.

Inner voice said, 'No more stupid bloody moves Kemosabe,

okay? You had your head up your arse in that last game.'

Ten minutes later his head met the pillows.

'And… a hundred leaping sheep… ninety-nine leaping sheep… ninety-eight leaping sheep…'

This time he got all the way to thirty-six before the night shift clocked on.

Chapter Nine

The alarm went off half an hour early. Snooze cruise was switched off. This wasn't just the start of another day; this time the hunt was on. No more letting The Ghost sit in the driving seat. No more doing things the old way. Now they were doing things the new way. Now there was a new team. A new set of brains. A new set of hunters. A new way of thinking.

The Ghost was still in the shadows. But they were coming for him. Tick tock... tick tock.

For as long as he could remember, the passage of time was something that McHale was always conscious of. It was always there. Front of mind, counting up or down. Keeping the score.

To other folk, time existed mostly in the background. Only jumping the queue whenever life's seconds, minutes, hours, days, weeks, months and years wanted or needed to be included in the conversation.

Not him. For him it was a North and South Pole kinda thing. Sometimes it was a firm friend. Other times, a sworn enemy.

Lateness was one of his few pet hates. And it was a Rottweiler, not a Chihuahua. That was no secret.

So, everyone was at Starbucks before 9am next morning. Wheelies in tow. Smart casuals on show. Limbic systems on go.

While the investigation carried on back at the murder house up north, the trio would be over two hundred miles away down South. All photography and forensics information would be fed through to a secure server at the Yard, for the team to access and investigate the hell out of.

For the next two hours, McHale, Toby, and Daisy would be held captive as their Virgin Pendolino class 390 train headed up to London at a top speed of 125mph, and an occasional bottom speed of dead stop. With carriages as tightly packed as budgie smugglers on Bondi Beach. With impatience nibbling at their vitals. With conversation limited to small talk; football, movies, soaps, reality telly, food, drink, and everything else apart from bloody work.

They pulled into Euston at 12.05pm. Thirty minutes later they were in a black cab on a short ride to the Wellesley Hotel.

As they drew up outside, McHale sorted out the fare and the other two went inside.

Inner voice was impressed. 'Well… thank Christ. It looks a very classy gaff from the outside. I hope the bloody sheets are clean.'

Victorian architecture. Neat and stylish on the outside. Bustling reception. All business on the inside. Pub-restaurant off to the side. Very appealing. Lift and stairs to bedrooms. Very convenient.

Daisy had everything organised, with no hiccups. Their rooms were all on the same floor. The third. All on the same side. The right. All next to each other. Numbers 145, 147, and 149. Not adjoining. Direction succession… not zig zag. Be thankful for small mercies, thought McHale.

'Bar and food about five,' he said. The other two nodded.

Key cards swiped. Doors opened. Shoes off. Telly on, sound down.

There was a note from Drummond waiting for McHale next to the room phone. It said: 'Welcome to London. I hope you remembered the Fairbairn-Sykes. Bugger off back up North if you didn't. See you Monday or sooner. The food here is good. C.D.'

He wasn't in a smiling mood.

He wasn't even in an unpacking mood.

Instead, he stripped, and stood under the pulsing shower for ten minutes, felt the hot jets pound his skin, and thought about a fifty-eight-year-old man with his chest cavity opened, his insides spilling out, and a knife sticking out of the top of his head.

He imagined the other two were probably doing much the same.

Some sights you just can't un-see.

They hang around and yell insults at you until they get tired and fade into the background.

But they never really go away.

Some dates are the same. They burrow inside your head and they stay there. Just waiting for the time when they can burrow back out again and make you smile or scare the shit out of you.

Like 1st September.

The day in 1985 when Charlie bit a stranger's finger through to the bone. Because she was stupid enough (or brave enough) to stick it inside the mouth of someone having their first 'grand mal' epileptic seizure to stop them swallowing their tongue.

Or 1st September. The day in 2007 when Charlie, who hadn't had a seizure for years, decided to have the biggest fucking one of his life, sat behind the wheel of an old Beamer. Just in time to plough into a lamppost at about 90mph.

Case closed. Along with the casket.

And now…

The team had twenty-six days left until another body was found with a knife in the head. Until somebody got another 10pm phone call. Only this time eleven months sooner than expected.

So why this September 1? What was so bloody special about this one? What made him fall out of favour with the other six August 1 dates?

At 4.45pm he was downstairs in the bar holding a fresh, cool pint of something that had lager attached to the name, thinking about dates in between two exploratory sips.

Not bad. Tasted worse.

The bar noise was somewhere in between too damned quiet

and the low hum of early evening conflabs.

Phone time.

He dialled a number. One ring. One female voice. Definitely not British.

'McHale.' Not a question. A fact.

'You hungry yet, Supervisory Special Agent Lightfoot?'

'Just Lightfoot.'

McHale smiled.

'You hungry yet, Just Lightfoot?'

Silence.

'How many have you brought with you?' she said.

'Two so far. More to come later. But just two for tonight. You want to make it four for something to eat?'

'Sure.'

He gave her directions.

'I'll see you shortly,' she said and hung up.

Two heartbeats. One gentle tap on his left shoulder. He turned around expecting to see Toby and Daisy. Saw a woman with a pair of the darkest eyes he'd ever seen standing a couple of feet away from him. Personal space invaded. Looking at him.

No blinks. No introduction. No hello and how the hell are you. No hello and who the hell are you. She had long black hair, parted in the middle. A dark cool-weather jacket over a denim shirt and blue jeans. A thick brown belt with a silver snakehead buckle.

She looked a shade under five-foot-ten.

'You sounded taller,' she said.

McHale double blinked. 'Just Lightfoot?'

'You know... I've tracked skinny-ass teenage heroin smugglers crossing over the US-Mexico border at night with no moon and through a network of tunnels six feet under the ground. Tracking you down to a hotel in London was easier than passin' wind.'

'So... Alice told you?'

That got the hint of a smile.

'I like her,' she said.

'Me too.'

He smiled and stuck out his hand. She had a strong grip and a strong voice.

Inner voice interrupted the moment. 'Damn. You think maybe she's got a sister?'

About 30 seconds before 5pm, Toby and Daisy joined the party. Everybody looked everybody else up and down. Drinks were ordered and guarded conversation begun. Most of it, naturally, was about the FBI.

'Right, let's eat,' said McHale.

He was about to have a quiet word in the ear of the concierge about local restaurants, when Daisy spoke up. 'Already checked it out. The best one's right here, through that door over there,' she said, nodding at a dark wooden framed glass door with a sign on it that said Salle à manger.

She looked at Lightfoot. 'I gather you like your beef with the hoofs removed.'

'My great, great grandfather used to eat buffalo meat. I prefer Aberdeen Angus.'

'So… no pizza, then?'

Lightfoot shot a right eyebrow up. It didn't have a reply at the end of it. But it did have the vaguest hint of a smile. One that disappeared as fast as it arrived.

They found a place in the restaurant far enough away from the madding crowd to talk business without being overheard.

McHale was the last to sit down. Daisy thought there was something of a gentleman in that. 'Okay… what do you think of our Ghost?'

Lightfoot took a sip of water from the glass in front of her on the table. She was sat across from McHale, with Toby to her right and Daisy to McHale's left.

'I like that,' she said. 'You don't waste time.'

'We don't have time to waste.'

'I don't think he does either, not anymore.'

'Ah... so you read the bit about September 1.'

'Something put his foot on the gas. I think he's been a man on a slow-burn mission for the past six years. Now, suddenly, the mission got real urgent, real fast.'

'You think he's strong?' said Toby. He felt like he was sitting at a table split down the middle with two real deals on one side. And two catch-ups on the other.

The waitress brought four menus, hung around hopefully for a couple of heartbeats, then left when it was obvious that nobody was paying her any attention.

Lightfoot raised an eyebrow. The nearest she had to a scoff.

'Not a matter of strength. Getting the knife in there is the easy part. Pulling it out is the hard part. It's all about suction.'

'Doesn't the side of the skull have the bone?' asked McHale.

'Yeah. It's harder through the top. But it's still doable.'

'Post mortem?' said Toby.

'I think so. This wasn't meant to kill. This was meant to say something.'

'Say what?'

Just then the waitress decided it was time to come back and try again. McHale took the hint and put the brakes on the conversation so they could order food and drink.

The kitchen had Aberdeen Angus steaks on the menu. McHale, Lightfoot, and Toby ordered a large one each with trimmings of potatoes, grilled onions and bacon skewers. Daisy ordered roast fillet of sea bass with crispy potatoes and roasted peppers.

Cops had three beers. FBI had one water. The waitress scribbled then left. Then they got back into it.

Daisy looked at Lightfoot. 'I'm curious,' she said. 'How come you've flown all this way to help us catch one of our killers when there are so many over on your side of the pond?'

'I didn't,' said Lightfoot. 'I flew all this way to solve a problem.'

'Now that was an answer I didn't expect,' said Toby.

The BAU agent took a deep breath. Looked at the faces

around the table. Made a decision.

'You all know what BAU stands for, right?'

'Behavioural Analysis Unit,' said Toby. 'I get the coconut.'

'Well, the National Centre for the Analysis of Violent Crime (NCAVC) has five BAU units, not just one.'

Toby turned to McHale. 'You knew this?'

McHale shrugged. 'What can I say? I read a lot.'

Lightfoot continued. 'BAU-1 deals with counterterrorism, arson, and bombing. BAU-2 is for threats, cyber, white-collar crime and public corruption. BAU-3 is for crimes against children. BAU-4 deals with crimes where the victims are adults. And BAU-5 is for research, strategy, and instruction.

'Then there's VICAP…'

'Violent Criminal Apprehension Programme,' said Daisy.

Lightfoot turned to McHale. 'You train your people well,' she said.

'She's new but she's a fast learner,' said McHale.

Lightfoot turned back to Daisy. 'It has the largest database of violent crimes, including murder, abductions, and sexual assaults, in the United States.'

'So which BAU are you?' said Toby.

'BAU-4. We get the real nasty fuckers. Some folk call it Serial Killer Central. Presumably the names Ted Bundy, Jeffrey Dahmer, Richard Ramirez, ring a bell.'

Daisy's eyes momentarily narrowed.

Inner voice joined in; 'I was wondering when this cosy little chit chat was going to get real juicy. Bring it on, Cherokee woman…'

Toby's stomach rumbled. He apologised for the sound. Blushed briefly. Then said, 'So that's why the BAU-4 is interested in The Ghost, eh? You're running out of yours so now you want to catch one of ours?'

'Some of those big cases are thirty years old, right?' said McHale.

'Sure. Those guys are rotting behind bars and they'll stay there until the day we nail the coffin lids closed and piss on their graves. Well… the ones who don't do everyone a favour and check out first. Or saddle up and ride the lightning. Or catch the vein train.'

'I can hear a 'but' coming,' said Daisy.

Lightfoot's eyes turned grim. 'But folk who know statistics more than they know people say there are around 200 active serial killers in the US at any given time. So, there's plenty more where they came from.'

'And how many people have you got in your BAU-4 unit?'

'I could tell you, but then I'd have to kill you.'

One heartbeat. Two heartbeats. A raised right eyebrow from Lightfoot to Daisy. Then a penny dropping. A smile from Daisy to Lightfoot. Ice well and truly broken.

'Just for the record, the number of serial killers active in the UK at any one time is apparently a grand total of two,' said Toby. 'I don't know whether that means you beat us, or we beat you.'

'Well, you're much smaller than we are. And you know about one of them,' said Lightfoot. 'I suppose the question is… do you know about the other one?'

Another pause while the three from the UK thought about that.

A decision.

A question.

'Okay. So, with all the evil bastards having fun in the colonies, why are you over here?'

'Ooh… ladies and gentlemen of the audience. We might actually be in danger of bloody well getting somewhere,' said inner voice.

Lightfoot took a sip of her water. Put the glass down. Told them a story.

'Most folk have no idea who we in BAU-4 are, what we do, or how we do it. Everything they know about us they get from watching too many programmes, on too many TV channels, about too many good-looking special agents.

'They think we're like a cross between Feds and US Marshals on steroids, wearing sharp suits and armed to the teeth.

'The truth is, ninety-nine per cent of the time we sit behind desks. We're not field agents. We're the ones you don't normally see. The ones who study other people. And most of the people we study are the ones who kill other people. Lots of other people.

'We make connections. We write reports. We draw conclusions. We connect dots. And if we're really lucky, if we're really good, we sometimes get to work out in the big wide world with other law enforcement agencies in an advisory capacity. But not often. And only when we're invited.'

Daisy and Toby had stopped chewing and were listening intently.

McHale half-laughed. 'The way I heard it; you didn't wait for an invitation before you jumped on a plane.'

Lightfoot grunted softly. 'You believe in coincidences?'

'Not in the conventional sense.'

'Good answer. When I joined the FBI, one of my mentors had a favourite saying. 'Coincidences mean you're on the right track.'

'So, what put you on the right track?'

'Something that was posted in Washington and delivered to the BAU at Quantico Virginia, on Monday 1st August 2005,' said Lightfoot. 'I was with Homeland at the time. The folk at the BAU didn't know what to make of it. It was just an envelope with a sheet of paper and two words.

'They didn't take much notice of the words at first. Then when they did, they didn't understand their significance. But they were curious enough to keep the envelope and its contents on file. Just in case.

'We do that a lot. We're curious people.

'Then, the following year, at the beginning of August 2006, the words popped up again. Right out of the blue. By that time I was back at the BAU. And we got a damned sight more curious. Real fast.

'This time they had another eleven words with them. Thirteen words in total. Exactly 54 characters long. Typed on a sheet of otherwise blank paper. Folded up and slid inside a standard envelope. Like the first letter, it was addressed to Supervisory Special Agent David Bernier, BAU-4, at the FBI Training Academy in Quantico Virginia.

'Like the first one, the paper was common laser printer stock. The words were reproduced in a Helvetica italic font. The font size was 18-point. Initial capitals. And they were centred about halfway down the page.

'The letter was posted in Washington DC. There was nothing unusual about the stamp, the franking, or the glue.

'There was nothing else. No explanations. No elaborations. No kiss my ass.'

'What were the first two words posted in 2005?' said McHale.

Lightfoot paused for effect.

She met McHale's gaze.

'Fairbairn-Sykes.'

He double-blinked. 'And the words posted in 2006?'

'There are none so blind as those who will not see. Fairbairn-Sykes.'

He double-blinked again.

'Told you you'd like it.'

'Fairbairn-Sykes as in Our Fairbairn-Sykes?' blurted Toby.

'Yup.'

'As in The Holy Ghost Fairbairn-Sykes?'

'Yup.'

'The same Fairbairn-Sykes with the stabbing and ripping of the chests and the knives sticking out of the tops of heads?'

Lightfoot held McHale's gaze. 'Yup.'

'Did you figure out what the other words meant?'

'At the time, we didn't have a clue.'

'And now?'

'Now we have six clues. Six letters. One for each year from 2006 to 2011.'

'And we're just finding this out now?'

Lightfoot shrugged. 'At the time they were just letters. Nothing more.'

'And now?'

Lightfoot nodded. 'Now they're something more.'

'Let me guess. Each one posted in Washington on 1st August each year?'

'Yep,' a ghost of a smile passed over her eyes.

'And each one exactly the same?'

'Nope.'

'No?'

There are very few awkward times for waitresses to bring plates stacked high with delicious-looking food to a table full of hungry diners. This was one of them.

McHale smiled.

'I think things just stepped up a gear. And we haven't even got started,' said Daisy.

'You talking about the case or the food?' said Toby.

Right on cue, approaching footsteps from the left. Hurried, but careful.

Conversation reluctantly slammed on the brakes as steaks and fish were dished out. Rumbling stomachs packed full of expectation and empty of protein decided that feelings about aromas and taste buds trumped talk about coincidences and double-edged knives. At least for the moment.

It was difficult for words to force themselves out of facial orifices when food was trying to get in.

However, once the foursome got past the first couple of mouthfuls, speaking and chewing got polite and took turns doing what they had to do.

Tomorrow would be about opening doors that had stayed closed for the past six years, or had never been opened at all.

It would be about getting all the machinery of an unconventional hunt up and running. It would be about looking The Devil straight in the eyes. And kicking him in the balls as hard and as often as possible.

But tonight, they would get down to the serious business of digesting food for bellies and food for thought. And getting at least some of the shit out of the way.

And talking about six letters received by the BAU over a period of six years.

The first that said; 'There are none so blind as those who will not see. Fairbairn-Sykes.' Postmarked Washington 1st August 2006. Received by Quantico 2nd August.

The second that said; 'There are none so deaf as those who will not hear. Fairbairn-Sykes.' Postmarked 1st August 2007.

The third that said; 'There are none so sorry as those who will not repent. Fairbairn-Sykes.' Postmarked 1st August 2008.

The fourth that said; 'There are none so dumb as those who will not speak. Fairbairn-Sykes.' Postmarked 1st August 2009.

The fifth that said; 'There are none so numb as those who will not feel. Fairbairn-Sykes.' Postmarked 1st August 2010.

The sixth that said; 'There are none so dead as those who will not live. Fairbairn-Sykes.' Postmarked 1st August 2011.

'So, when did the alarm bells start ringing?' said Toby.

'Thursday, 2nd August 2012,' said Lightfoot.

'That long ago?'

She looked at him. 'They weren't ringing very loudly at first. But the closer they got to now, the louder they rang.'

'You mean the more the bodies started piling up,' said Daisy.

McHale put down his knife and fork and looked at the BAU agent. 'Hang on a minute,' he said. 'You've got enough homicidal maniacs on your side of the pond. What makes you so interested in one of ours?'

Lightfoot hadn't taken her eyes off his.

'Unless,' he said slowly, 'you think he might be one of yours.'

She said nothing.

'So, you're really here to cover your own arse?' said Toby. 'Find out if one of yours hasn't defected across the pond and is happily giving us the benefit of his twisted expertise? Courtesy of Uncle Sam?'

McHale looked at Toby. 'Down Rover,' he said. 'The lady's here to help. And I, for one, am bloody glad to have it.'

Toby reacted like he'd been kicked in the leg, which he probably had.

Daisy's voice was conspicuous by its absence. Her right foot, however, had probably just made its presence felt.

'Okay. So, what makes you think your guy might be our guy?' said McHale.

The waitress returned and started clearing up the empty plates. The food had been delicious. But nobody had really noticed. She asked the usual enquiry, and got the usual answers. But they smiled, so she left happy with an order of coffees for everyone. All black.

'The signature,' she said.

'What signature? You said he didn't sign any of the letters,' said Daisy.

Lightfoot looked at McHale again. Paused. Waited.

Finally, he took the bait.

'You're not talking about the letters, are you?'

'No.'

He looked at Toby and Daisy. Then back at Lightfoot. 'Bugger. You've got a body, haven't you?'

She shook her head slowly, side to side. 'Nope.'

'But you think there might be one?'

She let out a long breath. 'Maybe.'

The coffees came, and with them came a polite lull in the conversation until the waitress scurried away out of sight and out of earshot.

Lightfoot picked up where she left off.

'We got a sneaky peek at all the crime-scene photos. The bodies and the way he posed them. The signature coup de grâce wound through the top of the head with the knife.'

'You think it's a 'he'?' said Toby.

'I've seen plenty of folk stick knives in other folk without even pausing for breath or offering up an excuse. I've seen them go crazy and lose track of the number of times they ventilated the skin of child-killing sons of bitches. I've seen them do it in the front, the back, the side, the throat, and the face. Sometimes all of the above.

'I've seen them try to cut ears off, noses off, and dicks off. And I once caught a sixty-three-year-old grandfather in the process of cutting the tongue out of his fifteen-year-old granddaughter.

'I even read a report of a cute blond who stuck a pimp right in the asshole with a flick knife. They had to sew him a new one and he couldn't sit down for a week without needing morphine for the pain. She said the pimp had always been an asshole. Now he was an even bigger one.'

Lightfoot's deadpan delivery was impressive.

Almost as deadpan as the coffee waitress.

'I've seen guys stick other guys through the side of the head. One with a meat skewer right in one ear and out the other one. I've seen guys get done with six-inch stilettoes through the eyes and into the brain. I saw heads get split with two axes and one Japanese sword. And I even saw one take a fucking big ass Bowie knife and almost cut another guy's head off just for looking at him sideways.

Lightfoot paused and looked around the table. As if by doing so emphasised the point she was about to make.

'But I never saw anyone stick anyone else through the top of the head like this. Not in sixteen years of folk sticking sharp things into other folk. Not once. Not even by accident. Then along comes your guy. And he's done it six times so far. Six times in six different locations all around the UK. And now he's about to do it a seventh.

'And I haven't figured it out yet. But somehow, it's all

connected to the letters that got mailed to us in Virginia from Washington DC years before he even got started. Or at least before we think he got started.

'So yeah… you could say I got interested enough to jump on a plane to see if your guy over here was just maybe connected to our guy over there.'

'Okay,' said Toby, ticking boxes off in his head. 'So… you don't have any dead bodies at any crime scenes with the same knife-in-the-head routine as our guy.'

He got the Lightfoot unflinching stare. 'Not that we know,' she said. 'But that doesn't mean we're not looking. And it doesn't mean we don't think there might be any bodies.'

'But we know what we think of coincidences,' said McHale.

'They mean we're on the right path,' said Daisy.

Lightfoot took a large gulp of still warm coffee. Paused. 'Did you bring it with you?' she said.

McHale knew that she meant the one Fairbairn-Sykes knife that he had brought with him down to London. The one that DCI Cyril Drummond had given him in Stockport. The one that had killed James Halliwell, in 2012.

'It's back at the hotel. I'll bring it Monday.'

Lightfoot shook her head. 'I'll come by tomorrow. I have a guy back in Quantico who loves old knives. He could be useful. I'll send him some shots, if that's okay.'

'Sure.'

'It's bloody sharp,' said Toby. 'He sliced himself with it.' He nodded at McHale's hand.

'Old war wound,' said McHale, dismissing the plaster wrapped around his index finger.

'Are they all the same?' said Lightfoot.

Pause.

'Nearly.' He smiled. 'They're numbered. One to six.'

Lightfoot double-blinked.

Inner voice said, 'Shit… she does the bloody double-blink

thing, too. There's no such thing as a coincidence, Kemosabe.'

'Got any photos of them?'

'I'll get close-up photos of the full set sorted for you when you come over tomorrow,' said Daisy. 'Morning? Or afternoon?'

'How does two o'clock sound?'

'Sounds better than three.'

'We'll be camped in Room 145. Knock three times and ask for Rosie,' said McHale.

Lightfoot double-blinked again.

'British humour,' said McHale. 'Or rather an attempt at.'

Lightfoot, still a bit jet-lagged, grabbed a cab outside and headed back to Winfield House in Regent's Park.

Crossing time zones was a bastard on the circadian rhythms. The other three had a slow drink at the bar and then early nights. It was 9.10pm. Deep sleep was a forlorn hope for McHale. Dreams of Fairbairn-Sykes knives stuck in bloody skulls were more of a reality. But not yet.

As they walked up to their rooms, Daisy did exactly what McHale hoped that she would do. Start to list everything. Every fact. Every scrap of information. Every supposition. Every impression. Every hunch. Every suspicion.

She emptied them into a large pot somewhere in the back of her brain and let them simmer overnight. Then she'd feed McHale breadcrumbs in the morning and throughout the next week. Breadcrumbs that would keep him on the right track and lead him and the rest of the team unerringly to The Holy Ghost. And the sooner the better.

So, she'd be up for an hour or two yet. Thinking and making notes. Unlike Toby. Toby did his best thinking by clearing his brain of every piece of clutter it had accumulated during each day, and concentrating on one thing only.

Tonight, that one thing was a question. And the question was this: *How old was The Holy Ghost?*

Chapter Ten

For those of a Christian disposition, Sunday had, until the last half-century or so, traditionally been a day of rest. A day when praying to whichever God happened to float their boat, whether it was a dinghy or an ark, allowed folk to take a break from the rigours of the previous six days. A day when kneeling in draughty, half-empty churches more often than not lead to arthritis of the knees, and a recurring niggly feeling that there might not be anybody upstairs or downstairs listening to them after all.

For those of a serial killer hunting disposition, however, there was no such thing as a day off. Traditional or not.

It was Sunday August 6. The UK's daily Express newspaper that day would report that nearly 400 police stations across England and Wales had closed in the past seven years, as a result of brutal cutbacks. New Scotland Yard, the most important police station in the UK, was always open for business.

A short stroll from it sat the Wellesley Hotel. In room 145 it was time to get up.

First, the time on the iPhone changed from 6.29am to 6.30am. Then, the phone alarm went off and a loud rock guitar riff did to the Sabbath what a certain Pete Townsend had done time and time again to his Fender amp setup over the years. It hammered the shit out of it. In this case at low volume.

McHale's hand attached to his hairy left arm reached out from under the bed covers and stabbed the alarm into snooze cruise mode.

Ten minutes later the alarm went off again.

Another day started; in a strange bed; in a strange room; in a strange hotel. In a city he'd only visited a couple of times in the last ten years.

Up. Piss. Shit. Shave. Teeth. Shower. Moisturise. Then dress. Painkillers. Black roast coffee. Instant. No sugar.

Make the bed, even though they were staying in a hotel. Even though they had maids for that kind of thing. Even though the maids would undo the bed and change the sheets.

It was the routine. His routine. Old habits die hard. New ones die harder.

Open the case, empty the contents and give the medicine box a quick once over. Two gulps of coffee, feeling the warmth slide down the throat.

Check the messages on the mobile. One from Daisy. One from Toby. One from Alice. Start from the top, work down.

Daisy had been a busy girl. Email timed at 1.58am. She was one of life's brain-dumpers; one of those people who have a compulsion to vomit, onto paper or screen, every thought that comes into their head. Relevant or irrelevant. She said this:

Hi Guv,

Brain dump number one. Long story short, I think there's a lot more to this guy than just someone who opens up people's chests and leaves trophies stuck in their heads. Anyway, there's a Word doc. attached that has a fistful of ideas. Probably lots of crap, too. Just to get the ball rolling. I can start knocking all the info we have into shape asap. See the two of you at breakfast. They begin serving at eight.

McHale left the Word doc. for later and went on to Toby's email. It was timed at 7.03am. It said this:

Morning Guv.

Slept like a bloody log. I think it's got to be full English for breakfast. See you downstairs about eight. By the way, I haven't figured out yet how old our guy is. But something's a bit odd. Can't put my finger on it yet.

No more emails. One voicemail from Lightfoot. It said this:

'Hi McHale. Change of plans. I'll be there about ten in the morning. I want to get the close-up shots of the knives and numbers over to my guy as soon as possible. Can Daisy put together a set of photos that I can choose from and email to him? A ZIP file would be great. Catch you later.'

Lightfoot definitely wasn't a back-seat driver, thought McHale. Front passenger seat, maybe, with hands on the wheel now and then. Somewhere inside of him, inner voice offered an opinion. 'Dammit, Kemosabe... just when you thought having a partner was a bad idea. This is one of those 'think again' moments.'

About 8.30am and three floors down, Sunday breakfast was a busy affair full of hushed conversations and loud silences. It was served up with cereal, fruit juice, toast, cooked food, and gallons of tea and coffee.

McHale and Toby attacked their 'full English' servings with all the desire their appetites could muster. Daisy had no culinary desire for anything other than buttered croissants and black coffee.

They all had heads full of thoughts. Bellies full of food were optional extras.

'You figured out what's odd, yet... apart from everything?' said McHale.

Toby frowned. 'Still digging,' he said.

He turned to Daisy. 'You?'

'Stopped digging,' she said. 'Too many questions... not enough answers.'

At 9.35am McHale's iPhone rang. Luckily the rock riff had been replaced with something a million miles away from anything by Pete Townsend and a damned sight closer to Count Your Blessings by Sonny Rollins.

The soft, breathy saxophone called from the table. Volume extra low. Interruptions welcome.

Lightfoot's voice on the other end of the line said; 'Morning, McHale. Another change of plans. Your guy has spoken to my guy and we're meeting here at Winfield House. Somebody knows how to pull strings. Colour me impressed. Eleven would be good. Earlier would be better.'

The phone went dead.

McHale smiled at the other two. 'Seems we're going to be guests of the Yanks for the day,' he said. 'Time for another coffee and then we hit the road in thirty.'

He outlined the change of plans and watched as the interest grew on their faces. Sonny Rollins blew a few more notes on the iPhone. Then Cyril Drummond said, 'Tom'.

'Morning, sir.'

'I was hoping to give you some space here at the new HQ today, but some awkward bastard has organised a bloody cross-forces talk in the room I booked for you guys. You've got it from tomorrow onwards. Today's buggered, but not to worry. You'll be spending Sunday at the house of the US Ambassador in Regent's Park. Lovely old mansion. Great grounds. They've got a nice set-up there. Loads of hi-tech toys. Should be fun. You should be getting a phone call any minute from that FBI lady. Watch your arse with that one. She's a bit sharp.'

'Already had the call,' said McHale.

'Good man. See you there.'

The line went dead.

They finished their breakfasts and went up to collect their gear. They stepped outside thirty minutes later and hailed a cab.

Forty minutes later they passed through armed security at

the gates and pulled up outside the main entrance to Winfield House.

'Now that is what I call a big-arse country pile,' said Toby.

And he wasn't wrong.

Except it was in a big-arse global city. Home to the largest financial centre in the world.

Every inch of the pile was drop dead gorgeous, all red brick and neo-Georgian architecture, full of class and Grade II listed; as big as an aircraft hangar on the outside. Big as three of them on the inside. With hi-tech gadgetry up the wazoo, and secure as the reputation of an elderly Mother Superior.

Twelve and a half acres of Regent's Park. Including the second largest private garden in central London. The first being Buckingham Palace.

McHale had to admit the Yanks never did anything small.

'Pros and cons, big man, pros and bloody cons,' said inner voice. 'Just remember what they did with the US Constitution... and iPads... and Wounded Knee, eh?'

The trouble with an inner voice, thought McHale, was that you never really knew when it was going to speak up. And when it did, you never had a fucking clue what it was going to say.

They unloaded their gear. The taxi drew away. The house's heavy black double front doors opened and Lightfoot stood in the entrance like she belonged there for the long haul, rather than just along for the short ride. No matter how bumpy it got.

She wasn't alone.

Three large black-suited men who looked in very good shape came from behind her and stood in front of the new arrivals. One was as dark as obsidian. They were all wearing coiled earpieces and throat mics. Even McHale thought they were the kind of individuals who would shoot first and not even bother about asking questions later.

'Protocol and security,' she said. 'Before you come through the door, they have to pat you down and go through your gear.

I already told them if they break anything of yours, I'll break something of theirs. So, I guess they'll be pretty careful.'

McHale nodded and the three agents did what they had to do without saying a word. Ten minutes later they were all cleared and given a digital visitor pass each.

Lightfoot led them into a cavernous entrance hall with a double stairway front and centre.

'You want the ten-dollar tour before we get to work?' she said.

The three looked around and tried not to appear gobsmacked. The grandeur of the place was almost overwhelming.

'Does the tour take in any of the toilets?' said Toby, slight physical discomfort showing on his face. 'Too many cups of coffee and not enough bladder control.'

A raised right eyebrow from Lightfoot, and the merest hint of a smile.

She pointed Toby in the direction of a door about thirty feet away. 'Have at it,' she said.

The young copper had at it with a serious measure of speed.

McHale and Daisy felt the eyes of history staring at them from furniture worth millions of dollars, collected by previous owners over hundreds of years. And the ten-dollar tour hadn't even spent its first fifty cents.

About half an hour later they still hadn't made a respectable dent in the walkabout. But it was obvious that the house was split up into 'go' areas, and 'no go' areas.

It was also obvious that their host knew when to stop and chat, and when to cut and get down to business.

It was time to ditch the former and do the latter.

'How about we grab some coffee and get to work,' she said.

'Sounds like a plan,' said McHale.

To the public, Winfield House was a three-storey thirty-five-room mansion that had been the subject of major renovation and restoration work over the years, and was now, almost, a work of art.

Behind the scenes, however, it was a very different animal.

As befitted the home of the Ambassador of the United States of America to the Court of St. James, it was a place that had, in its glamorous lifetime, entertained royalty, popes, movie stars, sporting stars, and a long line of major and minor celebrities.

It had also been used for an RAF Crew Reception Centre and an American Officers' Club during World War II,

Now, this small patch of US soil at the heart of mother Britain was packed with the very latest secure communications technology. Courtesy of a forward-thinking US Government in general, and a very canny National Security Agency in particular. With the grudging approval and cooperation of the British Government, naturally.

Nothing says 'I trust you' as much as the ability to see what your neighbours are having for breakfast from 22,000 miles above the surface of the planet.

Accordingly, two levels below the normal basement of Winfield House, in a suite of highly secure sub-sub-basement rooms dedicated to intelligence gathering and global communications, a team of highly trained men and women looked at, and listened to, the world, twenty-four-seven.

And listening into a telephone call placed from a house in Stockport, Cheshire, at 10pm on Tuesday, 1st August 2017, their impressive technology overheard something very interesting. Part of which it hadn't heard since Monday, 1st August 2016. And part of which it had never heard before.

The first part was this;

There was a man's voice.

Not young. Not old. English. No discernible accent initially. Delivery not rushed. Not excited. Strong. Good diction.

He spoke fifty-six words. They were these;

'Hello again guys. This is The Holy Ghost. I'm calling to arrange for the disposal of another piece of meat. The meat's name was Joseph Miller. It prayed before it died. You won't find me here when you arrive. But I've left a nice gift for you to add to the others. This is number six.'

There was a pause of about five seconds. Then the second part kicked in; same voice.

This time thirty-four words long. They were these;

'I was going to wait another year before leaving you another piece of meat to dispose of. Then I remembered Bobby and 1st September. Tick tock, guys. Tick tock. Look out for number seven.'

That was all there was. Ninety words in total.

By the time all that very advanced and expensive hardware and software had isolated those words from all the billions of other words and sounds and voices it was listening to and looking for every day all over the world, twenty-three minutes had elapsed.

By the time it had the chance to have a good long think about each of the words, another two minutes and seventeen seconds had elapsed.

By the time it decided that the words needed to be taken very seriously, the time lapse had turned into twenty-eight minutes and forty-four seconds.

By the time human ears and minds had been brought into the equation, forty-nine minutes later, the Senior Intelligence Commander in charge of Winfield House that day had been alerted.

And five minutes after that, at about 11.22pm, a call was placed to Detective Chief Superintendent Cyril Drummond. Sitting at home in an armchair, in a neat, detached house, in a quiet tree-lined road, in Hampstead, North West London.

His eyes were closed. His breathing was slow and regular. His left hand was holding a glass containing at least two fingers of Laphroaig Islay single malt Scotch whisky. Two sips down.

He was listening to the last ten minutes of a CD by the American composer Philip Glass. The CD was the soundtrack from the movie of the same name. The Illusionist. He was about halfway through the track when his mobile phone rang. He opened his eyes, cursed softly, switched off the CD, and picked up the call.

It lasted about thirty seconds. The caller said this;

'Cyril, this is Bob Masterson at Winfield House. Sorry as hell to be the bearer of bad news, but just over an hour ago, we got tapped on the shoulder. The Holy Ghost has just come up for air.' Drummond didn't even bother to ask him how the hell the NSA knew before he did about The Ghost surfacing.

Information is one thing. Intelligence is a whole different ball of wax.

'It's not like we weren't expecting him. The bastard is nothing if not predictable.'

'Not this time,' said Masterson. 'This time he brought some extra shit to hit the fan with.'

'Is MOTHER up to speed?'

'She hit the ground running an hour ago.'

'Good. I need to grab some stuff from the office and head up North. Time to hit that bastard's fan with some of our own shit.'

Fast-forward five days.

It was 11.33am. And Lightfoot, McHale, Toby, and Daisy, were two levels beneath the basement of Winfield House. About to walk through a set of secure, guarded, double doors into a suite of rooms that wasn't supposed to exist.

Beyond it, there was a hallway, off which were seven ash wood doors. There were two cameras. One either end of the hallway.

One door led to the major operations room. Three led to numbered hi-tech meeting rooms. One led to a suite of toilets and showers. One was a kitchen with dining facilities. And one was a storage cupboard.

Lightfoot led them to one of the meeting rooms. It had a small, dark grey, number 1 centred halfway up the door. She opened the door.

The room's lights automatically came on. She stepped through last. The room had neutral grey walls on three sides and a bank of black screens filling the fourth wall to the left. In the middle of the room sat a dark slab of a table around which were ten chairs. Four either side. Two either end.

On the table, in front of each chair, were pads and pens. Also, on the table were two iPads, one MacBook, a small hand-held remote-control unit, and a phone.

McHale slowly looked around and let out a long breath. 'I suppose next door is the flight deck of the Starship bloody Enterprise,' he said.

'Oh, we're way beyond that,' said Lightfoot, without even the hint of a smile. She picked up one of the iPads and swiped the small screen.

Suddenly the wall of large screens came to life. There were four banks of four. Each one larger than McHale's HD flat screen hanging on his wall at home. Each one blended into the one below or to the side, so the overall effect was one big fuck-off screen.

After a few seconds, the screen split vertically into two. Left and Right. On the left were two hyphenated words. Fairbairn-Sykes.

On the right were the ninety words picked up by Mother five days previously.

They were italicised, in Helvetica, and big enough to fill the whole right-hand screen.

'We haven't been formally introduced,' said a gruff voice behind them.

Like a well-drilled team of parade ground squaddies, they turned around as one.

Two men were standing just inside the open door.

The man on the left said, 'Hi. I'm Bob Masterson. And this,' he said, nodding to the screen wall, 'is MOTHER. The name stands for: Monitor, Organise, Talk, Hear, Evaluate, and Record. Which is exactly what she does.

'She doesn't eat. She doesn't sleep. She doesn't shit. She's scary smart, and she's here to help.'

Masterson was tall and rangy and had a long, almost handsome face underneath a short, dark buzz cut, greying at the temples. He had on a white, short-sleeved shirt, open at the neck. No tie.

No smile. No formalities. He wore dark grey trousers over black slip-ons and looked a million miles and about eighty years away from the real-life operating versions of old J. Edgar or Harry S. Truman. For example: he didn't look like he knew how to deliver a solid right hook. Which he did.

J. Edgar and Harry were long gone and Masterson was a different kind of agent for a different kind of president and a different kind of world.

Masterson was the kind who believed in the power of ones and zeros; the kind who preferred facts and figures to hunches and gut feelings. He was a data cruncher. A digital thinker. No doubt about it. But right now, McHale didn't just need people who could crunch or think. He needed people who could go off script. People who could think different.

He remembered seeing an ad campaign for Apple years ago. The slogan was 'Think different.' He couldn't remember all the words, but some of them stuck around for years after he first heard them. And they never looked like they were going anywhere soon.

There were twenty-four words. And they were these;

'Here's to the crazy ones. The misfits. The rebels. The troublemakers. The round pegs in the square holes. The ones who see things differently.'

These were the kind of people McHale needed to hunt The Ghost.

Toby interrupted his train of thought.

'Sorry Guv, I've got a question,' he said.

He looked at Masterson. 'Did you say 'Talk'?'

'Say what?'

'When you did the acronym thing with MOTHER, did I hear right? Was one of those words 'talk'?'

Masterson smiled like a proud daddy just finished introducing his brilliant 12-year-old daughter to a group of professors at Stanford, MIT, and Berkeley.

'Yep. You heard right. MOTHER speaks,' he said. 'She has voice recognition and vocalisation capability.' He turned to the screen wall. 'MOTHER, switch to conversation mode, please.'

Both screens went blank. The room was full of the noise of pins dropping. Almost immediately a logo appeared in the centre of the bank of screens. The typeface was anyone's guess. The letters were all upper case. Thin, not chunky.

The word appeared thus: MOTHER.

Tagged onto the end of it on the right was a small copyright symbol. The text was green on a dark black background surrounded by a slim, unbroken, oval line.

Masterson faced the screens and spoke. No remote, no raised voice, no slow careful diction as if speaking to someone who had the IQ of a trod-on chip.

His voice was calm and his diction was good. He was at least fifteen feet away from the logo. 'Hello, MOTHER,' he said.

No matter how well you prepare yourself for some things, they can still surprise the hell out of you when you hear or see them for the first time.

'Hello, Bob,' said MOTHER.

The voice came from hidden speakers that seemed to be placed all around the room. It was female, friendly, calm, unhurried, confident, genuine, and easy on the ear. MOTHER sounded natural, not artificial; like she came from everywhere in the US in general but nowhere in particular.

'You wee beastie,' whispered Toby. His jaw was on its way down to floor level. 'Forget Big Brother... this is Big Sister. And she rocks!'

'I need to bring you guys into the system,' said Masterson. So, as I introduce each one of you, just say your name. That's all. MOTHER will take care of the rest. From then on, she'll recognise your face, your voice, and whatever you say. Just speak naturally.

He turned to face the monitors. 'Room view please,' he said.

The large screen changed to a room interior view, showing

everyone sitting around the table.

Starting from the left and working clockwise, each of the four-team members present looked at the screen and said hello. And MOTHER said hello in return.

'Jeez… this is bloody weird. This time next year I'll be having private conversations with my coffee maker,' said internal voice.

'Right, that's it,' said Masterson. 'I'll leave you guys to get better acquainted. Pick up the phone if you need me. Or better still, ask MOTHER. Play nice.'

He nodded once to McHale, then turned and left the room. The man who remained, the one who hadn't said a word since Masterson walked in, was DCS Cyril Drummond, wearing the same tweed suit that he wore five days ago when McHale saw him for the first time.

'Right,' he said, walking further into the room and slapping his palms together. 'Who's for coffee, bacon butties, and brown sauce?'

In that moment, whether he realised it at the time or not, DC Toby Macbeth became a Drummond fan.

Old school meets new school meets say hello to the future school, thought McHale.

Daisy looked at the screens and smiled. MOTHER looked back at her from behind quite a few million dollars-worth of hi-tech ability.

Then Daisy looked at McHale, disappointment on her face.

'Are we just here for the day, Guv.'

'Maybe we are, maybe we're not,' said Drummond, winking, as a jacketless agent walked in the room, carrying a tray of hot bacon butties and two containers of sauce. One brown. One red.

'What about our own HOLMES system?'

'Say hello to Sherlock's big sister,' said Lightfoot.

Chapter Eleven

In 1985, an information technology system was developed for use by UK police forces. Its role was to help them improve effectiveness and productivity in crime investigations.

It brought together and managed mountains of information, helping to ensure that no clues, vital or otherwise, were overlooked. It also helped to record information about missing persons, casualties, survivors, and evacuees.

Its name, in a typically British blend of old-fashioned detective work and new-fashioned technology, was HOLMES.

And it had a flaw. Some called it a crucial weakness. Others thought it merely had teething problems.

Long story short: it wasn't all that clever when it came to exchanging information and linking separate crime incidents. Especially across police force boundaries. So, in 1994 it was upgraded to HOLMES 2.

The general opinion seemed to be that the new system was an advanced communications network version of the dog's bollocks. Used for everything from major crime investigation to disaster management.

After exhaustive testing and countless swearwords, it was finally released to the first UK forces in 2000. It reached the last ones in 2004.

By the time of the first Holy Ghost murder in Halifax, West Yorkshire, in 2012, HOLMES 2 was the go-to-guy for hunting down bad guys, locking them up, and throwing away the key.

But not all the bad guys.

Police forces are human. And humans, just like HOLMES,

have flaws. They make mistakes. They overlook things. They aren't perfect, nor would they want to be. It's not their fault. They have a million things going for them. They're dogged, persistent, talented, inquisitive, ingenious, articulate, courageous, disciplined, methodical, patient, perceptive, capable, determined... and a whole bucketful of qualities needed to make a good copper. And a damned good human, for that matter.

But they also have a whole stack of things going against them. And some of the really big things going against them are budget cuts. There just isn't enough financial breathing space to go around. There isn't enough fiscal elbow room to pay for the development, supply, and maintenance of the equipment and the systems that police forces need to do their jobs to the best of their abilities.

But sometimes the solution isn't about having more money to spend on the things you need. Sometimes it isn't even about needing more boots on the ground to catch more criminals. Sometimes it's simply about finding better ways to use what you've got more effectively.

The truth was, HOLMES 2 worked. And worked bloody well. Of course, it wasn't perfect. But it was a bloody large leap forward from the original. However, good as it was, there was always room for improvement. That's why, in August 2014, responsibility for the procurement of HOLMES 3 was transferred to Police and Crime Commissioners.

And that's why, in November 2014, the American Unisys Corporation's UK subsidiary announced that it had been selected by the UK's Police Service to implement the latest version of HOLMES, for major criminal investigations and incident management.

The British Police are a determined lot.

It was delivered to more than 40 UK Police Forces via a single browser-based application, hosted in a secure Unisys cloud service.

Clever money said it was only a matter of time before some

bright spark at New Scotland Yard kicked around the idea of developing a complementary information technology for fighting crime… and named it WATSON.

This was how legends were born.

One thing was for sure. Whichever incarnation of HOLMES was up and running at New Scotland Yard when the Ghost's words appeared on the multi-screen in Winfield House in 6th August 2017, he wasn't about to let a Yank named MOTHER get the better of him.

No matter how bloody good-looking she was. Not without a fight. Not without a clever compromise. Not unless he drew the short straw.

Working separately towards the same common goal was one thing. Getting down and dirty in a spirit of mutual cooperation was, as they said across the pond, a whole new enchilada.

HOLMES was British, after all.

Chapter Twelve

Five people. One bacon butty per person. Six butties in total. One spare. Brown sauce on five. Ketchup on one. Daisy was a tomato freak. A gallon of fresh, hot coffee and a pot of fresh, hot tea. No waste. No leftovers. Hardly any crumbs.

And ninety words beginning; 'Hello again guys. This is The Holy Ghost.' And ending; 'Tick tock. Look out for number seven.'

Drummond had a knack for providing the perfect way to kick-start the hunt for a serial killer who had kept himself pretty much invisible for the previous five years.

Or more.

The only clues to his presence were the bodies he left behind. Locard's exchange principle, on this occasion anyway, was a dead duck. Maybe.

Everyone sat around the meeting table spent the first five minutes reading and re-reading the Ghost's words on MOTHER's right-hand screen. At the same time, and with just as much concentration, they ate their way through a Sunday midday snack that smelled as good as it looked. And looked as good as it tasted.

Snack over, Drummond wiped his lips with a serviette, nodded at McHale, and stood up.

'I'm just an ordinary copper,' he said. 'I think it's time to hand things over to folk who can take ordinary and kick the shit out of it. If you need anything, just like Masterson said, ask MOTHER. Or call my mobile. I'll check in again in a couple of hours.'

Everyone else got a nod. Then he grabbed the spare butty, licked a dribble of escaping brown sauce from an edge, and walked out of the room.

McHale looked around the table. 'I think this is where we jump off the deep end,' he said. 'Who wants to start the ball rolling?'

'Is this the full team?' said Lightfoot.

'No. We have two more. Possibly three. The first two won't be here until tomorrow morning. The last one might not get here at all,' said McHale.

Lightfoot's right eyebrow went up. 'So, they'll have to play catch-up?'

'Don't worry. They won't be starting from scratch. I sent each of them good background, so they know what they're getting into. This isn't a brainstorm. This is a hunt. They don't know who they're hunting. But they know what they're hunting. They won't be asking twenty questions. They're not here because they want to catch The Ghost. They're here because they want to bury the bastard. Well, one of them is.'

Lightfoot's eyes narrowed. 'They sound like my kind of people,' she said softly.

'And here I was thinking you were all hi-tech and low profile,' said Toby, turning to Daisy. 'Looks like you were right after all. You owe me a tenner.'

Daisy smiled.

He turned back to Lightfoot. 'She said you were a badass.

'Nothing bad about my ass,' said the BAU agent.

McHale double-blinked. 'Okay... you can think it, but don't damned well say it,' said internal voice.

'Remember how I said I was thinking about age last night,' said Toby.

He paused.

'Yeah?' said McHale.

The young copper picked up his pen and scribbled something on the pad in front of him.

'And remember how I said I wondered how old The Ghost might be and I got bugger all?'

Pause. Two heartbeats.

'Well, I think I might have something.'

Another pause. This time for effect.

'It wasn't his age I got hooked on. It was their ages. All the victims.'

'Go on,' said McHale, frowning.

Toby looked at the screens, took a deep breath, and spoke.

'Hello, MOTHER,' he said.

'Hello, Toby', said MOTHER.

Toby grinned. 'MOTHER, can you clear the screen and bring up the names, ages, and year of death of all six Holy Ghost victims?'

'In sequential order?'

'Yes.'

The screen went blank and a list of text and numbers appeared. It was;

James Halliwell, aged 31, died on August 1, 2012.

Mary-Anne Nutall, 59, died on August 1, 2013.

Deepankar Ghatak, 67, died on August 1, 2014.

Calvin Miles, 47, died on August 1, 2015.

Barbara Lennox, 41, died on August 1, 2016.

Joseph Miller, 73, died on August 1, 2017.

Daisy was scribbling.

'No need to make notes, Daisy,' said MOTHER. 'All information is updated instantly and downloaded onto the Cloud every 60 seconds.'

Daisy blushed and put down her pen. 'Please don't make me redundant,' she whispered.

'Okay, Toby,' said McHale. 'Now what?'

'It's just a thought. There might be nothing in it. But... MOTHER, what's common about the dates?'

'They're all August 1,' said McHale. 'This is Blindingly

Obvious 101.'

'Now, what's common about the ages?'

'They're all prime numbers,' said MOTHER.

Now Toby stood up. 'Show me every prime number between 1 and 150.'

A list of numbers appeared on the screen. They were these;

2, 3, 5, 7, 11, 13, 17, 19, 23, 29, 31, 37, 41, 43, 47, 53, 59, 61, 67, 71, 73, 79, 83, 89, 97, 101, 103, 107, 109, 113, 127, 131, 137, 139, 149, 151.

'Now remove all numbers that don't correspond to the ages of The Holy Ghost victims.'

The numbers 31… 41… 47… 59… 67… and 73 remained on screen.

'Now change the numbers to match up with the ages of The Holy Ghost victims when they died and the years they were killed, first to last.'

The numbers changed to; 31… 59… 67… 47… 41… 73.

'You sure about this, Toby?' said McHale.

'I like prime numbers. Make that I love prime numbers. There are millions of them. Probably even hundreds of millions. Maybe even billions. I even have a poster in a frame at home with the first 1,000.'

Daisy scoffed. 'I can beat that.'

Lightfoot double-blinked. 'If you like we can compare knife and bullet wound scars later,' she said, raising a right eyebrow.

McHale picked up his pen and threw it at Daisy. She got the message.

'Why the change of order?' he said to Toby.

'Simple really. One, he starts at 31 and then skips a number each time. And two, their order. They're normally sequential, so you see them as 31… 41… 47… 59… 67… and 73. But the clever bastard mixed them up. I didn't twig straight away. He's playing a game.'

McHale did a head scratch. He had no ego when it came

to admitting he didn't quite remember anything about prime numbers. 'So,' he said, 'just for the people in the cheap seats, take us through Prime Numbers 101.'

Toby looked at Daisy and nodded.

He kicked off. 'Well, for a start, a prime number has to be greater than 1. Then it has to be divisible only by itself and 1.' She continued. 'For instance, 31 divided by 1 is 31. And 73 divided by 73 is 1. It's simple, really, when you know how.'

McHale scratched his head some more.

Lightfoot turned to face the screen. 'MOTHER, has anyone else picked up the term prime numbers and linked it to The Holy Ghost since his first kill?'

The wall went blank. 'No mention of prime numbers linked to Holy Ghost killings prior to 6th August 2017.'

'That's too bloody easy. How come we're the first to see this in six years? And how come we spotted it five minutes after we started looking.' He should have looked glad. Instead, he looked pissed off.

'Something's only easy to spot when you know where you're looking and you know what you're looking for,' said Lightfoot.

McHale figured she knew that more than most. He wondered just how many living, breathing, killers she had tracked when she was across the pond. And he wondered what happened when she caught up with them.

'MOTHER, bring the victim ages back on screen in order of their date of murder,' said Lightfoot.

The numbers 31... 59... 67... 47... 41... 73 immediately reappeared on the screen.

'So how does he choose them? Does he just pick prime numbers out of a hat?' said Toby.

'What do they have in common... or not?' said Lightfoot.

'I can't believe nobody's picked this up before now,' said McHale. He closed his eyes, opened his mind, and spoke as if reciting off a list printed on the convoluted surface of his brain.

'Their ages are all prime numbers. They're all single. They're both sexes. Their ages go from thirty-one to seventy-three. They're multi-ethnic. They're all different heights.

'They all had different likes or hobbies. Some liked modern music. Some liked classical. But… these are all things that were gone through with a fine-tooth comb the first, second, third, fourth, and fifth times around.'

'And still worth going through the sixth time,' said Lightfoot. She paused.

'When I joined Homeland's Shadow Wolves in 2009, I was patrolling along the Arizona-Mexico border, not far from a multi-billion-dollar fence and Predator drones.

'There was an agent who took me out in the wasteland early one morning. He was a Navajo and made me look for footprints where the dirt had reflected the light after the footprint had been brushed away. We were at it for hours. After we finished and went back to base, he said he was impressed because I spotted nearly half of them.

'I was just as pissed off then as you look now,' she said.

'So, looking isn't the same as seeing. I get that,' said McHale. 'Still don't know what these prime numbers tell us about The Ghost.'

'Well… maybe they tell us that before he hunted our six by age, he hunted them by mathematics,' said Toby.

'So, he's a numbers freak?'

'Remind me to tell you about the Golden Ratio.'

McHale held up his hands in apology. 'Bad choice of words. Let's just say he's a big fan of numbers.'

Toby nodded. 'Let's just say very big fan.'

'Okay now we know something else about him. So, he hunts them by numbers. What next?'

'Well, he has six ages earmarked from all the possible prime numbers. They're all adult ages. And they're all between 31 and 73,' said Toby.

'Why those ages?' interrupted McHale. 'Why does he start at 31'

Lightfoot spoke. 'Well, he has to start somewhere. He won't want to start too early. I don't think children or teenagers are in his profile. And I don't think he wants them too old.

'So, the two before thirty-one are twenty-nine and twenty-three. Then he hits the teens, which might give him a problem.'

'How so?' said Daisy.

'Too much of a handful. Maybe.'

'Okay,' said McHale. 'So... what about the top end?'

Lightfoot shrugged. 'Anything above eighty-five would be easier to control, so easier to kill, sure. But I don't think that's his game. Something he said about them being meat.'

Daisy spoke to the screen. 'MOTHER, show all text screens from August 6 relating to The Holy Ghost and number them.'

The screen wall was filled with mini screens.

'Highlight screen number 3 and bring to full size.'

The screen wall was filled with text. It was;

'Hello again guys. This is The Holy Ghost. I'm calling to arrange for the disposal of another piece of meat. The meat's name was Joseph Miller. It prayed before it died. You won't find me here when you arrive. But I've left a nice gift for you to add to the others. This is number six.'

There was a double space, then this; 'I was going to wait another year before leaving you another piece of meat to dispose of. Then I remembered Bobby and September 1. Tick tock, guys. Tick tock. Look out for number seven.'

'Right... another piece of meat,' said McHale. His cogs were spinning. 'He likes that phrase? Why?'

'I think he likes to kill his meat while it still has a bit of life in it, so to speak. I don't think he likes his victims too old,' said Lightfoot.

'My granddad's 86,' said Toby. 'He runs half-marathons for charity.'

McHale nodded. 'Okay. So... bottom end 31, top end 83. We've got our seven numbers. And we've got our seven knives.'

'What if he gets more knives?' said Toby.

'He won't,' said Lightfoot. 'We know there are only seven 1st pattern Fairbairn-Sykes knives that are numbered. We know he's already used six of them. We know he wants us to know he has the seventh one. And we know that he intends to use it on 1st September.

'Serial killers are either organised or disorganised. Some cross over. But most stick between the lanes.

'There are four main types: Thrill seekers; they like to think they're cleverer than law enforcement. Mission-oriented; they think they're doing society a big favour by getting rid of those they see as undesirable. Visionaries; they sometimes think that they've been told to murder by God or The Devil. And lastly, Power and Control killers; they love to see and hear their victims suffer and scream.

'MOTHER, bring up a list of the four types of serial killers. As they appear in the BAU's database.'

'Short list or expanded?' said MOTHER.

'Short.'

Four numbers and eight words appeared on screen. They were;

1.   *Thrill seeker.*
2.   *Mission-oriented.*
3.   *Visionaries.*
4.   *Power and Control*

Lightfoot continued talking. Everyone else looked at the screen.

'Our guy is highly organised. Unbelievably so. He's organisation on steroids. He's very intelligent. He doesn't overlook anything. He doesn't leave anything to chance. And he doesn't leave anything behind.

'He takes great pride in his work. When he kills it's at a time he wants and a place he wants.

'He'll kill exactly who he wants to kill. He'll use the method that he wants to use, and the equipment that he's brought with him. And he'll enjoy avoiding capture and seeing everyone trying to catch him fail. Time after time after time. He thinks he's cleverer than us.

'That's why if we want to catch him, we need to do things differently. We need to come at him from a place he won't see. A place he won't expect. We need to make him think that the people who are looking for him are looking in all the wrong places. We know that this makes him feel comfortable and not threatened.'

McHale was beginning to think of Lightfoot as less of a team member and more of a team joint-leader. He'd never been a joint-leader kinda guy. He didn't know if he wanted to start now. Then again, he didn't know if he didn't.

'Bollocks, Kemosabe… make your bloody mind up,' said inner voice.

'Time to stop playing by his rules. We need to start playing by ours,' he said. 'But there's one thing missing. His age. We haven't nailed that down yet.'

Lightfoot was in her element. This was her kind of territory. This was where she could sniff the air and pick up all the signals that came to her on the wind. Only thing was, the wind was on the other side of the world and the signals were cloaked and hidden and full of contradictions.

But a hunter was a hunter.

'You think he knows we're on his tail?' said Toby.

'I think he knows somebody is,' said Lightfoot. 'MOTHER, switch on news channels. Mute sound.'

The wall came to life and split into four banks of four screens. Sixteen separate live and recorded feeds from UK and international news channels.

'Show any channels with mention of The Holy Ghost murders.'

'National or international?' said MOTHER.

'National.'

Four screens remained on. The rest went blank.

Of the four, three were studio shots with interviews, and newspaper reports, and one was a recorded report from outside the murder house in Stockport.

'Not bad. Five days after his last kill and he's still newsworthy,' said McHale. 'I think we can knock out the Visionary, the Power and Control serial killers. Agreed?'

Lightfoot nodded. 'David Berkowitz was a Visionary killer. He said a demon speaking through his neighbour's dog told him to kill. So, he did. Six times. Eight wounded.'

'Son of Sam?' said Daisy.

'Yeah, that's what they called him. Later on, he admitted that he made the whole devil dog thing up. Said it was a hoax. Became a born-again Christian in prison.'

'MOTHER, where is Berkowitz now?'

MOTHER'S reply was almost instantaneous. 'David Berkowitz is serving six life sentences in Shawangunk Maximum Security Facility in New York.'

'I bet that place is tired of folk calling it Shawshank,' said Toby.

'Fictional US prison in a movie starring Morgan Freeman and Tim Robbins,' said MOTHER. 'Amazon's IMDb internet movie database lists Shawshank Redemption as the best movie ever.'

'I prefer Casablanca,' said Daisy.

Toby frowned and wished there was a window he could look out of. 'So, what kind of killer are we looking at here?'

Lightfoot thought for a couple of heartbeats and then seemed to come to a conclusion. 'I think we're looking at a Mission-oriented killer. There's no sexual element in his killings. But I also think that he likes the attention from the media. He commented on that in one of his messages. He likes to think that he's smarter than us, and he likes to think that we won't catch him. I bet there's a bit of a Thrill seeker in there, too.'

'And I bet we could all do with a break,' said Daisy. 'Coffees all round?'

'Sounds like a plan,' said McHale, picking up the phone and mumbling into it. Then he killed the call and put the phone down.

Toby turned to Lightfoot. 'Where's the, um…'

'Out the door first on the right.'

'Dammit… that was just getting bloody interesting,' said inner voice. 'I remember Son of Sam. Ugly bastard. They had another name for him. The .44 Calibre Killer.'

McHale pushed his chair back from the table and straightened his legs. Held his arms towards the opposite wall. Interlocked his fingers. Turned his palms outwards. Pushed. Felt the tendons stretch. Unlocked. Stood up and took a closer look at the screen wall. Came back and sat down again.

He noticed that Lightfoot hadn't moved much the whole time they were in the room, apart from the occasional head turns to look at the screen and the rest of the team.

She saw him looking at her. 'Old Cherokee trick,' she said. 'Stay still in one place long enough and the cavalry can't see you.'

McHale double-blinked and smiled, then got one back in return. Even a bit of a laugh. Result.

'I was beginning to wonder if you had your sense of humour surgically removed when you joined the FBI.'

'I did,' she said. 'We all do. We have to laugh every now and then just to keep up appearances. It's in the manual under do's and don'ts.'

Another double-blink.

Despite MOTHER'S assurances, Daisy seemed to have gone back to scribbling and was now lost in concentration. McHale estimated she had filled a few A4 pages with notes so far. Good girl, he thought. He trusted MOTHER, but no amount of software and hardware compared with the human element.

Daisy was the glue that held the team together. She was rapidly becoming a whole lot more than just a good-looking note-taker with a damned fine mind.

A couple of minutes later Toby came back, followed by an agent carrying two thermos flasks; one very large, for coffee, and one very compact, for tea. Just in case.

Americans liked to give folk the option. Even though it doesn't get taken up. They had hospitality in spades.

Another agent followed with two large serving plates full of sandwiches and biscuits. Neither smiled. Neither spoke. But as they left, Lightfoot called out a 'thanks guys'. She got a good-natured turn-and-nod in reply from the drinks agent.

It was 2.30pm. McHale thought they'd probably got more done in the past few days than the whole investigation had in the past few years. He kept that thought to himself. People who think different are sometimes viewed by others who think the same as a real pain in the arse.

Lightfoot looked at Toby. 'So… how come numbers?'

'Long story,' he said with a short laugh. 'My mother was a mathematics professor and my father was a musician. I tried making friends with guitars and keyboards but I guess I just grew up with numbers on the brain. All very boring.'

'All very fascinating,' said Daisy.

McHale made a mental note. Watch those two.

Then he felt an itch. Somewhere in the frontal lobe of his brain. Just under his forehead. It was the kind of itch he got when he wanted to reach out, grab a rogue thought, and scratch the hell out of it.

And the rogue thought was this;

Did he know The Ghost?

But before he had the chance to write it down or kick it around, Lightfoot asked him what he thought about the age of the Ghost… and the idea that he might actually know him disappeared into the fog of an afternoon full of conjecture.

'Toby had a think about that last night but came up empty. His focus was all on the victims. Why? What's on your mind?'

Lightfoot paused before answering.

'All my life I've watched people. I actually prefer watching them from a distance to interacting with them. Present company excepted.'

'Of course.'

'Now animals... that's a whole new level of interesting.'

'Wait... are you saying you prefer animals to people? Maybe even predict what animals do better than what people do?' said Toby.

It was meant as a friendly tease. It elicited a smile, followed by a frown.

'Probably,' she said. 'Depends on the environment and the circumstances... but yeah, human nature is mostly predictable. The more you watch the more you see. And the more you see the more you can tell. But I've always got on better with animals. Or maybe they've always got on better with me. Hard to say.'

'This is going somewhere, right?' said McHale.

'Flick your patience switch to ON,' said Lightfoot.

That drew a few laughs.

'MOTHER?' said Toby,

'Yes?'

'What is the age of The Holy Ghost?'

MOTHER was silent a heartbeat. 'Not enough information,' she said.

'Take a best guess.'

Another heartbeat. 'Twenty-five to thirty-five years of age.'

'What about physical condition?'

'Not enough information,' she said.

'Take a best guess.'

Another couple of heartbeats. 'Capable of overpowering each of the victims. Capable of inflicting all the wounds committed on each of the victims. Capable of escaping from the residences of each of the victims without being detected.'

'You ever heard of the Serial Killer Information Centre?' said

Lightfoot.

That got one yes and two nos. The yes being McHale.

'The SKIC was started by a guy called Doctor Mike Aamodt, a professor of psychology at Radford University in Virginia. He said that the average male serial killer had an IQ of 94.7%. That more of them were non-white than white. That they were in their mid-to-late-thirties.

'But then again, that was just in the US, and Aamodt's figures didn't quite match up to those from the FBI.'

'Doesn't exactly inspire me with confidence,' said Toby.

The next couple of hours was spent doing what McHale liked to call clearing away the sludge; getting rid of all the mental crap to give good quality thinking room to grow.

'Maybe it's time to call it a day and start fresh tomorrow. We'll have two more people joining us on the hunt. Every brain counts, right?'

That got nods.

Thinking different was over for the day. Covering the same ground would wait until tomorrow. When doors that had stubbornly remained closed today would be forced open or kicked down.

At 4.28pm McHale's mobile came to life with a fast touch of Charlie 'Bird' Parker.

'You like it there?' said Drummond. No preamble. No cracked it yet. No how the hell are you?

'If I said I did, would it make HOLMES jealous?' said McHale.

'Tell me you're getting somewhere.'

'We're getting somewhere.'

'Anywhere useful?'

'Hard to tell. We've only just kicked off. I need to divert our two arrivals due tomorrow. They're booked in at the Wellesley in the morning. I need them to join us over here as soon as.'

'Leave that to me. Are they DI Kelly and the Jesuit priest?'

'Yeah. Father Stephen Rice.'

'How's the Yank?'

McHale quickly looked at Lightfoot and saw she was looking at him. He quickly looked away.

'Tranquility base here. The eagle has landed,' he said.

'Tell her to sharpen her talons.'

'Will do, sir.'

'Speak in the morning, Tom.'

The phone went dead.

McHale awarded himself a small smile at the promotion to first name basis. He looked at Lightfoot who was looking at him anyway. 'Drummond said sharpen your talons.'

'I always keep them razor-sharp.'

He believed her.

'Are you burgers and fries guys?' she said, looking around the room.

'Does the Pope drink scotch?' said Toby.

'Depends which Pope,' said McHale.

'Depends which scotch,' said Toby.

Daisy consulted her iPhone for directions to the nearest burger bar.

'Never mind that,' said Lightfoot. 'Tonight, you guys are guests of Uncle Sam. The Ambassador wants to meet you upstairs. We're eating fast and messy. And lots of it.'

Ambassador Shaun Carpenter and his family were gracious hosts, full of questions, and empty of pretensions. Everyone steered clear of things that needed steering clear of. Any thoughts of the past few days, and the coming week or more, were carefully and politely side-tracked.

Arrangements were finalised for the team's extended stay downstairs. A black cab was called after food, a round of coffee and a small glass of something stronger for each of them.

By the time they got back to the Wellesley, it was just after nine, and their stomachs were stretched to capacity.

For all of them, except one, sleep came fitfully. Whatever dreams they had were fuelled by the kind of images that didn't need speaking of, and didn't really belong in the company they shared only a couple of hours earlier.

For one of them, sleep was mercifully postponed. It was Wednesday evening and McHale hitched himself up to needles, tubing, and a mechanical pump. Then 90ml of pure plasma, in five vials, said hello to the subcutaneous tissue of his abdomen.

This kind of self-medication was a ritual that didn't take no for an answer.

Chapter Thirteen

Monday, August 7th, 6.30am

The alarm went off and a Layla riff from Clapton's guitar chased bloody dreams away for another day. Then a groan escaped lips. A hand attached to a hairy left arm reached out from under the bed covers and stabbed the alarm into snooze cruise mode.

Then 10 minutes later the alarm came alive again. Then the hand stabbed the snooze cruise button to off. Then McHale's brain came wide awake.

Right... Press remote. TV on and low. Then piss, shit, shower, shave, teeth, dress, all the fun stuff that makes up the beginning of a new day in a still strange bedroom.

Part of him existed inside the skin of a creature of habit, and the other part a million miles away from one.

He wiped the condensation from the bathroom mirror and ran his fingers through hair that was a stranger to a serious comb. He looked outside. Wet, but hopeful. Checked his phone. Two emails. One from the Jesuit. Timed 11.16pm the previous night. It had twenty-eight words. They were these;

'Just a quickie. I'll leave the Heavenly uniform behind and dress casually grey. Sometimes the God Collar ruffles the feathers of those of a non-religious disposition. Best. Stephen.'

The second was from DI Siobhan Kelly. Timed 1.29am that morning. It had seventeen words. They were these;

'Time to settle the bill. And I don't mean the Wellesley. See you in the morning. S.'

To most the message would have appeared somewhat cryptic. McHale knew exactly what she meant.

Breakfast was a full-on English for Toby, as if anything else was an option. McHale joined Daisy in a Weetabix and fruit juice combo, followed by black coffees all round. All except for one.

McHale's medicinal infusion of the night before brought on his usual CIDP headache of the morning after. His breakfast liquid of choice was bottled water. Lots of it.

Then the hunt shifted up a gear. Or two.

By the time breakfast was over and they'd grabbed their gear from their rooms and met up in the foyer, the rain had stopped.

Clouds were beginning to drift away and patches of blue sky had decided to put in an appearance. It occurred to McHale that, most of the time in the UK, patches of blue sky were the best anyone could hope for. Every now and then, however, the patches got a lot bigger.

August was getting into its stride, and the summer weather in the capital city still had the power to make those who valued warmth remove their jackets. Or at least think about it. But it was mid-morning, and the sun still had a way to climb before the blue got bluer, and the pores began to leak sweat.

About forty minutes in a black cab later and they reached Winfield House. They pulled up at the front entrance and were greeted with a quick but well-practised pat down by security. Recognising someone as a friend didn't mean they weren't a potential enemy. The agents knew their job and did it silently and efficiently.

It was 9.55am.

Lightfoot was waiting for them by the open front door. McHale realised that smiling came difficult to her. But at least she wasn't frowning, which he took as a good sign.

Another good sign was the t-shirt she was wearing over her black jeans and black leather combat boots. It was black with the iconic Rolling Stones big red lips and tongue across the chest.

Just because you're 42 doesn't mean you can't be cool as Hell.

And when the BAU has your back, and Mick and the boys have your front, Hell is cool and hot in the same place, at the same time.

'You got two new best friends,' she said. 'They're downstairs already. Chomping their way through a bacon butty each. That's what you call them, right?'

'We're quaint that way,' said McHale.

'So I've heard.'

'Get a room you two,' said Toby, smiling. Lightfoot double-blinked and lead the way into the building.

The house's stunning interior was ignored as the four headed straight for the secure suite two floors down. Daylight was wasting, and as the Ghost had said; 'Tick tock.'

When they reached the entrance to the meeting room, there was no reason for Lightfoot to act the polite host any more. This was business as usual. If the hunt for the Ghost could be anybody's idea of business as usual. Accordingly, she walked into the room first, followed by Daisy, Toby, and lastly McHale.

Cops were still gentlemen. Well, some of them.

Sitting next to each other on the opposite side of the table, facing the door and with the screens on the right, were Father Stephen Rice of the Society of Jesus, and Detective Inspector Siobhan Kelly of the UK's National Criminal Agency.

The Jesuit was to their left. Kelly to their right. Both had empty plates in front of them and half-full mugs of black coffee. Milk wasn't in short supply. Just in short demand.

Father Rice was dressed in grey. Grey shirt, open neck. Grey trousers, same shade. And presumably, black shoes. Presently hidden from view behind the table. A matching grey jacket was hung over the back of his chair.

'Holy bloody moly,' said inner voice. 'The God Squad is in town. Jesuit alert... Jesuit alert!'

McHale ignored the warning.

Kelly was as far away from colourful as dyes, pigments, and imagination would allow.

She had on a casual black shirt tucked into black pants and a classy black leather belt with a small silver buckle. The belt provided a demarcation line between the two halves of a body that looked slightly lop-sided. She favoured her left side.

Whatever shoes she had on were out of view.

Her only two compromises to colour were her short, almost cropped, snow-white hair, and a deep red wooden walking cane propped up against the right arm of the chair to her left. Any makeup she had on was minimal and difficult to spot.

McHale and Kelly had never met each other until that morning. Some strangers have stronger things in common with each other than they do with their family and best friends.

Smiling, McHale stepped forward and stuck out a hand to the grey man. They both shook. Strong grips. Strong friendship. No need for an introduction.

He repeated the process with Kelly. This time he introduced himself. Same grip strength. Different history.

The priest was smiling. Snow White was wary. Both knew why they were here. He trusted McHale. She trusted nobody. Her eyes said she needed time to get to know these people. Or anybody.

They also said that time was something none of them had. Especially somebody somewhere in the UK who was eight-three years old and might have just a few more weeks to live.

The other team members followed suit with the handshakes and the introductions. Then everyone filled up on coffee. Bacon butties were politely declined. Lunch and snacks were in the future. Rice and Kelly were on the first-come-first-served queue, and the others had already eaten.

'Good to see you again, Father,' said McHale.

'Stephen,' said the Jesuit.

McHale nodded. 'Stephen.'

'I did some checking,' said Kelly. 'You put David Black away.'

'I had help,' said McHale, nodding towards Rice.

'Friends upstairs,' said Rice. Lightfoot and Daisy both looked to the ceiling. Then they twigged.

'The Head Office doesn't like it when one of their own goes rogue.'

'How did you two get here this morning?' said McHale.

'Checked into the hotel, then somebody called Drummond sent a car for us. Brought us right here. Didn't expect the strip and cavity search, though,' said Rice.

Daisy almost choked on a mouthful of coffee. Laughter breaks any ice.

For the first hour or two they went through the events, thoughts, and conclusions of the previous day. Bringing the newcomers up to date was a necessary exercise.

Most of the time Rice and Kelly sat quiet, taking everything in. They nodded in all the right places and occasionally asked the right questions.

Both of them were as impressed by MOTHER as the others had been the day before.

At 12.35pm Drummond walked in and introduced himself. He shook hands and smiled slightly to put the newcomers at ease. Then he made a little motivational small-talk, before making himself scarce.

At 1.00pm two agents, not the same ones as the previous day, brought in flasks of tea and coffee, a large plate full of sandwiches and a smaller one full of biscuits. As before, the tea went untouched. They brought it anyway.

Their motto seemed to be; better to have it and not need it, than need it and not have it.

The US Ambassador to the Court of St. James might have ruled upstairs, but down in the sub-sub-basement, the National Security Agency were the big dogs.

No expense was spared.

Software and hardware benefitted from the finest communications technology on the face of the planet. Cooked meals and multi-layered sandwiches had the finest ingredients available. Artificial intelligence was to die for. So were rib-eyes and pizzas. To be truly effective, according to Napoleon apparently, an army needed to march on its belly. And the NSA always kept their people, their minds, and their technology, well fed.

Napoleon might have known about bellies. But he knew bugger all about marching. He fought his biggest battles from a safe distance. Sitting on a horse. Again, apparently.

Fast-forward 196 years…

Father Stephen Rice, in between bites of a pastrami sandwich with mustard on rye bread, started the ball rolling.

'I think I have an idea. It might turn out to be a bit of a red herring. Then again, maybe not.'

'Every journey starts with the first step,' said Lightfoot.

Rice looked at her. Raised an eyebrow. 'And ends with the last one.'

He looked away and continued speaking.

'In 1960, I saw a recording of the coronation of Queen Elizabeth II filmed in Westminster Abbey in 2nd June 1953. We had an old television. I was only seven years old at the time, but I couldn't take my eyes off the screen. Even though it was really small. We had neighbours from either side crammed into the living room. All the grown-ups had alcohol and the kids had lemonade. Except a couple of sneaky ones.

'Anyway… when she was walking out of the Abbey, the Queen was carrying something in her left hand. It was an orb. I found out later it was called The Sovereign's Orb. I don't know if any of you have seen it. Maybe if you've seen the Crown Jewels it might ring a bell.

'It's a hollow golden ball or sphere just over six inches in diameter. It has gems around the middle and over the top. And it has a cross sticking out of the top.'

He stopped speaking and looked at everyone around the room.

Silence for a couple of heartbeats.

'Remind you of anything?' he said.

Life is full of moments where you can hear the sound of absolutely nothing of any consequence happening. But every now and then, a moment comes along that almost stops time in its tracks. A moment where you can practically hear and feel your heart skip a beat or two. A moment when the autonomic function of your lungs, which should do all your breathing for you without you even thinking about it, decides to think about it. A moment when the oxygen supply that your brain so desperately needs decides to slam on the brakes and wait a second or three, just so it can see you start to turn blue and pass out.

These moments are precious and should be treasured.

After double-blinking, twice, McHale was the first to speak.

'Holy fuck,' he whispered.

Kelly was the second.

'Make that a double holy fuck,' she said. All calm on the outside. Starting to feel a deep, dark kind of pleasure on the inside.

Daisy was the third.

'Way to go, Father,' she said.

'So, this is useful?' said Rice.

'Does The Pope drink Guinness?' said Toby.

'I thought you said he drank Jack Daniels,' said Lightfoot, turning to look at the screen wall.

'Depends which day of the week it is.'

'MOTHER, create two screens, portrait shaped. Left-hand screen display photo of the Sovereign's Orb. Right-hand screen, display close up of …' She paused. 'What was the last victim's name and where was he killed?'

MOTHER's calm voice was the antithesis of the excitement being felt in the room. 'Joseph Miller, 1st August 2017. Stockport, Cheshire.'

MOTHER thought about things for a second or two, then two images appeared onto the screens side by side.

On the left, there was the orb with a cross sticking out of the top of it. And on the other, there was Joseph's head with a

Fairbairn-Sykes knife sticking out of it.

Kelly stood up. 'Can we see all the head shots?'

After a few seconds, close-ups of all six victims appeared on the screen opposite the orb.

'Coincidences mean you're on the right track,' said McHale.

'MOTHER, split the left-hand screen into two squares. Top square, display the Sovereign's Orb. Bottom square, display Holy Ghost message transcript containing the name Joseph Miller.'

After thinking for a second, MOTHER complied.

McHale afforded himself a slow smile. It wasn't a happy smile. It wasn't a pleasant smile. It was the kind of smile that appears on the face of a hunter. The kind of smile that says; 'We're here. We're coming for you. And we're not going to stop until we get you.'

The kind that was replicated on the faces of everyone standing or sitting in a hi-tech room, in a hi-tech facility, in the middle of one of the most hi-tech capital cities in the western world. Where the hunt for a monster was beginning to take shape.

McHale decided it was time.

By the right side of his chair, sitting just in front of his right leg, was the bag containing his laptop. It also contained the Fairburn-Sykes knife inside its see-through container, wrapped in its protective cloth.

He leaned down and brought out the cloth. Placing it gently on the table in front of him, he unwrapped it, the blade's tip pointing towards the screens.

He slit the chain-of-custody label, opened the container, and withdrew the weapon.

He remembered how sharp it was and picked it up carefully, keeping his skin as far away from the edges as his grip would allow. Then he placed it gently on the table on the cloth. Naked to the world.

'Hello there,' said Lightfoot slowly.

She wasn't speaking to, or looking at, either Daisy or Kelly. In fact, nobody was looking at anyone else. The only star of this little show sat on the table. It was even more impressive in real life in front of them than it was on the large Ultra HD screens on the wall.

The Jesuit took a pair of gold rimmed spectacles from the left breast pocket of his shirt, cleaned them and put them on. He leaned over the table and took a closer look at the weapon.

'So, this is what all the fuss is about,' he said.

'Some of it,' said McHale.

'Which head is this from?' said Kelly.

The Jesuit sat back down. He looked at her and frowned.

'You're not big on tact, are you,' he said.

'I don't do tact,' she said. 'I do truth. Honesty. Justice. And painting a target on a murdering bastard's back.'

'James Halliwell,' said MOTHER.

'Pardon?'

'The knife was removed from the head of James Halliwell. He was killed on 1st August 2012. In Halifax, West Yorkshire. He was thirty-one years old.'

The fact that MOTHER had answered the question without being directly asked wasn't lost on McHale.

'And he wasn't James Halliwell any more when it was removed,' said Kelly. 'He was exactly what The Ghost said he was. A piece of meat.'

'Interesting,' said McHale.

'Like I said, I don't do tact.'

'What about punishment and revenge?' he thought. 'Do you do them?'

The room suddenly went very quiet. McHale and Kelly were looking unflinchingly at each other. Three heartbeats.

Lightfoot broke the spell. 'I like people who speak their mind,' she said. 'I find it difficult to trust people who don't.'

'You know... he referred to the victims as meat thirteen times in total, when he made the calls,' said Toby.

'Twice each call for all six calls. Except the last one, when he said it three times.'

'You really do like numbers,' said Lightfoot. Picking up the knife, examining it, then placing it gently back on the table. It sat there. Waiting to be picked up again.

'It's a curse,' he said, smiling. 'I've been thinking about the language. He's friendly. Informative. But he never gets personal. Not big on pronouns. Never says he or she. He does mention their names. But it's almost like it's not personal. Almost like he's saying words that have nothing to do with people. Nothing to do with anything living. So, I was just wondering…'

'If we had any records or stats of serial killers who impersonalised their victims after they killed them?' interrupted Lightfoot.

'On a day with a prime number,' said McHale.

The BAU agent let the cogs spin a bit faster between her ears. Toby could almost hear MOTHER's voice saying, 'processing… processing.'

After about 10 seconds, MOTHER replied.

'The only one who fits that profile so far is the one known as The Holy Ghost.

'Next question. What do the six victims have in common?'

'Apart from the facts that they all lived alone, that they were all victims of The Ghost, and they're all dead, of course,' said Toby.

Pause.

'Nothing,' said MOTHER.

'Fine.' He turned to the others in the room. 'We need to think off the wall. Throw the obvious out the window and kick around the kind of things that maybe slipped through the net.'

'I might be forced to break something,' said Lightfoot.

'Then say the first thing that comes into your head. As long as it isn't a mixed metaphor.'

Silence.

'Were they religious?' said Toby.

'Did any of them have birthmarks?' said Daisy.

'Good… keep going,' said McHale.

'Had any of them been depressed, attempted suicide, contacted the Samaritans?' said Rice.

'Good one,' said McHale.

'What about alcoholics? Were any of them 'Friends of Bill' or anything like that?' said Lightfoot.

'Friends of who?' said Daisy.

'Euphemism for Alcoholics Anonymous.'

'How would we ever find out if it's anonymous?' said Toby.

Good point, thought McHale.

'Maybe they had relatives either by blood or by marriage who linked them all together,' said Daisy.

Then McHale had a thought. 'Maybe the one thing that links them all together is that there's absolutely nothing to link them all together?' he said.

'Apart from the three things you mentioned, about living alone, being dead, and being killed by The Ghost,' said Rice.

Silence.

'Are you talking about hiding something in plain sight?' said Lightfoot.

McHale shrugged. 'I'm just shooting the breeze, as you Yanks say. I dunno. Maybe we're looking for something and there's nothing there to find.'

'Well, that's a depressing thought,' said Kelly.

'You been listening, MOTHER?'

'Yes.'

'Any of those ideas ring a bell?'

'No boxes, no churches, no Samaritans, no friends of Bill. Living alone, being dead, and being killed by The Holy Ghost are the only common links. Not enough information on hiding anything in plain sight. I'll keep looking.'

While trying to make connections of her own, Lightfoot's mind had drifted off to another place. And another time.

Chapter Fourteen

She was twelve years old.

Her great grandfather was eighty-three.

They were the same height.

His name was Nimrod Smith. Called after Nimrod Jarett Smith. Fifth Principal Chief of the Eastern Band of Cherokee from North Carolina. A veteran of the Confederate Army. Born 1837 and died 1893.

An important man whose Cherokee name was Tsaladihl.

The girl's great grandfather wasn't an important man. His Cherokee name was only important to him and to the girl.

It was Yonaguska.

The hair on his head was strong and pure white, and he wore it long. Fastened behind his neck not with a traditional strip of buckskin, but with an old knotted elastic band. He wore no hair on his face.

The skin on his face and the backs of his hands was dark brown and weathered. With more lines and folds and wrinkles than the hide of an African elephant she saw in a book.

His clothes were battered, worn and comfortable. But they carried no bad smells.

He spoke to her, not as an old man does to a young girl, but as someone coming to the end of his life to someone at the beginning of hers.

He had no children to teach. No boys who would listen to him and hear his stories. They were all pains in the ass with shit for brains.

Nobody cared about any contribution he had to make. And nobody gave a damn about anything he had to say. Not his children. Not even his grandchildren.

Nobody except the girl.

She was born, in 1975. The year when, amongst other things, the Vietnam War ended. Margaret Thatcher became the leader of the opposition for the Conservative party in the United Kingdom. And the blockbuster movie 'Jaws' was released.

He was born in 1904. The year when, amongst other things, Japan and Russia went to war with each other. St Louis police tried out a new investigation method… fingerprints. And the United States acquired control of the Panama Canal Zone for a measly $10 Million.

She was a new school Indian with an old school teacher

He was an old school Indian in a new school world.

His one claim to fame, told repeatedly to those who would listen, was that he met the famous actor, musician, and full-blood Cherokee, Wes Studi.

While this was technically true, it wasn't the grand coming together of like-minded individuals that the old man portrayed it to be. It was more like two people passing on a film set and nodding to each other. Once. Studi, a Native American movie star in his prime. Smith, an ageing Cherokee two-bit extra.

That was it.

But out of such small gestures, great stories were born. For those with many memories and a suitable imagination.

He would tell the girl his stories every time they went hunting. Stories of how the great Nimrod Jarrett Smith went hunting for the last time just eleven years before he, Yonaguska, was born.

Of how a grey wolf told him when he was thirteen that the spirit of Nimrod Jarrett Smith would always be nearby, looking out for him.

Of how, when he was fifteen, he tracked down a fine young doe and was about to kill it when the same wolf came near and spoke to him in the old Cherokee tongue. Asking him to spare the doe's life because she carried another life within her.

He always thought the wolf was the shape-shifting spirit of old Nimrod.

Yonaguska told her that, after killing a deer, hunters would throw the tongue and some of its meat into the fire as a sacrifice. And how blow-darts made of locust and thistle were good for taking down rabbits. But only if the weapons were blessed and prayed over before the hunt.

A lifetime of knowledge and memories and respect passed between the old man and the girl.

And when they went hunting for the last time, she was sixteen years old and he was eighty-seven.

He gave her the thing he valued most in the world. An old, thick leather band he wore on his right wrist. Tooled neatly into it was the image of a wolf howling at the moon. She strapped it onto her right wrist. It fitted just fine. It balanced the seven bands of small, dark coloured beads wrapped around her left wrist.

She gave him a rattler's tail attached to a necklace braided from her own hair. She said he had to shake it when death came for him. She said the noise would warn death that here was a brave warrior who had lived a good life and would die a good death.

She never saw him again alive after that night.

Her name was Grace Lightfoot.

She was a hunter.

Chapter Fifteen

'You want what?' said Drummond, loudly.

McHale tried to sound as nonchalant as he possibly could. He relaxed his posture and banished the worried look from his face, in the hope that neither would transfer themselves through the ether and out the other side where Drummond could see.

'It's not really a big ask,' said McHale. 'I don't see the problem.'

'It's part of the Crown bloody Jewels. That's the bloody problem.'

'It's a copy. A damned near perfect one, I'll give you that. But it has no monetary value. The jewels are paste and glass, and the gold is paint. It just looks like the real thing.'

'And the real thing just happens to be the Sovereign's Orb. You know how old it is?'

McHale sighed. 'Yeah… 356 years.'

'You know what its value is?'

'Potentially billions of pounds. I'm guessing it has lots of noughts on the end of it. In fact, it's probably priceless.'

The pair were talking on the phone on Monday August 6. It was 3.55pm.

'But like I said,' said McHale, 'I'm not asking for the real McCoy. Just the fake one. Who in their right mind would put the real Crown Jewels on display? Even if they were behind the toughest glass case in the world.

'Wouldn't the genuine ones be locked away in a bloody big safe in the Bank of England?'

There was a lot of huffing and puffing. But eventually Drummond said he knew a man who might know a man who could possibly know someone who might be able to help.

But no guarantees.

The six-man team was taking a leisurely stroll around the private gardens of Winfield House, where they had moved en-masse for a quick half an hour break. McHale thought it might turn out to be longer. Weather permitting.

The sun was out. The temperature was high. The gardens were well watered and tended. And the only clue to the fact that they were on a small patch of American soil was the large Stars and Stripes flag fluttering in the breeze at the top of a white pole high above the building.

Compared to Winfield House, the official American Embassy building a few miles away was nothing like as good looking, or as well kitted-out. The government of the United Kingdom could, on occasion, be very generous. They could also, on occasion, be very sneaky.

Security Service guards were always nearby. But they were keeping an eye on the property, rather than the people.

'Why the hell do you want it anyway,' added Drummond. His voice no longer agitated as his mind began to grapple with the possibility of borrowing a tangible symbol of the British Monarchy.

'For the same reason I want you to bring all the other Fairbairn-Sykes knives to Winfield House. Or, as I like to fondly describe it, Ground Zero Minus Two.'

Drummond's voice went up a couple of decibels again.

McHale pulled the mobile away from his right ear for a second or two and grimaced.

Then he put it back and said; 'Sorry… missed that. Bad line.'

'I said you want what?'

'The other five knives.'

'The real ones?'

'No, the plastic replicas… of course the real ones!'

'All of them?'

'Look. Seeing a photo of something and feeling it in the flesh, so to speak, are two different things. I want to put the orb, or at least a fake version of it, in the team's hands. I want them to touch it. With gloves on, of course. I want them to make the visual connection between it and the victims. I want them to use their imagination. Not their deductive reasoning.

'Same goes with the knives. I want one in the hands of each of the team. I want them to get used to the weight. The balance. The feel of those buggers in their hands.

'I want them to imagine what it must have felt like when the Ghost went to work on those poor buggers.

'I don't want them to just look at photos of folk with their guts ripped open and their skulls perforated, and treat this like another bloody investigation. Like I said… I want them to think different. That's how we nail this guy's hide to the wall. Not by doing things the same way they've done for the past six years.'

McHale stopped speaking. He realised that the others had stopped talking amongst themselves. He realised they were looking at him. And realised that, probably for the first time, he was beginning to think of them as a unique team. Not a bunch of very talented and very unique individuals. They weren't quite there yet. But they were on their way.

There was silence on the other end of the phone.

Two heartbeats grew into three. Then four.

Then Drummond sighed.

'You'll have your knives in the morning. How long it will take me to track down the fake Sovereign's Orb is anyone's guess. Maybe a day or two… maybe never. But like I said, I know a man who might know a man.'

There was a different tone to Drummond's voice now. That much was obvious. All the annoyance was gone. All the testiness had done a runner. All the gruff impatience had taken a hike.

In their place was the sound of a man who was beginning to see that he'd made the right decision at the beginning of the previous week. A million miles away. When he travelled to Stockport and started this very unusual ball rolling.

'Sounds like a plan,' said McHale.

Drummond grunted and ended the call. McHale, who had been standing next to a stunning purple Japanese Maple for the whole of the conversation, looked at the others looking at him.

He smiled and spoke to them.

'I got you some knives to play with,' he said. 'They'll be here in the morning. The orb might take a little longer. If at all.'

McHale thought about knives and flipped back in time. He looked at Rice. 'You remember what Black wrote in blood on the wall after he murdered the Kirkbrides?'

Just for a second or two, he saw the thousand-yard stare in the eyes of Rice. The same one that young GIs had when they returned from their time in the killing fields of Cambodia in the 1970s.

Then it was gone. Replaced by a look of intense sadness.

'I remember,' he said. 'Four words in red on the living room wall. Quote unquote. You can't save him,' said Rice.

'He wasn't talking about the Kirkbrides,' said McHale.

'No,' said Rice, lowering his gaze. 'That was Arthur, the other one. The one who is evil. Talking about Father Black. The one who is lost.'

'Who wants to put down another evil son of a bitch?' said McHale.

'That would be me,' said DI Siobhan Kelly. The only one of the team with three legs. The only one who grimaced every time she put weight on her shattered and arthritic left knee. The only one with a score to settle of a sadly personal nature, even though the score was a proxy one.

They carried on walking.

And talking.

And limping.

'How do you think he leaves nothing behind?' said Daisy.

'How come we can't find any transfer from him to them? Or him to the house?'

'I don't believe it,' said Lightfoot.

'You don't believe what?'

'I don't believe he left nothing behind. And I don't believe nothing got left behind on him. I just think we haven't found it yet.'

'Well, we've only got one crime scene left out of six, and that one has been trampled all over for the past six days.' said Toby. 'What if there's nothing there to find? What if Locard was wrong?'

'Just because you can't see something, doesn't mean it's not there. And just because you haven't found any evidence, doesn't mean there isn't any to be found.'

'And just because you think it must be there, doesn't mean it is.'

'What if he wore a wet suit?' said Daisy. 'Or something neoprene?'

'Or one of those full body suits that S&M folk wear, with a head mask with holes for the eyes and a tube in the mouth to breathe through?' said Toby.

'I think I'm officially worried about you,' said Daisy.

'My great grandfather could talk to the wind,' said Lightfoot. 'I saw him one time having a conversation with it at the top of a high ridge. I was fifty feet below him, but I could hear him clearly. He was asking the wind to show him which direction the crows had flown.'

'Had the crows landed on the ground?' said Kelly.

'Nope. No tracks.'

'Did they land on a boulder for a rest?'

'No boulders.'

'Did he see them fly past?'

'Nope.'

'Were there even crows in the first place?'

'Yep.'

'Okay. I give in. I get no coconut. How could he tell?'

They were passing a stretch of well-fed, well-manicured lawn. Around the edges and in the middle were sprinklers delivering much needed refreshment to the grass. Out of reach of the sprinklers a large tabby cat sat. Waiting. Looking for birds. Out of reach of the cat, sitting in the surrounding bushes and trees, was a large gathering of small birds. Waiting patiently.

Lightfoot pointed. 'The absence of birds on the lawn tells the other birds that the cat is there.'

'Clever birds,' said Kelly.

A slight frown wrinkled the skin just above Lightfoot's nose. 'Crows are cleverer,' she said. 'They're big, mean, intelligent, aggressive, resourceful and they can adapt.'

'The wind told my great grandfather to look not for crows but for owls. It reminded him that crows and owls were mortal enemies. If crows came across an owl they would fight to the death. And most of the time, the owl would lose.'

'So?'

'So, my great grandfather looked on the ground for an injured or dead owl. Then he knew where the crows had been.'

'Like hunting for black holes,' said Toby.

The Jesuit, who was being a gentleman and walking alongside Kelly, chuckled.

'What's so funny?' asked the walking stick blonde.

'The thought that maybe you can never truly see The Ghost. You can only see how everything else behaves around him. You can only guess where the black hole is by examining where it isn't.'

They had taken a path that wound around the garden in a circuitous route, starting and ending eventually at the front door of the building. They were only a couple of hundred yards short of the finishing strait.

'Okay,' said McHale. 'We're looking for the owl.'

'In order to see the crows.'

'What I don't get,' said Toby, 'is that owl's talons can rip the shit out of crows.'

'Yeah, but crows are also sneaky. When they go to war, they fight to win,' said Lightfoot. 'Owls are solitary. Crows come mob-handed. They come with murder in mind.'

It was 4.35pm.

It was time to talk to MOTHER again.

By the time they walked through the meeting room door in the sub-sub-basement, another itch that had been scratching a small raw patch in McHale's brain gave him a new question to ask.

He turned to Stephen Rice. 'Pub quiz question of the day, Father. How many versions of the King James Bible are there published in the English language? Have a guess.' Rice did the unexpected. He burst out laughing.

'I said something funny?' said McHale, looking around and shrugging.

Rice wiped the tears of laughter from his eyes. Then he calmed down, put his serious face on, and spoke.

'When Queen Elizabeth I died in 1603, James VI of Scotland took over the company and became James I of England. In 1604 he commissioned a new English version of The Great Bible that was written in the reign of Henry VIII.

'This new bible was started in 1604 and finished in 1611. It included the thirty-nine books of the Old Testament. Another fourteen books of the Apocrypha. And twenty-seven books of the New Testament.'

'You're a Jesuit, Father, right?' interrupted Kelly.

'Yes.'

'Roman Catholic?'

'Yes.'

'And the King James Bible is a Protestant book, right?'

Rice sighed.

'Isn't that a bit like working for the enemy?'

'Folk might speak different words, but to God they all sound the same,' said Rice.

'So, what you're saying is that trying to figure out how many versions there are is pretty dumb?'

'No. Not at all. Just very time consuming. I think the real question is what's different, or what's the same, about the six Bibles the Ghost left behind?'

McHale double-blinked and spoke to the screens. 'MOTHER, can you call the mobile phone of Detective Chief Superintendent Cyril Drummond and patch him through to my mobile?'

'Of course, Tom.'

About 15 seconds later, McHale's mobile, sitting on the table in front of him, rang. He picked it up and spoke.

'Afternoon, sir. Another request.' A pause. 'Yes, we're making headway.' Another pause. 'No, we haven't cracked it yet.' Another pause.

'We need the Bibles. All six of them.' Another pause. 'Tomorrow morning would be fine. Thank you, sir. See you then.'

Drummond killed the line.

McHale looked at the team. 'We can't get a fake Orb. We'll have to rely on photos of the real thing.'

He turned to Rice. 'Will you need a C of E scholar to help you have a damned good look at the Bibles? My guess is that they're not your average King James versions.'

Rice smiled. 'I am a C of E scholar. And a Roman Catholic one. And a few others.'

McHale nodded. 'Good. I'd like Daisy to help you.' He turned to Daisy. 'Daisy, I'd like Father Rice to help you.'

That got another few laughs.

The only laughs absent were those from Lightfoot, which was predictable since her laughs were as rare as white rhinos. And Siobhan Kelly, who was rubbing her leg and looking forward to her next Vicodin hit. Six on a good day. Eight on a bad one. Today was a good day. Three down, three more to go. Can't beat a good Schedule II opioid. In fifteen minutes, she'd excuse herself, slip to the loo, crunch up one of her Vicodin and take a break from the pain train. For a while.

In her wallet was a crisis and support line number. She hadn't rung the number in six months. That didn't mean she was pain-free. She wasn't. It didn't even mean she was prescription-free. She wasn't. It just meant she was conversation-free. It just meant she was all talked out. There were no words left that hadn't already been said to describe how she felt. She'd been there. Done that. Got the damned t-shirt.

Now, most of the time, she existed in the space between her ears. A space that had more noise than silence. A space that wouldn't let her forget the sights and the sounds that she tried to shut out but knew she never would.

Detective Inspector Siobhan Kelly had one thing on her mind. And it had bugger all to do with finding the person responsible for turning two beautiful little girls into buckets full of flesh. It's what made her useless, for the time being, as a field agent for the NCA. And it's what made her perfect for McHale.

This wasn't about looking for The Holy Ghost. That had already been tried. Repeatedly, and with a whole bunch of coppers who did things the right way for years.

This was about getting inside the damned head of one twisted fuck. Hunting him down, and bringing serious vengeance to bear on his sorry arse.

This was about payback for Ellie and Samantha Brasher, and the sooner the better.

New ideas were all tapped out for the team for the day. Everyone was on the merry-go-round of walking all over the same old ground. But that was the deal. You sat on the brightly painted horse as it went around and around in the hope that when the music stopped the horse would be somewhere it hadn't stopped before.

It was 5.28pm.

The Vicodin was working for Kelly and she was halfway through a final coffee in the room. As were the others.

'Right everyone. Last thought of the day,' said McHale.

'Something that has been brewing way down deep in the lobes but hasn't been said out loud yet. Just one thought from each of you. I don't want you to elaborate on the thought. Just get it out there. MOTHER will remember it. We'll see if it can open any doors overnight, and we can talk about it in the morning. I'll even start the ball rolling.'

He looked around the room and saw each of them looking back into themselves.

'What if The Ghost knows me?' said McHale.

'Wow… hold the phone,' said inner voice. 'Where the hell did THAT come from?'

Short silence.

Then Stephen Rice frowned and spoke. 'I think it might be an idea to go have a talk with David Black… or rather Arthur. He explained the relationship of the killer and the priest. Two distinct personalities in the same body. Arthur, who was aware of Black. And Black who had no idea that Arthur even existed and would be horrified if that door was opened.'

Longer silence.

Then Lightfoot spoke. 'I missed something. I keep going over and over things and I've just got the feeling I missed something. Like he knows I'm looking for something out of place that's there and shouldn't be. Or that isn't and should be. And he knows it. And he's fucking with my head. It's like something so damned obvious and it's staring me in the face.' She looked pissed off and fascinated at the same time.

More silence.

McHale looked at Daisy. She was flicking her pen against the table top like a drumstick looking for the right beat but finding only the wrong one. She had sound, but no rhythm. Her face was a mask of disappointment.

She shook her head. 'Sorry, Guv. I got nothing.'

Toby had something. And the more he thought about it, the more he thought it might be a big something.

'What if he's someone who suffers from Asperger's,' he said. 'What if his obsession with numbers is part of his condition?'

McHale double-blinked. 'Good one, Toby. Let that stew overnight.'

His gaze turned on Kelly. She had stood up and was taking a slow, limping stroll around the desk. At first, he thought she was heading in his direction. But she passed him by, mumbling as she went.

By the time she reached the screen wall and MOTHER, she stopped and looked at him.

'You said all the knives were numbered, right?'

'Yep. You've already handled the one he used to kill Joseph Miller.' He pointed to the Fairbairn-Sykes sitting on the table. 'It's the one with the number 6 engraved on the flat part just below the guard. Where are you going with this?'

'I'll tell you tomorrow when we have all the knives in front of us,' she said.

McHale was just about to wrap things up when Daisy interrupted him, 'I remember,' she said.

Everyone turned to face her, as if by doing so they would add more weight to whatever it was she forgot.

'We're assuming that the orb is a copy of the one used by the Queen in the coronation in 1953. But what if it isn't? What if it's another orb? How many other orbs are there?'

Toby, sitting next to her, smiled. He raised his clenched right hand and fist-bumped her. She threw a smile and a bump back at him.

McHale picked up the phone and after two rings a voice said 'Yeah?'

'DI Tom McHale for Bob Masterson, please.'

There was a pause of a couple of seconds, then Masterson said, 'Hi, Tom. Everything okay?'

'Everything's fine. We're closing down for the night. Is this room secure until the morning?'

Small laugh.

'That's room's secure until Hell freezes over, why?'

'I'm leaving a murder weapon on the table overnight.'

'That all? No bodies?'

American humour, thought McHale. 'Nope, nothing else. See you guys in the morning.'

The session broke for the day and Winfield House was left behind in the wake of a full black cab, taking five of them back to the Wellesley Hotel. The sixth, Lightfoot, would join them later.

They'd had a good day, so McHale decided that a reasonable meal was on the cards. As was a full-team bonding session.

He texted Alice from the cab, on the off-chance that Sonny Jello had managed to hop on a flight back to the UK and hook up with them. Alice texted back: 'Sorry. More chance of Cher than Sonny. Watch this space. A.x'

By 8pm, the six of them were in a reasonably private dining booth on the first floor of a restaurant called Charlie Brown's, about five-minutes-walk from the hotel.

On the walls of the ground and first floors, the owner, probably not named Charlie, had hung a selection of cartoons of the iconic comic strip Peanuts.

The fact that Charles Monroe Schulz was one of the most influential cartoonists of all time was way down the list of reasons why McHale chose the restaurant.

The fact that Peanuts was simply his all-time favourite cartoon strip was all the reason he needed to book a table. Snoopy Pizza, without the slightest hint of coconut, was on the menu. And on the plates. All washed down with a few bottles of red wine.

Conversation was loud. Stress levels were low. Relaxation levels were high.

Tomorrow was tomorrow and tonight was a light year away from any thoughts about The Holy Ghost.

They left the restaurant at 11.30pm, after some gentle nudging from some very polite staff.

Lightfoot hightailed it back to Winfield House, courtesy of a cab hailed from the middle of the road by McHale. Four knackered team members walked back to the Wellesley and were soon gratefully asleep in their respective hotel room beds.

The fifth member, Kelly, who had filled up with mineral water during the meal, was sitting up in bed, kneading her left thigh. She was watching an old black and white movie, and waiting for the effects of her sixth Vicodin – street name (or one of them) 357 – to kick the shit out of the pain in her leg.

Jagger was right. You can't always get what you want.

But sometimes, courtesy of a well-aimed 357 washed down by three fingers of Southern Comfort, you get what you need.

Chapter Sixteen

Tuesday, 8th August, 6.30am

A loud slice of Afro-Cuban Jazz shattered the silence and broke the spell. A hand attached to a hairy left arm reached out from under the bed covers and stabbed the alarm into snooze cruise mode.

Then ten minutes later the alarm went off again. McHale groaned and switched the snooze off.

Then the whole rise, wash, moisturise, dress, and coffee routine kick-started another day. Then email check. Nothing. Then weather check. Sunny. Then breakfast.

More coffee. Scrambled eggs on toast. Brown sauce. Pepper. Toby became Mister Predictable for the third morning in a row. Daisy had coffee and grapefruit segments. 'It's Tuesday,' she said. 'I have grapefruit on Tuesday. Good for the heart and immune system. Beats the hell out of eggs and bacon. And sausage and beans. And fried tomatoes and...'

'What about Wednesday?' said McHale.

'Weetabix. Keeps me regular.'

'Now there's an image I won't forget in a hurry,' said Toby.

The Jesuit made a beeline for porridge and strong, black coffee. In the world of Siobhan Kelly, coffee was reserved for any other time of day. Green tea was a ritual purely kept aside for the start of the day. Along with buttered toast.

Each had their single thought, shared with everyone before the end of the previous day, turning over in their mind. McHale knew the power of anticipation.

Their cab drew up outside the front door of Winfield House

just after 10.20am. The sun was just beginning to kick into gear. McHale longed for the cool aircon of the sub-sub-basement meeting room.

Two different agents were on pat-down duty. Kelly gave both of them the kind of look that carried with it a warning about invading personal space. The warning went over their heads at about treetop height.

Lightfoot was waiting at the open door wearing black combat trousers, dark grey Nike trainers, and a white, short-sleeved t-shirt. The shirt was open at the neck and baggy at the waist.

'You guys ever get up early?' she said.

'What makes you think we've been to bed?' said McHale.

That got a single eyebrow lift. 'You've got a box waiting for you,' she said.

'Oh goody,' said Toby. 'Do we have to write 'thank you' cards?' That got a hint of a smile.

'You keep your eyes to yourself, buster,' said inner voice. 'That goes for your hands, too.'

When they got downstairs and walked in the room, they saw the cardboard box sitting on the table. It was two feet square and taped up tighter than a duck's arse.

McHale looked to the screens and decided to accept MOTHER into his family of humans.

'Morning MOTHER,' he said.

'Hi Tom… hi everyone,' said MOTHER.

Everyone replied. Even though they were replying to a highly advanced machine. Even though the machine had no grey cells or vocal cords. Even though they were indulging in some good old anthropomorphism. They still regarded MOTHER as human. And female. With a brain the size of a planet.

Nothing like a little suspension of disbelief every now and then.

'I didn't want to open the box. It's addressed to you,' said Lightfoot. But it didn't stop her from reaching into her combats and pulling out a butterfly knife, flicking it open deftly with a twist of her wrist, to reveal a short, wicked-looking black blade. The double folding handle was just as black, with small holes along the entire length.

On the table was a box of powder-free latex gloves. The powder in many kinds of latex gloves had a nasty habit of inhibiting DNA analysis.

Lightfoot reversed the knife and handed it to McHale hilt first.

'I haven't held a Balisong for years,' he said. 'Don't tell me. You never leave home without it.'

He took it and felt the weight in his hand. It was a beautiful piece of deadly engineering and he had no doubt that the double-edged blade was sharp enough to cut fresh air.

'I don't suppose you have another one of those tucked away somewhere,' said Kelly.

Lightfoot paused. Deliberated. Then pulled a second, identical, Balisong from another thigh pocket. She handed it, unopened, to Kelly. 'Take care. Some things take a bit of getting used to,' she said.

With the same fast, practiced flick of the wrist, Kelly opened the second Butterfly knife with ease and admired the blade. She smiled for the first time that morning. Then closed the blade put the knife on the table and patted it gently twice.

A small, barely discernible wrinkle of interest appeared on the outer edges of Lightfoot's eyes. Coincidences mean you're on the right track, she thought.

Lightfoot slid the knife's edge along the box's taped flaps and opened it up.

'Right,' said McHale. 'Glove up.'

They all grabbed a pair of latex gloves from the box and put them on. Some with greater practice and ease than others. Others, like the Jesuit, with greater difficulty. When they had finished putting on their second skins, McHale reached into the box.

Sitting on top of the wrapped contents was a sheet of white folded paper. He picked it up and unfolded it. There was a single sentence, in cursive writing, in black ink. It had quotation marks front and back. A name. And a capital letter.

The sentence was this:

'Discovery consists of looking at the same thing as everyone else and thinking something different.'

The name was Albert Szent-Gyorgyi.

The letter was D.

Food for thought, presumably from Drummond.

McHale smiled and gently pulled out five Fairbairn-Sykes knives. Each one in its own see-through protective tube, sealed, complete with chain-of-custody label, and wrapped in thick cloth.

He handed them, one at a time, to Toby, standing next to him, who laid them gently on the tabletop.

The knives weren't visible yet, but there were no cigars for guessing the contents of each cloth roll.

Next came the Bibles.

Each one in an A4 jiffy bag. Sitting in its own little world. Each one the collected words of God. Depending on your viewpoint.

Each one written in Biblical Hebrew. Then translated into Greek. Then translated into Old English by a few select monks and scholars, from Latin Vulgate. Then translated into modern English by Heaven knows who. But the fourteenth century scholar and Catholic dissident priest William Tyndale was undoubtedly in there somewhere.

Last out of the box came an A4 size buff coloured, stiff-backed envelope. In it were six coloured photographs of the crime scenes. Specifically, the shots of the posed victims that McHale had first seen on the morning of August 2 the previous week. With the addition of a new one for Joseph Miller.

The photos were almost included by Drummond as an afterthought. McHale hadn't asked for them the previous day. But then again, he didn't have to.

Everyone helped with the unwrapping. All thoughts of coffee

were temporarily suspended, no matter how thirsty they were. The blades of Man and the words of God took precedence. At least for the moment.

McHale marvelled at how noisy busy hands and tongues can be one minute. And how silent they can be the next.

Fifteen quiet minutes later all five knives, complete with their dried in fluids, were naked and had joined the first one. Lined up on the table, each sitting on the folded piece of cloth that was its shroud; at the side of them, all six King James bibles were in a row. Each one with a number that corresponded to a knife of the same number. Each one looking, at first glance, exactly the same as its brother or sister.

And next to them, all six crime scene photographs showing each victim. Each photo numbered one to six with a yellow Post-It note.

But first glances can be deceptive. First glances can fool those who think that identical twins, or in this case, sextuplets, are physical mirror images of each other.

Then he spoke.

'Okay, take a matching numbered blade, book, and photo each. They're yours for the day. I want you to interrogate them. Question them. Let them talk to you. See what they have to show. Hear what they have to say.'

One by one, each team member reached out and took possession of their triple charges.

McHale was the last one to claim his.

'Right, Kemosabe, look at the number on the blade,' said internal voice.

He picked up the knife and looked at the flat section just under the S-shaped cross-guard. It had a number on one side. The number was four. His knife had been used on Calvin Miles. That's who his photo showed.

Toby had knife number two. His had been used on Mary-Anne Nuttall.

Rice had three. His knife had been used on Deepankar Ghatak.

Kelly had six. Her knife had been used on the latest victim. Joseph Miller.

Lightfoot had one. Her knife had been used on the first victim. James Halliwell.

Daisy had five. Her knife had been used on Barbara Lennox.

All of them, except one, put their Bible down, picked up their knife, and examined it. Tested the weight in their hands. Shifted it from right hand to left. Or, in the case of Kelly, who was a southpaw, from left hand to right.

The one who put down the knife and picked up the Bible was, of course, Father Stephen Rice.

Like all the Bibles, it had more than its fair share of blood spilled on it.

McHale could see the look of loathing on the Jesuit's face as he discarded the weapon. He almost felt the need to apologise for putting him through this exercise, until he remembered Rice's previous life.

The feeling came and went in the time it takes for a neuron in his brain to pass an excited electrical signal from one synapse to another.

The Bible sat in Rice's fingers, through a layer of protective latex, like a welcome handshake from an old friend. This was the world he understood. This was the world he lived in. Not the one where death visited innocents and did its level best to decapitate them.

And then a voice from within reminded him that the book he was holding in his hand was probably not just the greatest story ever told, it was probably also the bloodiest one.

An almost silent 'Hmm…' escaped his lips.

Each Bible on the table had a square, yellow Post-It note stuck on it that corresponded with the number on a knife, linking it to a matching victim.

The Post-It note on the black front cover Bible that Rice had in his hands had the large number 3 written in black marker on it. Which, of course, meant that the Bible was found in the lifeless left hand of Deepankar Ghatak.

Shortly after 10pm on 1st August 2014, Deepankar didn't give a damn who the hell it belonged to.

Rice took the sticky note and transferred it to the book's black inside front first page. All that remained on the cover now were the bloodstains and two words in gold capital letters. HOLY BIBLE. The only words on the spine were these: HOLY BIBLE King James Version. Cambridge. And the logo of the Cambridge University Press.

There were dried bloodstains also on the gilt edging of the pages, sticking some of the pages together. And on the material bookmark. All evidence of the horror that the softback edition had witnessed.

He closed the book and ran the fingers of his right hand slowly over the surface. He felt the texture. Sniffed the leather.

It smelled new. Apart from the faint whiff of the blood. Like an echo of a long-gone scream.

He opened it up.

Inside the cover, sitting at the base, were the words 'FRENCH MOROCCAN LEATHER' in gold.

He turned over the first page.

It opened to the section normally reserved for those who feel the need to personalise their Bible. Sometimes there are a few names, as the book gets handed down from family member to family member. Or even from stranger to stranger.

There were no names.

Just a single sentence in cursive writing in red ink.

The line was:

'There are none so sorry as those who will not repent.'

He picked up the pen sitting next to the A4 pad in front of him. Scribbled the line on it. Scribbled a question mark next to it. Moved on.

He flicked through the pages, coming to page 1235 and the last two words that, in any Bible, perfectly fitted the first three.

Those three were, of course, 'In the beginning.'

And the last two were, ironically, 'The End.'

The tale of an early Christian God perfectly book-ended by five words of the English language.

He glanced to his right at the Fairbairn-Sykes, sitting on the table waiting for him to interrogate.

Not yet, he thought. Not yet.

On either side of him, around the table, five almost mirror images of his borrowed knife were being examined closely and carefully. The earlier warning from Toby about the sharpness of one of the blades had been translated into the sharpness of them all.

No skin was coming into contact with metal. No fingers were holding any steel in front of the hilt. No blood accidentally spilled. No curses deliberately hissed.

'Presumably all the knives were thoroughly examined for trace?' said Kelly.

'Yep. Nothing except the blood and viscera of the victims,' said McHale.

'And the Bibles?'

'Same.'

'No blood belonging to anyone else?'

'Nope.'

'No strange latents, fibres, anything?'

'Nope.'

'And then the knives were properly bagged and processed?'

'Yep.'

'What about the difference in lab tech used in 2012 to now. Could they have missed anything?'

McHale turned to the screens. 'MOTHER?'

'Yes?' said the disembodied voice of their non-human seventh team member.

'Access all crime lab reports on file for The Holy Ghost

murders, starting with James Halliwell in 2012?'

'Which labs were used?'

Pause.

'All physical, optical, and chemical properties of the knives, plus all blood, fingerprints and fibres, were examined using the latest equipment at Bell Macaulay Laboratories in Battersea, London. Samples were taken and the all evidence from each crime scene was placed in storage.'

'Were all chain of custody protocols observed?'

'Yes.'

McHale knew they were the UK's finest and most reliable forensics lab.

'Thank you.'

'No problem.'

McHale smiled at MOTHER's conversational tone.

Toby examined the number on the flat piece of blade in front of the S-guard. There was a small number two stamped into it. He glanced at the photo sitting by his borrowed Bible. Both had yellow Post-Its with the number two on them.

Everything checked out so far.

Around the table, McHale, Lightfoot, Kelly, and Daisy were all still busy examining their knives. The Jesuit was browsing his Bible.

At 1.30pm the room door opened and a suited agent came in. His head was wearing a tan, a buzzcut, and a smile. 'You guys hungry? Thirsty?' he said.

'Gagging,' said McHale. 'Coffee and biscuits would be great.'

The agent disappeared with half a smile.

The voice of Stephen Rice came from across the table. 'Might be something. Might be nothing,' he said, looking at one of the Bible's first pages.

'My bet is something,' said Toby.

'I'm with him,' said Daisy. 'Never bet against a Jesuit.'

Rice smiled at her, then looked at McHale.

'Open your Bible at the beginning. There's a page reserved for the Bible owner to write their name in.'

Everyone stopped what they were doing and put down their knives.

'Okay… now what?' said McHale.

'Anything written on that page?'

'Yes. It says; 'There are none so dumb as those who will not speak.' Don't have a clue what it means.'

'Mine says; 'There are none so sorry as those who will not repent" said Rice.

The others were looking at their Bibles.

"There are none so dead as those who will not live," said Kelly.

"There are none so blind as those who will not… something," said Lightfoot. 'The line's unfinished. There's a piece cut out of the page.'

'Forensics,' said McHale. 'I bet they tested a sample of the ink.'

"There are none so numb as those who will not feel," said Daisy.

"There are none so deaf as those who will not hear," said Toby.

McHale frowned. 'This is old news,' he said. Apart from the latest killing, these Bibles have all been looked at under a bloody microscope. I don't think we're going to learn anything new from those lines.'

Daisy shrugged. 'No harm in asking, Guv.'

'MOTHER… do you have a record of all the sentences written on the inside pages of The Holy Ghost victims' Bibles?'

Pause.

'Of course.'

The six sentences, as they appeared in the Bibles, and before a sample of the page from the first bible was removed, came on the large screen wall. In order of first victim to last.

The complete line from the first Bible was; 'There are none so blind as those who will not see.'

'Ah… the missing word. What did they find when they tested

the ink?'

MOTHER paused a heartbeat, then said; 'The ink was manufactured by Waterman of Paris and available in 50ml glass bottles. The colour was Audacious Red.'

'Okay... now I'm presuming the lines were all taken apart, buggered about with, and put back together again at the time of the murders, just to see if they meant anything to anyone?'

Pause.

'They were,' said MOTHER.

'And?'

Pause.

'There is a report from a linguistics professor at Cambridge University that might be helpful. It was written in 2016. Would you like me to bring it up on screen?'

'How long is it?'

'Sixteen thousand two hundred and seventy-eight words.'

'Shit... does it have a synopsis section?'

'Yes. Four hundred and twenty-seven words.'

'Bloody hell. This is like pulling teeth. What about a conclusion section?'

'The conclusion is eighty-six words long.'

'That'll do nicely.'

The six Bible sentences were replaced by eighty-six words, which came up on the screen wall. They were these;

'These sentences appear to be written by the same hand. Language, grammar, and syntax seem consistent and one sentence in particular 'There are none so blind as those who will not see' can be traced back to John Heywood in 1546. Also mentioned by, amongst others, Jonathan Swift in his 'Polite Conversation' in 1738. Apart from their inclusion in the Bibles found at the six crime scenes I can find no obvious connection between these six sentences and the writings of the killer known as The Holy Ghost.'

'I recognise that sentence 'There are none so blind as those who will not see' from my seminary days,' said the Jesuit. 'It was on a wall in a lecture room for years. It's probably still there. It's one of those lines that stays with you.'

Just then the door opened and Agent Buzzcut plus one other came in with the usual flasks of coffee and unnecessary tea. Plus two large bottles of water. One still, one sparkling.

And instead of biscuits, there were two trays of assorted sandwiches, quartered mini pork pies, and mini sausage rolls.

They were all placed on a smaller round meeting table at the far end of the room. As far away as possible from the evidence sitting on the main table. Hunting serial killers was thirsty, hungry work.

Agent Buzzcut, nodded and smiled at Lightfoot. Just a slight nod. Just a quick smile. Lightfoot nodded back. The agent didn't see it. But Kelly did.

McHale raised his voice a touch to get everyone's attention. 'Okay... this is where I ask you to take your knives, Bibles, and photos, and cover them with the cloths that came with them. Then remove your gloves and place them in the trash can. He pointed to a large silver bin sitting against a wall near the screens. It had a flip top lid.

'We'll be eating standing up next to the food table,' he added. 'When we're fed and watered, we can glove up and go back to the business of feeling not quite so hungry.'

Laughter.

With evidence covered and gloves off, refreshments were poured and snacks shared and the first sips and munches of each slipped easily down waiting throats. That took fifteen minutes, with sandwiches and coffee enjoyed along with small talk and comfort breaks.

Then two agents returned and cleaned up. Then everyone went back to the hunt.

When they were all seated, MOTHER, who had waited patiently while bellies were filled, said, 'Picking up on Father Rice's comment about the sentence he recognised from his seminary days, I have other point. For those of you who don't believe in coincidences, and those of you who do – which just about covers everyone – all the sentences have something in common.'

Pause.

'Spill the beans,' said McHale.

Pause. It almost seemed like she was doing so for effect.

'They're eleven words long.'

'All of them?' said Kelly.

'Yes.'

'And?'

'Not really unusual. Until you consider that eleven is another prime number.'

Toby, even with a half of a chocolate digestive biscuit in his mouth, managed to grin. He slapped the table loudly with the palm of his right hand. Swallowed the biscuit quickly. Said; 'Bloody knew it!' forcefully.

The slap startled Kelly. Loud bangs were still the bringers of bad memories. She was over it in a second or two, but the effect hung around for a few seconds more, like a faint memory that made her right-hand shake ever so slightly. Almost too slightly for anyone else to notice. Except McHale and Lightfoot.

The memory also started a dull ache in her left thigh which she automatically rubbed. Her mind went to the child proof plastic tub of 357s in her shoulder bag. She had no children. The cap just made the pills that much safer. More difficult to access. A bit like safety speed bumps on side roads where children lived. And for as long as she lived, the two words 'children' and 'safety' would be inseparable.

The world above them was three levels up and three doors away.

Here, down in the bowels of a mansion set in the greenery of Regent's Park, there were no reminders. Nothing to make her palms sweat. Nothing to make her sheets damp.

The echo faded into the distance like a reticent memory.

It was twenty-three days before 1st September.

Chapter Seventeen

McHale opened the door on the team's overnight thoughts. It was one of those 'push me – pull me' doors. No handles to turn. No locks to fit keys into. All that was required was the desire to push your way in. Or the need to pull your way out.

'So last night I was thinking; 'What if The Ghost knows me?" he said.

Pause.

'That's a bit of a stretch, isn't it?' said Rice. 'Why should he know you? Are you being optimistic? Or pessimistic? Or are you just trying to kick-start the engine?'

'It just popped into my head yesterday. You know what they say. Some thoughts start off life as good babies. Other ones are just bad right from the start and they don't get any better.'

'Maybe you were separated at birth,' said Lightfoot. She did the single eyebrow raise thing. 'Evil Twin Syndrome.'

He smiled. 'One of these days that eyebrow will go up and refuse to come back down again, you realise that, right?' he said.

Pause.

'So… back on track,' said Daisy. 'What makes you think he might know you?' She had one of the remaining mini-sausage rolls held daintily between thumb and index finger of her right hand. It was hovering perilously close to her mouth. It looked like a dead roll walking. A second later it was a dead half-roll being munched.

'Chess,' said McHale.

'Ah, I forgot you play,' said Rice. 'You still do that internet chess thing?'

McHale smiled. The Jesuit hadn't forgotten. He was just being polite.

During the hunt for Father David Black and Arthur, he and Rice had played three games. Not online. The real touchy-feely kind.

McHale did what he did every time the subject of chess came up in any conversation. His mind went to a screen-grab of the board with his latest active game. 'Try to make a few moves every day.'

Pause.

'Made any today, Guv?' said Toby.

'One, so far.'

'Winning?'

'Only until I start losing,' said McHale.

'Who are you playing?'

'Ah… now there's the rub. With Internet Chess you can do one of two things. You can tell the truth and play under your own name, age, and sex. Or you can lie through your teeth and remain anonymous.'

'So, you do the former?'

'Superman doesn't lie,' said Lightfoot.

That got a few laughs.

'That means for all you know you could be playing the local vicar… or The Holy Ghost?'

McHale shrugged.

'Wait a minute,' said Lightfoot, immediately alert. 'You're thinking of Ted Bundy and the hunt for the Green River Killer?'

'Something like that,' said McHale.

'Okay,' said Daisy. 'I'm familiar with Ted Bundy. Remind me who the Green River Killer was'

Lightfoot carried on the story. 'The Green River Killer, or Gary Ridgway, was the most prolific serial killer in U.S.

History. In Washington during the 80s and 90s, he was convicted of forty-nine kills.'

Daisy quietly cursed for forgetting about Ridgway.

'In 1984, another serial killer called Ted Bundy, who was on death row in Florida convicted of killing at least thirty women between 1974 and 1978, approached the authorities and offered his help to catch him. He inserted himself into the hunt and gave investigating officers valuable insights into the minds of other serial killers. Including Gary Ridgway.'

'Hang on,' said Kelly. 'So, you think that David Black, sorry Arthur, can help us do to The Holy Ghost what Bundy helped the police do to Ridgway?'

'Not exactly,' said McHale. 'But he might be able to point us in the right direction. Or at least one that isn't completely wrong.'

He shrugged again. 'We're in the business of thinking different, right? This is the whole reason why we're here. To connect the dots that, so far, nobody else has been able to connect.

'Now this might be way off the beaten track. But who the hell knows what it might turn up?'

'But I still don't see how you think you might be playing chess with The Holy Ghost?' said Kelly.

McHale sighed. Stood up. Walked around the table and faced the screen wall.

'MOTHER, bring up a recent photograph of Alexander Pichushkin.'

A headshot of a frowning man in his early forties with dark hair and a crooked, probably broken, nose appeared on screen. He was clean-shaven and angry looking.

McHale turned around to face the team. 'Ladies and gentlemen, allow me to introduce 43-year-old ex-supermarket worker and brain-damaged Russian serial killer, Alexander Yuryevich Pichushkin.

'Better known as-'

'The Chessboard Killer,' interrupted Lightfoot.

McHale nodded to her. 'He's believed to have killed at least forty-eight people, possibly as many as sixty.

'Care to add?' he said to Lightfoot.

She put down the pen she was holding like a drumstick and bouncing off the tabletop. 'Sure,' she said. 'Pichushkin was convicted in 2007 and sentenced to life in prison, with a recommendation that the first fifteen years be spent in solitary confinement. When he was captured in 2006, he said that his aim had been to kill 64 people. The number of squares on a chessboard.'

'So, he's not The Holy Ghost,' said Rice.

'No,' said McHale. 'But here's the thing. A few months ago, I read an article in which Pichushkin was featured. It said that he belonged to an elite group of Internet Chess-playing serial killers. The writer of the article claimed that he had discovered how they were communicating using chess moves sent to each other via the post and the internet.'

'No crime sending a chess move to anyone. Serial killer or not,' said Rice.

'Are you fucking serious?' blurted Kelly loudly, then immediately regretted her outburst. Especially when it was made to someone sitting next to her; someone who probably wore a crucifix twenty-four seven. Someone who played footsie with the Vatican. Someone she actually liked.

She looked at him. 'Sorry,' she said. 'But any communication between serial killers has to have the phrase BLOODY DANGEROUS stamped all over it.'

Rice shrugged. 'I don't disagree. I just can't figure out how passing on moves might constitute passing on lessons for Serial Killer 101.'

McHale shrugged. 'Who the hell knows? What if The Ghost is part of the serial killer group playing chess on the net… and he recognised me because I play too and I always use my real name… and he did a little digging around and found out I was a copper… maybe he put two and two together. Then came up with the perfect way to insert himself into my game and into our investigation.'

Lightfoot picked up her pen and threw it lightly at him, hitting him on the chest. 'Might make a good movie script, but I think you've gone off the deep end with this one, McHale.'

'Wow… hang on a skinny minute,' said inner voice. 'No boss… no Guv… this is a dame speaking to an equal. Danger Will Robinson!'

McHale ignored the warning. 'The number of your Bible is 1, right?'

Lightfoot glanced at the yellow Post-It on the book's black leather cover. 'Yeah?'

'What's the sentence written in red ink at the front?'

'You know what it is.'

'Remind me.'

She flicked open the Bible and read the eleven words. 'There are none so blind as those who will not see.'

'Your photo is number one, right?'

Lightfoot picked up the photo and looked at it.

'Yeah?'

'What's on the coffee table in the photo?'

Lightfoot looked at the body of James Halliwell, sitting in his kitchen, slumped on his wooden kitchen chair.

She looked at the kitchen table. Looked at the mug, the ashtray and the cigarette packet. Looked at the portable chess set sitting open on the table.

Smiled. Looked back at McHale.

'Very good…'

'How many moves have been made in the game?'

Lightfoot squinted her eyes. Brought the photo closer to her eyes. Zeroed in on the board. Saw the opening move.

A single white pawn in front of the white King.

Her eyes looked from the photo to McHale then back again. She double-blinked. Twice.

'A Bobby Fischer favourite,' she said softly, showing the photo to the others.

She turned to McHale.

'What? You think you're the only one who plays chess?' she said.

'Coincidences mean you're on the right track,' thought McHale.

'Let me get this straight,' said Kelly. 'You think that killing Halliwell was The Ghost's opening move?'

'I have no bloody idea,' said McHale. 'It might be nothing. But if it's something, then it's definitely something interesting, right?'

One by one, the others picked up their own photos and examined everything in the scene apart from the corpse. After a couple of minutes, Toby shook his head. 'No chess set,' he said.

He was followed by Daisy, Rice, Kelly, and even McHale.

The only chess set in any of the photos belonged to the one in the James Halliwell photo. Number 1.

'Pity,' said Lightfoot. 'I thought you had something there.'

'Mind you,' said Toby. 'Just because you can't see something doesn't mean it's not there.'

McHale sighed. 'Okay. So maybe it was nothing. Let's put it aside for the time being and move on. Toby… what was your thought?'

The young copper skipped back a day in his mind and shoved the chessboard image out of view, bringing another thought to the front.

'Asperger's,' he said.

'Now there's a conversation stopper,' said Kelly.

He let the word permeate the air in the room and waited as it wormed its way as a new thought into the minds of the others seated around the table.

'MOTHER,' he said, looking towards the screen wall, 'How

many people suffer from Asperger's Syndrome worldwide?'

'In 2015 it was estimated that Asperger's affected around 37.2 million people worldwide.'

Toby's eyebrows both went up. 'That many? How many people suffer from it in the UK?'

'About 700,000.'

'Why Asperger's?' said Daisy. 'Isn't that a kind of autism? I don't understand how anyone with autism would be able to pull this off.'

Lightfoot was frowning.

'You obviously have a good reason for suggesting it,' said Rice. 'So?'

Toby took a deep breath. 'People with Asperger's are detail oriented. They're exceptional at recognising patterns and solving problems. They love order and precision. They can be passionate, even obsessive, about numbers.'

'Ah... now I get it,' said Kelly. 'Details... patterns... problem solving... order... precision... plus the prime number link.' She looked into his eyes. Unblinking. 'You know anyone with Asperger's, Toby?'

For the first time since they met yesterday, the young cop blushed. It was like she had opened a door slightly and glimpsed inside a room that was normally considered private and out of bounds.

'A cousin,' he said. 'She's thirty-something.'

'From what I'm given to understand, people with Asperger's are mostly loving, caring people. But they have difficulty with social interaction. Am I right?'

Toby nodded. 'She's all those things.'

'So, what makes you think our Ghost could have Asperger's?'

Toby paused. Collected his thoughts. Shrugged. Looked around the room. 'It could explain a lot. The only thing it doesn't explain is the killing.'

'MOTHER,' said McHale, 'are there any killers in custody in

the UK who suffer from Asperger's Syndrome?'

Pause.

'Peter Morgan,' she said. 'In December 2016, the 54-year-old multi-millionaire was found guilty of the premeditated murder of 25-year-old Georgina Symonds in South Wales. Giving evidence at the trial, Professor Simon Baron-Cohen, a director of the Autism Research Centre at Cambridge University, concluded that Morgan has Asperger's Syndrome.'

'So, it's possible that The Ghost might have Asperger's?' said Lightfoot.

'Let's say it's not remotely impossible,' said McHale. He turned to Toby and smiled. 'Good shout, sprog.'

Toby and Daisy did another fist-bump.

He looked at Kelly. 'Okay, your turn. You wanted to say something about the knives, right?'

'I just wanted to take another run at the numbers,' said Kelly. 'This is probably more Toby's patch than mine. But he's had his turn,' she smiled.

The smile was genuine.

'You have the floor,' said Toby. His smile was just as genuine.

Kelly faced the screen wall. 'MOTHER,' she said. 'Can you bring up photos of all six Fairbairn-Sykes knives used by The Holy Ghost? Close-up shots of the numbers on the areas just below the hilts? Show them numbered one to six, left to right, please.'

Close-up sections of all six knives appeared on screen. The numbers were small and neat, and the shapes had been punched into the metal at the centre of the flat section below the hilt.

The punching was carefully done. Not crude. Each number was small, almost modest. Created by someone proficient in the use of number or letter punching equipment. The product of a steady hand. Probably younger, rather than older.

'MOTHER, is there any information about the numbers?'

Pause.

'Yes. There was a report, prepared by metallurgists at Bell Macaulay. It wasn't definitive. They concluded that all the numbers had probably been punched into the metal surfaces using an engineering punch set. There was evidence that metal burs around the numbers had been removed and edges smoothed.'

'Is there any way to tell when the numbers were added?'

Pause.

'The condition of the first punching is consistent with the condition of the last one. The date when the knives were manufactured was established as January 1941. The manufacturer was the Wilkinson Sword Company. But Macaulay can't say with any degree of accuracy when the numbers were punched into the knives. It could have been immediately after they were made. Or it could have been any time between 1941 and 2012.'

'Dammit!' said Kelly.

She felt the pain return to her left thigh and the call of a small, white, oblong 357 felt like the sound of a friend whispering in her ear.

'Where are you going with this?' asked McHale.

'Nowhere fast, it looks like,' she said. 'I think I need a drink.'

'I'll call for more coffee.'

'I think I'd prefer it if you called for something a bit stronger. No… make that a lot stronger.'

'Single or double,' said McHale.

Kelly grimaced. 'Treble.'

'Hold that thought. Let's wind up here, get back to the hotel bar, and I'll open a tab.'

Sometimes, going nowhere fast was better than going nowhere at all, thought Kelly.

'Don't give up on the numbers angle just yet,' said Toby. 'That number keeps cropping up.' He started counting off on his fingers. 'Seven victims. Seven knives. Seven hunters including MOTHER. Seven is a prime number.'

McHale thought of the seven volumes written by Edmund Locard.

Daisy thought of the seven doors in the hallway outside the meeting room.

Lightfoot thought of the seven bands of small, dark coloured beads wrapped around her left wrist.

'Toby's right. Don't give up on number seven yet,' said McHale.

But it was 6.33pm.

And those were the kind of numbers that meant it was time to give their brains, and their imaginations, a rest for another day. But only officially. Unofficially, there would be plenty of time to rest when they caught the bastard.

Tick tock. Tick tock.

Supper that night for the team was battered haddock the size of small dolphins, chunky chips the size of doorsteps, and a steaming pile of mushy-peas. The hotel chef was a man of superior culinary talents. The kind that appealed to a person's soul. Not just their guts.

Even Lightfoot joined them.

The only one who went AWOL was Kelly, who limped off up to her room. Sometimes thinking was a painful process, made all the less painful by killers of a chemical persuasion and the promise of a large Southern Comfort, courtesy of McHale, in the bar around 8.30pm.

Sometimes a healthy appetite just got in the damned way.

Getting to know people was a process that held no interest for her. Except if that someone was The Ghost.

So, she went upstairs to her room. Had a conversation with a couple of 357s. Lay on her bed. Switched off the light. And reached out into the darkness for some kind of comfort.

Her 8.30pm date with Comfort of another kind came and went. When she opened her eyes, it was after midnight.

There was a message on her phone from McHale.

She played it and listened to the sound of his voice. 'Hope the pain takes a hike. I drank your Southern Comfort. See you at breakfast. Don't take too many 357s. Yeah… I know their name. I'm working up to them. Still on Paracetamol. Sleep well.'

She rubbed the ache in her left thigh and got undressed, then limped to the bathroom. Ignoring the mirror, she brushed her teeth and washed her face. There was no place for vanity in her life. She slid under the covers and eventually drifted off to sleep, thinking of a man barely visible in the darkness, holding a Fairbairn-Sykes knife in his right hand and a dead man's switch in his right. He had a block of C4 strapped to his chest.

She wondered why it wasn't called a dead man's button as that's exactly what it was. A small box with a button that was pressed down with a thumb to prime the switch. Then when the thumb moved off and the button moved up, the pressure was released, the connection was made, and the bomb went off. Simple.

As she looked at the man, she saw that his mouth was working. He was showing her his thumb on the button. She tried to hear what he was saying. She tried to understand the words. But all she could hear was the sound of two little girls screaming.

Then their world was ripped apart.

Then there was only the sound of silence.

Four doors along, about thirty seconds away on the same floor, on the same side of the corridor, McHale's bastard thugs had decided it was time to pay him a visit.

They decided that, in his case, absence wasn't meant to make the heart grow fonder. It was meant to make the pain grow stronger.

Accordingly, at 2.00am they decided to bring their jackhammers to the party and position them in the space between his ears. Any hope of staying asleep left Dodge on the fastest horse in the stable.

Bastard thugs left, smiling and joking, at around 4.30am, taking their jackhammers with them.

McHale's consciousness left for a coffee and a KitKat about fifteen minutes later.

Chapter Eighteen

Joe Strummer came on, and the opening riff of The Clash's London Calling beat the crap out of his sleeping synapses.

Between the time of the bastard thugs' arrival, and after the time of their departure, McHale had managed about an hour and 45 minutes sleep.

He groaned, stretched out a hairy arm, and stabbed the alarm into snooze cruise mode. As per usual.

Then, ten minutes later, he stabbed the snooze off and did the three things in his life that were predictable and reliable and routine and unavoidable and right.

One. He got up from the bed.

Two. He got ready for the day.

Three. He went through the whole piss, shit, shave, brush, moisturise, dress, and coffee, weather and email check routine.

Weather. London would be hot. Two emails. One from Alice, timed at 3.05am: It was said that Winston Churchill and Margaret Thatcher both survived on about four hours sleep a night. Churchill because he was at war. Thatcher because she was just bloody made that way. McHale believed that Alice could beat the shit out of both of them.

She was famously a three-hour a night person. Waking refreshed in the wee hours of the morning, while the rest of the world, or at least the rest of the UK, was still snoring. Barring shift workers.

Her email was twenty-six words short. It said this;

Sorry Tom. Sonny Jello will be a no-show. He sounded gutted. Really wanted to work with you. Hollywood won the day. Says maybe next time. A x

He fired off a reply. It said this;

Thanks, Wideawake Girl. T x

Next up was an email from Kelly. Timed 5.03am.
It was thirty-five words short. It said this;

You owe me a double-double SoCo. I owe you a couple of 357s. I had a weird dream about a guy holding a dead man's switch and one of the knives. See you at breakfast.

Before he left for food downstairs, he put his medical kit on the solitary bedside cabinet. It would be there when he got back, reminding him of his twice-weekly ritual. Tonight was the 80ml infusion.

Four vials. Four needles. One pump. Three hours, give or take.

He managed a short smile at his combination of routine and unpredictability. He liked the way they slept together curled up in each other's arms.

Breakfast was coffee. Then more coffee. Then more coffee. All black. No sugar. He had a short-lived wish that the hot, dark liquid was the product of Java beans, crunched into a fine powder in the hotel's kitchen, then served up to yell at his sleep-deprived body and mind.

He knew after the first sip that it was instant, granulated and served up to do no more than poke at him with a blunt stick. But even a poke was better than an ineffective nudge.

The others, apart from Lightfoot who had grabbed a cab about 11pm last night, were already sat down and munching.

It was 8.45am.

No hearty greetings were exchanged. No need. They were now a team.

A few well-placed smiles and head nods did the trick.

'Sonny Jello sends his apologies. He won't be joining us on the hunt,' he said as he sat down.

'I forgot all about him,' said Kelly. 'You get my email?'

'I did.'

'And?'

McHale waited until the waitress poured him a coffee, then left. 'And I think you're still having nightmares about the Brasher twins,' he said.

Kelly looked away and down at her plate.

McHale immediately regretted the words.

Toby had just taken delivery of his full English breakfast. The smell reminded McHale's gut of a time when his waistband was tighter.

The others were more eclectic. Rice, ironically, had Rice Crispies. Daisy had eggs on toast. Runny yolks. Black pepper. Kelly went the same route as McHale with the caffeine, with no nutritional benefits. She augmented it with two slices of rye toast and honey. Her inaugural 357 of the day was thirty minutes old in her stomach.

She looked back.

'He was trying to tell me something. I couldn't make out what it was.'

'Who was trying to tell you what?' asked Rice, just getting rid of a mouthful of snap, crackle, and pop.

Kelly told them about her weird dream.

'You get dreams like that a lot?'

Kelly stared at him. 'Often enough,' she said. Her eyes went down. The coffee cup came up.

Daisy finished her last mouthful of scrambled egg. 'I had a dream about the orb, last night,' she said. 'What's it called again?'

'The Sovereign's Orb,' said Rice.

'That's it, The Sovereign's Orb.' She took a gulp of coffee. 'Anyway, in my dream it was hollow and I unscrewed the top half from the bottom half and when I pulled the two halves apart there was something inside.'

'What?' said Toby.

'I can't remember.'

'Little factoid of the day. The Sovereign's Orb actually is hollow,' said McHale. 'The Archbishop of Canterbury probably stashed a small supply of whisky in there for the Queen. I bet she had a swig during the ceremony, just to keep her going.'

Laughter was a good way to start any day, thought McHale, as he downed the last mouthful of his Java wannabe.

Traffic from the hotel to Winfield House was a bad-tempered bitch. By the time they drew up outside the front entrance it was 10.40am and the air was already getting sticky. The pat down was a well-practiced formality and Lightfoot, in black combats, black trainers, and show-off black BAU t-shirt, was leaning against the door-jam holding a half-empty mug of black coffee.

He had a vague memory of watching her fling the contents of three or four large shot glasses full of Jack down her neck the night before.

Just before she headed off to hail a cab.

And here she was looking fresh, rested and ready to go on the warpath.

'You believe in luck, McHale?' she said.

McHale, who was as casually dressed as a cop could be without still looking like a cop, said; 'Coincidences I have a problem with. But luck? I'll take all that I can get.'

They were heading in and downstairs to the meeting room. The others following in their wake closely, in case they missed any of the conversation. Police forces everywhere are curious. And so are priests.

'You remember that colleague back at BAU-4 I sent the close-up shots of the knives and numbers to?'

'The one who got in touch with you this morning?'

'You been reading my emails, McHale?' she said softly, just as they got to the meeting room.

'Lucky guess.'

By now MOTHER was a colleague and each of the team said hello as they walked in. MOTHER, of course, returned the greeting?'

On the screen was a head and shoulders image of a lab technician. She was about mid-forties. Extremely short black hair. Black t-shirt under white lab coat. She was smiling. She was also moving. The feed was live and the woman was waiving.

'Hi guys,' she said.

She had a voice that was husky but not unpleasant.

Lightfoot indicated the screen with a sweep of her left hand. 'I'd like to introduce you to my friend and colleague, Forensic Scientist Doctor Hannah White.'

Doctor White was black. God was ironic. She had features that, even on a bad day, could be described as stunningly beautiful. She was also as thin as a rake.

'You'll have to forgive the good doctor if she seems a little ragged. It's just before 6.00am over there in Quantico and she's been up for a couple of hours.'

White, a notoriously bad sleeper, looked a million miles from ragged.

Lightfoot turned back to the screen. 'Tell us what you've got, Hannah.'

'It's probably better to show you what I've got,' said White. 'And what I've got is a lot.'

'Why don't you start at the beginning?'

'Okay… but before I do, you guys better pour yourselves some coffee. This might take a while. I'm going for a refill. Back in five.'

She disappeared sideways and the team was left with the image of a backdrop screen showing the six close-up shots of the knives, sent to Quantico by Lightfoot.

The door to the room opened and two agents brought in flasks of coffee and biscuits. They put them on the small round table at the far end of the room. They were learning. They left with a smile.

Five minutes later, all team members were sat around the large table, facing the screen wall, coffee sipped and biscuits dipped. White came back on screen. She had a remote in her hand. She turned to face her own backdrop screen and pressed a button on the remote.

The images of the knives changed to images of letters.

'First… the letters.' She looked down and her hands came back up into shot holding six envelopes, displayed in a fan. 'There are six of them. From August 2006 to August 2011.' She turned to the screen behind her and all six letters were displayed, opened, on her screen.

'I've emailed them to you guys so you can download and print them out. They're also available on Cloud so you can examine them in detail on screen.'

White brought up all six letters, one at a time, to fill the screen behind her.

She left each one up on her backdrop long enough for the team to read, digest, and discuss.

'I gather these words are familiar to you?'

'We know them,' said McHale. 'Do you know about the Bibles?'

White nodded. 'Grace briefed me about an hour before you guys arrived.'

McHale did a quick mental double take. As did the others on the team.

It was strange hearing Lightfoot's first name spoken out loud. Even though he never referred to Alice, Toby, and Daisy as Kennedy, Macbeth, and Nash, calling the BAU agent Grace still seemed a bridge too far.

They went through them one by one, first to last.

First up on screen was the one delivered to Quantico on August 1, 2006. The line was: 'There are none so blind as those who will not see.'

'Our guys had some fun with this one,' said White. 'I think we might just adopt it as our lab's motto.'

Rice spoke up. 'I'm familiar with the line. And I gather there are two literary references that we know of. One from John Heywood in 1546 and another from Jonathan Swift in 1738.'

He stopped speaking and went back to drinking his coffee.

'Absolutely,' said White. 'And we found it over here in the Works of Thomas Chalkley in 1713. Apart from that, we got zilch. Sorry guys.'

'What about the other lines? Any joy there?' said Kelly.

The thought of mentioning joy and Kelly in the same breath seemed just wrong to McHale.

The other five lines expanded to full screen size behind the American forensics expert.

'There are none so deaf as those who will not hear.'

'There are none so sorry as those who will not repent.'

'There are none so dumb as those who will not speak.'

'There are none so numb as those who will not feel.'

'There are none so dead as those who will not live.'

One by one the team spoke about the sentences. Kicked them about. Turned them upside down. But, like stubborn young thugs being interrogated by stubborn old cops, the words refused to give up anything in the way of information or recognition.

'The only thing any of them have in common is the name Fairbairn-Sykes tagged onto the end of each one,' said White. 'But we're still looking. We're not the kind of people who give up easily, so we'll be in touch if we find out any more.'

White took a breath. 'Okay... now onto the juicy bits,' she

said. And she raised her right hand.

In her clenched fist she was holding a Fairbairn-Sykes knife. Toby was the first to react. His surprise was predictable. As was his choice of language.

'Holy fuck,' he said. A little louder than he expected.

'Is that what I think it is?' said McHale, slowly.

A smiling White said, 'Yes… and no.'

McHale frowned. Excitement was something he normally didn't display. His face wore a mask of serious professionalism. Inside he was punching the air. 'Why don't you start at the beginning.'

'Okay,' she said, putting the knife down out of shot. 'Well, I have some good news and some bad news.'

Lightfoot, who hadn't touched her coffee, shook her head. 'You've got a Fairbairn-Sykes knife. Nothing about that is bad news, Hannah.'

White nodded. 'Cool. Well, in that case I have good news… and great news.'

From the far end of the table, Toby's voice interrupted White's flow. 'This sounds like a Dirty Harry moment,' he said.

McHale twigged immediately and laughed.

'Sorry… you've lost me,' said the Jesuit, looking slightly confused.

'Make my day,' said Lightfoot.

Rice still looked confused.

McHale thought quick. 'It's a bit like the water into wine moment at Marriage at Cana, Father,' he said.

The penny dropped.

Rice smiled.

'How did you get the knife?' said Daisy.

'We're jumping the gun,' said McHale, although he wanted to see the knife again and talk about it as soon as possible. 'The beginning, please…' he said, reluctantly, nodding at the screen.

White carried on.

'As I said, we're not the kind of people who give up easily. After we received the first letter in 2006 and filed it away, we didn't just forget about it. Well, I should say one of us didn't forget about it. His name was Special Supervisory Agent Seymour Marshall. He was an older guy, nearing retirement. But a bit of a legend in the organisation. Not because he tracked down anyone dangerous or famous. But because was a bit like a Canadian Mountie. He always got his man.'

Inner voice joined in; 'Now he sounds like my kinda man, Kemosabe. Old school lawman. Doesn't take any shit. They don't make them like that any-more.'

It was good to hear inner voice again, thought McHale. He'd missed his constant company over the past couple of days.

'I saw Marshall once,' said Lightfoot. 'Tall, bald guy. Always wore a black three-piece suit. Looked like a funeral director with style.'

'He's still tall and bald,' said White. 'Only now he doesn't wear the suit and he retired last year. He lives in a cabin in the Catskills with his wife and two large mutts.'

'Why do I get the feeling you like to tell a good story,' said Rice, smiling.

White laughed. 'I get that from my mama,' she said. 'Anyway. Seymour kept a watching eye on that first letter. But nothing happened for a year. He thought maybe it was just a one-off. Some crazy who came and went in the blink of an eye. Then, when the second one arrived a year later, he started sniffing around. Again… no joy. Then, by the time the third one came in the post in 2008, he started sniffing so hard he sounded like a guy with a streaming damned cold.'

White broke out in a seriously powerful belly laugh. Daisy joined in. She couldn't help herself. The laugh was infectious. It took both of them a minute or so to calm down.

White took a deep breath and then had a large swig from a glass of water, then continued.

'Anyway, Seymour opened up his own file on them and spent all his spare time trying to get under the skin of the guy who wrote the letters. I say wrote. Typed would be more accurate.'

'Manual typewriter?' said McHale.

White seemed genuinely surprised. 'How did you guess?' she said. Then she looked at Lightfoot. 'Now him I like,' she said.

Then she looked back at McHale and narrowed her eyes. 'Not many folks would have said that right off the bat. What did you say your name was again?'

McHale smiled. 'Tom,' he said.

'Naaw... the other name. The one that sounds like it came from Scotland or maybe Ireland.'

Lightfoot said, 'McHale.'

'That's it,' said White.

McHale said, 'But you can call me Mac.'

'And you can call me whenever you damned like, Mac,' said White, before Lightfoot shut her down. Friendly but firmly.

'Tell us about the typewriter, Hannah, before your knees buckle.'

Hannah regained her composure and got back to business. 'Okay. Um... are you a book reading man, Mac?'

McHale thought of the shelves groaning with the weight of all the books sitting on them back home. He thought about the number he had read. And the number he bought intending to read but just never got around to it.

'I suppose you could say I'm a Fifty-Fifty guy. Half read. Half unread.'

'You ever read anything by a writer called Cormac McCarthy? He was a Mac too. Just like you.'

McHale smiled. 'I have,' he said, picturing the book sitting at the bottom of the pile of books on the floor next to his nightstand at home.

'No Country for Old Men, right?'

'Right.'

'You know what typewriter he wrote that on?'

'Yes ma'am.'

McHale held his breath.

She turned, pressed a button, and the photo of a small, blue, manual typewriter came up on the screen behind her.

'A light blue Lettera 32 Olivetti,' she said. 'He bought it in 1963 for $50. It sold at auction for $254,500. It was pretty beat up by then. But I guess, if you pardon my French, his fingers had beat the shit out of its keys by the time they were done.'

She laughed quickly. Then the smile disappeared as McHale double blinked and she saw the look in his eye.

'You look like you seen a ghost,' she said.

'More like an old friend.'

Pause.

'Anyway. Like I said. Old Seymour was a never-give-in kinda guy. And the more he looked at those letters, the more he felt there was something hinky, as we say, going on.

'You ever had that hinky feeling, Mac? When you know in your bones there's something going on. When you can feel there's something coming but you just can't see it yet?'

McHale nodded. Oh yeah, he thought. 'I bet everyone here has had that feeling, Hannah.' He looked around the table, stopping at Kelly.

Her eyes were looking down. The kind of down that involved time travel. The kind of down that took her back to a day in November 2014. To a house in West Hampstead, a mad man called Stubbs, two five-year olds, and three members of her hostage rescue team.

Then he stopped at Stephen Rice.

The Jesuit's eyes were looking directly at McHale but his mind was a million miles away, thinking about a priest with a monster inside him.

White's voice brought him back to the present.

'Two things about Seymour you should know. One: he loved

197

things that just didn't fit. And there was something about those letters that just didn't fit. And two: sitting on his desk at home he had a manual typewriter. He was restoring it to its former glory. It was a black Underwood Standard portable typewriter.

'The typeface on the Underwood reminded him of the one used on the letters. It was a similar Pica typeface. But not the same.

'So, he got hold of all the makes of portable typewriters he could. There were six. Olivetti, Remington, Corona, Imperial, Smith-Corona, and Underwood. And he compared the shit out of them.

'The one that jumped out at him was Olivetti. So, he got all the Olivetti portables he could get his hands on. And the one that smacked him in the face was the same model used by good old Cormac McCarthy... the Lettera 32.'

White took a deep breath.

McHale's mind was racing. It was racing because White had just slammed the investigation up another gear. And because he thought of another Lettera 32. The one sitting on a shelf above the desk in the small bedroom in Stockport that he used as a home office.

Coincidences mean you're on the right track.

White turned to the screen behind her and pressed her remote. The typewriter on her screen disappeared, to be replaced by the first letter received by the BAU. The words were large on the screen.

White continued. 'This time, Seymour took a real good look at the first letter. And he noticed something that, until then, nobody else had. Something about every letter 'a'. They were ever so slightly lighter than all the other letters. It didn't have anything to do with the ribbon, because that wouldn't account for only that one letter being lighter on the paper than all the other letters.'

McHale, who was sitting back in his chair, legs out straight under the table, hands clasped on his stomach, relaxed but alert, looked down at the little finger of his left hand.

'Then he had a bit of a lightbulb moment,' said White, 'and he wrote this on his pad.'

She pressed the remote and the page of a notepad appeared on the screen. It was blank apart from three words. Written in black ink and circled. The words were;

'Damaged left hand.'

'I know it doesn't sound a lot,' she said. 'But after the fourth letter came in August 2009, it was enough for Seymour to ask his Unit Chief to lend him a couple of agents.

'He got one. A nice Mexican rookie by the name of Angel Romero. He was fresh out of the FBI Training Academy. But the unit chief figured Seymour could use a break, so Angel became his go-to guy. And the first thing he did was the best thing he did since joining up. He started looking in medical records for males aged twenty-five to forty-five years of age, living in the State of Virginia, who had a partial disability of the little finger in their left hand.'

'Jeezus… talk about a miniature needle in a damned big haystack,' said Toby.

'It took them over a year.' White pressed another button and some numbers came up on her backdrop screen. She spoke while referencing the numbers.

'Virginia then had a population of just under 8,500,000 people.

'By November 2010 Seymour and Agent Romero had tracked down 1,972 individuals who fitted the profile. Of those, 328 had congenital disabilities present since birth that also extended to other fingers. Of the remaining 1,644, 592 were the result of accidental breaks and misaligned bones, through childhood or in adulthood. That left 1,052.

'Of those, medium-to-long-term ligament damage to that particular finger accounted for 1,014. That left thirty-eight individuals. Of those, seventeen died in car accidents between 2012 and 2013, bringing them outside of the scope of the hunt for your guy.'

She took a loud breath.

'That left us with twenty-one.'

'I was going to suggest a coffee break,' said McHale. 'But the suspense is killing me.'

'Actually,' said White, 'I wouldn't mind giving my voice a rest. A comfort break, a coffee and a quick breakfast snack sounds like a great idea. How about we pick this up in ten minutes?'

Slamming on the breaks in any investigation was always a sore point with McHale. But he, like the other members of the team, was very impressed with White's contribution. However, ten minutes was only ten minutes, and nature wasn't the kind of lady who was easily denied without a fight. So, he agreed.

'Good call,' he said, secretly wishing they were carrying on without the break. 'See you in ten.'

White disappeared sideways leaving her backdrop of the breakdown of the 1,972 profiled individuals up on her screen.

McHale looked around at the team.

One look at the pain on Kelly's face told him that there was a 357 in her tablet tub ready and willing to disappear down her throat with the help of a black coffee. She was the first to rise, grab her bag and head for the loo.

Rice was up next. It's true, he thought. The older you get, the less your bladder is able to hold onto its contents without complaining painfully.

The coffee break Agents must have been on red alert, because a couple of minutes after Kelly left the room, they entered with the usual refreshments.

It was 1.45pm UK time. Hungry and thirsty was hungry and thirsty wherever you were in the world.

By 2.00pm the team was back sat around the table and White was, once again, the star of the show. For the time being, anyway.

McHale was trying not to think of the bastard thugs. But he

could hear them in the distance, tapping their steel toe-capped Docs like the good skinhead boys they were.

A couple of 500mgs paracetamol at the next coffee break should do it, he thought. Maybe three. Or four.

Lightfoot did the pick-up.

'So, Hannah, you were saying. That left thirty-eight individuals. Take away seventeen who died between 2012 and 2015, so we can discount them. That means we've got twenty-one still in the mix.'

'Not quite,' said White.

She brought up some new numbers on the backdrop.

'Eight were out of the country, working abroad.

'Five were in prison.

'Three were in wheelchairs.

'And two were cancer patients suffering from acute lymphoblastic leukaemia.'

'That leaves three,' said Lightfoot.

Toby couldn't stop himself from turning to Daisy and giving her a fist-bump. 'Yes!' he hissed.

'Not so fast, my young enthusiastic friend,' said White. 'Two of the remaining three were gunshot victims in 2013.'

'Better still,' said Toby,' shrugging. 'That only leaves one.'

'And he went missing in January 2011.'

The anti-climax was visible on the faces of everyone in the room. It was a painful feeling. A gut-wrenching feeling. One of those so-near-and-yet-so-bloody-far feelings. The kind that made you want to scream at the nearest wall and go look for someone to punch.

'Bollocks!' shouted McHale, slapping the tabletop.

But White was cool, calm, and collected.

She might have worked in a lab, but it wasn't an ordinary lab. It was a kick-ass FBI lab. And although she wore a white coat, she was still in the business of catching bad guys. And she had a BFG. And it wasn't a Big Friendly Giant; it was a Big

Fucking Gun. And she hadn't used up all her bullets. She still had two left.

And now it was time to use them.

So, she used the first one, and told them about the name.

'Funny thing about that guy who went missing…' she said.

Doctor Hannah White loved the feeling of talking to a roomful of people and having them in the palm of her hand. She loved having the feeling that something she did or said could turn an investigation that was dead in the water into one that was suddenly alive, and damned well kicking.

McHale felt a tingle. And it had nothing to do with his nerve ends. 'Tell me you have a name,' he said.

'I have a name,' she said. 'And a face.' She also loved the feeling of stopping people in their tracks and turning an abundance of negative vibes into a surfeit of positive ones.

She turned around to face her screen, pressed a button on the remote, and the black and white photo of a man appeared.

There was something very familiar about him.

'Okay, this is going to sound weird, but I feel I know this guy,' said Daisy. 'I think I've seen him recently.' She was sitting upright in her chair. The fingers of her right hand were holding her pen and she was bouncing it off the surface of the table. Her eyes were searching her memory. She didn't have to search long.

'His name is Riemann,' said White.

No… it's not, thought Daisy. Mind racing.

Nearly there. Nearly there. Memory on overdrive.

'You've come across his twin brother.'

Nearly there. Nearly there!

'George is older by two minutes. His brother's name is…'

There!

'James Halliwell,' exclaimed Daisy, almost too loudly.

'Fuck,' whispered Toby.

Coincidences mean you're on the right track.

As bombshells go, this was a fairly big one. It took a few

seconds for the team to digest White's words, during which time a very loud silence invaded the room and sat glaring at everyone from one of the corners.

White looked pleased. 'Thought you'd like that,' she said.

The only one whose jaw hadn't hit the floor was Toby. He was smiling.

'You recognise him?' said McHale.

Toby shook his head slowly, still smiling. 'Sort of, Guv. But I definitely recognise the name Georg Friedrich Bernhard Riemann,' he said.

'Give that guy a cigar,' said White, grinning, from the screen.

'Okay, I'll bite,' said McHale.

'He was a German mathematician,' said Toby. 'Born September 17, 1826. If you're interested in Number Theory, particularly prime numbers, as I am – and as I think The Ghost is – then you know about Riemann. You also know about Fermat's Last Theorem, about Stephen Hawking, Andrew Wiles, and a whole bunch of other very brainy folk.'

He stopped talking.

They were looking at him. All of them.

There's a feeling that people get when they realise that other people are cleverer than they thought, and that they've underestimated them. And that they need to give them a bit more respect. That's the feeling that everyone around the table had for Toby pretty much the moment he zipped his lip.

Internal voice spoke up; 'Well tickle me sideways with a bottle brush and call me Doris, Kemosabe!'

'Every now and then somebody comes along who surprises the hell out of me,' said Rice. He was looking at Toby like he would a grandson he was suddenly proud of.

'What's the connection, Toby?' said McHale. 'Tell me what you're thinking.'

Toby took a breath.

Then he looked at the others.

Then he took a chance.

'I think if James Halliwell had a brother, and if his name is George Riemann, then I think Riemann is The Ghost. I think at some point in his life, he moved to the States, changed his name to an Anglicised version of one of his maths heroes, until something happened that opened the door and let a monster out into the world.'

Sometimes you stick your toe in the water. Sometimes you just have to jump in feet first. Toby wasn't big on toe dipping.

'Impressive,' said Lightfoot, looking at Toby. Then she turned and looked at the screen wall. 'MOTHER, I know it's old ground, but can you look up everything we have on James Halliwell. Grandparents, parents, any siblings, place of work, place of worship, hobbies, every address he's ever stayed at – the works. And can you print it out. Six copies, please.'

Pause.

'Got it,' said MOTHER.

Kelly got up stiffly from her chair, grabbed her cane, and started walking slowly around the table. It was the kind of exercise she did in hospital, after the bomb blast, to get her leg used to the idea of putting weight on the damaged muscles and joints. It was the kind of rehabilitation that made her curse and helped her think.

Lightfoot noticed the design on the cane for the first time since they met. The wood was deep redwood, polished to a warm lustre. Curling around it, climbing its way to the top, was a superbly carved image of an Eastern Diamondback Rattlesnake. The most dangerous rattler in North America.

When she was sixteen, she'd been bitten by one. Luckily it was only a small one. A mere four feet long. Half the size of a fully-grown adult. But the fangs were still massive and the pain was still intense, and the bleeding was still profuse.

And the scar was still there on her lower right calf.

She knew the only reason that Kelly was walking her circuit

was that it was past her time for a 357 tab, but she didn't want to break off and lose track of the conversation. So, she walked the walk, while the rest of them talked the talk.

Everywhere Kelly went, the Diamondback went too.

After she'd completed about a dozen laps of the table, she sat down. Slowly. At that point, White decided to use up her second bullet. 'Now, let's go back to the typewriter,' she said, turning and pressing a button.

Another Lettera 32 Olivetti model came onto her backdrop screen. It was just as old, just as blue, and just as battered as the first one.

'Now this one isn't McCarthy's machine,' she said. 'It looks like it. It feels like it. It even types like it. Almost.

'This is the Lettera 32 that we believe The Ghost typed those letters on and sent them to us.'

She paused, almost for dramatic effect.

'This,' she said, 'is Agnes.'

She pressed another button and a second image of the typewriter came up on the screen. This time a back view. And there, in black paint, in small, perfectly formed, stencil-like lettering, over the blue casing, was the name AGNES.

It was the kind of personal touch that changes a something into a someone.

It was the result of a ceremony of naming that confers a unique personality onto a previously impersonal and inanimate object.

AGNES belonged.

AGNES mattered.

AGNES lived.

She was nowhere near as valuable to McCarthy, and to the literary world, as her more famous sibling. But she was potentially a damned sight more valuable to Supervisory Special Agent Seymour Marshall and greenhorn agent Angel Romero.

'You really think this belongs to The Ghost?' said McHale.

'Well… we really think it might have belonged to George Riemann. And if Riemann is The Ghost, then yes, we think we can connect the dots,' said White.

'What if we're wrong,' said Kelly. Her face was pale with pain and she was rubbing her left thigh.

'What do you mean?' said McHale.

'I mean what if The Ghost isn't George Riemann. What if the guy we're looking for wasn't one of the 1,972 we profiled. What if he slipped through the net and we've just been wasting time chasing the wrong guy?'

Rice, sitting to her left, sighed heavily. 'Then we go back to square one, I suppose. But too many things seem to fit with him. What is it you coppers say,' he said, looking at McHale. 'I like him for it.'

'Me too,' said McHale. 'I think we're looking at the right man. Or rather, we will be looking at him when we find him.' He turned to Lightfoot. 'What about you?'

The BAU agent was deep in concentration, looking at the opposite wall. Thinking about clues. Following tracks. Finally, she spoke.

'I like the typewriter,' she said. 'And I like the damaged finger.' She was counting them off on the fingers of her left hand.

'And I like the link to James Halliwell.'

That was three.

'Potential link, so far,' said Toby.

'Okay. Potential link. And I like the knives.'

That was four.

'And I like the link from the knives to the Sovereign's Orb. But I don't know where we go with that.'

That was five.

'What I don't get yet,' she continued, 'is why, if he killed Halliwell, he also killed the others.'

'What if he killed the others to cover up Halliwell's murder?'

said Daisy. What if he was the target all along and the others were just a deflection?

'What if this has all been about hiding something in plain sight?'

McHale seemed to consider this. It got the pouted lips and raised eyebrows treatment.

It was a new thought that hadn't been put into the equation before now, and it earned her a fistful of brownie points.

'Okay… put it in the pot and stir it around.'

He turned to White. 'How did you get the typewriter?'

White smiled. 'I'll tell you in ten, Mac. Time for a coffee break.'

'Make it fifteen.'

That got the nod and White disappeared off-screen.

It was 4.05pm. Everyone was hungry and thirsty, so coffee came with sandwiches. Lots of them. One thing McHale was sure of: the Yanks sure knew how to feed their guests.

Fifteen turned into twenty. Small talk included. And just before 4.30pm they got back into it.

'Okay, onwards and upwards, guys,' said White. 'As you probably guessed, Seymour was a bit of a workaholic. Well… a lot of one.' She laughed. She wasn't the only one.

'They knew the make and model of the typewriter they were looking for. They just didn't know where it was or who had it.

'Before George Riemann disappeared in January 2011, his last-known address was a neat, white-painted house in Baltimore, Maryland. In between Washington and Philadelphia. He had lived there with his mother. By that time, they had both changed their name to Riemann. He changed his first name to George, she to Elizabeth. Then, when she died in 2010, he had continued to live there alone.

'By the time agents got to it, the house had been empty for months. No George. No activity. Neighbours said mother and son kept to themselves. Most of them couldn't remember the

last time they saw the Riemanns, or their car. The car was some
kind of a Honda, but they didn't know what kind. Inside, the
house was immaculate. Not a thing out of place. And when I
say that, what I mean is it was, like, OCD tidy.

'Then we got lucky. The kind of lucky that only happens once
in a blue moon. Or it could just be that we asked the right kind
of question to the right kind of person at the right kind of time.

'Anyway… one of the neighbours mentioned that a week or so
before she saw him for the last time, George had knocked on
the door about 8pm one night. He apologised for calling so late.
He was carrying a portable typewriter in its case and he said he
was upgrading it to a fancy new computer with a keyboard. But
he didn't want to just dump the typewriter. He said it had been
a reliable machine and he wanted to make sure it went to a good
home. As it happened, the neighbour was an old-school kinda
guy and liked the look of the typewriter. So, he accepted it with
thanks and promised George he would take good care of it. Then
George left and the neighbour never saw him again.

'The neighbour invited the Agent in and showed him
AGNES sitting on a writing desk. He didn't want to part with
the machine, but after hearing that the FBI wanted to talk to
George, the neighbour couldn't get rid of the typewriter fast
enough.'

'Sometimes the harder we work, the luckier we get,' said
McHale.

'You know what I think?' said Lightfoot, 'I think he was
closing up the shop. I think he'd typed all his letters and he
didn't need anything lying around that could link him to them.
But I think he couldn't just throw it away. That would have
been too messy. Too impersonal. He needed to do something
that would get the machine away from him, but something
that kept it safe.'

'But that doesn't fit,' said Kelly. 'Up until August 10, 2017 you
people had only received six letters. There were seven knives. So,

if we think he had all seven, then it makes sense that he had seven targets in mind. So why did he get rid of AGNES if he had another letter to write?'

Then Toby had his lightbulb moment.

'What if he already typed the seventh letter back in 2011?' he said. 'What if he kept it with him when he left the States? A damned sight easier than carrying the typewriter around. What if he killed six people over here between 2012 and 2017? Then nipped back over to the States after the last murder and posted the letter from Washington, just like the others, just to throw us off the scent?'

'Then he would have had plenty of time to come back to the UK for murder number seven on September 1,' said Daisy.

She looked at Toby.

Toby blushed.

The room was silent.

Sometimes you tell the story that fits the facts. Sometimes it's the other way around.

Eventually Lightfoot shrugged and said, 'I like it.'

Just then, Daisy got a text message from MOTHER.

She looked at the message. Looked at McHale. Wondered whether to mention it. Decided to see what MOTHER had to say first. She said this;

'Hello Daisy. Sorry to interrupt. I've attached a ZIP file containing all the background information about James Halliwell I have on file. I've also requested that six printed copies of the file be delivered to you personally for you to distribute as you see fit. You should have them by first thing in the morning. M.'

To have any of the other humans present regard her as an important team member was gratifying in itself. To have MOTHER, with all her advanced hardware and software, single her out for the first time as someone who could be a trusted ally… that was something else entirely. Somewhere inside she smiled.

She would look at the data tonight, and then report to McHale in the morning.

Although she was communicating with a highly intelligent machine, she fired off a quick 'Thank you'.

She saw McHale look at her quizzically, so she just smiled and stuck up a positive thumb. He shrugged and turned away.

'I haven't been able to figure out how anyone who was so precise, so neat, so obsessive about not leaving any evidence of his presence, should decide to murder someone in a way that left blood and guts in plain view,' said Toby.

'Not only does it not make sense, it seems completely out of character. It doesn't fit. This is a man who doesn't like mess.'

'Unless the act of making the mess is in some way a vital part of the ritual,' said Rice. 'He wouldn't be the first person who made a bloody mess as part of a sacrificial ritual.'

With his left hand, he picked up the Bible sitting in front of him. Patted it softly twice with his right hand.

'You're talking about the Crucifixion?' said Toby.

'Why not?' said Rice. It has at least some of the ingredients. A unique individual… sacrifice… blood… torture… and someone called The Holy Ghost. The only things missing are betrayal, death, resurrection, and redemption.'

'No, Father… the only thing missing is putting him and me in a locked room together for five minutes,' said Kelly. There was rage on her breath. But there was also the strong whiff of revenge. She reached for her Diamondback Cane leaning against the wall behind her, stood up, and began another circuit of the room. Muttering as she went.

'Six letters. Six years. Six bodies. Six knives. We know there are seven knives. And we know he hasn't finished.'

She stopped walking. Turned around to McHale. 'Where's the seventh letter? What's the seventh line?' she said. 'We only got six letters with six lines, sent to Quantico. Then he starts killing here in the UK. What made him leave the States? Or who? I don't buy it. Not yet.'

She started walking again. Talking out loud. Talking to herself and to everybody in the room. Including White on the screen. 'First one in 2012. Last one in 2017. First one in 2012. Last one in 2017.' Repeating the words over and over. 'He's thrown his old timetable out the window. He's given us a date for the last one. September 1. What's so damned special about September 1?'

The penultimate 357 of the day was sitting in its plastic container in her bag, calling to her.

She stopped walking and looked at White.

'Check your mail,' she said.

'Email?' said White.

'No… your post. Have you checked today's post?'

Urgency in her voice.

'Hang on,' said White, and disappeared off-screen.

She returned a couple of minutes later. Blurted out, 'Got something.'

Held up a white envelope.

'Don't open it,' Kelly said, as loud as she could without shouting.

White immediately understood the warning tone and put the letter down like it was a red-hot coal.

'Who is it addressed to?' said Lightfoot. 'Is it SSA David Bernier, BAU-4? Like the others?'

White merely looked at the envelope. Her fingers didn't go near it. 'No,' she said. 'This one's different.' She paused and looked up at Kelly. 'It's addressed to SSA Seymour Marshall.'

'Good,' said Lightfoot. 'That means he doesn't know Seymour has retired. That means he's acting on presumption, not on up-to-date knowledge. That means he's vulnerable.'

'Is the address handwritten or typed?'

'Typed. Like the others.'

'Got a magnifying glass handy?'

'Way ahead of you there,' said White. She bent down off-screen and looked at the typed letters on the front of the envelope.

'Yeah… it's him. Slightly lighter letter 'a's on the Marshall.

'What's your protocol for dealing with a suspicious letter?'

'We leave the damned thing alone and call in the cavalry,' said White. 'Or in this case, we let the folk in the labs with brass balls examine the hell out of it, pardon my French.'

'Good. Why don't you do that and get back to us, okay?'

'Sounds like a plan, Mac. What time is it over there?'

McHale decided that working on US time seemed appropriate. Given where they were and who they were satellite linked up to.

'Just after 17.40,' he said. 'We're calling it a day here. We've got lots of things to think about now and we'll probably be up half the night kicking them around. Can we continue this in the morning?'

He looked at Lightfoot, who nodded.

'Helluva day, Hannah. Speak tomorrow.'

'Bye all,' said White. And just before the link died, she looked directly at McHale and winked.

McHale turned to Kelly. Nodded. 'Good call,' he said.

She nodded back, then she grabbed her bag and made for the smallest room in the house. Time to kill the biggest pain in her body.

Lightfoot arranged to meet them as usual for a meal later. McHale politely declined. As did Daisy. Tonight, he had a date with Mister Hizentra, and four strategically placed micro-needles. And she had a date with a fistful of background data on James Halliwell, sent to her by MOTHER.

During the cab trip back to the hotel, McHale thought about how far the team had come in just a few days. He wondered if they would have come so far if he'd done things by the book; with conventional thinking and conventional coppers on his team. The question answered itself.

Just over forty-five minutes later he was standing naked, flesh being pounded by the jets of the power shower in his room.

Heat was a natural aphrodisiac to his skin. It seeped, like a drug, through his muscles and ended up giving his bones a high temperature hug.

He turned up the controls as high as they would go without the risk of third-degree burns. Then he let every thought inside his head go to sleep for ten blissful minutes.

Eventually, a single, errant thought shook itself awake before all the others, and pulled itself up to the surface of his consciousness. And the thought was this;

'Who the hell is AGNES?'

And like all clever thoughts, it wriggled its way into the juicy part of his cerebral cortex and had some fun. It was still there having fun half an hour later, while 80ml of pure plasma was worming its way under his abdomen. Kicking the living shit out of his CIDP symptoms.

About an hour into his medical infusion, he got an email from Daisy. Like her, it was short, sweet, and to the point. It was also funny. It said;

'Take your medication or the hostage dies.'

He laughed out loud. Fired back an answer. It said;

'You'll never take me alive, copper. All hooked up.'

Five minutes later he got another one. It said;

'Last thought for the night. Attached is a ZIP file from MOTHER containing all the info she has on James Halliwell. Best grab a coffee, there's quite a bit.

'The big news is that he did have a twin brother. Charles. Parents separated in 1997, when the boys were 12. Father, Thomas Halliwell, stayed in the UK with James. Charles went to the States with Mother, Suzanne. She remarried one year later. New hubby's name was Victor Lomax. See you at breakfast. D.'

McHale opened the ZIP file, downloaded it, then spent the next half hour skimming it.

His plasma ran out around 1.00am. His eyes gave in around 2.00am. His consciousness followed shortly afterwards.

The last few words he thought of before sleep came were these; 'Wherever you are, Charlie boy, we're coming for you. That's our breath on your neck. That's our hand on your shoulder.'

He repeated the phrase 'We're coming for you' over and over in his head as he drifted off to sleep. He thought it might make a good slogan for a t-shirt.

He wondered whether Lightfoot might think so too.

Chapter Nineteen

The fifteen seconds orchestral intro to The Beatles' All You Need Is Love pulled McHale out of a dream he didn't even get the chance to say goodbye to.

Then he groaned, farted loudly, reached out a hairy arm, and stabbed the alarm into snooze cruise mode.

Then, ten minutes later, he told the snooze to go to hell and tried to remember that he was in a hotel in the middle of London, not a neat semi in the outskirts of Stockport.

Ablutions were the same old things, done in the same old way, in the same old order. His body was used to the routine. His mind just went along for the ride.

Today, just like the last nine days, he would get up and get on with the job of hunting monsters. No protest. No complaint.

He looked out the window. London was always awake. Today it was getting ready to sweat.

His topsy-turvy world of the predictable and the unpredictable allowed him to make his bed, even though he knew that, at some time today, hotel maids would come in and re-make it with clean sheets.

It allowed him to sit on the edge of his made bed and read the morning's new emails, even though he would re-read them over breakfast.

No new ones. Only Daisy's from last night.

He switched to his MacBook Pro and skimmed the

information about James Halliwell that Daisy forwarded to him the night before. He was ten minutes into it when his mobile sprang to life.

'I hear good things about you guys,' said DCS Cyril Drummond.

'And good morning to you, too, sir,' said McHale, in as friendly a tone as he could muster. A headache first thing in the morning after a medical infusion the night before was the rule, not the exception. It was what it was.

The bastard thugs were stirring, but he'd already taken four paracetamols to head them off at the pass. He figured 2,000mgs would do the job. It was starting to.

'That's quite a team you've got there,' said Drummond. He didn't mention that half of them were his suggestions. He didn't have to. 'I'll have to keep an eye on that young lad of yours.'

'Don't turn him into a conventional cop, sir. One day he'll beat the crap out of all you Met guys.'

Drummond laughed heartily. It was good to hear. 'See you later,' he said. The phone died before McHale could return the goodbye.

Breakfast was its usual eclectic self. But McHale decided to throw caution to the wind and give his cholesterol level a kick up the arse. Ten minutes after joining the others, he was tucking into a full English, with extra bacon. Washed down with two large mugs of straight-up strong black coffee.

Finished off with a double espresso.

Sometimes rocket fuel was de rigueur when a hunt was picking up speed. It was the same when he was closing in on Black.

The taxi got to Winfield House at 10.16am.

The pat down was fast and efficient.

The team walked through the meeting room door three floors below at 10.29am. McHale smiled. The game was afoot, as little Billy Shakespeare said, he thought. Adding... sorry Mister Doyle, the bard got there first.

He smacked his hands together, rubbed them enthusiastically, and said, 'Morning all. Are we ready to go Ghost hunting?'

On the screen wall, a smiling Dr. Hannah White said; 'Hi guys.' She got the expected greeting from each member of the team in return. MOTHER was silent, but McHale knew she was listening in the background.

One by one, the team took their usual seats, then went to the small, round table at the far end of the room, where hot coffee and tea were waiting for them.

White waited until they had all sat down. Then she spoke.

'So… the good news is that the letter and its contents are doing fine. We didn't find any suspicious substances. It all looks very safe.'

She held up a sheet of white A4 paper. 'And the great news is that we have a seventh line.'

She pressed a button on her remote and an image of the letter came up on the screen behind her. It was punched up as big as possible. The line was the usual eleven words long. The words were;

'There are none so hateful as those who will not love.'

It was followed by the words Fairbairn-Sykes. Just like the other six letters.

But unlike the other six, it was followed by three more words. They were;

'Nice try. Goodbye.'

There was a lull in conversation in the room while they all digested the farewell addendum.

'So,' said the Jesuit. 'It seems that we'll have one chance to catch this guy. After September 1 he'll be gone.'

'What? He'll stop because he'll have used up all his knives?' said Kelly, angrily. 'Sorry… I don't buy it. I don't think people like that can just switch on and switch back off again whenever they want. Just because they feel like it.'

'He's beaten us six times already,' said McHale. 'If he plays his cards right, he'll beat us again. He's done everything he's set out to do. He fooled us. Now he's probably laughing at us. All the manpower of the Great British Police. All the manpower of the FBI. Six years of hunting and looking for even the slightest bit of evidence. And we've drawn a blank.'

He raised his eyebrows, held out his arms palms up and shrugged like an old Jewish tailor he used to know with a shop near the centre of Manchester.

Then he relaxed his shoulders and brought his arms down. Smiling, he slowly said, 'At least he thinks we have.'

He turned to Daisy. 'We'll have those files now,' he said.

Daisy nodded, got up from her chair, and was about to leave the room when the door opened. A black suited Agent walked in carrying folders containing the background MOTHER had prepared on the Halliwell family.

He handed them to Daisy, smiled at Lightfoot and left.

Forty-five pages of data. Stapled in the top left-hand corner. Times six copies. Times six blue plastic folders with pockets. Each with a team member's name on the front. Uncle Sam being thorough; the devil, after all, was always in the detail. He handed them to Daisy. Daisy handed them out to everyone.

The files had been updated and now contained all the information the FBI knew about his brother Charles, including everything they knew about his latest incarnation, George Riemann.

It was more information than both law enforcement organisations either side of the pond had ever had on either of them. But it still wasn't enough.

It still slammed on the brakes in 2011. Until now. Until the latest letter. Posted in Washington and received by the mail room at Quantico on August 10, 2017. Why the gap?

'This is your suggested reading for today,' he said.

He nodded at Daisy, who handed a file copy to each of the team.

'I think it would be a good idea if we spent this afternoon, or at least part of it, going through the file. Learn as much about these people as you can. It's a lovely day outside. Go sit in the sun. But this morning, I'd like Hannah to talk about the star of the show, so to speak.'

He looked at the screen wall. 'Sure thing,' said White. And she held up a Fairbairn-Sykes knife.

'Remind me to get myself one of those when this is over,' said Lightfoot, softly.

'This,' said White, 'is a Fairbairn-Sykes First Pattern fighting knife. It has a 7-inch two-sided blade – that's 18 centimetres in new money. Total length 11.5 inches. That's 29 centimetres. It has a flat area, or ricasso, at the top of the blade. It has an S-shaped cross-guard and a ring pattern grip. It was designed by William Ewart Fairbairn and Eric Anthony Sykes and produced by The Wilkinson Sword Company in 1941.

'Some folk call it a stiletto. Most folk call it the best damned fighting knife ever designed or made.'

'Can you show us a close up of the ricasso, please?' said McHale.

'Thought you'd ask that,' said White.

She brought the knife up as close as possible to the camera. The ricasso section took up most of the screen.

There was no number on it.

There was, however, a Wilkinson Sword logo etched into the steel.

'Now can you show me the grip?'

It had a diamond-knurled grip. Not a ring pattern.

Lightfoot was drumming a pen against the edge of an empty white mug that minutes ago held hot, black coffee. She looked at the screen wall and double blinked.

Okay, thought White, *let's see how good you really are.*

'Where did you find it?'

No pause. Immediate answer.

'Buried in the top of the head of a man in an old, dilapidated house in Williamsburg, Virginia.'

'When did you find it?' said Kelly.

Ah… warmer, thought White.

'Officially, local police found it January 15, 2011. Technically, local kids found it first, on January 13. They were trespassing on the property. Police didn't hear about it until two days later.'

McHale had felt an itch, deep inside his head, from the moment White had started speaking. He didn't waste any more time.

'Tell me the body was posed,' he said.

'The body was posed,' she said. 'When this is all over remind me to have a box of fine Cuban cigars delivered to you guys. Courtesy of Uncle Sam.'

She turned around to face her screen and pressed a button on her remote.

The black and white image of a body appeared. It was sitting on an armchair. Judging by the clothing it looked like a 'he' and he had been dead for weeks. Somehow, he was still managing to hold what looked like a book in his left hand. The chest had been ripped open and collapsed inwards. Maggots and bacteria had been having a banquet. What was left of the body had slumped to the left. Skeletonization wasn't far off.

And there was a knife, stuck in the top of his head, almost to the hilt.

White hadn't spoken a word since she put the photo up on her screen. She just let the image, and the story it told, sink in. And she waited. A dropping pin made more noise.

About fifteen seconds into the silence Kelly spoke. 'What was the book?'

Pause.

'A King James Bible,' said White.

The sound of more pins dropping.

'Identity?'

White frowned. 'We know the body was male. We know he was between fifty-five and sixty-five years old. We know he had fifteen teeth left in his mouth. We know he was approximately 5 feet 10 inches in height. That's about 167 centimetres, give or take. We know that at some point in his life he had suffered a bad fracture of his tibia and fibula bones on his left leg. Midway between his knee and his ankle. We know he had two dollars and fifteen cents in his right trouser pocket.

'And that's it. We don't know who he was or where he came from. We named him Angus.'

She finished speaking and sighed heavily.

Life's a bitch and then you die, thought McHale. He liked the name. He had an uncle called Angus.

'This was a practice run,' said Lightfoot. 'The knife isn't exactly the same as the numbered P1s, because he didn't want to waste the seven real ones on anyone but the real kills. He needed to see the knife working. He was too much of a perfectionist to leave things to chance. The kills had to happen with the right weapons. Used in the right way. At the right time. In the right place. And the body had to be posed in the right way. And the Bible had to be held in the left hand. To begin with, anyway.

'All the boxes had to be ticked, before he even started.

'This is our guy. And he's here.'

'Check the deeds to the property, I bet it's owned by George Riemann,' said McHale.

'Nope,' said White. 'Land and property are owned by someone by the name of Ada Lovelace. We tried to track her down. She seems to have disappeared into thin air.'

Toby gave a short laugh. There was no humour in it.

Everyone turned to look at him.

'What's the joke?' said Kelly.

'Ada Lovelace... or to call her by her full title, Augusta Ada King-Noel, Countess of Lovelace... was the only legitimate daughter of the poet Lord Byron. She was a famous nineteenth century English mathematician.'

'So, this was another one of Charles Halliwell's aliases?'

said Rice.

'A name-change and a sex-change, too?' said Daisy.

'Only on paper,' said Toby, offering up another fist-bump.

McHale turned to the screen wall. 'Hannah, this is great work,' he said.

White grinned. 'No problem,' she said. 'I left out the news about the practice run and the knife from everything I sent you yesterday. I didn't want to let the cat out of the bag until I spoke to you today. I'll update the files and resend everything to Daisy later this afternoon your time.'

It was 2.10pm.

Just before she cut the connection, the door opened and DCS Cyril Drummond strode in. Had he been frowning; he might have simply walked. Had he been thoughtful, he might have merely strolled.

But he was smiling, so he strode in like a man on a mission. And the first person he spoke to was over 3,600 miles away.

'Hannah, my dear, how the hell are you?'

White looked as though she'd just met up with into her favourite uncle. 'I'm fine, Cyril. Good to see you again,' she said.

'Not as good as it is to see you,' he said.

Favourite uncle my arse, McHale thought. *The old bugger's flirting.*

Two minutes later, after some polite small talk, the old bugger said so long and White did the same before cutting the link.

The only ones left in the room had bodies, not pixels.

Drummond was wearing the same grey tweed two-piece suit he had on the last time he was there. If anything, he seemed to have grown in size over the past few days. It was almost as if any progress made by the team was reflected in his posture.

He nodded at McHale, who nodded back. Then he spoke to the team.

'A week or so ago, the folk above me didn't think you people had a bloody cat in hell's chance of catching this bastard. Then

I politely reminded them that you'd done more in a week that a football stadium full of coppers had done in six bloody years. And I also reminded them that when it came to catching serial killers, they knew fuck all, and you people were the dog's bloody bollocks. They shut up after that. That's all I wanted to say. Time for me to piss off and let you do what we couldn't. I just wanted to say 'well done'.'

He looked at McHale. 'Tom… a word.' And he turned and strode back out the door.

The others looked at McHale, who shrugged and followed Drummond into the corridor. Before he reached it, he turned to the team and said, 'I think this is a good time to do some reading. Get out in the fresh air. See you back here in an hour or so.'

Then he went to join Drummond.

Chapter Twenty

When McHale caught up with him, Drummond was halfway into a room on the other side of the corridor, about twenty feet away from the room with the team. As the DCS walked in, the light came on.

As McHale walked in, he saw that the room was half the size of the one he'd just left. As was the table. It was oblong and had six chairs around it. Two chairs were already occupied; in one was Bob Masterson, and in the other was a woman he hadn't seen or met before. Both stood up. Both were smiling.

McHale was immediately on his guard. The smiles looked as genuine as a £9 note.

Internal voice said, 'Watch the dame, Kemosabe. She looks like a bloody spook. Count your fingers after you shake her hand.'

Drummond did the introductions. 'Tom, you already know Bob Masterson.'

Masterson shook McHale's hand.

'And this –'

He didn't get to finish his sentence.

The woman smiled, stuck out her hand, and said; 'Molly Spencer.'

She was a wavy-haired redhead who looked about thirty-five, maybe forty. McHale suspected she was probably about forty-five, maybe fifty. Still, she looked good for whatever age she was.

She was wearing tight cream chinos under a beige blouse, two buttons open at the top, under a light grey jacket. No lapels.

She had a gold chain around her neck and some kind of medal dangling just where McHale didn't want to look.

She shook McHale's hand and they all sat down. Almost immediately a dark-suited agent knocked on the door and walked in without being invited. The knock was a courtesy. It didn't require an invitation. He was carrying a tray with four mugs of black coffee, a small jug of milk, and some sachets of brown sugar. He put the tray on the table and left wordlessly.

Masterson played mother and, thirty seconds later, Spencer opened her mouth. It wasn't to drink.

'We're not people who are easily impressed,' she said. Her accent said she was originally from somewhere North of Hadrian's Wall. The years had taken the edge off it.

'That's a compliment,' said Drummond.

She continued. 'We're also people who get annoyed when somebody pisses on us from a great height because they think we can't do our job properly.'

She took a slow sip of her black coffee. McHale quickly did a fast about-turn and decided he liked her. The decision was instinctive. It didn't happen often, and he was very rarely wrong.

Okay, thought McHale. Well, so far you could have been describing me.

He judged the coffee to be just about gulpable, so he took a swig. It was the real McCoy. Not some granulated, low-grade, caffeine that was rolled out for the ordinary folk.

His right eyebrow went up. Roger Moore would have been proud. This was high-grade astronaut fuel.

He decided to pop her balloon.

'Well… for the past six years you haven't,' he said. 'You should have done what you're now doing at least four years ago. Maybe three. Definitely two. But you already know that. So, I'm here either because you want us to keep doing what we're doing… or because you want us to stop. So, which is it?'

Spencer looked at him long and hard. Then she smiled and

looked at Drummond. 'You were right, Cyril. I do like him.'

She turned back to McHale. 'Before long you're going to need some help. Maybe lots of help. I'm not talking about brains. Your team's very well equipped in that department. But how would you feel about having another dozen or so very bright coppers who can pick up some of the legwork. You think you could use them?'

Take your time, thought McHale. Don't make any daft agreements. Don't let anyone walk in and take over the show just because they have some bloody political agenda that you don't know about. She's giving with one hand. What the fuck is she taking with the other one?

'I'll even throw in unrestricted access to MOTHER, if that helps,' said Masterson.

Pause.

'Three conditions,' said McHale.

'Name them,' said Spencer.

'One: keep your mitts off my team. We stay the way we are.'

'Agreed.'

'Two: I only call for help when I need it and if I need it.'

'Agreed.'

'Three: I need a secure mobile number I can reach you on, and a favour.'

'I normally don't do favours,' she said. 'I normally have favours done for me.' But she looked interested.

Spencer picked up a wallet sitting on the table in front of her, dug out a card, wrote a number on it and handed it to McHale.

He didn't look at it, just slipped it into an inside jacket pocket.

'What's the favour?' she said.

'You'll know when I know.'

'Sounds like a mystery,' she said.

McHale finished his coffee in one gulp, put the mug down, held out his hand for Spencer to shake and said; 'Sounds like a plan.'

He nodded to Drummond and Masterson.

Then he turned, walked out the door, and went back into the team room to collect his copy of MOTHER's background info on the Halliwell family.

Five minutes later he was sitting on a bench, on his own, in a secluded part of the garden of Winfield House. The sun blazed out of a blue sky; a large, overhanging oak offering welcome shade. He read about James, whose father showered him with love and affection. And about Charles, whose mother married a vindictive alcoholic called Victor Lomax who beat the hell out of him at the slightest provocation.

Victor regarded Charles as stupid, uncommunicative, mentally defective, and unwilling or unable to learn. The more he regretted becoming the boy's stepfather, the more he regretted marrying Suzanne Halliwell. And the more he did that, the more he drank. And the more he drank the more violent he got.

What he didn't know, not that it would have made any difference, was that Charles suffered from Asperger's Syndrome. One of the Autism-spectrum disorders.

What he didn't know was that, although Asperger's usually becomes apparent in toddlers, Charles was an exception, not a rule. He wasn't of normal intelligence; he was highly intelligent. And he wasn't physically clumsy, he was highly athletic. Apart from the slight muscular weakness in the little finger of his left hand.

What he did know, however, was that Charles had a profound and deep-seated hatred of his twin brother, James. He knew this because he helped Suzanne Halliwell put it there.

She knew there was something different about Charles. She always knew. But she wanted him to fit in. She wanted him to be the same as everyone else. So, she kept her mouth shut. And she poisoned his mind. And she home-schooled him. And she compensated for him. And he ended up compensating for himself.

But the older he got, the more difficult it became to deny that Charlie had Asperger's Syndrome. He was officially diagnosed in 2003 when he was seventeen.

But he didn't receive the quality medical care and the kind of schooling that understood his disability, and that would help him accept the world and the world accept him.

From early teens onward, his mind had been a toxic dump, poisoned by a woman who felt nothing but murderous rage for the man who cast her aside. And, eventually, also for the man who beat her regularly.

But he hid his true nature well.

By early adulthood he was a young, friendly, approachable man who, on the outside, looked and acted a bit different from most other folk, but was basically okay.

On the inside, however, he was vicious, sneaky, warped, and unapologetically murderous.

McHale knew this because the writer of the report he was reading on the bench in the garden that afternoon knew this. And the writer knew this because Suzanne Halliwell kept a diary.

And in her diary, she wrote down every poisonous thought, every tortured feeling that she felt towards Thomas Halliwell. And, because James Halliwell had fought and screamed to stay in England with his father at the time of the separation, all those poisonous thoughts were, by osmosis, transferred to her son.

The one she left behind.

The one who betrayed her.

In December 2010, Suzanne Halliwell died of ovarian cancer. And, as a final 'fuck you', she mailed her diary to Victor Lomax, by way of his lawyer. It catalogued years of physical and psychological abuse, violence, and barbarity. It was, of course, completely biased.

The lawyer's curiosity got the better of him. He read the diary, then contacted his local police force.

And they did what all good police forces should do... and sent the diary to the FBI.

The law sometimes travels a circuitous journey. Justice doesn't always travel the same road. It doesn't even use the same clock.

By the time two FBI agents visited the house Charles and his mother had stayed in, it was January 2011. Charles had gone, and they found the place in the process of being forensically strip-searched by more FBI agents.

On March 22 that year, Thomas Halliwell received a savage beating at the hands of a couple of goons in the employ of a local loan shark. After spending a month in hospital recuperating, Thomas decided that staying anywhere within a 100-mile radius of Halifax might not be good for his health. So, he left twenty-five-year-old James behind to make what he could of his life, and headed out of Dodge on the fastest horse in the stable.

Fast forward to 4.50pm in the quiet garden of Winfield House, on Thursday August 10, 2017.

McHale finished reading the report, returned it to its folder, closed his eyes, and for ten minutes, let the tail-end of the afternoon sun cover Regent's Park in a warm summer blanket.

Internal voice joined him under the tree. 'No wonder the kid turned out a raving bloody psycho.'

On the way back into the house, he met up with Stephen Rice and Siobhan Kelly. They were deep in conversation. 'Having fun?' he said.

Rice looked sad. 'I need a favour,' he said.

'Name it.'

'I need a video link with Father David Back. He's in Broadmoor.' The Jesuit didn't sound enthusiastic at the prospect of coming face to face again with someone who, on the outside, was a man of God, and on the inside, was a monster of The Devil.

McHale knew how much Rice's last encounter with Black had affected him. But he also knew that the Jesuit wouldn't be asking if he didn't think there was something to be gained from the meeting.

You can't see if you can't look. And Rice had to look at the priest face to face.

He nodded. 'I'll have a word,' he said, walking in behind the two as they made their way down to the meeting room.

Before he got there, he stopped in the corridor outside the room, letting the other two enter.

Time Drummond earned his pay. Again.

Time to wake up a sleeping monster. Again.

He pulled his phone out of his inside jacket pocket. Speed-dialled a number. Waited two rings.

'Hello, Tom,' said Drummond. 'Caught him yet?'

It was a game that he and the DCS played.

'I need a favour,' said McHale.

There was a pause. 'Go on?'

'I need a video link in a quiet room here between Stephen Rice and Father David Black in Broadmoor. And I need it set up today. How possible is that?'

There was a longer pause. Then a sigh. 'You're full of surprises,' said Drummond. McHale could imagine him frowning on the other end of the line.

'That's why I ask the big questions and you get the big bucks.'

'Leave it with me.'

'Appreciate it.'

Drummond killed the line and McHale went to join the others.

When he walked in the room everyone was there except Lightfoot. Coffee had just been brought in and most were in the process of filling up mugs.

This was American soil.

Mugs by choice. Cups and saucers by request only.

He looked at Lightfoot's vacant chair.

Looked at Daisy, who shrugged.

'We'll give her ten minutes,' he said. Coffee smelled good. He filled his mug. Sat down. His mobile rang.

'You know someone called Molly Spencer?' said Lightfoot.

'Met her briefly, why?'

'She just collared me. Wanted to know if I would be interested in joining the team after the Ghost hunt.'

McHale sighed. 'Sorry about that. I'll have a word. Forget it for now. Just concentrate on catching the bastard. You coming in?'

'Five minutes.'

McHale killed the line. He looked around the table. 'So… you all had a good read in the sun?'

'Part of me feels sorry for him,' said Daisy. 'I think it's got something to do with the Asperger's. That Lomax guy was an evil bastard.'

Kelly turned to the screen wall.

'MOTHER?'

'Yes Siobhan?'

'How many people in the UK suffer from Asperger's Syndrome?'

Pause.

'Asperger's belongs in the Autism spectrum. In the UK around 700,000 people are diagnosed as autistic. They come from all nationalities, cultural, religious, and social backgrounds. Asperger affects about 1 in 200 people. And it appears to affect more men than women.'

Kelly turned to Daisy. 'Don't feel sorry for him, love. He doesn't deserve your sympathy. Keep that for his victims. Being a serial killer doesn't make you an Asperger's sufferer. In the same way that being an Asperger's sufferer doesn't make you a serial killer.' She turned away.

Daisy blushed and looked down at the tabletop.

The door opened and Lightfoot walked in. 'Miss anything?' she said.

'Only me getting politely bollocked, and rightly so,' said Daisy. Kelly shrugged.

McHale held up his copy of the report in the blue folder. 'I'd like you all to have another look at this between now and first thing in the morning. Just let it simmer. See if anything else comes to mind.

'Meanwhile, before we shut down, I want to run something

by you all. It has to do with what I was saying the other day about me being playing chess.'

'Ah,' said Stephen Rice. 'I wondered when you'd get around to that. How's your latest game progressing?'

'Slowly,' said McHale. 'The idea I'd like to bring up is this: so far, The Ghost has used two aliases. And both of them have been based on long-dead mathematicians. So... what if he carries on in the same vein? What if this alias game he's playing is part of his signature? And if so, how can we use this to our advantage?'

'I think you know something,' said Lightfoot. 'You know something or you've seen something that's put you on this track. Spill the beans.'

McHale always fostered an atmosphere where all comments were allowed and none were held back. Not that Lightfoot needed any persuasion to say what was on her mind. She was getting nearer to standing by his side, metaphorically speaking. He decided that he liked the thought.

Time to put his money where his mouth was.

'Remember my comment a couple of days ago about killers inserting themselves into investigations?'

'Ted Bundy, yeah,' said Lightfoot.

'I have one game of internet chess on the go at the moment. This is the first time I've played this guy. We've only made a few moves so far.

'He calls himself Arnie GM. GM is chess-speak for the title Grand Master. So, he's either legit and keeping himself under the radar, or he's bullshitting and just wants to look better than he is.'

'Is he good?' said Kelly.

'Too early to say.'

'Is he hinky?'

'Don't know yet.'

'I think you know something,' said Lightfoot, again.

'I think I think something,' said McHale.

'Who's playing black?' asked Rice.

'He is.'

'Your first move?'

'e4…'

'His?'

'c5…'

'Your second?'

'Knight to f3…'

'His?'

'e6…'

'Your third?'

'd4…'

'His?'

'c5 takes d4.

'Your fourth?'

'Then my knight took his pawn on d4.'

'His?'

'Moved his pawn to a6'

'That's it?'

'So far, yeah.'

'Could be anything. Maybe a Sicilian Defence, that's all.'

'Did I ever tell you about my favourite ever chess game?' said McHale, not even waiting for an answer. 'It was played in 1972 in Reykjavik, Iceland. It was between Bobby Fischer and Boris Spassky. But really it was between the USA and Russia. The was the ultimate Cold War game. It went to 41 moves, then Spassky resigned. Fischer became the first American-born World Chess Champion.'

'And?'

'And the day Fischer won was September 1, 1972.'

Pause while the date sunk in.

'Fuck,' said Toby, softly

'That's not all,' said Lightfoot.

'No. That's not all. The game I'm playing mirrors the game Fischer won.'

'Double fuck,' said Toby.

'This is getting very spooky,' said Daisy.

'Want to go for three?' said McHale.

You know that moment when you have a room full of people and they're all looking at you? Not because of something you said, but because of something they think you're about to say?

'What was the name of your opponent again?' said Lightfoot.

McHale smiled. 'Arnie GM.'

Toby held up his hands. 'Wait… wait…' he said. He grabbed his pen and scribbled on his pad.

Looked up at them.

'It's an anagram,' he said. 'Arnie GM is an anagram of Germain.'

'And?'

'That's the surname of Marie-Sophie Germain… 18th century French mathematician. Bloody hell, the cheeky bastard.'

'You sure?' said Kelly.

'About the name?'

'No… about the damned anagram. Maybe it's just a coincidence.'

McHale grinned at Toby. 'Coincidences mean you're on the right track.'

'I think he thinks he's playing you. This is our one chance to play him,' said Lightfoot. 'This is big, McHale.'

'Not finished… not finished… here's twist number one,' said Toby. 'They called her Sophie Germain Prime, because of her work with prime numbers!'

McHale began a slow hand clap of respect. Then the others joined in.

But Toby wasn't finished.

'And now, for the Grand Finale, twist number two… Germain has seven letters. And, as you all know, seven is a prime number. Seven knives… seven letters… seven lines… six kills with one left to go. Does this mean that I get the big fat Cuban cigar?'

'No,' said McHale, giving Toby a fist-bump with an extra finger-splash. 'But it does mean that I pay for the meals tonight. And I think you deserve a damned fine steak for that.'

As it turned out, there were four steaks served up that night for the team, plus one grilled chicken and one sea bass, in the hotel restaurant.

As usual, they were in a talkative mood. And as usual, the restaurant manager placed them at a table as far away from everyone else as possible.

They were talking shop. With alcohol. There were sharp weapons involved. And dead bodies. And one very homicidal serial killer.

It was a bit of a late night. McHale didn't even remember Lightfoot leaving. If indeed she did.

Chapter Twenty-One

Friday, 11th August, 6.30am.

Martha Reeves and the Vandellas came on the radio, and fifteen Motown seconds of Nowhere to Run started off another sweaty day in London, hunting for a serial killer who could be anywhere.

Then McHale reached out a hairy arm, and stabbed the alarm into snooze cruise mode. Ten minutes later, he nearly sent the iPhone flying across the room with a swipe of his hand. The bastard thugs had come to welcome in the day with a headache the size of Alaska.

Ablutions were a slow and painful affair, only made slightly easier by 2,000mgs of paracetamol. Four oblong whites. Okay. Six. 3,000mgs. Washed down with a large gulp of cold coffee he couldn't remember making the night before.

The thought of a full English anything wasn't even remotely on his radar. Last night's enjoyment left him gagging for chilled water followed by the strongest caffeine on the menu.

One slice of toast and strawberry jam was all he could manage. The others were cheery and hungry.

McHale noticed that Lightfoot joined them for breakfast. He started to wonder exactly who she had spent the night with. But the bastard thugs were still making both thinking and moving at the same time a painful process.

Mercifully, by the time their two taxis reached Winfield House it was 10.12am, the thugs had buggered off, and all that remained was the vague tail end of a dream about a bloody chessboard, disappearing like smoke in the wind.

Ten minutes later they were all sat down around the meeting table, coffees distributed. Ready to carry on the hunt. Feeling a damned sight closer to The Ghost than they did the morning before.

Like any good open forum, everyone had a voice and nobody had a monopoly on being heard.

But everyone naturally looked to McHale to start the ball rolling.

'Right,' he said. 'The more I thought about it last night, the more I liked the idea of my friendly neighbourhood chess mate being The Ghost. So, I'm going to do two things. First, make another move today that mirrors the Spassky/Fischer game. Then I'm going to start up a bit of a conversation with him. Nothing much.' He turned to Lightfoot. 'Just shooting the breeze as you guys say.'

'Don't do that,' Lightfoot said. 'Let him say something to you first.'

McHale considered that and nodded his head. 'Okay. Explain.'

'Do you have a set time limit for each move?' she added.

'It varies. But this game is set for a day a move. That's 24-hours.'

'How long has it been since his last move?'

McHale got his laptop from his bag and fired it up, opening the chess programme. Looking at his board, he said, 'He made a move last night. Pawn to a6.'

'How long until you have to move?'

'Eleven hours.'

'Right… make a move now.'

Internal voice joined the game. 'Now don't piss about. Move your knight to c3. This is the Sicilian bloody Defence… remember The Godfather!'

McHale moved his knight to c3.

'Now… whatever he does, don't make another move yet. Take up your full 24 hours. You don't want to be reacting to his moves. You want him reacting to yours.'

Almost immediately Arnie GM moved his knight to c6.

McHale double blinked. 'He doesn't usually reply this fast,' he said.

'Good… now he's reacting to you.'

'I didn't know you played.'

'My grandfather taught me. He used to say that hunting and chess are the same.'

'Remind me never to challenge you to a game.'

She smiled. McHale hadn't realised what a beautiful smile she had.

He also hadn't realised how much that thought pleased him.

'That would be a shame. I think you'd be an interesting opponent,' she said. 'Right… now we wait.'

'Are we thinking that he's now here in the UK?' Daisy said.

'Not necessarily. He's got 20 days until his final kill. So theoretically he could be anywhere,' said Toby.

'Of course, that supposes it really is his final kill,' said Rice.

McHale's mobile rang.

Drummond said; 'Morning, Tom. Black has agreed to a video link with Rice. 11.00pm on the dot. I'll collect him myself about ten minutes before.' He killed the call.

McHale turned to the Jesuit. 'Looks like your video link with Black is on. You've got until just before midday before you see him face to face. If you want to bugger off upstairs to sit in the garden and prepare, now might be a good time.'

'I'm fine,' said Rice. 'Anyway. Talking to Black would never be a problem. It's Arthur that's the problem. I wonder which one of them will show up.'

'You ever taken Black's confession, Father?' said Kelly.

Surprise on Rice's face. 'Many times,' he said.

He wasn't expecting that.

Siobhan had a knack of cutting right to the chase, thought McHale.

'Not the kind of question you should ever ask a priest.'

She ignored the answer.

'What about Arthur? Has he ever confessed his sins to you?'

Rice suddenly looked sad. 'Only once,' he said.

'One thing always bothered me about confession,' she said. 'How the hell do you know if somebody's being honest with you?'

Rice shrugged. 'Everybody lies,' he said. 'Even people who think they're telling you the truth. Anyway, it doesn't even matter if they only think they're telling you the truth. HE knows the difference. You can fool you; you can fool me... but you can't fool HIM.'

'What if HE lies, too?'

'Then we're all screwed,' said Toby.

'Ever the optimist, eh?'

'What if Charles Halliwell is here? What if he's already sorting out his next victim as we speak? All we're doing is knee jerking to his actions. There must be something in this background that MOTHER prepared that can at least point us in the right direction.' Saying that, she picked up her copy of the blue folder and began to read.

No sooner had she started than she stopped, looked up, faced the screen wall and spoke.

'MOTHER... is there any way to check all incoming flights to the UK from the US over, say, the past month? And see if any passengers with the names Charles Halliwell, George Riemann, or S. Germain show up? Check all ports, too?'

'Into the UK from the US only?'

'No... better make it from everywhere.'

'I'll get back to you.'

Daisy liked the idea of having a special relationship with MOTHER. She liked the thought that MOTHER viewed her as more than just another member of the team. The one worry that had nibbled away at her confidence over the past ten days was that MOTHER would somehow make her presence on the team unnecessary.

Nothing could have been further from the truth.

Daisy was now MOTHER's first port of call with information gathering and disseminating.

Ten minutes later, Daisy received a text from MOTHER. It was twenty-two words long. It said this;

'Hi Daisy. No record of any of the names you gave me entering or leaving the UK during the past month. MOTHER.'

It was 11.50am.

The door opened. Drummond stood at the entrance and looked at Father Stephen Rice. When he caught his attention, he motioned him to follow.

Rice looked at McHale. Raised his eyebrows. Grabbed his pad and pen. 'See you on the flip side,' he said. McHale liked the analogy. It went well with the collection of hundreds of vinyl 45s he had at home.

He nodded slightly, said 'good luck', and watched Rice walk out the door to hopefully pick the brains of a killer.

The Jesuit's briefing from Drummond was mercifully short. They were in the room where McHale had met Molly Spencer. The room now had a large HD monitor mounted on the right-hand wall.

The table had a tray with a glass of water, a mug of black coffee, and a King James Bible. Black leather. Gold lettering.

The monitor was switched off.

Rice drew back a chair, sat down opposite the screen, and Drummond sat next to him. He pointed up to the four corners of the room where the walls met the ceiling.

The lights on four small cameras were blinking red. He looked directly at one of the cameras and made a throat-cutting motion with his right hand.

The camera lights went off.

'Right,' he said. 'You're flying solo. Same with Black on the other side. What you say to each other during the next half an hour is between the two of you and God Almighty. Nobody else.

I have no bloody idea who's going to turn up to the party. Let's hope Arthur's there somewhere and feels like having a chat.'

He patted Rice on the shoulder twice, then got up and left the room.

Almost immediately, the monitor came alive and Father David Black, minus dog collar, was sitting at a table in a bland room in Broadmoor prison, staring back at him.

He was now 62 years old and his hair was shorter and whiter than Rice remembered, since they last saw each other in 2011. His face looked grey and sad. But his eyes were almost shockingly just as bright blue as they must have been when he attempted to decapitate poor old John Kirkbride in 2010.

'Hello, Stephen,' he said. Trying to smile but failing miserably. 'It's been a while.'

Rice had more success, and at least managed half a smile. 'Hello, David,' he said. 'At least I presume I'm speaking to David?'

'It's me. I've been told about Arthur. I know he's in here with me somewhere. But I can't feel his presence. I suppose it must be a bit like being possessed by The Devil and not being able to tell when he's going to put in an appearance. Not what I signed up for.'

Black shifted in his seat and grimaced slightly in pain. 'Slight case of haemorrhoids,' he said, shrugging. 'I think this must be God's way of punishing the innocent.' He sighed.

'You're not innocent, David,' said Rice.

Pause.

'You're looking well,' said Black, ignoring the comment, reaching out of shot, lifting a plastic beaker to his lips and taking a sip.

You're not, thought Rice, but didn't let the words out of his mouth. Instead, he said, 'Do you know why I'm here?'

Black nodded. 'I do,' he said. 'And I want you to know I'll do everything I can to help you.'

'I know you will. But now I need you to take a back seat,

David. I need to speak with Arthur.'

Black let a solitary laugh escape his mouth. It came from a place where no humour existed. 'I know you do. Why else would you be here except to speak to the stranger inside me? You do realise that before you caught me, I had no idea that Arthur even existed. He hides himself very well.'

Rice felt a surge of sorrow for Black well up inside him.

Then the warning bell sounded.

No, he thought, *don't even go there*. Don't even think about the costume that the monster wears. Don't be seduced by a single word spoken by someone who used to be a man of God.

So, he said something else instead.

'In that case, I'd like to invite Arthur to speak to me, if he wishes. I'd like to hear what he thinks. What he has to say. I think he'd like to hear what I have to say.'

Black closed his eyes and faced his tabletop. There was a long pause. Rice counted out almost five minutes in his head. Then Black took a large breath as if he were filling his lungs to their full capacity. Then he let the air slowly out.

He raised his head and looked at Rice. The transformation was astonishing.

His eyes which, mere seconds ago, had been sad and at least accepting of his predicament were now darker, angrier, more cunning. Almost feral.

Then he blinked and the look was gone. The David Black that Rice saw when the screen was switched on was back.

Only he wasn't.

'Well, well, well,' said Arthur, smiling. 'This is a nice surprise, I must say. Come here often? Oh no, wait. You don't, do you? Poor old David. A bit pathetic, isn't he?'

Rice began to feel his skin tingle.

It was the same feeling that he had when he accompanied McHale to the crime scene in Altrincham, before they took away the bodies of the Kirkbrides.

The same feeling that he had when he spoke to Arthur immediately after he had been brought to Broadmoor. When he was sitting on the floor in the corner of a secure, bare room.

Face white. Clothes white. Rocking backwards and forwards. Mumbling. Scratching his arms bloody.

Years ago, Rice spent some time talking to a man trying to break his fentanyl addiction. He'd spent decades in extreme pain. He hadn't put any of his patches on for a week. He was describing how the spiders crawling under his skin were making him feel.

First the tingling. Now the crawling.

'Hello Arthur,' he said. 'How are you?'

'Me?' said Arthur, a look of betrayal on his face. 'How the hell do you think I am? You never call… you never write… anyone would think we weren't friends.'

'You think we're friends?' said Rice.

The look changed to a smile, but the eyes were a million miles from happy.

'Sure we are. Best buddies. Apart from the bit where you helped to catch your best buddy and lock him up and throw away the key. How is my other best buddy? How is Mister McHale? I always liked him.'

'I'm helping him again, Arthur,' he said. 'We're trying to catch somebody who might think like you. We want to ask if you'd like to help us.'

'Oh puleeese,' said Arthur, in a slow, sarcastic manner. 'Nobody thinks like me. You above all people should know that, Stephen. Nobody thinks like me, talks like me, or acts like me. Of all the billions of little people out there, not one of them is like me.'

'That's because you're unique, Arthur. You're one of a kind.'

Arthur's smile widened. 'That's very nice of you to say so, Stephen.' Suddenly the smile vanished. 'Now… say it again. And this time, say it like you mean it.'

Pause.

Rice smiled. 'You're unique, Arthur. You're one of a kind.'

Arthur seemed to consider this. Then he nodded his head. 'Tell me about him.'

'He's a very sick man,' said Rice.

'You don't look so healthy yourself.'

'I have a healthy mind. The body is a different matter.'

Arthur looked sad. 'Do you still have the nightmares?'

'I don't have nightmares. I used to have nightmares but now I sleep like a baby.'

'You still have nightmares. I can see it in your eyes,' said Arthur, shaking his head slowly. 'It's nothing to be ashamed of. Your God won't love you any less.'

'He likes numbers,' said Rice.

'Who, your God?'

Pause.

There was no sound in either room at either end of the video link. But Rice could hear the sound of his heart beating. He could hear the sound of his blood rushing through his veins. The sound of air, coming in and going out of his body.

'The man we're hunting. He likes numbers and he likes killing people. One a year on the same day every year for the past six years,' he said.

'He sounds like a busy man. A busy bee. Does he take off their heads?' said Arthur.

'No. He sticks things in them.'

'Are they sharp things?'

Pause.

Breathe. Sometimes you have to give a bit to get a bit.

'They are.'

Pause.

'Do you have photos?'

'Do you know anyone like that?'

'Do you have photos?'

'No. No photos.'

'Sorry. Then I don't know anyone like that.' Arthur yawned and stretched his arms above his head. 'I'm feeling very sleepy,' he said. 'Maybe if you come back tomorrow, we can talk again.'

'I'm sorry, that won't be possible.'

Suddenly, Arthur leaned into the monitor until his face filled the whole screen, and he whispered. 'Do me a favour. Don't tell him about our little chat, eh?'

'Who?'

'You know… Pathetic Dave. That's what I call him. Pathetic Dave. Will you tell him?'

'Not if you don't want me to,' said Rice.

Arthur sat back in his seat and seemed to consider this. He made a pouting motion with his lips and nodded his head a couple of times.

'A favour done is a favour owed, that's my motto,' he said. 'You still play chess?'

Rice's pulse skipped a beat.

'A little, why?'

'Your friend play chess, too, does he?' he said.

Rice's pulse skipped another beat. Careful Stephen, he thought… be very careful.

'Now and then.'

'Give Mister McHale my regards,' he said. Winking with his right eye and tapping the right side of his nose twice with the index finger of his right hand. 'Tell him I hope his headaches get better.

'Oh… before I forget… I know a bloke who lives in Portsmouth. He used to play a bit of chess now and then. Not any more though. He's getting on a bit. He got a right hiding years ago. Never been the same since. Mister McHale should look him up. His name's King. Harry King. Mea Culpa, Father. Time to go.'

With that, Arthur closed his eyes and let his head roll forward to leave his chin resting on his chest. After a couple of seconds, he breathed in deep and let it out slowly. Then he sighed. Raised his head up. And opened his eyes.

David Black looked at Rice and blinked. 'Sorry, Stephen... I must have dozed off,' he said. 'That was very rude of me. What were we saying?'

'We were talking about Arthur.'

'Really? How much time have we got left?'

Rice looked at his watch. 'About ten minutes,' said apologetically.

'I have a favour to ask.'

'Of course.'

'Is there time for me to confess my sins?'

Rice smiled. 'There's always time for that,' he said.

Ten minutes later, the video feed to Broadmoor was cut and Rice sat in the chair, in the room deep under Winfield House, gathering his thoughts. He was about to get up, walk out the door, and re-join the others, when it opened and Drummond walked in.

'You get what you needed?' he asked.

Rice frowned. 'Maybe,' he said. 'One thing's for sure. He knows more about us than we think he does.'

'Black?'

'No. Arthur.'

'I don't think I like the sound of that,' said Drummond, grimacing. He was carrying a mug of coffee. It was half drunk.

He put it on a coaster on the table and stuffed his right hand in his right coat pocket. He pulled out a box of migraine tablets and Popped two out of a blister pack, then washed them down the hatch with a gulp of warm caffeine.

'How many do you get?' asked Rice. Nodding to the pack still in Drummond's hand.

'More of the little ones, less of the big ones,' said Drummond.

'Like McHale?'

Drummond shook his head once from side to side. 'From

what I understand, he gets them the other way around.'

Rice looked thoughtful.

The two left the room. Drummond went left, Rice went back into the team room across the corridor.

'Welcome back from the flip side,' said McHale. 'How was Arthur?'

'Cryptic. And surprisingly pleasant. He knows you play chess.'

'I don't think I like the sound of that.'

'That's what Drummond said.' The Jesuit walked over to the small table at the far end of the room. 'Is this coffee fresh?'

'About half an hour old, but still very drinkable,' said Kelly. All it needs is a little Southern Comfort. Or maybe a lot.'

'And he said something that could mean something just before he went to sleep and turned back into David Black.'

'How does that work?' said Toby.

'Black isn't aware of Arthur, although he has been told about him. Arthur, on the other hand, is fully aware of Black,' said McHale. He turned to Rice. 'So... what was the something he said?'

Rice closed his eyes and allowed his recall to kick in. 'He said he knew somebody in Portsmouth who played chess. He said he was getting on a bit and that he got a hiding years ago and he hasn't been right since. He said you should look him up and that his name was Harry King. That name mean anything to you?'

McHale did the thousand-yard stare while he opened up his memory files. He was like that for a good couple of minutes. Eventually he drew a blank.

Zilch. Nada. Zero. Not a bloody thing...

He recognised the name Larry King. But then so did millions of other folk who watched the eighty-something year old US TV and radio celebrity on Larry King Live on CNN. But no Harry.

'That was it?'

'No, there was the whole getting-to-know-you-again bit at the beginning. And then there was the other bit right at the end.'

'What other bit?'

'The bit where he said 'Mea Culpa, Father. Time to go' then he went to sleep.'

'Maybe he was just fucking with you,' said Kelly.

'I don't think so. It was like he said it as an 'oh and by the way' kinda thing. Like it was a last-minute thought. But I got the feeling it was probably the most important thing he wanted to say.'

McHale looked at the screen wall. 'MOTHER?'

'Yes, Mac?'

'Wow… what happened to Tom?' said McHale, who, by now, was way past the point of thinking that having a decent conversation with a machine was either a good or a bad thing.

A voice was a voice. If there was something thinking behind it, then there was nothing wrong with having a conversation with it. Or her. Or him.

'I like Mac better,' said MOTHER. 'Is that okay?'

McHale thought about it and smiled. 'Sure. It's okay.'

'Your question?'

'Right. Could you access your databank for all white males living in Portsmouth who are between the ages of fifty-five and seventy – and whose name is Harry King, or Harold King?'

Pause.

'Done. There are eighteen males who fit the search parameters. One is paraplegic. One is unsighted. Four are ex-Royal Navy. Two are retired. And the other ten are either married, single, or in a gay and loving relationship.'

'Out of the ten, how many live alone?'

'Four.'

'Okay. This one's a bit left field. How many of The Ghost's victims lived alone?'

Pause.

'All six.'

'And how many of the six had Internet access and Facebook accounts?'

Pause.

'All of them.'

'And how many of them were registered as players with the Internet Chess site called Your Move?'

Pause.

'All of them.'

Toby was going to say 'Fuck', but he managed to keep his lips tightly shut.

'Good job. Can you list all eighteen with any contact details? And can you highlight those last four who lived alone.'

'I have emailed Daisy the list and copied you in. Details are also now on screen.'

Eighteen names, addresses, and telephone numbers appeared on the screen wall. There were colour photographs of all eighteen. Presumably either passport or driving licence mugshots.

They were all ordinary looking. There was nothing striking about any of them. Not one of them was very handsome. Not one was extremely ugly. They were all middle-of-the-road.

And not one of them bore any resemblance to the black and white photo of George Riemann that Dr. Hannah White showed them via satellite link from Quantico two days previously.

Not even the four highlighted.

The Ghost wasn't there.

It was 2.40pm.

A black-suited agent popped his head around the door. 'Hungry?' he said with a smile.

'I don't know about you guys, but I could eat a whole hog roast,' said Lightfoot.

'Bring it on,' said McHale. Nodding to the agent, who nodded back and disappeared.

Pause.

'So, either we didn't get the right Harry King,' said Toby, 'or Black really is fucking with us.'

'Or Harry King isn't The Ghost. He's the one The Ghost is hunting,' said Lightfoot, her gaze focussed on the screen wall.

'I like it,' said McHale. 'Keep going...'

'What if The Ghost needed someone to flush out his prey. Think about it. He's set himself a short timetable. Much shorter than he had with all the others. So, he doesn't have the luxury of taking his time to look for the right Harry King, if he wants to keep to his timetable.'

McHale could see where this was going. So could Kelly. She got up from her chair, grimaced, and grabbed her Diamondback. Then she started pacing slowly around the table, talking to everyone in general and herself in particular.

'Right... he's not a man who makes mistakes. He's a planner. He can't guess. He needs to be sure. So, what does he do... what does he do... what does he do,' she mumbled as she walked.

Lightfoot broke into her reverie. 'My great grandfather was a man called Yonaguska. He was born at the turn of the last century when the old Cherokee world was meeting the new one. He used to tell me stories about his father and grandfather hunting buffalo.

'Back then, the largest of the seven traditional Cherokee clans was known as Waya. Waya is the wolf. When they were hunting buffalo, my people would watch the wolves. And the wolves would watch for the weak and injured buffalo.

'Then the wolves would howl and the buffalo would get scared and try to escape. They would run but they ended up on their own with no other buffalo to help them. The hunters would talk to the wolves and take the buffalo. A weak buffalo on its own is an easy kill. It could put the rest of the herd in danger. Waya is a protector. It protects the future of the herd by leading the hunters to the injured and leaving the healthy. The hunters would make sure that enough meat was left for Waya.'

Lightfoot turned to McHale. 'The hunters are The Ghost. The wolves are you. The weak, lone Buffalo is Harry King. All you need to do is let The Ghost believe that you've found the right Harry King.'

Pause.

'You ever howl like a wolf, McHale?' said Kelly.

'I've squealed like a stuck pig a couple of times. But a wolf? No.'

'Hang on,' said Daisy, double-blinking, 'this is where I get to say something either really stupid or really brilliant.'

'Bugger me,' said inner voice, 'now she's bloody double-blinking, too. Damned thing's contagious. Maybe it's a disease or an affliction. Shit.'

Just then the door opened and two black-suited agents walked in carrying food and drinks. A large plate of sandwiches. Two flasks of coffee. And one large bottle of water.

'Hold that thought,' said McHale. I suggest we grab a bite and a slurp and reconvene in five minutes. Everyone okay with that?' There were nods of agreement all around. Even from Daisy, who had slammed on the brakes so hard, the airbag almost inflated.

She scribbled something quickly on her pad, then rose to grab a couple of sandwiches and some much-needed caffeine.

It was 3.10pm.

Eating was done on the hoof. Daisy's thought was bursting to get out into the room and mix it up with all the other thoughts.

'Okay… out with it,' said McHale

Daisy finished chewing a mouthful of chicken salad sandwich and swallowed. 'Well… what if Grace is right and we actually have found the real Harry King?'

Silence.

She had a good grip of her audience and she wasn't about to let go. Lightfoot turned to the screen wall where the eighteen Harry King photos were still visible.

'Maybe we were a bit too hasty in dismissing them,' said Daisy. 'MOTHER, I'd like another look. Close up this time. And can you do a split-screen? King photos on the right. And the head shot of George Riemann on the left. Bring up the King shots one at a time to compare with Riemann. Leave the highlighted four until last.'

Twenty seconds on each shot. They got to shot fifteen. Riemann cheese… everyone else chalk. Then they came to the last four.

Harry King. Aged 59. D.O.B. 3.7.1958.

Harold King. Aged 62. D.O.B. 17.10.1955.

Harold J. King. Aged 68. D.O.B. 14.4.1949.

Harold King. Aged 71. D.O.B. 9.12.1947.

Each one brought up in turn to sit next to Riemann. MOTHER left them up a little longer this time. Six brains. Six sets of eyes. Six gut reactions.

No. Maybe. No. No.

'Dammit,' said Kelly.

'Wait… go back to the second one,' said McHale.

The screen changed.

Harold King, aged 62, sat next to George Riemann, aged 36.

'Hold on that screen,' said Lightfoot.

Everyone got up from their chairs. Moved closer to the screen wall. Nothing was being said. Everything was being thought.

'Helluva good call, Daisy,' Lightfoot said softly, moving even closer to the screens. 'Now MOTHER… focus on the eyes. Big as you can get them.'

The pupils of King's eyes were different colours. Left eye brown. Right eye green.

So were Riemann's.

'Ghost eyes,' whispered Lightfoot.

'Pardon?' said McHale.

'Heterochromia. Different coloured irises. Some Native American cultures believe that people with different colour eyes can see into heaven and earth at the same time. They say these people have 'ghost eyes'.

'So, they've both got the same different coloured eyes?'

'Looks like it.'

'You can say 'fuck' now, Toby.'

Toby was grinning. 'Odd eyes like Bowie,' he said.

'No. Bowie's was the result of an accident. Think more Jane Seymour or Simon Pegg,' said Daisy.

Toby looked at her, surprised. She shrugged. 'My aunt Eileen had it, only the other way around. Left green, right brown,' she said.

'MOTHER, is Heterochromia inherited?' said Lightfoot.

Pause.

'Not always, but often,' said the voice from the screen wall.

'So, what we're saying here is that these two are father and son. That Harold King is really Thomas Halliwell and George Riemann is really Charles Halliwell, right?' said McHale.

He looked at the team.

'He killed the brother first and he's going to kill the father last. If it wasn't so monstrous it might almost be poetic.'

'What about those other poor buggers in between?' said Rice.

'Collateral damage,' said Kelly. Her thoughts were of little Ellie and Samantha Brasher, and the three members of her rescue team who saw Monday November 17, 2014. But didn't see Tuesday.

'And deflection,' said Lightfoot. 'It's 7-card street Monte. Find the Queen. Only there are two of them. And they're not Queens, they're Kings. And they're hidden in amongst all the other five. And even when you find them, you're not sure if they're the right Kings because all the other cards are Kings, too.'

'But we found them,' said Toby.

'Yes, we did. So why am I just waiting for the other shoe to drop,' said McHale. 'I better call Houston. Tell them we have lift off.'

He went to his jacket, fished out his mobile, and speed-dialled a number.

'How soon can you get in here?' he said. 'We know who The

Ghost is and we know who his next kill will be and where he is.'

'I'll be there in ten minutes,' said Drummond.

There was a collective sigh of relief in the room. Not because there was still a killer to catch, but because they now had him in their sights. He was no longer a stranger barely seen through the fog.

He had a face, a history and an MO; a signature, a voice and a personality; a target, a weapon and a timescale.

McHale couldn't remember the last time he'd had a decent sleep. Or even a half-decent one.

The bastard thugs were kicking the shit out of an old wheelie bin somewhere over his right eye.

'I have another thought,' said Lightfoot. 'What if Toby's right and Halliwell really is fucking with us? What if he's known all along who Harry is and where he was?'

'That's three thoughts,' said McHale.

He could feel his fingers tingling.

It was 4.20pm.

Chapter Twenty-Two

Friday, 11th August, 4.35pm - Twenty days to go

Drummond came through the door of the team's meeting room like his arse was on fire.

He was flushed and the energy was practically sparking off his fingertips. 'Nothing makes me fucking horny like the thought of catching a murderous bastard, Tom. Pardon my French, ladies. Tell me what you've got.'

McHale, with frequent interruptions and explanations from the rest of the team, brought Drummond up to date.

They went through the whole story from day one to the moment McHale called him in.

The murders. The knives. The call from White. The aliases. Angus, the unidentified body in Williamsburg. The discovery of Harry King and the link to Portsmouth. The link with the Sovereign's Orb. The connections to August 1st and September 1st. The chess game. Whether McHale's secret opponent was The Ghost.

The full Monty. From Aardvark to Zyzzyva and everywhere in between. Including all stops along the way.

At the end of the briefing, Drummond clapped his hands together and rubbed his palms vigorously. 'Right,' he said. 'I think we should take Molly Spencer up on her offer and send a team down to pick this King fella up. Bring him back here.'

'That would be a big mistake,' interrupted Lightfoot.

It didn't sound like she meant a probable mistake. It didn't even sound like she meant a possible one. This was a very definite one. An 'ignore if you want to end up with your gonads in a vice' sort if mistake.

'Holy fucking moly, Kemosabe,' said inner voice. 'I wouldn't like to come up against her when she's pissed off.'

By the look on Drummond's face, the interruption had the desired effect.

'If I didn't know how bloody good you are hunting these bastards, I might be inclined to tell you to shut the hell up and go with the flow,' he said. 'But I do know how bloody good you are. So, I'll shut the hell up instead.'

Then he smiled. Leaned against one of the walls. Folded his arms. Crossed his ankles… and said; 'Okay, you guys are in the driving seat. What now?'

Grace Lightfoot, almost-partner to Tom McHale, took over.

'Now I think we do everything from a distance,' she said. 'Charles Halliwell, or whatever he's calling himself, is a very careful, very meticulous guy.'

'He's also a bloody clever one,' said McHale. 'All we have to do is get to Harry before he does.'

Lightfoot continued, 'Remember… he's a background person. He doesn't like drawing attention to himself. He likes to blend in. Become part of the furniture. If you asked anyone who saw him what they remembered about him, they'd probably say he was an ordinary-looking guy. Neat. Polite. Quiet. Kept himself to himself.

'Another thing. When we catch him – and make no mistake we will catch him – don't be surprised to find that he's wearing contact lenses, with one lens coloured to correct the look of his Heterochromia. That's just another part of his MO.'

'Why didn't he wear them when he had his photograph taken,' asked Daisy.

'Because he's probably adapted his MO as time went on. He might have had the photo taken before he started killing. We don't know. It's a behavioural variable.

'I think it's also probably true to say that this next kill means more to him than even the first one. Those two kills are the only ones he cares about. I don't think he cares anything at all for the other five. But he does care about how we view them. His ability to get the better of us is very important to him.

'One thing probably scares him more than anything else, and that's the possibility of not being able to complete what he sees as his mission. The possibility that he might be found before he can do what he was meant to do.'

'And that is?' said Drummond.

'Kill the one man left alive responsible for the death of his mother.'

'Hang on... so he thinks Halliwell was the other one responsible for her death?'

'No. I think the other man responsible for her death was the first man he killed. The unidentified man in Williamsburg, Virginia.

'What... Angus?'

'I think Angus was Suzanne Halliwell's second husband, Victor Lomax.'

Drummond's eyebrows went up. 'You can prove that?'

'Nope. But I like it. It fits. It was the first part of the jigsaw. The last part is Harry King.'

Drummond double-blinked. Considered this new thought. Unfolded his arms. Stroked his chin with his right hand, then nodded. 'Okay... let's say I buy that.'

'Shit,' said inner voice. 'Another fucking double-blinker, Kemosabe!'

'What do you need from me?'

McHale had been sitting quietly throughout Lightfoot's analysis. Now he spoke.

'Two things,' he said. 'First, I need to have a little talk with Molly Spencer. We need a pair of solid undercovers. A pair that looks like a couple. We want them to sit on Harry King. No contact. Keep it all very quiet. We need them there now. And we need them armed.'

'Agreed. And second?'

'We need a car. Big enough to take all six of us.'

Pause.

'Portsmouth?'

'That's the plan,' said McHale.

'You sure you don't want more undercovers, just in case?'

McHale shook his head, looked around at the team. 'No. We're the ones doing the hunting this time. We don't want any conventional cops getting in our way.'

Drummond frowned. 'Suit yourself,' he said. 'Just don't forget. He's a clever bastard.'

McHale smiled. 'We've got some clever bastards of our own.'

Toby's smile widened. His enthusiasm was infectious. It was also dangerous.

'Down, boy. You get to go out to catch a killer. Plain and simple. No glory. No fun in that. You're just doing your job. This is why your sheriff gave you a nice, shiny badge and God, in all his wisdom, gave you a nice sneaky brain,' said Lightfoot.

McHale caught Kelly rubbing her left thigh. She was mentally counting out her supply of Vicodin 357 tabs. She returned his look, pain on her face.

Thank God she had access to scheduled 2 narcotics that were blistered. Not many were. She had good friends in high places.

Kelly visualised her supply. Ten tabs in a blister strip. Five strips a box. Four boxes in her case. One strip in her bag. Four tabs down. Two left for tonight. Four left for the morning. Total... 176 tabs left.

Best case scenario: six tabs a day. Twenty-nine-days-supply left. Worst case scenario: eight tabs a day. Twenty-two-days-supply left. Hope for the best. Plan for the worst.

She forced a smile. 'We'll catch him before I need to re-stock,' she said.

He nodded. 'MOTHER, how long is the drive from here to

Portsmouth,' he said.

'About three hours, depending on traffic and comfort breaks. But don't quote me on that.'

Pause.

'We leave tomorrow afternoon. That okay with everyone?'

He got nods all around.

He turned to Drummond. 'Daisy will be driving. Can your people sort out the paperwork and the car?'

'And if possible, make it one of those MPVs. And make it black. And make it dirty and uncared for,' said Lightfoot.

Drummond frowned.

'We need a good night car that doesn't stand out and won't look nice and neat and clean. Halliwell likes nice and neat and clean. We don't want him to look twice at it. In fact, we don't want him to look at it at all. He likes to blend in. So that's just what we'll do.'

'Weapons?'

McHale thought a couple of heartbeats. 'Have a word with Molly Spencer. We'll need three Glock 17s. Three clips each. Three belt holsters. Two right, one left.' He looked at Lightfoot and Kelly. 'I presume that's not a problem for you two?'

'Bring it on,' said Lightfoot, grimly.

'Ditto,' said Kelly. McHale thought she looked like someone who was coming awake after a long time asleep. Her eyes were narrow and filled with a sense of purpose.

He looked at Toby and Daisy. 'Sorry guys. No big boy's toys for you.' Stephen Rice wasn't even in the running. McHale figured that the Jesuit had more firepower on his side than mere man-made 9mm ammunition.

Toby and Daisy looked relieved. No firearms experience equals no skill. No skill equals no gun. No way, Jose.

It was 6.10pm.

Drummond shook everyone's hand and nodded to McHale. 'You'll have everything you need, firepower and stab-proof vests, by lunchtime tomorrow.'

McHale nodded back and watched as the senior policeman left the room to arrange their supplies.

He turned to Daisy. 'I need you to find us a hotel in Portsmouth. Six rooms. All together if possible. If not, at least all on the same floor. If not, then we'll take pot luck. Try for the same price as the Wellesley. Book it for seven days and we'll take it from there. Text me when you've done it.'

They went back to the Wellesley Hotel where dinner was a muted affair. Full of private thoughts and long silences.

Daisy disappeared upstairs to track down hotel rooms. Before they hit their various sacks about 11.00pm, McHale took the others into the hotel bar and had the barman line up six shot glasses full of Southern Comfort. The extra one was for the absent Daisy. Then he doled them out and offered up a toast. Like pouring every sailor a tot of rum just before a navy battle. Lightfoot drank Daisy's.

'May you be in Heaven half an hour before the Devil knows you're dead,' he said. Then he emptied his glass in one gulp and slammed it down on the bar top. The others followed suit.

'Nice toast,' said Lightfoot, smiling.

'Old Irish saying,' said McHale.

Before they could turn to go, Lightfoot had asked the barman to refill their glasses. The extra one was given to Kelly. Then she raised hers and said: 'With all things, and in all things, we are relatives.' Then she emptied her glass in one gulp and, like before, slammed it down on the bar top. The others did the same.

'Old Cherokee saying?' said McHale.

'Sioux,' said Lightfoot. 'We share lots.'

When they left the bar behind it was 10.55pm.

As far as McHale knew, Lightfoot took a taxi back to Winfield House.

As far as Lightfoot was concerned, she left a lot later.

In his room, McHale dug out Molly Spencer's card and

dialled.

Two rings.

'Hello,' said Spencer.

'I presume this line is secure,' he said.

'Always,' she said. 'I presume this is the favour.'

The call lasted ten minutes.

Then McHale had a shower.

And Spencer had a think.

And wheels were set in motion.

Chapter Twenty-Three

Saturday, 12th August, 6.30am – Nineteen days to go

Keith Richards came on, and fifteen memorable guitar riff seconds of Jumpin' Jack Flash later, the hunt for the Ghost hit the road. Well, nearly.

First the alarm suffered a healthy stab from McHale's hairy digit. Snooze cruise mode knew better than to argue.

Then, ten minutes later, with the bastard thugs jumping up and down to Jagger's scrawny vocals, McHale slung his legs over the side of the bed, reached for four paracetamol, and swigged them down with two large gulps of bottled water.

Waiting for the thugs to disappear before attempting any further movement was a pointless exercise. So, he ignored the pain and spent the next 30 minutes doing what a man's gotta do, which included putting his best head on, and getting ready for the road trip.

Halfway down to breakfast he realised the thugs had done a runner and a decent breakfast began to sound like a good idea.

He was first at their usual table. That in itself was another first. So, he ordered a Full English, gulped down a small glass full of squeezed orange juice, gave his taste buds a helluva shock, and seriously thought about mainlining caffeine.

Before the others joined him, inner voice popped in to say hello. 'Time to put the fucker away, Kemosabe,' he said. 'And I don't mean talk to him nicely and persuade him to slip on the handcuffs.'

One gulp of very warm black coffee later, the rest of the team showed up, almost as a bunch. All except Daisy, who was still upstairs, and Lightfoot who made it back to Winfield House at 2.00am and would meet them at the hotel after breakfast.

His eyes immediately went to Kelly and was relieved to see that the pain that was on her face the night before had backed off. She looked revitalised, energised, buzzing, anticipatory, almost as if breakfast would simply get in the way of what she was here to do... give the dead little Brasher twins some sort of payback. Even though it was by proxy. Even though nothing would ever bring them back. Even though she'd live with the guilt for the rest of her life.

Today felt like the start of the journey back from Hell. From now on, fucking up wasn't an option.

Toby was wearing the demeanour of a professional, yet unconventional, cop. His face was serious but his eyes told a different story. They were bright and excited. He was a member of an elite team hunting a monster, and what they did over the next nineteen days, if indeed it went that long, could earn them a million brownie points.

What wasn't to love?

Stephen Rice was wearing blue jeans and a casual blue shirt, open at the neck. McHale could just about make out the black rosary he wore around his neck, next to his skin. It was as if he wanted to get as far away as possible from the garb of a man of God.

Not that he could ever get away from God himself.

But at least he was smiling, and that was something. He looked behind him, expecting to see Daisy bringing up the rear.

Almost on cue, McHale's mobile 'pinged' and told him he'd received a text notification. It was from Daisy. Then all Hell broke loose.

The text said this;

'Shitstorm, Guv. The Ghost has made a move. September 1 is a bust. It's much sooner. See you in five. D.'

McHale could feel the enthusiasm drain away from his face like sink water down a plughole.

But something else took its place. The morning of the day he caught David Black in 2011, he woke up with a tingling in his toes. It quickly spread to his feet. Then his legs. Then his fingers started to tingle.

It hung around for about an hour then disappeared.

He thought it was just his nerves reacting to the arrival of the final act of his search for the priest. He found out the reality four weeks later when the tingling came back. Then the shocks. Then the numbness.

They came and went. Good days and not so good days.

Then he was diagnosed with CIDP. Then he started treatment. Then he got his life back.

Now, sitting at the breakfast table in the Wellesley Hotel in August 2017, he felt a tiny, vague tingle in the little toe of his left foot. That's where his CIDP had started. That digit was the bloody culprit.

Inner voice swore. 'Fuck's sake, Kemosabe. Get that fucking pinkie toe under control. No time for tingles. Pull your bloody finger out and readjust the plan.'

The tingle did as it was told. It buggered off.

McHale told the others about Daisy's text. But rather than deflate the mood, the news only seemed to brighten it. Now things were going to happen a damned sight faster than they thought. Thinking was still in the driving seat. But action was now an enthusiastic passenger up front.

Daisy joined them. She was travelling at a rate of knots, and she was pale-faced and carrying her laptop.

It was 8.45am

She waited until she sat down, and the hovering waitress had taken her order of black coffee. Nothing else. Then she opened the laptop, pressed a few keys, and was about to speak.

McHale's mobile 'pinged' again. It was a text from Lightfoot.

It said:

'Got the news. Be there in five. Locked and loaded.'

He turned to Daisy. 'Grace is nearly here. Take a breather, grab a drink, and you can brief us all together, okay?'

Daisy took a long, deep breath and nodded. Almost on cue, a fresh black coffee appeared on the table. She added a little water from a jug on the table then took a large gulp. The caffeine was warm and relaxing on the way down her throat.

Lightfoot appeared and sat down. She nodded to everyone. She was calm on the outside, but McHale suspected that on the inside, she was pumped as hell.

'Okay, you're on point, Daisy. Have at it,' he said.

Daisy took another gulp of coffee, then spoke.

'About half an hour ago, 3.45am their time, Quantico received an email. It was red-flagged the second it hit their server.' She looked at the laptop screen. 'The subject line of the email had the following five words:

'You won't win. Tick Tock.'

'I'll let you read the email content for yourselves.'

She swung around the screen so, with a bit of seating adjustment, everyone could read.

It had a message and a photograph.

The message had eighty-nine words. They were these;

'Hello again guys. This is The Holy Ghost. I see you've been busy looking for me. But your little band of hunters is a little band of losers. I'll get to the meat before you get to me. Number seven was always the big one.

'Meanwhile, I've decided to give you another chance. I know you miss our little conversations. So how about a puzzle. See if you can solve it before the big day. Here's a clue. It's not September 1 anymore. Tick tock, guys. Tick tock.'

Below the words was six sets of numbers, each set separated by three ellipses. The numbers were;

2011… 1876… 1534… 1998… 1057… 2017

And below the numbers was a JPEG file.

'Ready for this?' said Daisy.

'Open it,' said McHale, holding his breath.

The photo was taken with a telephoto lens. It showed the six team members, coming out of the main entrance of Winfield House.

'Holy fuck!' whispered Toby, saying aloud what most of the others were thinking.

Sometimes when you go hunting for monsters, they go hunting for you.

'I forwarded this to all your emails. We've got some thinking to do in the car.'

McHale looked at Daisy. 'Where is the car?'

'Half an hour out,' she said, looking at her mobile and looking at a text.

'Right. Everyone pack up and get ready to move. Daisy, sort things out with reception.'

'Already did,' she said. 'Drummond picked up the tab. We're good to go. Everyone meet in reception at 9.45.'

He looked at Lightfoot. 'You got everything you need?'

'What you see is what you get. How do you think I got my name?'

They all finished off their breakfasts, which were more liquids than solids, and disappeared upstairs to pack up their gear.

When McHale got to his room it was just after 9.30am.

Inner voice yelled at him; 'Bloody hell... it's chess time! Make your damned move, Kemosabe.'

McHale fired up his laptop, went to the chess programme, looked at the board, and made the next move in Fischer's winning game. Bishop to e3.

Within about a minute, Arnie GM responded, Knight to f6.

Right, you bastard, he thought. Time to find out if you take the bait. There was a section in the game page where players could comment on their moves, or congratulate a winning opponent.

McHale decided to take a chance. He had to be careful, so his comment needed to be innocuous, interesting and friendly.

His mind went to the subject text in the email Daisy showed them. The one sent to Quantico early that morning saying, 'You won't win. Tick tock.'

Was this a veiled prediction about the chess game? Was The Ghost really Arnie GM?

Coincidences mean you're on the right track.

He typed in; 'I have a friend who calls this the Sicilian Kan. I've always called it the Paulsen.'

Again, fast reply.

No hesitation.

'I prefer Paulsen. Better thinker,' said Arnie GM.

McHale smiled and closed his laptop. Twenty-three hours to his next move. He went downstairs.

The Wellesley Hotel had a good-sized underground car park. At 10.00am the six-strong team was in it, standing next to a black Citroen Grand C4 Picasso. Seven-seater, 2 litre turbo-diesel. It was a big, nifty, six-speed automatic that hadn't seen the inside of a carwash in a month.

Most onlookers hadn't seen the inside of the C4, due to the darkened windows in the rear and on the tailgate.

The fact that it was somebody's MPV of the year in 2017 didn't matter a monkey's wank.

It was dark, nippy, roomy, in great condition, dirty, and obviously not an 'official' car for anyone. This made it ideal for the team, and invisible to The Ghost.

Parked next to it was a Met unmarked pool car with a woman sat in the driving seat.

A tall, well-built man was standing at the rear of the pool car and the boot was open. He had just opened a very large black nylon holdall and was showing the contents to McHale.

The car park was half full or, as McHale preferred for the handover, half empty. There were no onlookers.

The holdall contained three Glock 17s. Three clips each. Each clip holding 17 rounds of 9x19mm Parabellum ammunition. Three belt holsters. Six stab vests. And, by special request of one very dangerous ex-member of the Homeland Security Shadow Wolves unit, one black Ka-Bar combat knife. Seven inches of partially serrated, double-edged, fixed blade. Synthetic rubber grip. Lightfoot's favourite close quarter friend.

'You one of Molly Spencer's boys?' said McHale.

The man smiled. 'Everyone's one of Molly's boys,' he said. 'And now I think you are too.'

'Think again,' McHale said. He nodded once lifting the tactical goody bag out of the car boot while Toby lifted up the C4 tailgate, and McHale stuffed it in alongside everyone's gear. It was a tight fit.

At 10.15am they hit the road.

On-board navigation told them to head for Portsmouth via the A3, through Guildford. Satellite technology told them it was faster than the M3 motorway.

They would be there in about two and a half hours.

But London was London. And Saturday was Saturday. So, all bets were off.

Daisy made a good wheelman. She and the Sat-Nav immediately bonded. The others fired up their laptops.

'By the way, when you need them, all the laptop and phone chargers are in my case,' said Daisy to anyone listening.

McHale, sitting in the front passenger seat, turned to Toby two rows behind. 'Toby... switch on your mathematical mojo and see if you can figure out what those numbers in the email mean.'

'On it, Guv,' said the soft Scottish voice from the rear.

'Everyone else... have a good look at that email message,' said McHale, and he brought it up on his screen.

The eighty-nine words stared at him. He ignored the numbers.

'Hello again, guys. This is The Holy Ghost. I see you've been busy looking for me. But your little band of hunters is a little band of losers. I'll get to the meat before you get to me. Number seven was always the big one.

'Meanwhile, I've decided to give you another chance. I know you miss our little conversations. So how about a puzzle. See if you can solve it before the big day. Here's a clue. It's not September 1st any more. Tick tock, guys. Tick tock.'

'Who wants music, who wants silence,' said Daisy.

'I like silence outside my head when I'm trying to be noisy inside it,' said Kelly.

Everyone else was busy with the eighty-nine words, so music was conveniently forgotten about.

'He wants us to know that, whatever we do, he'll win and we'll lose. He's feeling very sure of himself. Almost cocky,' said Rice. 'It's like he's saying, "You can try as hard as you like, you'll never be as clever as me. I'll outsmart you all".'

'And there's the photograph,' said Lightfoot. 'That's him saying he knows every move we make. He's saying that wherever we are, he can get to us. He knows everywhere we go.

'I don't think anyone has come this close to catching him before. And maybe the thought of that excites him.'

'You mean he got bored of everyone failing to catch him after all the other kills?' said Daisy.

'I think he has his audience,' said McHale. 'One that's listening to every word he says. Maybe for the first time. And we're not only listening to what he says... we're acting on it.'

'If I didn't know any better, I'd think he was bugging us. He seems very interested in the team. You think he knows more about us than just what we look like?' asked Toby.

'I thought you were trying to figure out what those numbers meant,' said McHale.

'I was. I mean, I am. I get the feeling that there's something I'm missing. Something about the photograph. It's like it's staring me in the face and I can't bloody see it for looking.'

McHale, Lightfoot, and Kelly immediately clicked on the

JPEG photo and stared at the image of the team coming out of the front entrance of Winfield House two days previously. The photo was colour and good quality. It was probably taken when they went outside to sit in the sun and read MOTHER's background info on the Halliwell family.

The fact that a Halliwell had probably taken the photo was an irony not lost on any of them.

On the surface, it was just a shot of a group of six people leaving a building and walking out into the sunshine.

McHale was at the front, along with Lightfoot. Then came Rice and Kelly. Then Toby and Daisy. Three couples. But not by design. More by accident. More because that's just how they walked out.

But McHale knew that when it came to body language, and physical or intellectual attraction, or conversational interest, the dynamics of human interaction was totally predictable one minute, and completely unpredictable the next.

So why the team came out the way they did was anyone's guess.

But the inescapable fact was that the first two out were the two most skilled hunters. And the last two out were the most junior members. And the middle two out were the man of God and the woman who had lost her faith.

Coincidences mean you're on the right track.

'Is it anything to do with numbers?' asked Daisy.

Both eyes on the road. Hands at ten and two. Doing forty-five in a fifty zone. Time: 10.40am.

'What d'you mean?' said Toby.

'Well, when I saw the photo this morning, the first thing I noticed that it wasn't just a group of six people, it was three groups of two,' said Daisy.

'YES! That's what it was,' shouted Toby. Too loud even for a soft Scottish voice in a confined space. 'It wasn't the people; it was the groupings. Nice one Daisy!'

'No problemo, Numbers Boy,' she said. 'Everybody's mojo needs a little help now and then. So... what does it all mean?'

'Haven't the foggiest. Yet. The only thing I do know for sure is that there were six people in that photograph. And there are six groups of numbers. So, they must be connected somehow.'

The next fifteen minutes was spent in silent contemplation.

This feels like the 7th cavalry riding to the rescue, thought McHale.

Or maybe it feels more like a last-ditch attempt by six very intelligent minds to make sense of a stack of words and numbers, while sitting in a small space, travelling at a fairly high speed, in an attempt to stop one very smart human being from killing another in a particularly gruesome manner.

That was probably nearer the mark.

The 7th cavalry, after all, was slaughtered to a man at the battle of Little Bighorn. The dashing George Armstrong Custer dying heroically surrounded by his fallen men. Or at least that was the romantic version of history. The truth was no doubt somewhat different.

Cue another greedy white man re-writing history at the expense of the indigenous population.

What was the name of the 7th cavalry's marching tune again? Gary something, he thought.

He brutally reigned in his imagination and got back to the task at hand.

'Hang on a minute,' said Toby, slowly. 'That last set of numbers, 2017... that's this year. Two thousand and seventeen, right?'

'Um... yeah?'

'Maybe the others are?'

'Are what?' said McHale, his mind only half on numbers. 'Keep counting.'

'Well... if one set is a year, what if they're all years?' His fingers were dancing across the keyboard of his laptop. The tip of his tongue peeking out from between his lips like a mole poking its nose up from a hole in a lush green lawn.

'You think he's been keeping an eye on us all along?' said

Rice. 'I don't think I like the sound of that. I thought we were tracking him, instead of the other way around.'

'He'd be disappointed if we weren't tracking him,' said Lightfoot. 'So, he'll be tracking us, too. It's all part of the game. The trick is to let him think that he can out-think us.'

'Absolutely. We find Harry, then he kills him right under our noses. He wins. We lose. His ego won't accept any other outcome.'

'Doesn't that ring any alarm bells with you?' said the Jesuit. 'Aren't we just playing his game?'

Silence.

'I think it's time for a road trip story,' said Lightfoot.

Rice frowned and shook his head, looking down at the words on Kelly's screen.

But the suggestion got a couple of cheers. Road trip songs were par for the course. Road trip stories were few and far between. Especially for people with death on their minds.

Lightfoot took a swig of bottled water that had lost its coolness in the increasing warmth of the late morning. 'Okay,' she said. 'I'll tell it using the words that my great grandfather used to tell it to me.'

'There's an old story about a large white wolf who was being tracked by a band of hunters. The hunters wanted to kill the wolf because he was attacking and killing too many deer. Not because he was hungry and wanted to eat his share, which the tribe would have been fine with. But because he had a devil inside him and the devil killed again and again, just for the pleasure of taking lives.

'So, they spoke amongst themselves and they decided that the wolf, whose name was Unega, had to be killed.

'They hunted him for five days. But Unega always kept ahead of them. No matter how smart they were, he was always smarter.

'One time, he doubled-back and came up behind them in the night, and took one of their young hunters and ate his heart.

'Then one of the four remaining hunters did a clever thing.'

She was interrupted by Kelly, who had dug into her bag and was in the process of handing out road trip Jelly Beans. McHale's eyebrows automatically went up. A gesture like that seemed out of character for the damaged, guilt-ridden cop.

Nobody refused a baby except Lightfoot. Storytellers needed a mouth that was only busy with words. She continued.

'Then one of the hunters did a clever thing. He walked out alone on the fifth night. Rubbed the scat of a female wolf into his skin. Knelt down on all fours and howled at the moon. The sound was sad and lonely and the wind carried it to the ears of Unega.

'The howl made Unega forget about the hunt and about the devil inside of him, and he came to see if he could help the other wolf.

'Then when he came close, the hunter jumped up and killed Unega with a single arrow.

'As he lay dying, Unega said—'

'Shit!' interrupted Toby.

'What? The wolf said shit?' said Daisy.

'No... no... I mean, I think I might have figured out something.'

'Can't it wait until the story's over?'

McHale pulled rank. 'Sorry. The story can wait. This can't. Out with it.' He glanced at the Satnav. They had just passed Guildford and the traffic was building up.

Roadworks ahead.

The holidaying public was heading to the south coast.

The working public was making life difficult for them.

'Well,' said Toby, 'we've got a photo with six people. And we've got six sets of numbers that could be years. And we've got six murders and six knives and six weird lines written in six bibles. Anybody up for some wild guesswork?'

'One day you just might make a reasonable tracker,' said Lightfoot. 'Go ahead. Connect the dots.'

'Everybody knows I like numbers. Not everybody knows I also like history. Every now and then, just to pass the time, I dip into a website called BrainyHistory. It has over two-thousand years of significant events in human history, and shoves them on the Internet so people can browse them over a cup of coffee.'

'Long story short, Toby,' said McHale.

'That's exactly what it is. Just a couple of lines for each event. But overall, it gives you the big picture of human development.' Toby grabbed a bottled water and took a slug.

'So... what if we took the order of the team in the photo, coming out of Winfield House, and matched them up to the order of the years? So, for instance, 2011 was you, Guv. Then 1876 was Lightfoot. Then 1534 was you, Father. Then 1998 was Kelly. Then 1057 was me. Then 2017 was Daisy.'

The traffic outside had come to a standstill. Up ahead, McHale could see temporary lights and roadworks that told their own story of a lane out of action. Inner voice whispered; 'Okay, Kemosabe. What bloody happened to you in 2011? Pick a date. Don't show it to me. I know you know this one. You can't phone a friend. You have thirty seconds starting from now!'

McHale drew a blank.

Three hundred and sixty-five days in a year. What happened on one day six years ago wasn't just a big ask. It was like watching water spill through his fingers. Even time in the past didn't like to stand in one place for too long.

'Tom,' said Rice softly, 'wasn't 2011 the year you caught Black... or rather, Arthur?'

Click.

McHale went back in time to an old Volvo estate parked outside St. Margaret's Catholic Church in Macclesfield. Black sitting in the driver's seat. McHale and six armed men standing next to the car. Weapons drawn. A look of fear and confusion on the priest's face.

Pause.

'So… let's take another year,' said Toby, turning to Lightfoot. 'What about 1876?'

Lightfoot closed her eyes.

'A bit before my time,' she said. 'But…' and she took a deep breath, opened her eyes, took an open laptop from McHale, logged into the net. And looked for significant events in 1876.

Outside, the traffic had started moving again and they were now only a hundred yards or so from the lights.

Toby and Kelly were also looking.

'This is a bit off the wall,' said Kelly. 'But in 1876, the US government removed the Oglala Lakota Sioux Indians from the Black Hills in Dakota after gold was found. Is that a significant event?'

'Well… it was for them,' said Lightfoot.

'Fuck…' said Toby, softly.

'That can be your new favourite word,' said McHale. 'What about you, Stephen? What does 1534 mean to you?'

Rice double blinked. 'Every Jesuit knows that. It was the year the Society of Jesuits was formed by Ignatius Loyola.' Pause.

Lightfoot spoke as if she was talking to The Ghost. 'Very clever, Charles. Very, very clever.'

'1998 Siobhan?' said Toby.

'I'm still looking,' she said. Then she cursed. 'Shit. The bastard. The evil fucking bastard.' She spat the last three words out as if they were poison on her tongue.

'What?' said McHale.

'Omagh. The Omagh bombing. Worst ever terrorist incident in the history of the troubles. Killed twenty-nine. Injured two-hundred and twenty.'

She closed her eyes and pressed her back harder in her seat. She thought of the Brasher twins. They weren't Irish. But one of the twenty-nine killed in the bomb was a woman pregnant with twins. That was close enough.

'Toby?'

'You know, the first time I came across my namesake was in secondary school when we read Shakespeare. I thought it was a cool coincidence. For a short while I was a star amongst my classmates. From then on, the year 1057 was tattooed on the surface of my prefrontal cortex. The year Macbeth was killed in battle by Macduff.'

'Your name's Macbeth?' said a surprised Kelly.

'It's a curse,' said Toby, shrugging.

They all looked at their wheelman. The only one left without a personal connection to the year 2017. 'How the hell can I look at anything except the road?' she said.

'Guv?' said Toby.

He said it quietly at first. Then louder.

Everyone went quiet.

'I know your birthday, Daisy,' he said. 'Don't ask me how I know, I just do. Tell everyone else when it is.'

Pause.

'August 15,' she said. 'Why?'

'Because that's when Macbeth died.'

Silence as fingers checked August 15 against all the six events. The date was the common denominator.

They had it. That was the date of Halliwell's final kill.

'Toby, you're a bloody genius,' said McHale.

'Possibly an apprentice genius,' said Rice.

Toby blushed.

Daisy felt something she hadn't felt before. She wasn't sure how to deal with it. So, she decided to put it on the back burner and deal with it later.

About forty-five minutes out of Portsmouth, the bastard thugs put in an appearance. This time they brought Mister Queasy with them. Ever since the CIDP came knocking, his time behind the wheel had been slashed by about fifty per-cent. It was a voluntary choice. He had been tested by the best police drivers in the country and was declared fit for duty.

The problem wasn't the hands or the legs. They were fine.

The problem was he liked being driven about by others, leaving him time to wrap his mind around what he did best. Catching people. Locking them up and throwing away the keys was up to other folk.

Mister Queasy always popped in to say hello whenever he was in the passenger seat reading something.

The action of his eyes going from side to side was somehow incompatible to the action of the car going forward or going around bends or turning corners. Add a hot day and bastard thugs into the equation and the result was a recipe for throwing up on the side of the road and looking a bit on the white side.

Luckily, they drew in and parked about fifty yards from a café. A black coffee, six paracetamols, and thirty minutes later, they were able to resume their journey. Windows partially open.

Not for the first time in his dealings with CIDP, McHale felt like a bit of a wuss.

Inner voice tried empathy. 'Extract the digit, Puke Boy! Tell the bastard thugs to fuck off and get some food down yer throat. You'll be fine.'

Half an hour later, they hit the outskirts of Portsmouth. Another half an hour after that, they drew up in the parking lot behind a hotel called The Mary Rose. About a mile or so away from the purpose-built museum that was the final resting place for the sixteenth-century flagship of King Henry VIII's navy.

It was an older, refurbished and renamed hotel with a brand-new block of rooms at the rear.

Toby nearly said it was ship shape. Good sense stepped in and zipped his lips for him.

'You arranged this last night?' said McHale, impressed.

'Drummond came up trumps again,' said Daisy, smiling. 'Somebody in the Met called somebody in the Hampshire Constabulary and strings were pulled. We're here for a week. Six rooms. I don't know what condition they're in. Don't ask how many palms were greased or favours were promised. They even threw in food.

As if on cue, McHale's stomach rumbled. As if in sympathy, so did Kelly's.

'I guess they have a good relationship with anyone in a blue uniform.'

'I guess they have a good relationship with anyone taking a serial killer off the streets of Portsmouth,' said Kelly.

Daisy checked everyone in at reception and McHale, standing nearby, noticed that the receptionist was almost overly helpful. Rather than let them find their own way to the rooms, she arranged for someone to be their guide.

As McHale suspected, the rooms were in the new block to the rear of the hotel. Rooms 80 to 86 on the ground floor. Next to the fire escape.

They were small, they were single, and they were clean and brand spanking new. Nicely done, Drummond, thought McHale. Very nicely done.

Five minutes after walking through the door of his room, his mobile rang. No lyrics. No music. Just the sound of an old telephone. He imagined it coming from a heavy black Bakelite phone with a silver circular dial and coiled cord. Classic never grows old.

It was Alice.

He smiled. 'People will talk.'

'How's Daisy holding up?'

'I'm thinking of asking her to change her name to Alice. You think she might go for it?'

Alice laughed out loud. 'Good to hear.' Pause.

'You be careful down there,' she said.

'That's the plan. See you soon.'

Alice killed the call. McHale looked at his watch. It was 3.38pm.

So much for two and a half hours to Portsmouth.

Chapter Twenty-Four

Saturday, 12th August, 3.50pm

McHale had been standing under a hot shower in Room 80 in The Mary Rose Hotel for five minutes, trying to figure out what was wrong.

It wasn't that he minded being stuck in a metal box with five other people on a hot day for five or so hours. It wasn't that his head hurt and he felt nauseous for the last quarter of the journey. It wasn't even that, between them, the team was now closer than ever to catching Charles Halliwell, before he managed to kill his father.

Then it clicked.

What was wrong… what was really wrong… was AGNES.

AGNES was the loose end.

AGNES was the unknown.

AGNES was the name painted neatly in black on the back of the blue Lettera 32 Olivetti portable typewriter that Halliwell, a.k.a. George Riemann, a.k.a. The Holy Ghost, used to type the six letters sent to the BAU. One for each year from 2006 to 2011.

Each letter containing a single sentence followed by the name Fairbairn-Sykes.

Each sentence written in the front of a black, leather King James Bible, found in the left hands of six murder victims.

He had those sentences safely locked in his memory. They were; 'There are none so deaf as those who will not hear.'

'There are none so sorry as those who will not repent.'
'There are none so dumb as those who will not speak.'
'There are none so numb as those who will not feel.'
'There are none so dead as those who will not live.'

And he had the latest sentence in there too. The seventh one. The one also typed on AGNES. The one that said;

'There are none so hateful as those who will not love.'

He kept repeating the lines and the name AGNES over and over. As if by doing so, some kind of an answer would pop into his head.

Zilch.

Nada.

He decided it was time to lather up and emptied half a mini bottle of shower shampoo into his hair, and worked his way down his body until his skin and hair felt squeaky clean.

That, and another few minutes' hot rinse made every square inch of his body tired and crying out for sleep. But sleep, if it came at all, was at least six hours away.

Time was running out, and as Halliwell himself had said... tick tock, guys. Tick tock.

At 10.00pm in three-day's time, Harry King would be killed by his remaining twin son. Unless McHale and a favour from Molly Spencer decided otherwise.

So... no pressure.

He dried himself off, had a shave and a brush, and did what every girlfriend he'd ever had told him to do. Religiously. Moisturise, moisturise, moisturise.

He remembered one girlfriend who used to repeat; 'a moisturised skin is a happy skin' every morning in front of the bathroom mirror.

He grinned at the mental image that came with the words. Then he wrapped the towel around his waist, sat on the edge of his bed, and called Daisy.

She answered on the fifth ring. 'Sorry Guv... just out of the shower.'

'Too much information,' said McHale. 'You're a good wheelman. You did good today. You feeling okay?'

'Nothing a large steak and a good night's sleep wouldn't cure,' she said.

'Well, let's start with the former and put the latter on the back burner for a while. It's four-thirty now. Might be an idea if we grab a bite to eat in an hour or so, then have a look around. How does five-thirty in the restaurant with the gang sound?'

'Better than the butler in the library with the candlestick.'

Pause.

Laughter.

'Sounds good,' she eventually said. 'Want me to call the others?'

'I thought you'd never ask. Let me know if there are any no-shows.'

'Will do.'

McHale killed the call. It immediately sprang back to life.

'Did I ever tell you about Joseph Black,' said Lightfoot. 'He was a Lakota Sioux. His people live in South Dakota. He was my team leader when I was with the Shadow Wolf unit of Homeland Security.'

McHale knew that somewhere within the next few minutes there would be an important point to the story.

'When he was a boy Joseph had a dreamcatcher. It was small enough to fit in the palm of his hand. It was given to him by his father, who got it from his father, who got it from his father.

'Whoever held it was protected by the forces of good… and untouched by the forces of evil. Or so the story goes.'

McHale, like all good listeners, kept his mouth firmly shut.

'Anyway… when I left the unit, Joseph gave me his dreamcatcher. He said it would protect me when I went into battle.

'It's time to pass it on to someone else.'

Then she killed the line.

'Shit a brick, Kemosabe. I think you've just been nominated,' said inner voice.

But before McHale had the chance to look around the room for Lightfoot's dreamcatcher, his phone pinged. It was a text from Drummond. It was six words long. They were; 'How much time do we have?'

He replied immediately. 'Three days.'

His mobile rang. 'Fucking hell,' said Drummond. 'How did you figure that out?'

McHale mentally shrugged. 'Because we're a bloody good team, and we don't do conventional; we followed the breadcrumbs he left for us. We're pretty damned sure it's the 15th. We're just hoping he keeps to his 10.00pm timetable.'

'And if he doesn't?'

'The thought of pulling this off right under our noses even though we know the day, the place, and the time, will be absolutely irresistible to him.'

'You know it will be your arse and mine if he does pull it off.'

Which, in Drummond-speak, basically meant that McHale's would be the only arse hung out to dry.

'He's good. We're better,' said McHale.

Pause.

'Rooms okay?'

'Yeah. Nicely done, Guv,' he said.

'Bury the bastard,' said Drummond, and killed the line.

McHale spent the next five minutes looking around the room for the dreamcatcher. It was nowhere to be found. He began to think that maybe Lightfoot's gift, wherever it was, wasn't meant for him.

Bloody idiot.

He spent the next ten minutes unpacking his case, checking and sorting out his medication for the next night's infusion, and getting dressed. Beige chinos and a plain black XL t-shirt sounded about right. Looked about right, too.

It was only when he got to the bottom of the case that he came across a small, white envelope. On the envelope was written a sentence.

It wasn't his envelope. It wasn't his writing. They weren't his words.

The sentence was eleven words long. They could have belonged to the same family as the words written in each of the crime scene Bibles. The words were these;

'There are none so brave as those who will not surrender.'

Inside the envelope was a small, circular, object about two inches in diameter. A spider's web mesh with an edging wrapped in hair, with a hole at the centre of the web. It was ancient and it was beautiful.

Tied to it was an old leather lanyard.

McHale smiled, nodded in agreement with the line, and hung the lanyard around his neck. Under his t-shirt. The dreamcatcher settled perfectly on his chest. Next to his skin. It felt warm.

He left the room and went to meet the others.

Portsmouth was warmer than London. Even in the late afternoon. The forecast for the weather was hot and humid. The forecast for the investigation was unpredictable.

At 5.30pm the six of them made their way from the new hotel block through to the restaurant. The doors were open but the kitchen wasn't.

A black suited, white tied, man in his forties recognised Daisy from the reception when they checked in earlier, and he approached them smiling. Obviously, the word had spread that these were the people who had to be taken care of.

He introduced himself as George, told them he had set aside a table for them in a quiet area of the restaurant, and told them that meals would be ready to order from six onwards.

'By all means wait in the bar,' he said. 'Please enjoy a drink there with our compliments. Or, if you prefer, you can take your seats at the table and I'll bring your drinks in.'

McHale could see the bar from where they stood. It looked a little on the busy side.

Small talk only.

'We'll sit at the table,' he said.

The restaurant was mostly open plan. But there were two areas separated off from the main room. Their walls were mahogany-looking panelling halfway up and frosted glass the rest of the way. Each area was, in effect, a small, intimate, dining room with a table big enough to seat eight.

Perfect for the team.

Both were unoccupied.

McHale chose the one on the left. For a fleeting second, he wondered if people who were right-handed tended to choose things that the left side of their brains had more of an affinity for. And more control over.

The moment came and went as he walked through the room and entered the private dining area. It was warm, cosy, and gave them the kind of privacy that told prying eyes and ears to politely fuck off.

'You make your chess move this morning?' said Lightfoot. 'Forgot to ask.'

She didn't mention the dreamcatcher. Neither did he. There wasn't any need.

'Yeah, decided to leave him a little comment. Nothing too heavy. Just enough to let him suspect I know the game we're playing.'

'How long until your next move?'

'About nine in the morning. Probably just a few minutes before.'

George gave them five minutes to settle in then came and took their drinks order.

Lagers for McHale, Lightfoot, and Toby. Guinness for Rice. Chilled White wine spritzer for Daisy. And a diet Coke and ice for Kelly. All perfect for a warm summer evening.

The table was circular, and by accident not design, Kelly was on McHale's immediate right. During the settling-down chitchat, he leaned close and whispered, 'How's the leg?'

Without looking at him, she folded up the thumb and pinkie of her left hand, leaving three fingers outstretched, indicating three Vicodin 357s taken since first thing this morning. He gave a swift thumbs-up sign and a small smile. Today was a good day.

'You?' she whispered. He gave her a 'fifty-fifty' wiggle of his right hand.

Everyone has something broken somewhere, he thought. Whether it's on the inside, the outside, or both. We deal with it the best way we can. It is what it is.

Food orders were taken just after the kitchen officially opened. By about 6.30pm they were tucking into the kind of meals that put smiles on taste buds and stretches stomach linings.

In between chewing they managed the kind of conversation reserved for those who didn't give a damn about speaking with their mouths full.

McHale looked at Daisy. 'You got Harry King's place fed into the Satnav?'

Daisy looked at him and frowned. *Yeah, stupid question*, he thought.

'I think we should do a drive by later. Park up somewhere within sight but not too close. Only for ten minutes or so. Just to get a feel of the place. That okay with you?'

'All of us?' said Rice.

'I think so. It should be dark about nine. I think we should check it out at night first, then some of us can come by in the morning and see what the darkness hides.'

'You're not going to warn the bait?'

'Nope. Too risky.'

'Agreed,' said Lightfoot, after swallowing a well-chewed

mouthful of prime rib beef. 'By the way, do we know what happened to the pair of undercovers that are supposed to be here?'

McHale double blinked. Fished his mobile out of his pocket. Speed dialled Drummond.

Two rings.

'Do we have our undercovers in place?'

'That was my understanding,' said Drummond. 'I'll get back to you in five.'

McHale killed the call and frowned.

'What?' said Lightfoot.

'You ever get a funny feeling about something? Like an itch you can't scratch.'

'All the time,' said Lightfoot.

'Ditto,' said Kelly.

'Me too,' said McHale. 'And I've got one right now.'

'It's your 'Spidey Sense',' said Toby.

He smiled at the young cop, but there was no real humour in it. The itch was growing stronger.

His phone pinged.

A text from Drummond.

'No time to put undercovers in place tonight. Due there tomorrow. Fuck it!! You're on your own until the morning. Got problems of our own here. Holmes might have been hacked this afternoon. Supposed to be bloody un-hackable. We think somebody came in and sniffed around. Mind your back. Keep me informed. D.'

Coincidences mean you're on the right track. McHale thought of Molly Spencer.

It was 7.10pm.

George sent a waitress to remove the empty plates and came to take orders from the dessert menu. There were no takers. 'Any drinks from the bar?' he asked. Again, no takers.

The only drinks ordered were black coffees for everyone.

'Instant? Or the Real McCoy?'

Silly question. No contest.

McHale told the others about Drummond's text. The silence was deafening as everyone got busy with their own thoughts.

Eventually Kelly distilled all their thoughts into one sentence. 'So,' she said, 'now the bastard might have our details.'

'You think it's him?' said Toby.

'You think it's not?'

More silence.

'More coffee,' said McHale, and motioned to a nearby waitress.

'Here's a thought,' said Lightfoot. 'Maybe he just wants to make us think he hacked our details. Maybe this is just another one of his damned games.'

McHale considered this.

The coffees came.

Decision time.

'Maybe he did. Maybe he didn't. Nothing we can do about that now. We're not going to play his game. This is our game. So, we carry on as if Holmes is still secure. Okay?'

Nods all around.

For the next hour or so, before the night-time reconnaissance, they spoke about AGNES.

'I'm sure there's a link between AGNES and the seven lines Halliwell sent to the BAU. I don't know whether we're talking about a 'she' or an acronym. The name doesn't crop up anywhere in connection with The Ghost except on the back of the typewriter.'

'There's a Saint Agnes,' said Rice, burping loudly and then apologising profusely.

Laughter.

'Good manners in Bahrain. Bad manners in Japan,' said Toby.

'Saint Agnes, or Agnes of Rome, is the patron saint of chastity, gardeners, girls, engaged couples, rape survivors, and virgins.'

'How can anyone be the patron saint of engaged couples and virgins? Seems to me there's a conflict of interest,' said Kelly.'

More laughter.

Daisy had cleared a space in front of her on the table, and was busy surfing the net.

'There's a movie called Agnes of God, made in 1985, about a novice nun who gives birth without losing her virginity.'

She continued looking.

'Oh… this is good. How about Agnes Macphail. Another 'Mac'. She was the first woman ever elected to the Canadian House of Commons. Oh no, wait… she died in Toronto in 1954?'

More looking.

'How about Agnes Waterhouse. Executed for witchcraft in Essex in 1566?'

'What if AGNES isn't a she? What if it's an it?' said Kelly. 'People give names to all kinds of things.'

'I had a car called Max,' said Toby.

'And B.B. King named his Gibson guitars Lucille,' said McHale. Adding, 'I think we need a large brain.' He fished his mobile out of his pocket, pressed the speakerphone button, put the phone in the middle of the table and dialled a number.

One ring.

'Hello, Mac,' said MOTHER.

Toby's eyebrows rose up in one synchronised movement.

'Hello, MOTHER. Are you up to speed?'

'Fully. Daisy and I are in perfect sync. What she has on her laptop, I have in my databank.'

'Excellent. Can you check your databank for any reference to the name AGNES in connection to Thomas and Suzanne Halliwell, their sons Charles and James Halliwell, or any relations? Can you also include the names Georg Friedrich Bernard Riemann, George Riemann, and Victor Lomax? Can you make your search parameters between the years 1940 and 2017 and consider AGNES not only a Christian name, a product name, or a title, but also an acronym?'

'Sure. I'll send Daisy an email this evening and copy you in on it. If AGNES raises any red flags, I'll text Daisy with details.'

'Thank you.'

'You're welcome.'

McHale killed the call.

'You two need to get a room,' said Lightfoot.

'We're just very good friends.'

'That's how it always starts. Then before you know it, she'll be introducing you to her motherboard.'

Toby nearly choked on the last gulp of his coffee.

Later, when he looked back on it, McHale would remember every moment, every detail, of this meal. He couldn't pinpoint exactly when, but at some point, over the past week, they'd changed from being just a team of gifted, damaged individuals.

They were now the magnificent six plus one. And McHale's bastard thugs only had a vague idea who the bloody hell Yul Brynner was.

An hour and a half later, they were sitting in the C4. Parked on the opposite side of the road and a hundred yards away from the small semi-detached house where Harry King lived alone.

It was dark. There was a full moon. The street was tree-lined. There was a downstairs light on King's house. Harry was home. Or at least that was the impression.

The team was quiet. Watchful. Patient. The car was warm and crowded. Speaking was down to a minimum and they were as far away from the prying glare of the nearest streetlight as possible.

At 10.00pm, Lightfoot announced, 'I'm going for a walk.' She had brought with her a dark grey hooded top and, before she got out of the car, she pulled the hood over her head. She had on a black t-shirt, black tracksuit bottoms, and dark grey trainers.

Years of training with the FBI and with Homeland left her with a good appreciation of the dark corners of life. And being brought up amongst elders in a modern-day Cherokee tribe gave her a hatred of confined spaces and an almost uncanny expertise when it came to tracking all living creatures.

She could handle herself and almost anyone else unfortunate enough to come up against her.

She got out of the car. Closed the door slowly and quietly. Walked head down and unhurriedly in the direction of Harry King's house, away from the front of the car.

She looked for all the world like someone who belonged exactly where she was and knew exactly where she was going.

McHale watched her disappear into the night.

Ten minutes went by.

Twenty.

He looked at his watch. The luminous dial marked the growth of concern, not just the passage of time.

Then, around the twenty-five-minute mark, she surprised them all. Reappearing from the opposite direction behind the car.

She opened the door on the pavement side behind the front passenger seat, got in without saying a word, and quietly closed the door.

Then she spoke softly. Almost in a whisper.

'The curtains aren't drawn and there's somebody in the front room. Couldn't see who exactly but a guy for sure. TV is on. House next door has lights on downstairs and upstairs.

'And another thing. My Spidey Sense is acting up too, McHale. Something's got me itching. I couldn't see or hear anyone. Couldn't even smell anyone.'

'You think you got made?' said McHale.

Lightfoot shook her head with certainty. 'Nope. Seen? Maybe. Made? Not a chance.' It was warm in the car. The body heat of six adults persuaded her to unzip her fleece top and pull back the hood.

The warmth of her exercise burst into the car interior, raising the temperature by at least a smidgen of a degree.

The darkened windows didn't give away the fact that the metal box parked in the dark held hunters.

Toby whispered. 'Mind if we let a bit of fresh air in here,

Guv? I love the warmth but I think my oxygen level is seriously up the bloody creek.'

McHale lightly tapped Daisy's left forearm. Daisy pushed a button. The offside rear window behind her slid down an inch.

Just then McHale's mobile pinged. A text. Unknown number. It had eleven words. They were these;

'There are none so lost as those who will not find.'

'Shit!' McHale cursed. 'Another line.'

He showed the others the text.

He looked at Lightfoot. 'Did you get a good look at Harry?' She frowned.

Then the penny dropped.

In one smooth motion she opened the car door and, before McHale's trainers had even hit the pavement running, she was twenty yards in front of him, sprinting down the road in the direction of Harry King's house.

Glock drawn.

If he ever dreamed of being able to catch up to her, he quickly woke up. She stopped short of actually going onto the property and instead stood looking through the window into the living room.

Curtains still pulled back. TV still on. Only now there were two people in the room. One an elderly woman.

Something wasn't right. Harry King lived alone. He didn't have visitors.

They heard a screech of tyres behind them as the car containing Daisy, Kelly, Rice, and Toby, braked hard in front of the house.

Doors flung open. Bodies spewing out.

By the time they reached the garden gate, Lightfoot and McHale were at the front door, urgently hammering on wood.

McHale was just about to kick the door in, or at least try to, when a light went on in the hallway, and the door slowly opened.

Lightfoot quickly holstered the Glock and covered it up with her fleece top.

The face of an old, wrinkled, white-haired man appeared around the edge of the door. The rest of his body followed shortly afterwards.

He was about five-foot-eight tall. He looked suspicious and frightened.

McHale grabbed his mobile. Brought up the photo of sixty-two-year-old Harold King.

This wasn't him.

An old woman appeared behind him. Standing in the hallway at the entrance to the living room. 'Who is it, Bob?'

'I don't know,' said Bob, who suddenly decided that he would put on a brave face, even though the two strangers standing in front of him looked bigger and more frightening than he had ever looked in his life.

Then he saw the other four strangers, and his bravery evaporated.

The two at his door were breathless and worried looking. The man spoke first. He held up a wallet with a badge. 'I'm sorry to bother you, sir, but we're members of the Metropolitan Police. We're looking for Harry King.'

The woman smiled, which made Bob relax.

'My name is Detective Inspector Tom McHale,' said the man. 'It's very important that we speak to Harry King. We understand he lives here.'

'He did until yesterday morning,' said Bob. 'Then they came and took him away.'

'My name is Detective Inspector Grace Lightfoot,' said the woman, who looked quickly at the man and then back again to Bob. 'Who came, sir?'

Inner voice said, 'Oooh… liar liar pants on fire!'

'Buggered if we know,' said Bob. 'We only got moved in here this morning. We used to live in a flat. Too bloody high up.'

'The woman next door said two men came and took him

away. They said Harry had, oh what's it called, Margaret?' said Bob, turning to look at the woman behind him.

'Dementia,' said Margaret. She said it like she knew the word but didn't know the meaning.

'Where did they take him?' said McHale.

'Green Gables Nursing Home,' said Bob.

'We even got all his furniture,' said Margaret. 'Rubbish, most of it. We told that other man.'

'What other man?' said Lightfoot.

Bob sounded defensive. 'He said he was a policeman.'

'What did he look like?' said Lightfoot.

'We don't know,' said Bob. 'He phoned.'

Lightfoot's voice grew soft and friendly. 'How long ago was this?'

Bob relaxed. He smiled.

'About ten minutes,' he said, turning to Margaret, who thought, then nodded in agreement.

'You've been very helpful,' said a smiling McHale. 'Goodnight.' And he turned away from the door, Lightfoot following, joining up with the rest on the pavement.

Behind them, they heard the front door close.

As the team filled up the car, McHale fished out his mobile and speed-dialled MOTHER.

Two rings.

'Hello, Tom.'

He brought her up to speed.

'I need the fastest route to Green Gables Nursing home from our location,' he said.

'Send the location to all our mobiles, fast.'

'I don't do slow.'

All the mobiles pinged.

'Done. Tell Daisy to break the speed limit.'

McHale killed the call and turned to Daisy. 'Put Green Gables in the Sat-Nav. Harry's got Dementia. I don't know whether to feel sorry for him or happy. Even if he saw Halliwell again, he probably wouldn't know him from Adam. He probably has no idea whether he's coming or going, or how to look after himself. Poor bastard.'

Daisy programmed the Sat-Nav. 'Green Gables is just outside a place called Funtington, near Chichester. Clarice says it's 12.9 miles away. We can be there in twenty-four minutes. Give or take.'

'You've named the Sat-Nav Clarice?' said Lightfoot.

'I get it. This is one of those Silence of the Lambs moments, right?' said Toby.

Daisy shrugged, started the car, and left rubber on the side of the road outside Bob and Margaret's house.

It was 10.55pm.

They had three days left. Or twenty-four minutes, depending on your ability to sense impending danger.

The journey took them a gnat's whisker over nineteen minutes. The entrance gate was wide open. The MPV raced up the driveway and screeched to a halt eight feet from an open front door.

The porch light was on. The front door was kicked in. There were lights on inside.

This was the end game. No need for stealth. The Ghost had no plans beyond killing his final target. His father.

Lightfoot was first through the door, in a semi-crouch, making herself as small a target as possible. Two hands on her Glock. Eyes taking in everything in a single sweeping glance.

McHale, Rice and Kelly followed fast behind. McHale hissed 'Stay there,' to Daisy and Toby.

They did as they were told.

The home was as silent as a grave. No yells. No screams. No gunshots.

No people.

There was a closed door to the left, a carved banister next to the reception desk, with stairs going up, and a lit corridor to the right. Three doors either side.

All the doors were open. No lights inside.

Then a confused shout split the silence.

'Where is he?'

Then the voice grew to a scream. Full of anguish and anger. 'Where's Harry King?'

Then a man slowly walked out of the last darkened room on the right. Saw the team.

Glock in his left hand, pointed at the floor. Fairbairn-Sykes knife in his right. Pain and defiance on his face. He was looking straight at McHale.

'Where is he?'

McHale raised his gun and aimed it centre mass at Charles Halliwell. 'He's somewhere safe,' he said. 'And you'll never do to him what you did to the others.'

Halliwell looked at the team and saw guns pointed at him. In that split second, he knew there was no way out.

'It's over,' said McHale.

But it wasn't.

He was twenty-five feet, give or take, from the team who had tracked him down. Half a dozen steps from the people who had destroyed the final part of his plan.

He let out a snarl like an enraged wild animal and ran at them. Raising his gun and firing. Three times.

But his bullets didn't reach McHale.

Instead, they reached Kelly, who pitched herself sideways in front of McHale, shielding him with her body. The bullets hit her in the chest and she collapsed in a heap on top of McHale. Still breathing, but mortally wounded.

She wasn't wearing her bullet-proof vest.

Halliwell was still ten feet away when Lightfoot's bullets hit him.

He was five feet away when he sank to his knees, dropping

the Fairbairn-Sykes weapon in front of him.

He was ten seconds from Hell when Lightfoot screamed with rage, darted forward, picked up the dagger and in one swift movement, plunged it into the top of his head.

Halliwell's eyes rolled and blood poured from his nose and mouth.

Then he gasped, gurgled slowly, and died.

Behind them, Toby and Daisy had ignored McHale's order and had rushed in to join the rest of the team.

As they did so, Rice gently moved Kelly off McHale and laid her on the floor.

Her breathing was shallow and ragged.

The priest was leaning over her and mumbling softly. Then McHale, kneeling by the priest's side, realised he was praying.

He was also saying goodbye.

Lightfoot dropped to her knees by the side of the stricken Kelly. She had tears in her eyes. She bent down and clasped Kelly's right hand. Then she leaned forwards and kissed her gently on the lips.

Then Kelly sighed and smiled. It was the kind of smile that says, 'Job done.'

The kind of smile that appears when someone who doesn't deserve to be breathing the same air as normal, good folk, gets put down.

The kind of smile that carries with it forgiveness for not saving the lives of two small innocent girls and three colleagues who left behind wives and children.

It was also the kind of smile that says, 'I love you.'

Then Detective Inspector Siobhan Kelly, NCA, sighed, and slipped away.

Rice closed her eyelids gently with his fingertips, then made the sign of the cross on her forehead with the thumb of his right hand.

It was over. Kelly was gone. Halliwell was gone.

Everyone has a time for dying. This was theirs.

For some folk it's too soon. For others, not nearly soon enough.

The Ghost had been caught and some kind of justice had been dispensed. Not the kind that involved capture and handcuffs and courts and judgement and incarceration. Not even the kind that involved balancing scales and atonement and making right what had gone wrong years before.

This was the kind that involved taking out the trash, mourning a dead colleague, and living with the consequences.

Then McHale had some explaining to do.

He told them that, with the threat of Halliwell knowing their every move, he had to figure out a way of making him think he had the upper hand.

He told them about the favour he asked of Molly Spencer. That a soon-to-be-demolished Green Gables would have one last part to play in a trap to catch the deadly serial killer.

He told them that everyone... excluding himself and including Drummond... had to believe Harry had been taken to the nursing home and that's where Halliwell would find him.

In truth, he had been whisked away to a safe house, out of reach of the son he never really knew.

He also told them that a vital role of the trap was the part played by retired police officers, the elderly couple known as Bob and Margaret.

All the while they'd been sitting in the car outside Green Gables, while inside, a clean-up crew was hard at work.

He apologised for keeping them in the dark and waited for someone to speak. Lightfoot threw a Jelly Bean at him, breaking the tension, before she turned on the engine and drove home.

Epilogue

Mick Jagger sang You Can't Always Get What You Want into the morning air and McHale's hairy arm reached out from under the duvet.

For the first time in a long time, he cancelled the snooze cruise button. Then, instead of dragging himself out of bed and doing the ablute routine, he relaxed, rested his head back on the pillow and thought.

The last fortnight had come and gone in the blink of an eye. Maybe two blinks.

Losing Kelly was a punch in the gut that he never saw coming. He knew her a fortnight but it felt like years, and he still felt raw and angry. The funeral was in a week's time and the rest of the team would be there.

Even Lightfoot.

He never figured Lightfoot for the romantic type. Then again, he never figured her for the one person in the whole damned world who would hook up with Kelly.

Stephen Rice had promised to officiate at Kelly's funeral and McHale figured there probably wouldn't be a dry eye in the house.

After holding Daisy tight as Kelly lay dying, Toby decided that a very good friendship was worth cultivating. Where it went from there was anyone's guess.

Maybe nowhere. Maybe somewhere. Only time would tell.

When McHale looked for reasons why Kelly had thrown

herself in the path of the Ghost's bullets, he could only bring up an image of the Brasher twins. Before their lives were so cruelly destroyed.

One way or another, she had settled a debt. And in doing so, she also might have saved his life.

Drummond organised the clean-up. He handled the media storm, and he handled the aftermath.

Then, when the time was right, he asked McHale if he would be interested in forming his own unit. With his own team. Hunting the kind of killers that other folk didn't have much luck tracking down.

McHale said he'd think about it. As long as he could have a say in where the unit was based. Winfield House was mentioned.

The words; 'We're coming for you' slipped gently into his consciousness again. He couldn't think of a better description of the work the team did. And he couldn't think of a better way to remember Kelly.

The bastard thugs hadn't put in an appearance since Saturday. He figured that underneath their rowdy, punkish, yobbo exteriors, lay the hearts of unapologetic hooligans using reverse logic.

He figured that they wouldn't put in an appearance, on principle, if they knew that kicking off was exactly what he was expecting them to do. So as long as he didn't expect to have a headache, then they'd stay away.

He hadn't been expecting a headache for three days so far.

Just then his mobile pinged.

One email.

A notification from Arnie GM.

He double-blinked.

He logged onto his chess site and saw Arnie's message. It was forty-two words long. The words were these;

'Guess you knew this was the Fischer-Spassky game all along. Can't fool you. Fancy a proper game? We'll make this one a McHale-Arnie special. We'll just have time before I hop on the plane and visit my daughter and family in Ontario.'

He fired back a reply; 'e4. Enjoy Ontario.'

Then he closed his eyes.

Many questions remained unanswered long after the authorities closed the book on the hunt for The Holy Ghost.

But only three of those questions were large enough, and important enough, to warrant years of sleepless nights.

One... who was AGNES?

That question would probably develop a life all of its own. With imagination the only limit to the number of possible answers.

Two... how did Charles Halliwell choose his victims? The first, second, and last, were no brainers. But how he cherry-picked the other five remained a mystery. Almost.

The only things known for sure were, they were single, they lived alone, they played chess, they had internet access, they had Facebook accounts, they were Halliwell's victims, and they ended up very dead.

Five points on that list were also common to McHale.

It wasn't a comforting thought.

And three... how did Charles Halliwell manage to not only evade capture for the six years from 2012 to 2017, but also prove Dr. Edmond Locard wrong. And leave no trace evidence, or evidence of any kind, of his presence at any of the crime scenes?

Except for the murder weapons... and his voice.

In the aftermath of the murders there were many theories about how, in this case, the word impossible lost its first two letters.

If indeed it ever did.

Maybe the only reason evidence wasn't found was because those looking for it hadn't looked hard enough.

The only person who could have provided definitive answers to all those questions was buried in a small country cemetery in the South of England.

Not a million miles away from an empty nursing home, where he never had the chance to murder his father.

D.I. Tom McHale will return in another mystery.

Keep reading for an exclusive extract of
A House For Monsters **by Bryce Main:**

*We have always had our monsters. They live for the spilling of
our blood and exist in the darkest places of our soul.*

*They seek us out, sharp-fanged and grotesque in their shape.
Our only saviours are those who hunt.*

*Driven creatures who seek out our monsters with
harsh vengeance and unyielding determination.*

*To put them down and send them back to Hell.
Until the next one comes along…*

Prologue

Sometimes the difference between life and death is as simple and as final as a change of expression on the face of a middle-aged woman.

Sometimes seeing a face transform from a calm exterior into a twisted grotesque mask in a split second is persuasion enough to grab a large kitchen knife and plunge it ten times into the body of another human being. Before they decide to do the same to you.

It was just after 4.00am

It was Saturday August 17, 1991.

It was a small room in a small house in a town called Madan in the Smolyan Province, at the southern edge of Bulgaria. Not far from the northern Greek border.

In the room, a woman was lying awake in a double bed. Her husband was sitting on the other side of the bed, smoking a foul-smelling cigarette and drinking foul-tasting whisky. He was a bad sleeper, even when blind drunk.

The woman's hands were pressed over her ears. The medication she was taking and the voices she heard inside her head were helping to contort her facial muscles. The voices had been shouting at her all night.

They were telling her that she was shit. That she was ugly. That she was stupid, and that nobody in their right mind would want to love her.

One of the voices, a young man who had been hissing and growling at her non-stop for days, was beginning to scream.

'You're a fucking whore. You're a fat, ugly, fucking whore. Who could love you? Why don't you just kill yourself. Go to the bridge and jump off. Nobody wants you. Not your husband. Not your kids. Nobody! Everybody hates you. Go on. Piss off. Do it, you fucking bag of shit!'

He screamed it over and over and over again.

The woman's name was Svetlana Lazarov and she was fifty-five.

Poor, simple, uneducated, and overweight, she had brought three sons into the world, one of whom, Ivan, died at birth. He was the one they named but never mentioned again. Ever. The one they tried to banish from their memories, but never quite could.

And for as long as she could remember, Svetlana had suffered from schizophrenia.

She did the best she could to bring up her remaining family, but passed her condition on to Anton, the youngest of her surviving sons. The other son, Dragan, dodged that bullet. There was another one waiting for him, though. Further on up the road. That one wouldn't miss.

She was constantly terrified, depressed, confused, anti-social… and her grip on reality was unreliable and tenuous at the best of times.

Worst of all were the voices. Male, female, young, old, polite, scary, friendly, happy, and dangerous. Sometimes off and on. Other times twenty-four seven.

And worst of the voices was the hissing, growling, cursing, evil young man who called her a 'fucking whore.'

And then there was The Devil.

Svetlana also suffered from Tardive Dyskenesia. The condition was a side effect of the antipsychotic medications she took for her schizophrenia.

It made her body sometimes jerk and writhe uncontrollably. It made her grimace and stick out her tongue and smack her lips.

Her face would twist and contort and her husband, Radomir, would say she had The Devil inside her.

Radomir was a smelly pig of a man who was mean spirited and violent towards his wife and sons.

He was a paranoid schizophrenic who didn't suffer from TD and who came to believe that The Devil inside his wife was planning to kill him. So, that night, he came to a decision.

He went to the work shed behind the house and fetched his father's old bone-handled knife. The one he used to skin rabbits. It had a six-inch blade and it was razor sharp.

When he got back, Svetlana was still in bed, moaning and hitting the sides of her head repeatedly with her bunched-up fists. She was mumbling words Radomir didn't understand.

Then she suddenly stopped and looked up at him. Eyes wild, lips snarling, and lungs gasping for air.

That was when Radomir acted swiftly and, with the help of the bone-handled knife, separated Svetlana from himself, their sons, and her tragic life. Savagely and permanently.

But in doing so he made three big mistakes.

The first mistake was stabbing her ten times. Eight more than was necessary to result in her quick death. There was no coming back from the two stab wounds to the heart. All the others had nothing to do with murder and everything to do with fear and favouritism.

Radomir had no medical knowledge. He had very little general knowledge of any meaningful kind.

But in that moment, he knew six things.

He knew what an awful lot of blood looked like. He knew that Svetlana stopped breathing very quickly. He knew that ten was his favourite number. He knew that ten was also Anton's favourite number. He knew that Anton was his favourite son.

And he knew that the roar he felt in his throat was the roar of freedom.

The second mistake was wrapping the bloody body in bedsheets, dragging it to his battered old car, driving to a remote spot in a nearby forest, and burying Svetlana in a shallow grave. He buried her face-down to stop The Devil from escaping back into the world and seeking revenge on him. He learned this from his grandfather, who hung himself when Radomir was in his early teens.

But the third, and biggest, mistake was believing that neither of his sons, who were out for the night and would return the following day, would find out what he did.

So, he cleaned up the mess as best he could and waited for them to return home. And waited… and waited.

When they eventually did return, he blurted out the truth. He couldn't help himself. To his horror, the words came out of his mouth as if they had a will of their own.

He feared his sons would kill him. Or at least attack him. Even Anton. After all, they loved their mother. Not him.

But his sons were far more intelligent, and far more cunning, than their father ever imagined or gave them credit for. Or at least one of them was.

If anyone had cared to measure it, they would have seen that Anton had an IQ of about 150. Only ten less than Einstein. Between Anton's ears sat the brain of a warped, broken genius. And it was constantly up to no good.

He was the taller, and stronger, of the two sons, and bisecting his right eyebrow, giving him a cruel, dangerous look, was an old scar, a leftover from an argument with a broken beer glass in a barfight. The scar was two inches long and settled halfway down his cheekbone.

His sight was undamaged, but the wound merely served to place more emphasis on the peculiarity of his right eye.

Anton had Heterochromia.

His eyes were different colours. Left one dark brown, right one bright blue.

He was also a leader. Dragan, his older brother, was smaller and quieter. He followed where Anton led.

Dragan had always been proud of his brother's ability to say the right thing at the right time and in the right circumstance.

Hence, Radomir was fooled into believing that the boys understood what he did, understood why he did it, and understood that this was a family secret that could never be revealed.

So, the three got drunk that night and, after the sons persuaded Radomir to tell them where their mother was buried, they all made a pact never to speak of the deed again. If anyone asked where she was, they would say she had gone to stay with a friend in the northern town of Lukovit and they didn't know when she would be back.

And since the immediate family kept to themselves, had no friends, and had only distant relations, they were sure that no one would find anyone to answer any awkward questions. The deed would remain as buried as Svetlana.

Everybody lies.

When Dragan awoke the next morning, he found Anton curled up in a foetal position, fast asleep on the threadbare rug in front of the dying log fire, wearing only his underpants.

Radomir was gone. So was his large black travelling bag.

Dragan shook his younger, smarter brother awake, told him their father had left, and listened to what he had to say. Theirs was hero-worship of a different kind. He had always followed where the younger Anton led.

Anton told him to go immediately to the local police station. He reassured him everything would be fine. He was very persuasive.

He told him to say that his father, Radomir Lazarov, had confessed to killing his mother and burying her in a shallow grave in a nearby forest. Then, Radomir had run away.

The eldest son did as he was directed and told his story well. He looked suitably shocked and worried.

The police discovered Svetlana's body, buried face down where Dragan said it was, and they immediately issued an arrest warrant for Radomir, who was never found.

That night, while Anton slept, he dreamed he was in another man's body. And the other man was standing outside his house, in his back yard, looking at a black cat. And the cat was speaking to Anton in his mother's voice.

She said she was glad to be free of The Devil inside her at last.

She said the torment was like living in Hell every minute of every day. But she said that The Devil was also now free. Free to spread his evil throughout the world, and it was now up to her precious son to find him and stop him wherever he was.

She made him promise to hunt down The Devil.

So, Anton knelt down in a puddle in the wet yard and prayed to the Holy Virgin Mary. It was cold and moonless and the rain had just stopped falling. But like a good son, he did what his mother told him to do. Even though she looked like the cat from next door.

Svetlana said all this while sitting on the top of a stone wall slowly licking her fur clean. She would lick for a while. Then speak for a while. Then repeat the whole process over, and over, and over.

'How will I recognise The Devil,' he asked.

The cat blinked. 'His face will be twisted and he will want to kill you,' said Svetlana. 'So, you have to find him and kill him first. But the Devil is a liar with a hundred lives. Even if you kill him once, he will rise again. So, you have to hunt him down and kill him again and again until he has no lives left.'

'Where will I look?' he said.

'Everywhere,' she said.

She said that The Devil was now inside Radomir.

That's when he told her that Radomir was dead. That he had killed him to avenge her murder.

'Does Dragan know this?' she said.

'No,' he said. He kept his face as still and expressionless as possible.

'Good boy,' she said, licking her fur some more. 'Now… where did you put Radomir's body?'

'Under the logs in the woodshed,' said Anton. 'I have to find a better place.'

The cat looked at him and blinked slowly. And she told him about a clearing in a remote part of a nearby forest. She said it was the ideal size for the job he had to do.

'Then what?' he said.

That's when she told him about his mission.

And about his older brother Ivan.

That's when she told him that Ivan wasn't dead, that he lived inside him, and that they would always protect and take care of each other.

And that's when Anton, who had just killed for the first time, was born for the second time in his life. From now on, he would spend the rest of that life, hunting and killing the Lord of Hell.

Chapter One

The thing about prisons the world over is that most of the people put there probably deserve to be there. Many of the others are victims of a prison system that has nowhere else to put them. So, they get put where they don't fit and don't belong. And the folk who put them there don't look you in the eyes.

Some are victims of their own damned misfortune or stupidity for being in the wrong place at the wrong time.

An unlucky few simply fall between the cracks. They're completely innocent but, for one reason or another, have absolutely no believable way to prove it.

The vast majority of prisoners will keep their heads down, keep their noses clean, do their time, and walk out the front door. Some of them will be so scared shitless they'll never offend again. Others, once they get out, will happily repeat whatever they did that caused them to be banged up in the first place.

A small elite few, however, will never taste freedom in the outside world again. At least not as long as they have a pulse.

For this band of brothers (and sisters) there will be no parole. No redemption. No forgiveness. No rehabilitation. And sure-as-hell no release.

This is why most of us living on the outside of prisons sleep easier in our beds at night.

We place our trust in the long (and occasionally short) arm of the law to hunt those who need hunting. Punish those who need punishing, and put them in places where the sun doesn't reach, never mind shine.

317

Because for us, prisons are more than mere storage facilities. More than just warehouses of incarcerated flesh.

They're the places where we keep our monsters. At least the ones we know about. At least the ones we manage to catch.

It was Friday March 23, 2018.

It was 3.00pm.

It was Broadmoor high-security psychiatric hospital in Crowthorne in Berkshire, England. Not the brand spanking new purpose-built Broadmoor that was both a million miles and a stone's throw away from the old Victorian Broadmoor. This was a redeveloped, ultra-modern, ultra-maximum-security wing inside the tired old fifty-three-acre facility that was built in 1863 and initially contained 95 'insane' female prisoners.

In January 2013, with appropriate ceremony and publicity, the new wing was officially opened by the then Home Secretary; a plain-looking woman with a dedication for law and order infused into her bones like the words running through a stick of Blackpool rock.

Speeches were said, hands were shaken, photographs were taken, a ribbon was cut. And, in theory, good folk could start feeling safer.

The facility was dedicated to housing the most insane, most dangerous, male serial killers who, for their sins, would never be allowed to mix with any general prison population. Or anyone else, for that matter. Ever again.

It was very exclusive, and informally known, by those being held there, those guarding them, and those who put them there, as The Monster House.

It contained twelve solitary-confinement cells. Each one a six-sided box. Floor, ceiling, and three walls made of 2-inch-thick steel panels. The sixth side, the front, was made of half-inch thick polycarbonate ballistic glazing. Total floor area was 12-feet by 14-feet. The steel ceiling was 10ft above the floor.

Built into each glass wall was a meal and documents hatch,

and a wireless audio feed switched on or off from outside the cell. The microphones could pick up the sound of a pin being dropped anywhere in the cell. Or a voice coming from anywhere within a ten feet radius of the outside.

The cells were in two lines, back-to-back, with a 6-feet gap all around between each one. Through the glass, each occupant could see a blank wall eight feet away across a corridor.

Each cell had a double door security 'porch' built into the right side of the see-though wall with a 5-feet space between each door. Once inside the porch, the outer door was electronically locked before the inner door was opened. Same routine on the way out.

Each see-through wall had a privacy 'smart' mode, controlled from outside the cell. This allowed the wall to become opaque at the touch of a button.

This happened at 10pm every evening until 6am every morning, during which time, inmates were afforded a certain degree of privacy. Or so they thought.

Hidden micro-cameras inside the cells took that privacy away. Not that any occupant was aware of this. When it came to privacy with maximum security, perception was one thing. Reality something else entirely.

Each cell had a bed, a toilet, a wash-hand basin, a shower cubicle, a TV with cable channels, a bookcase containing the books and magazines, a desk and chair, a small chest of drawers, a rug, a keyboard and monitor with access to an intranet server monitored by prison staff, and bottled water plus tea and coffee making facilities on a small round table.

For one hour each day, and always with four armed guards present, each member of The Monster House would have free reign of the dedicated exercise area. There, they could take advantage of exercise machines, but no free weights.

Even monsters, apparently, had rights. Irrespective of the number of people they had killed. Or how they had killed them.

That was 2013.

This was now 2018.

Detective Inspector Tom McHale was sitting on a metal chair on the outside of what was known as Cell 3.

Sitting on the inside, on the other side of the glass wall, was Father David Black.

Only he wasn't.

Arthur was awake.

He looked a shade over 5ft 10ins. About an inch taller than Black. This perceived height difference was, in reality, the result of Arthur's desire to remain almost rigidly straight-backed at all times. Except when he was supine; except when he was asleep.

Black, however, had adopted a noticeable old man's stoop over the years.

Although the priest had aged seven years since entering Broadmoor, and was now sixty-three, Arthur had remained the age he always thought he was. Twenty-five.

He was, of course, cleverer than Black, with an IQ of 136. By comparison, Black was a dullard.

Although the priest also had short, white hair, Arthur viewed this as a physical anomaly. But not unattractive.

He thought it distinctive, distinguished, even attractive and unique in a man so young. His wrinkles were merely the result of his skin prematurely ageing. He had an answer for everything and an apology for nothing.

They had been staring at each other for the five minutes that had elapsed since McHale first sat down. Both wanted to speak. Neither wanted to speak first.

McHale's mind began to wander, his memory going over the journey that had led him all the way to where he was at that precise moment.

There are a million reasons why people make the decisions they make, and set off on the journeys they take through life.

When McHale was small and thin, he had a best mate called Fat George. McHale was the brains and George was the brawn.

Fat George's dad was a butcher. And, when the time came, Fat George followed in the old man' footsteps. He was deliriously happy right up until the instant he died at the age of twenty-six, when he wrapped his motorbike around an obstinate tree after consuming too much alcohol. He was on his way home from his favourite pub around eleven one night. Witnesses estimated he was travelling about seventy miles an hour.

The tree had no intentions of travelling anywhere, fast or slow.

Long before George's meeting with fate, a thirteen-year-old McHale moved with his parents to London. Ever since the he was a pre-teen he'd had one goal in life. To join the police force. Not merely to maintain law and order. Not just to catch criminals. Not only to protect the life and property of an often-ungrateful public. More than anything, McHale wanted to catch killers.

Above everything else, he wanted to take away the freedom of anyone who, by any and every means, took away the lives of folk who died too early, too fast, too easy, and too hard.

So, on his 18th birthday, March 18, 1994 he applied to become a member of the thin blue line. Or, as some critics unkindly (and wrongly) described it, the thick blue line.

Over the years, as he rose from being a raw copper fresh out of Hendon Police College (before it was rebuilt, reborn, and renamed The Peel Centre) to being a seasoned Detective Inspector in Stockport, Cheshire, he saw that line get stretched thinner and thinner.

But McHale was a man who knew the value of patience.

He also knew the value of being unconventional in his thinking. And as often as not, because of that patience and unconventionality, he succeeded where others had failed. He was blessed with a surfeit of creativity and imagination. Something that couldn't be said for many of his peers.

No doubt that's why, in 2010, he was chosen to lead the hunt for Father David Black. The Catholic priest suspected, caught, and convicted in 2011, of killing John and Annie Kirkbride, an old couple, in Altrincham, Cheshire.

Black was diagnosed with Dissociative-Identity-Disorder. He had a sleeping subordinate personality inside him called Arthur.

Arthur was taller, better looking, and more intelligent than Black. At least that's how he viewed himself.

Black was a caring, funny, 56-year-old man of God. Arthur was a clever, manipulative, cold-blooded killer.

At that moment, one of them was looking at McHale through the reinforced screen with a smile that brought him out of his reverie and slammed him, fast forward, into the present.

'Wake up, Kemosabe. Time to call the bastard's bluff,' said McHale's internal voice.

He looked at his watch, came to a decision, stood up from his chair, and started to walk away.

It was 3.35pm.

'I win,' said Arthur, through the intercom speaker in the glass wall.

The voice was deep and menacing. Nothing like the soft, lighter voice of the priest.

McHale, facing away, smiled. Turned. Walked back to the chair and sat down.

He looked at his watch again. 3.10pm.

'You got somewhere you need to be?' said Arthur.

'Oh, you know. The usual,' said McHale, his face a mask of disinterest. 'Memories to catch up on. Places to go, people to save, murdering bastards to catch.'

Arthur tutted and shook his head sadly from side to side. 'So impatient,' he sighed.

'Well… tick tock, Arthur,' said McHale, quoting words from the letters written to the FBI's BAU unit by the serial killer known as The Holy Ghost.

Arthur smiled. 'How is the padre?' he said. He was referring to the Jesuit Father Stephen Rice. One of the members of the small team who tracked him down eight months earlier.

McHale changed tack.

'Spill the beans, Arthur. What do you want?'

Arthur looked annoyed. 'See, there you go. Always answering a question with a question. Do you have any idea how fucking annoying that is?' His voice had drifted up a notch in volume.

Hearing the priest swear was initially shocking to McHale. It was almost sinful. Then he remembered that Black wasn't the one who was talking.

'That's the first question I've asked you in years, give me a break,' he said. 'I think I'm doing pretty damned well.' He forced out a small laugh. There was no humour in it.

Arthur crossed his legs, right over left. Then crossed his arms over his chest. Left over right. 'How can we hope to have any kind of relationship if you don't engage in a bit of friendly banter?' he said.

Pause. Four heartbeats.

McHale sighed. His inner voice spoke up. 'Might as well humour the bastard, Kemosabe,' he said. 'See what he has to bloody say.'

'Fine.' He raised his eyebrows and tilted his head to the left. 'How are they treating you in here? Miss the outside world?'

Arthur grinned. 'See how easy that was?' He uncrossed his arms and legs and stood up. Held his arms wide apart and turned around in a circle. 'I am lord of all I survey. Master of my own tiny world. Why do I need to go anywhere outside,' he said, 'when I can go anywhere I fucking want in here, eh?' and he tapped his right temple with the forefinger of his right hand.

He walked over to the small chest of drawers. On the top was a bowl overflowing with oranges and bananas. He picked up a bunch of bananas and broke off a fat yellow finger. Walked back to his chair and sat down. Peeled open the banana and took a large bite.

Through the mashed pulp in his mouth, he said, 'Always remember to get your prebiotics, Mister McHale. 'It's good for the gut flora. Did you know that?'

McHale nodded. 'So is garlic,' he said. 'Also good for keeping vampires at bay.'

Pause. A couple of heartbeats.

Then Arthur burst out laughing. As he did, bits of mulched banana flew out of his mouth, one or two landing on the inside of the see-through wall.

When he finished laughing, he said, 'You know… I think under different circumstances we could have been good friends, Mister McHale.'

McHale shook his head slowly from side to side. 'We could never be friends under any circumstances, Arthur.'

'Because?'

'Because you're a psychopath who likes killing people.'

Arthur cocked his head to the right. His eyes took on a dead look. The look McHale had seen in sharks.

No emotion. No feeling. All predator.

His voice became soft and inquisitive. 'I wonder why that is, Mister McHale? You think maybe it's because I was abused as a child, eh? You think something inside me is fucked up and broken and can't ever be fixed, eh?'

Even though they were separated by one inch of almost unbreakable plastic wall, McHale could feel a small trickle of sweat run down the back of his neck.

There was something about the tone of Arthur's voice that made him want to shift his chair back a foot or two. He ignored the feeling.

'You were never a child,' he said. 'You were fucked up and broken right from the word go. It just took time to come out.'

Arthur stared at McHale and sighed. Then he finished eating the banana and, like NBA legend LeBron James in his prime, threw the empty skin with unerring accuracy into a waste basket sitting next to his desk about ten feet away. It didn't even hit the sides.

McHale gave him a couple of slow handclaps.

Arthur took a mock bow, then returned the handclaps. 'I hear you haven't been booted up the pecking order yet,' he said.

He was referring to McHale's lack of promotion from Detective Inspector to Detective Chief Inspector, following the hunt for The Holy Ghost, aka. Charles Halliwell, the previous year. It was a hunt in which Black had played a vital role. His tip had led McHale's specially formed team south to Portsmouth where The Ghost was stalking his final victim.

'I guess I was born lucky,' said McHale with a half grin. 'I got to stay where I could do the most damage.'

'With a little help from your friends.'

McHale's right eyebrow went up. 'You think this is one of those "we couldn't have done it without you" moments?' he said.

'A 'thank you' would be nice.'

Pause.

McHale shrugged. Nodded once. 'Fair point,' he said. 'This is me saying thank you! Now, can we do away with the small talk and get down to business?'

'Tell you what, how about a nice cup of coffee, eh? I can arrange it.'

'No thanks.'

'Sure? It's none of your instant crap. It's the real deal. Only the best for you, Mister McHale.'

There was nothing genuine or sincere in his tone of voice.

'Oh, bugger this. You're just pissing about. Bye, Arthur.' McHale got up from his chair and this time he got about five feet further away from the cell than he did the first time, before he heard Arthur's voice chasing after him.

'Only, I was thinking, while you're drinking your Java, I could tell you a little story,' he said. 'It's about a clearing roughly quarter the size of a football pitch in the middle of a forest.'

McHale stopped and turned.

Long pause.

'And?'

Arthur smiled. 'And I need a drink of water,' he said. He got up from his chair and walked to the small table, filled a plastic cup with still water, sipped it, then brought it back carefully to his chair and sat down.

Then he took a deep breath and continued.

'Now… where was I? Oh yeah. The clearing in the middle of a forest. Right.'

'Where's the forest?' said McHale. Walking back to his chair and slowly sitting down.

Arthur didn't like being interrupted. That much was obvious. His face grew flush with colour and his eyes narrowed. There was a temper sitting just under his skin. The kind of temper that didn't need much of an excuse to come out into the open to do a little GBH.

But he held it in check. The demeanour of his face changed. The muscles around his jaw relaxed. He blinked slowly, breathed deeply, and when he opened his eyes again, the temper had gone.

'The forest is in Bulgaria. Now, no more fucking talking.'

'Fine.'

'So… in March 2015, a helicopter was flying over a remote, forested area in the south of the country. They were taking aerial photos for one of those surveys. And when they looked at the photos, they noticed something odd.

'A clearing deep in the forest had what looked like vague oblong shapes in the ground. Twenty of them.

'They were lined up in two rows of ten. Very curious. So the men in charge of the survey sent a couple of people to have a good look at the shapes. They took ground penetrating radar gear with them. That's when all fucking hell broke loose. Turns out the shapes were shallow graves. The graves were only a couple of feet deep.'

Somewhere in the back of McHale's mind, a faint alarm bell began to ring.

'All in all, they found twenty bodies. Some had been in the

ground for more than a decade. They didn't look much like bodies any more. Some had only been there a year or two. A couple of the graves were only a few months old.'

The alarm bell got louder. McHale couldn't help himself. 'Dumping ground,' he said softly.

This time Arthur showed no annoyance. 'Give that man a coconut,' he said, almost proudly. 'And now for a bonus point…'

Pause. Four heartbeats.

'Bulgarian mafia?' said McHale, slowly.

Black stared at him.

A few years previously, McHale received an internal memo about a conference at The Met's new headquarters at New Scotland Yard on Victoria Embankment, London. The conference was about organised crime.

One of the keynote speakers was a high-ranking officer from Bulgaria's National Police Service. McHale missed the conference but he read the transcript of the presentation.

It mentioned the bodies buried in the wood.

Barely a month after the speech, the officer and his wife were blown to fleshy smithereens when a bomb exploded under their car.

Apparently, organised crime and certain inhabitants of Bulgaria went together like death and taxes. Or so some folk thought.

Arthur downed his water in two large gulps and held the empty beaker in his right hand. 'Good guess, Mister McHale. Good… but wrong. No bonus point for you.

'You see, it wasn't those nasty gangs that put all those people in the ground. It was just one man. One very ordinary looking man. Average height. Average build. He was a regular Joe fucking Schmo. Except for the fact that he killed at least twenty people. Or so the authorities thought.'

McHale wished he'd said yes to the coffee. His throat was dry and his taste buds relished the thought of a kick up the arse from a mouthful of double-strength caffeine.

He was still wrapping his head around the fact that he was looking at a sixty-four-year-old priest, and listening to a killer who, in his mind, would always be a damned sight younger.

'You mean he killed more?'

Arthur looked smug. 'He actually confessed to killing another ten, but he wouldn't give up the other burial sites. They're still looking for them.'

'So, they caught him?'

Arthur shook his head slowly. 'Wrong again. He walked into a police station in Sofia in September 2015 and gave himself up. Stupid bastards put him in prison with all the other crazies. He became a big celebrity. He was also murdered on his 58th birthday, April 21, 2015. The guy who killed him became an even bigger one.'

The alarm bell ramped up its decibel level.

'That's not why you asked to see me is it?'

Long pause.

'No Mister McHale. The man's name was Dragan Lazarov.'

'And?'

'And he didn't kill anyone.'

Another decibel.

'And you know this, how?'

Arthur smiled. 'Because the man who did kill them is his younger brother Anton. And he's right here in the UK. And I think you'll find he's already started killing again.'

Twenty-three words. Ninety-five letters. Millions of possibilities.

'Oh… something else,' said Arthur. 'Something that anyone with a healthy dose of curiosity would find very interesting.'

McHale sighed. 'Okay, I'm officially curious.'

Arthur smiled. 'They were all buried face down. Just like the brothers' mother.'

It was 3.40pm.

Six days after McHale's forty-second birthday. And his arse was aching from sitting on the hard metal chair outside the cell.

He was trying to stay poker faced. He wasn't succeeding.

Black was looking at him. Neither had said anything for about thirty seconds.

McHale was trying to figure out what to think next. What to do next. What to say next. That, plus trying to imagine what twenty graves next to each other in a small clearing in a remote forest looked like.

Finally, he broke the silence.

'You seem to know an awful lot for someone banged up in solitary with no physical contact with the outside world. How the hell do I know you're not just yanking my chain?'

'Who needs physical contact when you've got the internet, Mister McHale. I call it my world in a box.'

'I thought you only had access to the intranet... not the whole internet,' said McHale.

'Have I?' said Arthur, mysteriously.

McHale's brain put that juicy question on the shelf for the time being.

Arthur's eyes narrowed and the smile disappeared. He made a fist with his right hand and crushed the empty plastic cup he was holding. Then he closed his eyes and his head lolled forwards slowly onto his chest. He sighed softly. Then his breathing slowed and his shoulders relaxed.

Long pause.

He raised his head and opened his eyes. Only it wasn't Arthur who looked and blinked. David Black was back.

'Hello, Tom,' he said in the soft, tired voice that McHale instantly remembered. 'You're looking well.'

'It's good to see you, Father. I wasn't sure whether we'd get to talk this time.'

Black raised an eyebrows 'Arthur and I are not the strangers we once were,' he said. There was more than a tinge of sadness in his voice. 'He shares more with me than he used to. I think he finds it lonely in there all by himself.

'I can't tell you much. But I can tell you that poor old Dragan only had one visitor in the short time he was in jail, just before someone took great delight in slitting his throat. His younger brother Anton came to see him and stayed for about an hour. It was Dragan's birthday. When the younger Lazarov left, he was smiling.'

'And?'

'That's it, I'm afraid. The well, as they say, has run dry. For the time being.'

McHale noticed that the stoop had returned to Black's upper body. He was back to looking his chronological age. And feeling it, too. Any vitality that had found a home in Arthur's face had abandoned the features of the priest.

'Is it worth me asking how you know all this?'

'I could tell you, but then Arthur would have to kill me.'

Pause.

'That was my feeble attempt at humour,' said Black.

Neither was smiling.

'So… you're not going to tell me?'

Black smiled kindly, as if he was being asked to divulge the secrets of the confessional. 'No. I think it's best if you take my word for it and know that your chain isn't being yanked in any direction. Everyone has their dirty little secrets, Tom. Arthur has lots of breadcrumbs. He likes to throw them to the waiting pigeons a few crumbs at a time.'

'So, I'm a pigeon?'

'Oh, not you, Tom. Arthur thinks you're a bit of a raptor. He saves the best handouts for you. They still have warm flesh attached.'

McHale's eyebrows lifted and he grunted softly.

'I bet you and Arthur have had some interesting chats,' he said. 'Has he told you about Luntz?'

The disgust on the priest's face was instant.

Two months after he came to Broadmoor he came across

Donald Luntz, a convicted paedophile who had sexually molested and then strangled four young girls. One of them only two years old.

Luntz was a hulking bear of a man who sweated too much and didn't bathe enough.

He was caught when he tried to snatch a nine-year old girl from a playground. He was in the process of sexually assaulting her in the back of his beat-up van when her father heard her screams.

For all his size and aggressive behaviour Luntz was, at heart, a coward. Faced with a six-foot well-built man frantically trying to save his daughter, Luntz crumpled into a tearful heap, before receiving a savage beating inflicted by the father and several onlookers.

The adult human body is composed of 206 bones. The girl's father, with help, broke 43 of those belonging to Luntz.

But even that was nothing compared to what Arthur did to him. Even though Black was late middle aged, his dark passenger felt he was in the prime of his life.

The harming, either physically or psychologically, of children was Arthur's line drawn in the sand. He was on one side and Luntz, for the brief remainder of his life, was on the other.

Seven months after the beating, three months after Luntz entered Broadmoor, and just under nine months before the completion of the prison's new Monster House, Father David Black invited Lunz to join him in the small prison chapel for a session of prayer and spiritual guidance. He was very flattering and very persuasive.

Number of prisoners in attendance… two.

Number of guards on hand… zero.

Number of doors locked so Luntz couldn't escape… one.

Once inside, Black took a coffee break and Arthur took over. Luntz never saw it coming.

An hour later, long after the screams had died away, the

guards returned and unlocked the door.

Arthur was sitting in a far corner of the chapel, smiling.

Luntz was everywhere else.

Nine months later, in February 2013, Arthur became the first permanent member of the new Monster House facility.

At the time, he had twelve empty cells to choose from. Two rows of six, back- to-back. Each cell numbered. His new home address was cell number three, as per his request. He didn't explain why. It was granted without question.

That was then. This was now.

There were two other occupants in the cells on the same row as Black. Cells one and five. McHale didn't know who they were. Or what they did to warrant membership to The Monster House. Or how many of the cells on the other row were still empty. He didn't ask.

The only thing he knew about the occupant of cell number five was that he liked the taste of human flesh. Too much information.

'Thank you for not feeling sorry or for expressing regret at my circumstances,' said Black.

'It is what it is,' said McHale.

'Indeed,' said Black, sighing heavily. 'Right… I think it's time to go. Bye for now, Tom. Give my best to Stephen.'

Father Stephen Rice was the Jesuit priest who had helped McHale capture Black. He was also an off-again-on-again member of McHale's team. One of his on-again collaborations with the team led to the successful hunt for the serial killer Charles Halliwell.

McHale nodded once.

Black closed his eyes, lowered his head and sighed. When he raised his head and opened his eyes again, Arthur was back.

'That's quite a trick,' said McHale.

Arthur shrugged. 'Every little helps,' he said.

'Except this is Broadmoor, not Tesco.'

'Broadmoor has a supermarket,' Arthur whispered. He winked, then tapped the right side of his nose twice with the forefinger of his right hand, like he was passing on a confidence.

Time to go, thought McHale, and he stood up.

'There's something for you in the hatch,' said Arthur. 'A little going away present of sorts. Something to get the ball rolling and keep you busy until the next time.' Then he smiled, stood up, went to his desk, sat down, and started writing.

'There's going to be a next time?'

'There's always a next time.'

The reunion was over. McHale glanced at the hatch and walked over to it. There was a slip of folded yellow paper sitting in the tray. He picked it up and unfolded it. There were two words, carefully printed in black ink.

Eight letters.

Grey John.

It meant nothing to McHale. He didn't know whether the first word was a first name, or a nickname, or a colour. He didn't know if the first name and last name were in the right order. He didn't know what it had to do with Anton Lazarov, if anything.

But it obviously meant something to Arthur. So, he refolded the paper and slipped it into the inside left breast pocket of his jacket.

McHale wasn't a suit man. Too conventional. Today, the jacket was a Harris Tweed single breasted number with brown leather elbow patches and two leather buttons at the front. Eight years old. Never fastened. Tomorrow's outfit? Black leather jacket, maybe. Never fastened.

It was 4.29pm.

He walked away from David and Arthur, drove away from Broadmoor, and headed back the forty or so miles towards the city that had been his second home for the past six or so months.

London. In all its cosmopolitan, impersonal, cultured, dangerous glory.

He had free use of a tidy, refurbished, fully-furnished, Victorian end terrace in Battersea. Bay windows. High ceilings. A ton of original features. Plus a few very stylish new ones… like the luxury Poggenpohl kitchen.

Old England meets new Germany.

He'd rented out his house in Stockport and put the money in a high yield interest account for a rainy day. Or preferably a dry, hot day somewhere abroad.

The second home was within spitting distance of Battersea Park and a mile from the iconic, Grade II listed Battersea Power Station. One of the most innovative repurposed developments in the City. Some might say the country.

He was the head of a new unit, inside a new department, based in an old capital. A unit with a singular mission, to hunt serial killers, wherever the hell they were.

The official head of the new department was Detective Chief Superintendent Cyril Drummond, with McHal acting as the unofficial head.

It was Drummond who brought McHale on board to hunt down Charles Halliwell, and it was Drummond who arranged for the keys of the Victorian end terrace to drop nicely into McHale's outstretched right hand. No questions asked, no answers expected.

The way Drummond figured it, laying out a few quid to finance a team like the one McHale put together was time, money, and effort well spent.

His methods might be unconventional. But nobody in their right mind argued with his results. And results were the name of the game.

However, before the new unit got the green light there was the small matter of location, location, location. It couldn't be in the high-security complex where the hunt for Halliwell mostly took place. That was underneath the official residence of the US Ambassador to the Court of St. James. Winfield House in Regent's Park. A small plot of Stars & Stripes bricks and mortar inside a much larger plot of Union Jack greenery.

That was too much like having your next-door neighbour always in your home. Eating your food. Watching your telly. Rifling through your underwear drawers. And it couldn't be in the newly-refurbished New Scotland Yard building on Victoria Embankment. That was too much like having your hands zip-tied behind your back by folk who normally did things by the book. From A all the way through to Z. And sometimes back again. No detours.

McHale had a habit of throwing books out the window. Open or not. It had to be somewhere nearby. Very private. Very secure. Very unconventional. Very Uncle Sam meets John Bull. And very full of the latest hi-tech communications systems.

That somewhere was Lassiter House. And it was hidden away in a quiet back street about a mile from the Yard. It was a fifty-fifty joint US-UK collaboration, where everyone's share of the communications pie was the same size, same quality, and same taste as everyone else's. Give or take. Most of the time. Theoretically. It was a handsome Edwardian building, refurbished inside and out, and spread over six floors. Four above ground and two below. It was stuffed full of twenty-first century digital innovation and law enforcement technology.

And the top floor was up for grabs.

There was only the other small matter to deal with before they moved in. Intelligence.

Not human intelligence. Not the kind that sat between ears. More like the kind that married one silicon chip to another. The artificial kind. In the shape of two highly advanced information systems. One developed by the forces of US law enforcement. The other by the long arms of the UK police.

The former was called MOTHER. It was an acronym for Monitor, Organise, Talk, Hear, Evaluate, and Record. McHale and the team used it to bring down Charles Halliwell.

The latter was called HOLMES. It stood for Home Office

Large Major Enquiry System. It was used predominantly by UK police forces for the investigation of major incidents such as multiple murders and high value frauds. The Americans always seemed more inventive and creative with their acronyms than the British. The British always seemed more traditional.

There was no point letting the two systems duke it out to see which one was standing when the dust settled and the coughing stopped. Both had wicked left jabs.

What was needed was a stunning right cross. Something that looked like the street-fighting love-child of MOTHER and HOLMES... but felt like the fairies had left it on the doorstep overnight. Something that would cherry pick the best from each of them and merge them together to create a new hybrid system. One that would be uniquely designed to hunt serial killers and nobody else, that was rammed full of piss and vinegar. With a 'fuck off' attitude and a mind of its own.

It took close to eighty very clever people six months to cross-pollinate and develop and three weeks to install. All hands-on deck. When they had finished Stage One, they named the system SKIN. It stood for Serial Killers Intelligence Network. Simple. Straightforward. No nonsense.

And on paper, it kicked arse.

It just needed a case that could take it out for a test drive. And ten days after his visit to Broadmoor, McHale gave it one. Courtesy of Arthur. Via Father David Black. It was called Lazarov. Not Anton, not anything else. Just Lazarov.

Drummond pressed all the right buttons, so, a week later McHale and his team officially moved into Lassiter House.

Acknowledgements

There are probably thousands of people (give or take) who I should thank for helping me give birth to *A Time for Dying*.

They won't all know who they are. In fact, apart from a cherished few, most won't even have any idea they helped at all. But believe me, they did.

From those who lit the spark that grew into the flame that burned a love of words into my little grey cells. To those who critiqued my early efforts and gave me the enthusiasm to continue. From those who enjoyed (most of) my writing, to those who, like my publishers and editors at Northodox, saw, in me, a love of the crime genre that, perhaps, was a little bloodier, and a lot more enjoyable, than I had initially anticipated.

Without you, my output would be merely indecipherable scribbles on a page with no beginning, no end, and a distinct and uninteresting lack of middle.

Thank you all.

NORTHODOX
PRESS

HOME OF NORTHERN VOICES

 FACEBOOK.COM/NORTHODOXPRESS

 TWITER.COM/NORTHODOXPRESS

 INSTAGRAM.COM/NORTHODOXPRESS

 NORTHODOX.CO.UK

SUBMISSIONS
ARE OPEN!
WRITER &
DEBUT AUTHOR [ ]
NOVELS &
SHORT FICTION [ ]
FROM OR LIVING
IN THE NORTH [ ]

THE

FATAL

FORMULA

REVENGE IS A SCIENCE – AND CHEMISTRY IS THE KEY

MALCOLM HAVARD

Sometimes doing the right thing is the greatest mistake of all.

PAUL D COOMBS

THE
GREAT
ORME

Printed in Great Britain
by Amazon

36196628R00199